BY KIM WILKINS

Daughters of the Storm
Sisters of the Fire

SISTERS OF THE FIRE

SISTERS OF THE FIRE

KIM WILKINS

Del Rey | New York

Published in the United States by Del Rey,
an imprint of Random House,
a division of Penguin Random House LLC, New York.

DEL REY and the HOUSE colophon are registered trademarks
of Penguin Random House LLC.

LIBRARY OF CONGRESS CATALOGING-IN-PUBLICATION DATA

Names: Wilkins, Kim, author.
Title: Sisters of the fire / Kim Wilkins.
Description: New York: Del Rey, [2019] |
Series: Daughters of the storm; 2
Identifiers: LCCN 2018039372 | ISBN 9780399177507
(hardback: alk. paper) | ISBN 9780399177514 (ebook)
Subjects: | BISAC: FICTION / Fantasy / Epic. |
FICTION / Fantasy / General. | FICTION / Action &
Adventure. | GSAFD: Fantasy fiction.
Classification: LCC PR9619.3.W547 S57 2019 |
DDC 823/.914—dc23
LC record available at https://lccn.loc.gov/2018039372

Printed in the United States of America on acid-free paper

randomhousebooks.com

9 8 7 6 5 4 3 2 1

First Edition

Book design by Virginia Norey

For Bek, Charlotte, Fi, Lizzie, Nic, and Meg:
the best sisters I never had

SISTERS OF THE FIRE

PROLOGUE

Rowan kept many secrets. Some were big and some were small. Some she had been told to keep, and some she kept to protect herself. By the time she was seven, she had so many secrets that she decided to draw a special code to remember them all. After supper one evening, she took off into the sapling grove behind the house with her bone-handled hunting knife and a stick of charcoal from the fire. Carefully, while the day cooled off the land and the evening breeze thickened in the oaks of the Howling Wood, she drew her diagram in the corner of the fence Snowy had built.

She mustn't tell Papa about the sword her aunt Bluebell had given her on her seventh birthday. And *absolutely*, should she ever see her mama again, she mustn't tell Mama that Bluebell knew where she was all along. Mama was represented with a soft round outline, indistinct as she was in Rowan's memory; Papa was a strong square.

She mustn't tell Sister Julian that Snowy took her hunting every afternoon when she was supposed to be practicing her sewing, and she should certainly never mention how her bow shot was finer and more accurate than her stitching by a hundred miles. She drew Sister Julian with her headscarf over her eyes, to indicate she wasn't allowed to see the beloved elm bow Snowy had made for Rowan, precisely the right size for her child's hands. "Sapwood for the back, heartwood for the belly," he'd said, stroking the inside curve. "Let the world believe you fearless, but keep your heart soft."

She mustn't tell Bluebell about the prayers to Maava she said every night, just as Papa asked her to. And, of course, she mustn't tell Papa about the prayers to the Great Mother and the Horse God that she said every night, just as Snowy asked her to. A long straight rectangle for Bluebell, with her dog at her side.

Pleased, Rowan sat back to consider her drawings. Her hands ached a little from carving, and her fingers were black with the charcoal she had rubbed into the lines.

But how to represent the last secret, the big secret? Perhaps she didn't have to. Once, she'd overheard Snowy telling Sister Julian that Rowan had forgotten about her mother already, and it was better that way. But she had not forgotten; she curled up against her mother's back every night. All it took was to close her eyes and send her shimmering self (that was what she called it—she didn't know the real word, or even if there was one) out and above the world, where it found Mama and plummeted toward her like a hawk hunting. She found the warm curve of her mother's back, and she pressed herself against her and slept dreamless every night. Woke up in her own bed every dawn. She knew Mama was sad, but Rowan had no way to tell Mama she was there or to comfort her. Anyway, Mama had another child now, though Rowan couldn't see him, just feel him when he was there in bed with Mama. The three of them all curled together, a family that nobody could see.

It wasn't the only time she sent her shimmering self places, either. Some nights she flew over the Howling Wood, looking for the source of the beautiful singing she heard from time to time. But then the wood coiled in on itself like a labyrinth within a labyrinth, and she couldn't find it. She would never stop looking, though.

That was Rowan's very own secret.

CHAPTER 1

The music and laughter and free-flowing mead made her father's hall seem so alive that Bluebell could hardly believe this feast was to mark a death: the king's counselor, Byrta, who had served their family for sixty years. But for Bluebell and her hearthband it was a party, a chance to catch their breath and eat heartily after the privations of life on the road.

"And then I sat on him," Gytha was screeching, "until he said yes!"

A loud roar of laughter went up, and Bluebell gulped her mead and laughed with them. Gytha, the only other woman in her retinue, was telling the story of how she had convinced her new husband to marry her.

"I suppose you'll be off having babies now," Sighere, Bluebell's second-in-command, said. "Just when your spear arm was becoming legend."

"Depends on who has the greater claim on my womb: the Great Mother or the Horse God." She shrugged, took a gulp of her drink. "What will come will come." But Gytha had already been to see Bluebell to ask how to avoid a pregnancy, something Bluebell herself had avoided since—when had she started fucking? Sixteen? Seventeen? A long time, in any case. Gytha didn't want to leave the road any more than Bluebell did. Life after the road was dull and circumscribed, waiting around to die.

Bluebell glanced around the room. Firelight and smoke and movement. Her eyes were drunk and exaggerated everything, and she smiled at nobody and everybody. The wise women of the village crowded around a table near the hearth—their bones so cold from age that even summer couldn't warm them—telling happy stories of Byrta's life and laughing in defiance of death. The rest of the crowd was made of old warriors, young stable hands, musicians and tale-tellers, Byrta's friends from town, and others who had known and loved her—many of whom were unused to being in Athelrick's hall and were full of marvel and excitement rather than mourning. It was a happy occasion.

"Where's that little serving wench?" Ricbert slurred.

"Over there," Lofric said, pointing across the crowd to the other side of the hall.

Bluebell's men had become infatuated with one of the new hall girls. She was tiny, perhaps a foot shorter than Bluebell, with curling ringlets and a poppet's face, but enormous breasts.

Ricbert stood, holding up his empty cup. "Hey there! Hey!" And when she didn't hear over the din, he put down his cup and lurched off after her.

Sighere was straight-backed, alert.

"Relax," Bluebell said. "Enjoy yourself. No harm will come to us today."

"Your father," he said. "The king. He's nowhere to be seen."

"He probably went outside to piss."

Then there was a shriek and Bluebell saw that Ricbert had picked up the little serving girl and was carrying her back to where the hearthband was sitting. Indignant, the girl dumped her jug of mead all down his back. The other men were laughing and whooping, calling to Ricbert to toss the girl to them. They began to pass her around, lifting her over their heads and crowing about how strong they were.

Bluebell finished her drink, stood up, and boomed, "If you are so keen to lift a woman over your head, try it with me!"

Lofric placed the woman on the ground, and she scurried to the fire.

"Come on, then. Lofric? Ricbert? No?" She spread her arms. Bluebell never drew attention to her sex. She was sure, for the most part, her men thought of her as they might think of another man. She was a more powerful soldier than any of them, taller than all but Sighere, and made them call her "my lord" rather than "my lady." But it was the sign of a craven spirit in a man to exercise his power over somebody weaker outside of battle, and she disdained it furiously. Would they be so cruel to children, or to dogs?

"Ricbert," she said, with cold threat in her voice. "I want you to try to pick me up."

Ricbert knew better than to defy a direct command. Sheepishly, drunkenly, he took a step forward and reached for her. Thrymm, Bluebell's dog, leapt to her feet and growled low.

"Down, girl," Bluebell said.

Ricbert's arms went around Bluebell's waist, and as hard as he pulled her up, she planted herself ever more firmly on the ground. It was no contest. She was bigger than him, and he was drunker than her.

"Anyone else?" she asked.

Gytha laughed and piled on with Ricbert, then it became a joke and they were all crowding around her, falling over one another as they tried to pull her off her feet. Thrymm barked nervously and Bluebell laughed and laughed as they failed to move her. She was made of stone. She brought down her arms with one swift movement and swept them all off. Some landed on the floor among the rushes and the dogs. A crowd that had gathered laughed and hooted, and Sighere put a cup of mead in her hands and she called them all fuckers under her breath and sat down again.

"He's not back," Sighere said.

For a moment she didn't understand what he meant, but then she glanced up at the high table and realized he meant her father hadn't returned.

"I'll see if I can find him," she said, and patted Thrymm's flank so the dog would follow her.

Bluebell slipped out of the hot, noisy hall into the long summer twilight. If her father had sought peace, he wouldn't have headed to town, but rather around toward the stables. She followed the path and saw him soon enough, standing under an oak tree at the top of the hill, looking out over fields beyond the giants' ruins. The oak was thick with foliage except for the topmost branches, and a dozen rooks had perched up there: black fruit. The sky was washed yellow-gray as the day finally gave way, late as it always was this time of year.

"Father!" she called, and he turned and waited for her to join him, patient and still. Thrymm ran down to him and licked his outstretched hand.

"Are you unwell?" she asked as she approached over the dewy grass.

"I suffer from what every old man suffers when a good friend dies," he said.

"And what ailment is that?"

"An unshakable feeling that my death is near."

The cold touched Bluebell's heart, but she pretended to laugh his comment off. "Byrta was fourteen years older than you. A crone. You are still—"

"I am not *still* anything, Bluebell. I have seen sixty-two winters. I have old injuries that ache more with each passing year. Byrta lived to an old age because she had a life indoors, in quiet rooms and soft spaces. I have worn my body out in service of my people. I cannot be too far behind her."

Bluebell realized that her father's morbid ramblings were his way of grieving. Four years ago, he had fallen into a deathly sleep for many long weeks; he already knew the darkness that was coming. He had never been the same since. He had lost some of his steel.

"You are still hale," she said gently. "You are still our king. My king."

"But if there was a war, Bluebell, could I lead the army? Or would you do it? I'm good for visiting shearings and settling land disputes and placating people who think they've paid too much tax, but not much else." His eyes went back to the fields laid out all around the town of Blickstow, crops of different shades of green ripening in profusion. "It's already over," he muttered.

"Nothing is over," she said.

"I had hoped to die by steel, not by winter."

He turned back to her and she saw the deep lines on his face, the sag of his eyelids and the silver of his beard, and felt a pang.

"Death will come to you, too, one day," he said.

Bluebell's spine stiffened. As it did, she could feel the strength and suppleness in her muscles and joints, and she dismissed her father's words without letting them settle inside her. "If death comes for me, Father, I'll cut its fucking head off."

Athelrick laughed, light returning to his eyes. "That you would, my girl. I can imagine it all too well. Well, at least I can say I raised a good child."

"Five good children."

His smile retreated. "Well."

"Three, then. Ivy and Willow were a waste of your seed, I'll admit that."

He nodded. "Ash," he said. "I want her back. I always thought she would take Byrta's place. She trained for it."

"She never finished her training. And now she's taken herself into exile, and we aren't to reason against that. She believed it the right thing to do."

Her father's expression told her he disagreed, but he didn't pursue the point. "You know I have eyes all over Thyrsland looking for her."

"You should leave her be."

"I only want to know where she is. I won't bring her back against her will. But I liked it better when I knew where you all were. What you were all doing. I long for us all to be reunited. How long will Rose stay with her aunt? I expected her to return ages ago."

Bluebell bit her tongue so she didn't interrogate his choice of words. "Her aunt." Why not *my sister*? He had refused to explain their estrangement, and there was no point in pressing him now. Bluebell wouldn't mention his bastard grandson. Instead, she said, "Rose fears your disapproval."

"As she should. She behaved foolishly, but not all is lost. She gave up Rowan; the peace still holds. For now."

For now. Nettlechester, long their foe, was in the protracted process of converting to the trimartyr religion, as Tweening already had. If Littledyke also went down that road, nearly half of Thyrsland would have adopted the cruel faith. A faith that said women couldn't rule.

"Have you given thought to Rowan's future?" Bluebell asked suddenly. "One of King Blackstan's sons might make her a good husband, and secure Littledyke."

"Ask him next time you go north. How old is the girl now?"

"Too young to wed. Seven, I think. But a promise might be made. If Wengest is amenable." Wengest, who was too stupid to see Rowan wasn't from his seed.

Athelrick nodded, opened his mouth as though about to say something, then thought better of it.

"Go on," she prompted. "You can tell me anything that's on your mind."

"It would be much easier if *you* wed."

But Bluebell was already shaking her head.

"And if you had your own heirs."

"They wouldn't grow inside me. Everyone says my womb is made of steel," she joked.

"Bluebell . . ."

"The Horse God made me this way."

"Take a year out, while I'm still alive—"

"No babies." Bluebell's pulse was thudding in her throat. He had never said it directly to her before, though of course it had been implied a million times. His wistful mood must have made him say it. He was grieving. He felt old and longed for his family to be biddable little girls again.

Not that Bluebell had ever been biddable.

"Rowan will be a good queen. She's in good care and far enough from the trimartyr fervor of her father's court," Bluebell said. "I go north as soon as the mourning is over. I will send ahead to Blackstan for a meeting." She glanced up to the hall. "Will you come back inside?"

"I am enjoying watching the day dwindle," he said. "I'll be along in my own time."

"Very well." She turned and began up the path.

"Don't forget," he called after her urgently, "that you will die one day."

"Don't forget," she replied, without turning around, "that you are still alive."

chapter 2

The Howling Wood, at the bottom of Greyrain Range, was dense and gloomy, and Skalmir's first glimpse of his little house at the end of a long working day always made him smile. Out into the long sunshine after a shadowy day tracking, trapping, hunting, into the fresh air after the cold tang of blood by the stream then the choking air of the smokehouse. Yes, he was muddy and bloody and his hair smelled of smoke, but inside were clean clothes and sweet-smelling herbs hung from the ceiling beams and, of course, Rowan. His dogs wrestled and growled around his feet, happy.

Skalmir opened the door and there was Rowan, sitting by Sister Julian. The shutters were all open to let the afternoon breeze in, and yellow sunlight hit Rowan's hair and found auburn highlights. She looked up at the same time as Sister Julian. Rowan's first instinct, he could tell, was to bounce out of her seat and hug him hard around the middle, winding her little legs around his ankles and demanding he walk around the house with her hanging off him, a limpet—her favorite way to greet him. But with Sister Julian's eyes on her, she sat still.

"Snowy!" she cried instead. "You're home!"

Strike and Stranger jumped up on her lap, wagging their tails happily.

"That I am, little one," he replied, sitting at the freshly lit hearth and taking his boots off.

"Good afternoon, sir," Sister Julian said, eyes returning to her stitching.

"Good afternoon, sister."

Sister Julian came from the village daily to mind Rowan, to teach her to sew, and to tell her stories about Maava, the god of the new religion that hadn't quite spread as far as the Howling Wood. She rarely spoke more than a few words to Skalmir, but seemed kind enough with Rowan, and Wengest had insisted on hiring her for Rowan's care and instruction.

"I'll clean myself up. You may go," he said to her.

She nodded, but he couldn't see the expression on her face below the headscarf she always wore over her long, fair hair. He sometimes wondered if she was embarrassed by him, as if the fact of her being a spinster and him being a widower meant they should never look at each other directly.

"Rowan, can you water the dogs?" Skalmir made his way across the room and through to the back door, which opened on overgrown weeds and a stone slab with their water barrel on it. He ladled water over his head and hands, then stripped to the waist and left his clothes in a bundle for Sister Julian and Rowan to wash tomorrow. A robin chirped above him, and he glanced up. "Good afternoon to you, too," he said.

He ran his eyes along the length of the eaves, checking for loose parts and gaps where the rain could get in. He had built this house with his own hands ten years ago, when his wife Mildrith had been expecting their first child. He knew every nail, every inch of oak and elm, every handful of mud, every flat stone collected from the stream. He had never worked so hard as he worked that year, watching his wife's belly grow, keen to keep them all warm. But the first child had not survived the birth. The small anteroom off their bed chamber remained empty. No, not empty: hollow.

By the time Mildrith's belly swelled again, they were raising Rowan together, King Wengest's daughter in hiding, deep in the ancient woodland reserved for Skalmir's work as king's huntsman. This time the birth was more brutal, and neither his child nor his wife lived through it.

But the house still stood, sturdy as ever.

Skalmir found a sunny bank of grass to lie on and closed his eyes, filling his lungs with afternoon air.

A few moments later, Rowan was there, flinging herself on top of him. "She's gone! Today was very long," she declared.

"Why is that, dear heart?" he asked, spitting her long hair out of his mouth.

"Because Sister Julian is very old and very boring."

"She's the same age as I am," Skalmir said, although even he found it hard to believe that a woman of only thirty could have such a pinched face.

"Yes, but you're my lovely Snowy and she is just an old bore." Rowan wriggled off him and grabbed his bare arm, trying to pull him up. "Take me shooting."

"I don't want to go out again."

"In the sapling grove, then. Please. I've been sitting still all day and I'm *dying*."

He dragged himself to his feet. "Go on, then. Get your bow."

With an excited yelp she hared off inside again, while Skalmir waited with the afternoon sun on his bare shoulders. The sapling grove had once been land cleared for farming. Mildrith had had the Great Mother's touch with plants, and her small vegetable and herb patches weren't enough to keep her busy. She had wanted to grow food to sell to the markets. She had wanted to be busy and productive, and raise her child to be the same. After her death, Skalmir replanted the space with saplings, so he wasn't reminded every day of the dreams that had died with her. Now it was Rowan's favorite place to go: safe and close enough to home, but still wild, with its rabbits and its chatter of birds and gleam of insect wings.

The door slammed behind her again, and a moment later her hand was in his and they were walking the muddy path into the sapling grove, the dogs at their heels. Sparrows pipped in the low branches.

"So what did you learn today?"

"How to be a good trimartyr," she said grimly. "Which is a great deal the same as how to be a commonsense good person, but far more boring and with lots of talk of death by fire."

"Well, always remember, nobody sees inside your heart. You may believe what you want to believe." Though Skalmir hoped she believed in the old ways.

"I know, Snowy. I can keep all of the gods in my head at once. Don't worry."

He didn't worry, not really. Rowan was almost preternaturally able to present the perfect face to every person she encountered. With King Wengest she was the demure princess; with Bluebell she was the raging warrior-child; with Sister Julian she was the patient trimartyr pupil. Skalmir liked to think she was herself with him. Somehow his grief and Rowan's had found in each other a sweet harmony. They both knew Rowan wasn't his, that one day she'd be taken from him, but as far as Skalmir and Rowan understood life, that was the nature of loving someone.

He stood by her in the dying afternoon light as she shot arrow after arrow into a painted target he had built for her out of a larch log. Every afternoon she would do this, for hours. He sometimes believed she wouldn't stop if he didn't tell her to. She didn't tire of it, or grow bored, as she did with everything else. She was all focus and energy, running back and forth to fetch her arrows and unleashing the whole quiver again and again. Then, in the evenings, she would sit happily by the fire after supper to replace arrowheads and mend fletchings and wax her bowstring.

"Give me a challenge, Snowy," she said after a while. "I'm sick of shooting at that target."

"All right," Skalmir said, grasping her hand and walking her up a hillock. "See that ash over there?"

"That one?" she asked, pointing with an arrow. "With the ivy growing up it?"

"Yes. The lowest branch is very narrow, but you have a clear shot. Can you hit it from here?"

She nocked the arrow without a word. Became still. He never saw her so still as she was when shooting.

With a soft swoosh the arrow sailed away and thudded into the branch.

"Well done!"

She pulled out another arrow. A soft rustle in the undergrowth behind them caught her attention. Skalmir had time to register the fact that a rabbit had emerged from its hole a hundred feet from them—moving, half hidden by wildflowers—before the arrow had left Rowan's fingers and found its mark.

She gasped. "Did I hit it?"

The dogs, trained for precisely this task, streaked off after it. Skalmir and Rowan began to run back through the undergrowth, the long tickling grass. Skalmir found the little body, warm but limp, Rowan's arrow protruding from its back.

"I hit it!" she shouted. "Snowy, I hit it. I caught us dinner. And from so far."

"Not only that, it was moving," he added, trying to sound more encouraging than astonished. He reached out to stroke her hair, but she ducked away, too full of excitement for affection, and snatched her rabbit off him.

"Now you can show me how to skin it and gut it, and then we'll roast it with some turnips." Already she was heading back to the house, her proud little spine straight and square, quiver bouncing over her shoulder, the dead rabbit dangling from her hand.

Skalmir followed, brimming with pride, even though she wasn't his to be proud of.

Late, late in the night, a boom of thunder woke Skalmir from a confusing dream about a deer that could speak, once it had taken an arrow to its brain. He blinked in the dark and saw the flash of lightning through the cracks around the shutter. Another boom. Rain hammered down.

He turned over, told himself to go back to sleep, but then remembered that Rowan liked to sleep with her shutter open on warm evenings, and it had been cloyingly warm at bedtime. So he kicked the dogs off his feet and rose to open the door between their chambers. Yes, the shutter was open, and the rain was gusting through it in swells. Another bolt of lightning momentarily blinded him, leaving a flash on his vision. He closed the shutter. Tomorrow he and Rowan would have to take out these wet rushes and put new ones down. He turned to where she lay, sleeping on her side. In the dark, he could make out her white nightgown, her shoulder rising and falling with her breath.

Skalmir went to her bed and crouched down. It seemed she had slept through the thunder. Gently, careful not to wake her, he reached out to stroke her shoulder.

She was icy cold.

Puzzled, his heart speeding a little, he let his hand rest there a few moments. She was definitely breathing. So why was she so cold? The shutter had been open but the night was muggy. He reached under her blanket to feel her back. Again, icy.

Now he began to doubt himself, doubt his eyes. She was as cold as the dead, so he shook her lightly and said her name. "Rowan?"

She moved. Of course she moved. She was breathing, she was alive. She made a small mumbling sound, then said, clear as a bell, "Mother?"

Skalmir didn't know what to say. He couldn't answer. If she was dreaming happily about her mother, he would not be so cruel as to remind her that she was stuck here in a dark, ancient wood with him, and would perhaps never see her mother again. Wengest had put Rose aside—Skalmir didn't know why for certain, but the rumors were of infidelity—and ordered her never to see her daughter again if peace was to hold between Almissia and Nettlechester.

Rowan's question hung there in the dark, unanswered. But she was breathing regularly and deeply again, and still as cold as frost under his hand. He pulled her blanket up higher and tucked it around her tightly, trying to warm her up. He was surprised she remembered her mother; perhaps she only remembered her in her sleep.

Skalmir stood. Leaving her small, sleeping body behind him, he closed the door and let her dream.

chapter 3

Bluebell never brought her entire retinue to Nether Weald. She always left them under Sighere's command at Withing, a town much better equipped for dealing with eleven men, their warhorses, and their packhorses. Nether Weald had one inn, small enough to burst at the end of an ordinary day; her hearthband simply wouldn't fit. Besides, Nether Weald was chosen precisely because it was so far from anywhere, so quiet and so forgettable. A perfect place for a young princess to hide until she came to womanhood. Not even Sighere knew that Rowan was in the Howling Wood. He was easily deflected with a claim of "the king's private business."

The elderly woman who ran the stable at Nether Weald received both Bluebell's roan-gray stallion, Torr, and Bluebell's money gratefully. "I'll take good care of him," the woman said, reaching up to rub Torr's withers.

"The extra coin is for your silence," Bluebell said.

"I know. You and King Wengest will always have our silence." She smiled, her face crinkling pleasantly.

Bluebell always forgot her name and always felt vaguely guilty about it. She nodded toward Torr. "He doesn't like many people, you know. But he likes you."

"He's a good judge of character," the woman replied proudly. "Come on, big fellow. I have some lovely oats for you."

Bluebell emerged from the stable, whistled for Thrymm, and set off down the road on foot. The way to Skalmir's house would be quicker on horseback, but there wasn't enough there for Torr to eat—he had a mighty appetite to go with his mighty heart—and she was unsure how long she would stay. In the past, she was almost guaranteed to spend at least one night. But things had changed.

She followed the path into the woods. The deep ruts of carriage wheels had collected muddy puddles that stank and buzzed with insects. Either side of the road, the hedges were covered in banks of wildflowers: cow parsley and roses and flowering blackberry vines. Nettles and thistles straggled among them. The canopy was thick, admitting only threads of sunlight. Thrymm stopped to sniff everything, but Bluebell kept her purposeful stride. She heard hoofbeats behind her and turned. Rowan's teacher, Sister Julian, on her bay palfrey. Bluebell moved into the middle of the road and held up her hand, and Sister Julian stopped.

"My lady," Sister Julian said.

"It's my lord," she said. "Or Bluebell." Nobody who spent any time with Bluebell would mistake her for a lady.

"My lord," Sister Julian said, the faintest pull of disapproval at the corners of her mouth.

"Have the day off," Bluebell said. "I'm going to spend some time with Rowan."

"She oughtn't miss her lessons."

"I'll teach her . . . some kind of lesson," Bluebell said. War strategy? The quickest way to kill a man? How to shit in the wild? She would come up with something.

Sister Julian already knew she was defeated. "Could you at least make sure she finishes hemming the apron she made? And check her fingernails? She had blood under them the other day from gutting a rabbit, and she hadn't even noticed."

"Absolutely. Absolutely I will do those things. You go ahead and enjoy your day off."

Thrymm had disappeared into the undergrowth chasing something. There was a squawk, a rattle of leaves.

Sister Julian offered her a cautious smile. "It is marvelous weather. Maava has blessed us."

At that moment, Thrymm tore out of the undergrowth with a half-dead pheasant in her mouth. She dropped it in the mud at Bluebell's feet, and it flopped around pathetically. Bluebell would have to cut its head off with her knife, but guessed this might be too much for Sister Julian's sensibilities.

"Bad dog," she said, as the bird continued to flap about on her feet. Thrymm sat back and licked her lips, her big head resting on Bluebell's thigh, eyes turned upward guiltily.

"Good day to you then, my lord," Sister Julian said, turning her horse around.

"You too."

As soon as the horse retreated, Bluebell pulled out her knife, crouched, and cut the bird's head off. Blood under the fingernails? Bluebell had once had to wash somebody's blood out of her ear. What would Sister Julian make of that? She rubbed Thrymm's muzzle. "This will roast up nicely," she said to her. Thrymm wagged her tail so hard it made an impression in the mud.

Together they walked the mile into the forest to Skalmir's house, then Bluebell whistled Thrymm forward and the dog went bounding to the door, pawing at it until it opened and a little voice said, "Thrymm!"

Rowan poked her head out a moment later and waved happily. "Bluebell's here!" she called. "Snowy, Bluebell is here!"

Skalmir's two little hunting dogs ran out and joined in a sniffing frenzy with Thrymm; then the three of them began to play, even though Thrymm was three times their size.

Bluebell jogged the last twenty yards. Rowan ran out to the front gate and Bluebell swept her up in a ferocious hug. The older Rowan grew, the more she looked like her mother, Rose. For Bluebell, it felt almost as though she had traveled back in time and was looking at her sister instead of her niece.

"Watch this," Rowan said the moment Bluebell put her down, and she began cartwheeling on the path. After four she fell on her bottom and picked herself back up, scooping one of her dogs into her arms. "My record is eleven."

"Double it and you'll be strong enough to lift up Thrymm," Bluebell said, making a show of feeling the little girl's arm muscles.

"Would she let me?"

"If I told her to."

"How many cartwheels would I have to do to lift Torr?"

"Even I couldn't lift Torr. But if you get to fifty in a row, I will take you riding on him."

"Hello, Bluebell." This was Skalmir, who stood at the threshold.

"Snowy," she said, looking up with a smile. Would her visit be awkward? Well, what did she care? Plenty of people were awkward around her. She strode forward and grasped his hand firmly, then let it go and handed him the dead pheasant. "Thrymm caught us some dinner." She slipped past him into the house. "I told Sister Julian to stay home. I'll watch Rowan today and we can cook together, can't we, little one?"

"Yes, and you can come home early and have a proper dinner with us, Snowy," Rowan said.

"I do as I'm told." Skalmir shrugged. He was a good-looking man with golden skin and white-blond hair. It was Bluebell who had given him his nickname, and not just for his snowy hair. His appearance suggested that he drew his bloodline from the raiders who inhabited the far north, although he had no knowledge of who his parents were. He had been found as a baby, abandoned outside the great study halls of Thridstow, then adopted and raised in Nettlechester by one of King Wengest's thanes.

Bluebell liked him. She liked the fact that he looked like a raider—tall, strong, fair—but wasn't throwing an ax at her as they usually were. She also liked the fact that he was always willing to get naked with her after Rowan went to sleep, though after last time, she vowed she would be a little more cautious.

"Not in the house, Rowan," Snowy said, and Bluebell looked around to see that Rowan had sat on the floor and was energetically plucking the pheasant.

"Go on, you take it outside and give its guts to the dogs," Bluebell said.

"Come on, doggies," Rowan said, and Thrymm, Strike, and Stranger followed happily.

Bluebell undid her sword-belt and let it drop on the bench that ran the length of the house. "Have you been well?" she asked.

"Have you?"

She spread her arms. "As you see me."

"Heading north?"

"Yes, to Blackstan's court. I'm hoping to open negotiations about Rowan marrying one of his sons. How many does he have?"

"Six, I believe. And a daughter. Isn't Rowan a little young?"

"To marry? Yes. To be promised to a family? Not really. You know I was promised to Wengest when I was eight. Then when I was sixteen he got a look at me and asked for Rose instead."

They both laughed, then Skalmir ventured, "He would have been lucky to have you."

Bluebell shook her head. "Enough of that."

"Sorry." He smiled tightly, then turned to the door, where he found his shoes and bent to lace them on. "I have to go to the village today," he said. "The smokehouse is full and Wengest will be expecting some fruits of my labor, no doubt, so I'd best go talk to the meat merchant. I can be back for dinner, if you're determined to cook."

"Rowan can do the cooking. I'll watch."

He nodded. "Will you take her out shooting?"

"I'm not much of an archer."

"No, but she is. More impressive than the cartwheels, I promise. Take her. She'll want to show you."

Bluebell sometimes wished Skalmir was a warrior rather than a hunter; then he might have taught Rowan something more useful, like how to lift a sword. "Very well, I will."

He straightened, fixed her with his blue gaze. "She's excited to see you. You haven't visited us in a long time."

"I get here when I can. Go on with you. Don't you have business in the village to attend to?"

He clearly wasn't afraid of her steely tone. Of course he wasn't. That was the problem with fucking them.

"I'll be back in a few hours, then," he said, before heading off down the front path.

Bluebell and Rowan spent the morning salting and spitting the pheasant, buttering the cabbage, and steeping the marrow in broth. Only when everything was prepared and ready to cook over the hearth did Bluebell invite Rowan out into the wood to show off her archery.

They roamed off into the mouth of the hunting wood: a narrow muddy path, crowded on all sides by hedges and overhanging branches, laden with thick summer foliage.

"Do you know your way around the wood well enough to get us back?" she asked Rowan.

"Yes, of course. Snowy leaves little markers. See?" She pointed out two round gray stones balanced on top of each other. "Wherever there's one of these, there's another hunting path. Come on, let's go down this one."

Then they were tramping over thick undergrowth and deep leaf-fall, picking their way down rocky slopes. Bluebell could hear the trickle of running water. Rowan led her down to the edge of a stream, where the rushes grew thick on one side, and the elms bent over it on the other.

"Snowy lets me swim here on very hot days," Rowan said, marching up to the thick trunk of a birch and pulling out a piece of charcoal. She marked three crosses on the bark, one under another, then tramped back. Twenty feet. Fifty.

Bluebell followed at a distance. "Really? From this far?"

Rowan pulled herself up straight and queenly. "Really," she said, and waited until Bluebell was standing at her side. Then she retrieved three arrows from her quiver and kept them in her little palm. Nocked the first while the other two protruded between her fingers, waiting. She went very still.

Thwack. She nocked the next one. *Thwack.* And then the last. *Thwack.* It took less than five seconds for her to send an arrow sailing squarely into each cross.

Rowan turned to Bluebell, beaming.

Bluebell had to laugh. The girl was seven. *Seven.* "Good work, little chicken. Though I am disappointed you haven't picked up that sword I gave you."

"It's too heavy." She handed Bluebell her bow. "This is light. Snowy made it for me."

"Run and fetch your arrows. See if you can do it again."

So she did, and this time one of them missed but Rowan was jiggling with excitement now, so could be forgiven. They ran through the whole process a few times then remembered they had better cook dinner before Snowy returned. Rowan slid her hand into Bluebell's and they trod in the impressions left by their feet on the way in.

"Bluebell, why haven't you been to see us in so long?" Rowan asked finally, as though she'd been wanting to ask it all along but waiting for the right moment.

"I have been busy. It's busy work being a king's daughter. When you are older, you'll see."

"I thought you and Snowy had a fight."

"No." The opposite. The perfect opposite. He had declared he loved her, but she wasn't a thing to be loved.

"He was sad after last time. Did you make him sad?"

"I don't know the inside of Snowy's heart," Bluebell muttered. That was the other problem with fucking them: Sometimes they fell in love. No matter that she was no prettier than a millstone and her nose was smashed to bits. But she'd never expected such folly from Skalmir. He had been her favorite, damn it. Far too much her favorite. "But I did nothing to make him sad."

Rowan's hand slipped out of hers, and Bluebell walked a few paces before realizing the girl was not following her. She turned, wondering what sulky nonsense Rowan was indulging in, but Rowan was not sulking. She was standing, very still, her head cocked slightly.

Bluebell narrowed her eyes.

"Can you hear it?" Rowan asked.

Bluebell listened. Robins. Rustling leaves. Soft paws in the undergrowth. She shook her head. "Hear what?"

"Singing."

Bluebell strained her ears. Now she could hear her own pulse, but no singing. A shadow walked her spine. "Come on. Inside now."

"I hear it sometimes. Nobody else ever can."

"Nobody lives in the forest, and deer don't sing. You must be imagining it."

"No, it's not a person singing," Rowan said, skipping to catch up. "It's . . . something else."

"I don't know what you mean."

"Why do they call it the Howling Wood?"

Bluebell shrugged. "Perhaps it used to be full of wolves, before your great-grandfather enclosed it and hunted them out."

Rowan walked along beside her, her head bowed so her long dark hair fell over her face. "I don't know. Sometimes I imagine it's the wood singing."

"Woods don't sing."

Rowan didn't answer. Bluebell glanced at her. A strong line of second sight ran in her family; had Rowan inherited it? At times like this, she longed for Ash's company, her quiet wisdom.

Bluebell was about to suggest it might be poachers, but she didn't want to alarm Rowan so instead she said brightly, "Perhaps it's the wind in the trees. Then you'd be right; it would be the wood singing."

"Perhaps," Rowan answered, sounding entirely unconvinced.

"Come along. We'll start the fire and while the bird is roasting I'll get that sword into your hands for a bit of practice."

Rowan groaned and followed her to the house.

Around the wood and across the river in two days' comfortable riding, Bluebell and her hearthband reached Fifelham, the main town in the northern kingdom of Littledyke. But even though they had sent a messenger five days ahead of them, even though they approached with Almissia's standard high, nobody came out to greet them. The guardsmen at the tower recognized Bluebell and let them through, and their stewards took the horses and told her and her men to go and wait in the king's hall, but it was empty, the hearthpit cold, the tables all pushed against the walls. Ordinarily, the hall would be bustling with preparations for a feast to welcome them.

"What is this?" Sighere asked her in a quiet voice as they waited. "Did our messenger not arrive?"

"I need food and drink," Gytha grumbled.

"Hush now," Bluebell said. "Until we've spoken to Blackstan, we can't know why they are so unprepared for our visit." She glanced around the hall, so much smaller than her father's, with the double hearth and low roof favored by the northern kingdoms as proof against the cold. The door swung in, admitting light and a small, slight man dressed in green and amber.

"My lord Bluebell," he said, shuffling toward her with head bent. "You will not remember me. I am Wulfgar, eldest son of Blackstan."

Bluebell sized him up. Rowan couldn't marry this one—not because he was almost twenty, but because he looked as though a strong wind might snap him in two. "We sent a messenger," she said, taking his hand.

"I . . ." He looked around, and she noticed dark shadows under his eyes. "I don't know where my father is."

"You don't know?"

"He was meant to be back by now. He took my mother and my brothers up to North Hall—our northern residence—for some time away hunting and fishing. He left me and my sister in charge down here. But he's not back."

Alarm rose in Bluebell's blood. North. Raiders. "When were you expecting him?"

"On the turn of the summer."

"That's ten days behind us."

"Yes. I have wanted to ride north to find him but Annis . . . my sister . . . she is afraid to be left here without me." He dropped his voice, almost as though he suspected Annis was nearby, listening. "I fear the worst. North Hall is close to Merkhinton."

Merkhinton was a stronghold in the mountain foothills, set up precisely to keep raiders from Iceheart out of Thyrsland. But it was a robust stronghold with eight hundred men. If it had fallen, word would have reached them by now. Wouldn't it?

"Nothing and nobody would have gotten past Merkhinton," she said reassuringly. "But we will travel there now to see that all is in order, and if you give us directions, we will also stop to pay our respects to your father and brothers at North Hall."

The relief was visible in his posture. "My lord, I would be so grateful." His eyes were shining with unshed tears. Lofric sniggered behind her. She held her tongue. Life would eventually teach that idiot about compassion and humility.

"It would be our honor," she said to Wulfgar. "Put all worry out of your mind."

Within an hour, Sighere had the route to North Hall mapped out, and Bluebell was saying goodbye to a pale and shaking Prince Wulfgar near the gatehouse.

"Close your gates until I send somebody back to you," she instructed him. "It will be either King Blackstan or one of my men with news. You are well fortified here. You need fear nothing for your own safety, or that of your sister." She turned to her hearthband. "Back on the road," she commanded, and urged Torr forward.

Sighere kept pace with her. When the town gates were a long way behind them, he finally asked, "What do you think has happened to Blackstan? Raiders?"

"It ought not be. Not through Merkhinton, unless the world is ending. But I almost wish it was raiders—I know what to do with them. I always fear worse the thing I cannot see, the thing I cannot predict."

"I suppose we will find out soon enough."

"That we will," she said, then shouted to her hearthband, "North!"

CHAPTER 4

Between the hood of gray cloud and the broad plains, the sun burned low and orange, infusing the world with ambered twilight. Ash glanced at the sky and knew they would not reach home before dark. Unweder trudged ahead of her, heedless of the coming night. Upward and upward, past granite tors cooling in the dusk. Her legs ached. Every day for the last month, her legs had ached. Unweder led her over every inch of moorland, through yellow-blossomed gorse that caught on her cloak and dense curling bracken that grabbed at her ankles. This time he was certain, he said. This time he knew they would find it. He had taken bird form yesterday and flown for miles, finally spotting among the tors what he was certain was a barrow. These moors were dotted with barrows. Most of them were tiny, gaping open to the elements, stone lintels fallen, containing little more than mud and animal droppings. For a month they had been in and out of them all. Fruitless. But a bird couldn't open a barrow. And Unweder knew he couldn't protect himself from whatever lurked within it, not without Ash.

"We're close," he called, his voice swept east by the wind. He stopped and turned in a slow circle, his good eye shrewd as a bird's, assessing the landscape. "Definitely close," he said. "Everything looks different on the ground."

"It's growing dark."

"I'm not afraid of the dark. Nor should you be. Especially you."
His eye still roamed. The other was hidden under a patch perma-
nently now. "That way," he said, nodding at a steep grassy slope.

"I will follow," Ash said. She always had.

"Good girl."

Within half a mile, she saw it herself. A hump in the land, with
granite slabs laid out atop it. To anyone who wasn't searching, it
would disappear between the naturally occurring rock formations.
A narrow alley between rocks led steeply down to the entrance. The
path itself had been laid out with small square stones, overgrown by
grass and weed. They found themselves in a crevice where layers of
cold gathered and lingered. The lintel stood a foot above Ash's head.
A large slab leaned crookedly across the entrance, cracked directly
through the middle, left to right.

"We'll have to move this," Unweder said, and looked at her
knowingly.

"Let's try with our hands first."

"If you say." He shrugged one shoulder, reminding her that one
of his hands was all but useless. It was a sore point between them.

"Do what you can," she said.

They positioned themselves on either side of the slab and heaved
against it. It wouldn't budge.

"Ash?"

"Once more," she said, not meeting his eye.

Heave. It gave a little. Ash moved her feet out of the way. One
more heave, and the top of the slab overbalanced. Unweder leapt
back. The rock slammed to the ground with an enormous thud.

"Now we can climb over," Ash said.

"We'll need light."

"I know." Ash hoisted herself up and over the remains of the
door, her feet landing in a shallow puddle of icy water. She stood a
moment, stilling her mind and her hands, with her right fist
clenched. *Concentrate a little, just a little.* Slowly, she unfurled her
palm. A small circle of soft blue-white light shone from it. Shadows
ran as Ash extended her palm in front of her. There were strange

carvings on the walls of the barrow, circles and lines that belonged to a time long before hers.

Unweder dropped softly to the ground beside her. "Here we are," he said, and she could hear the suppressed excitement in his voice. Unweder wanted to find a dragon, and dragons were known barrow-dwellers. He knew all seventeen locations in Thyrsland where dragons had ever been seen, and Ash had followed him to fifteen now. Unweder wanted to adopt the dragon's body as his own, shift his shape into something mighty and sublime. Ash wanted to find a dragon, too, but for different reasons; hidden reasons.

"It's deep," Ash said. She could feel it in the way the chill air moved.

Unweder took a deep breath. "Can you smell that?"

Ash could only smell old stone, limey and inert.

"It's the smell of centuries. Lead the way with your little light, Ash."

She reached for his hand and held it firmly, her other palm still extended. The barrow tapered to a tunnel, and he had to walk behind her, tightening his fingers in hers. The dim light barely penetrated the darkness as they left the entrance behind. Ash's shoulders brushed against the carvings, and she shuddered involuntarily, as though some ancient hand had touched her.

Unweder spotted it first, his gasp both awed and disappointed. The tunnel opened to a large chamber whose walls curved away. She imagined they must form a large circle, but couldn't see that far. In front of them were bones.

Dragon bones.

Relief was warm and liquid through her limbs. They had found one, and it was already dead. Long dead.

Unweder released her fingers and squatted on the cold floor with his hands pressed mournfully into the creature's skull. Ash moved closer to provide light, even though her hand was beginning to ache. The dragon's body was perhaps the length of two horses; the bones of its tail, if laid out straight, would make it twice that length

SISTERS OF THE FIRE   33

in total. Its head was smaller than she had imagined. Two sharp ridges rose on either side of its skull.

Ash's light caught the glimmer of precious objects in small piles all around the skeleton. Coins and cups and plates.

"How did he die?" Ash asked.

"She," Unweder answered. "Only the females are this small. And she died of old age." He ran his fingers inside the creature's jaw. "Many teeth missing, the rest worn down."

Ash imagined the dragon, curling up here around her paltry treasure, solitary and old. A pang of sadness, familiar and marrow-deep. "To be alone is a terrible thing," she said, so softly that Unweder didn't hear. He was poking around at the walls, looking for other chambers.

"Nothing, nothing, nothing," he said, exasperated. "They sometimes mate, and when they do, it's for life. I'd hoped there might be a male around here, but it seems she was an old spinster. No evidence of anything having lived or breathed here in many years."

"I can't hold the light much longer," Ash said.

"You underestimate yourself."

"Can we go?"

Unweder scooped up a handful of coins and filled his pockets.

"Careful," she said. "There may be old magic."

"Too old to hurt us, like this poor old lady. Get some gold, Ash. You know we'll need it."

She did as he instructed with her free hand, filling the deep pocket on the front of her apron. It clinked softly, weighing her down. The trek home would be long and tiring.

Unweder turned to the skeleton and put his hands around the skull again. "I want to bring this."

"What for?"

"A keepsake."

"I'm not helping you carry it."

He tried to scoop it toward his chest with his good arm, lifted it, then dropped it again, laughing. "You're right. It's too heavy, too far. If only we hadn't had to sell the horses."

The horses. Ash had bought them from a stable near their fifth location. She'd walked them home happily enough, only to find that neither of them would tolerate Unweder anywhere near them. A week later she'd returned them and only gotten half her payment back. So it was on her own feet that she had traveled the length and breadth of the west country, through forests and across plains, in and out of barrows and caves, up and down hills and valleys. All to find, at their third-to-last location, one dead dragon.

"I'm leaving now," Ash said, because Unweder seemed so reluctant to abandon the skeleton.

"Very well, very well. If you must rush me."

She led the way again, out toward the daylight. Gratefully, she extinguished the light in her hand, and cool clarity returned to her temples. She climbed over the broken door, helped Unweder over.

Then felt the rumbling.

"Unweder?" she said.

"Old magic," he gasped.

The rumbling came from behind them, from the barrow, shaking the ground. The sound of beasts in stampede, wild whinnies and snorts.

"Run," Unweder said, and Ash ran, up the narrow crevice and out onto the tor, where dim evening had taken hold. She glanced behind her to see ghostly horses pouring from the barrow, gravel rocketing up behind their hooves. There was no way she and Unweder could outrun them. She seized her companion's arm and pulled him behind her as she faced them down, arms twisted back and around Unweder. The thought was half formed before the word poured out of her, a word she didn't know and would never remember later—something between *stop* and *stone*. It echoed sharply for miles and up to the clouds. A cold thud gathered around her, little half glimpses of phantom hands, gray as carved stone but moving softly to connect over her and Unweder, hands that disappeared from her sight if she looked at them directly.

The ghostly horses sensed the invisible barricade and reared up, parting around it, pouring past Ash so fast and so loud that she felt them like wind on her cheeks. Their mist-white manes streaked behind them. Speed and power. It rattled her clothes, making the coins in her apron jingle. Her blood thundered with the thrill of it.

Moments later, they were gone. The barricade dismantled itself as the elementals dispersed back into the rock and ground. She released her arms and turned to Unweder.

"Right," he said. "Let's head home."

Home was a grass-roofed hut fashioned from a hollow in the ground and woven sapling trunks, with an earthen floor spread with rushes, under a huge oak tree whose roots made the hut's foundations. Half a house and half a grotto, Ash mused. After their seventh location, they spent less and less time building their homes and making them comfortable. They usually didn't stay for long, although the four long wintry months in a cave on the grassy southwest downs of Micelmold had passed agonizingly slowly. Which year had that been? The first? The second? They blurred into each other sometimes, the locations, the seasons. It had been four years and two months since she had last seen her family, and she was barely the same person anymore.

Ash curled up on her side on her old blanket. Unweder sat by the fire, counting coins. A charm he wore around his neck had worked free of his shirt and swung as he moved. He had eaten some rabbit-and-parsley soup, but she had no appetite; she never had any appetite after performing magic. The breeze came from the west, fanning the smoke back into the hollow and making her eyes sting.

Sleep wouldn't come. Her scalp itched. Her scalp had been itching for seven weeks now. At first she'd thought lice had bred in her hair, and she'd packed her scalp with oil infused with stavesacre and sweet wormwood. Then, when the itching didn't cease, she took a knife and shaved off all her hair. But still, the itch.

Slowly, she had come to believe this was a new symptom of using magic. Over the years, she had outgrown the worst of the gut aches and head fogs, and she knew that if she didn't try to stretch her undermagic too far, to things that she had no natural talent for, she would mostly be comfortable. But now this crawling feeling across her scalp. In some ways it was worse than the other ailments, given it was constant, and driving her to madness.

Her dark hair only half an inch long, her shins and elbows as sharp as knives. No, she wasn't the same person anymore. Or at least would never be recognized as the old Ash, should her sisters ever see her again.

"We have a lot of gold here," Unweder said. "We will be well furnished at our next location."

"Our second-last location," she muttered, knowing that Unweder would stay away from society and the money mightn't buy them more than a few new blankets from a trader on the route.

He fell silent a few moments, then said, "Yes, yes, Ash. I'm aware of that."

"And after that there is no more hope." No more fear.

"The vision was clear, and you know I paid dearly for it."

Ash did know. She had nursed him back to health after the long night he had spent, half poisoned on god-eye toadstools and nightshade, sweating in a trance by the fire, pupils huge and black. Afterward, waking from a deep sleep, his blind eye had turned milky and ghastly, but his mind could now reach out to the memories that still quivered in the vast web of knowing and follow the threads to every dragon sighting for centuries. Seventeen. A number that had once seemed impossibly high, but had dwindled to almost nothing.

Two more locations. And if there was no dragon, then her dreams would have been made into lies and she could return to her family, her old life, and know both were safe.

If there was a dragon . . .

Ash had seen her future. She had seen fire and fear.

The vision rose in her again, its dread details never far from her mind. The town high above a harbor. The fear and panic. The scarlet monster rising from the water, coming for her, spewing its blinding fire on everyone in its path. Looking for her. Always looking for her.

If there was a dragon, then she would destroy it, before Unweder found it or became it; before it or he could destroy all she loved.

"Do you know where we will go next?" she asked him.

He sat back and gazed at her a moment. "You look tired, Ash."

"I am always tired."

"After all these years, eh?" He considered her a little longer. The two of them had spent every waking moment together for four years, but they were not lovers. They were not even friends, really. She needed the knowledge he had, certainly, and not just about where dragons may lie. A century of practicing undermagic meant that he was wise in ways she simply couldn't be yet. Without him, her own magic would have killed her at the start.

But lately things had shifted: He was far more dependent on the power she possessed. He inhabited a stolen body that would rot all around him without a regular supply of her blood. He also relied on her command of elemental spirits to keep them safe. She often wondered if it had occurred to Unweder that she might not need him anymore, that she might have her own aspirations for their journey that ran counter to his, rather than still being the compliant apprentice.

But for now, he trusted her and didn't seem to know that she had always kept her heart wary. "You're a good girl, Ash. Get some rest."

"My scalp is itching."

He shifted, sat next to her, and laid his fingers gently on her head. "Here, this will help." He often stroked her hair while she fell asleep. She closed her eyes.

"Ash," he said, after a long silence. "I need some more."

Ash sat up and looked at him, her pulse flicking hard in her throat. "Already?"

He shrugged, almost sheepishly. Ash calculated in her mind: four weeks. It had only been four weeks since the last time he had taken her blood. At the start, many months would pass between her gifts to him.

"Can you wait another week?" Ash asked. "The last wound is barely healed."

"My body is not what it once was. You know I have other choices." This was said diffidently, almost a challenge. Unweder badly wanted a new body, but it meant murder and Ash wouldn't have it. She'd agreed to provide the blood so he wouldn't kill, but it never stopped troubling her that killing was always on his mind.

"Very well, then," Ash said, rolling up her sleeve. Pain had long since lost the power to trouble her.

"I will be strong and hale tomorrow," Unweder said, reaching for his knife. "And then we will head toward the sea."

They struck out in the cool of the following morning. Ash had long since lost her sense of direction and distance from home; she had followed Unweder, obedient, from one side of Thyrsland to another. They were back in her father's kingdom of Almissia, but in the far southwest, which was sparsely populated because of poor pasture-land. Undermagicians like Unweder avoided other people; they demanded isolation. He insisted they walk the low roads, the green paths, the holloways. Ash had embraced the knowledge that she was an undermagician, too. The friends she had trained with in the common faith would certainly say she was. But Ash missed people. She missed the sweet daily whirl of chatter and activity by which most people lived their lives. Also, her high sensitivity meant that she could see things on the low roads that Unweder could not.

Every child grew up in Thyrsland knowing to stay on the road, that bad things lurked off the main routes. Now Ash could see them. Not directly; more like the bright flickering impression left on her eyes after staring at a flame. But they were there. And not just bad things. Not just the mournful spirits of the lost dead and impossible creatures formed of bones and feathers that lurched along beside them awhile, staring with uncanny intensity through hollow eyes. But wonders, too. A seven-foot man with the head of a deer accompanied them for half a day. Ghostly women of aching beauty wrapped themselves around low-hanging branches and called to her by name in bell-like voices, only to snarl and turn to vapor when she refused to answer. And of course there were her elementals, the tiny, pointy-faced piskies who had taken her as their queen.

No, that wasn't right, for a queen could be loved. The elementals did not love her. They believed themselves enslaved. Somehow, her voice and thoughts could command them. Even Unweder couldn't explain it.

On the third day, after sleeping in balmy evenings under shady elms and oaks, the sky filled with gray and rain set in. They kept moving. They had walked in rain before, in colder weather than this. But as the afternoon deepened and so did the rain, they passed into a tiny village on the edge of a wood. A hunters' village, little more than an unpaved road, a collection of small houses, and a tiny wooden inn.

Rain was dripping off the tip of Ash's nose when she turned to Unweder and said, "Can we sleep under cover tonight?"

Unweder's brows drew down. "Worried about a little rain?"

"Please? We have money. Imagine. A roof over our heads. A hot meal. Beer."

Unweder nodded. "Beer."

"It's only for a night. This rain won't last."

"I don't know if predicting the weather is one of your talents," he said with a half smile. "All right, but we must hide the gold. I'll keep a pocket of change to pay, but the rest . . ." His eye roved up and down her body.

"I can pin the purse to my underdress."

They retreated into the trees and Unweder helped her pin the heavy leather purse under her pinafore, up near her hip where her dress would skim loosely over it. She hitched her pack so it rested on that side, and together they walked back down the muddy road to the inn.

Inside, the smell of mold and wet dog. A little weak illumination straggled through the shutters, but most of the light came from the low fire in the grate. The stone floor was so cold, Ash swore she could feel it through her shoes. Summer seemed as though it had never come here. The inn was empty.

The smell of sweet steam and stewing meat came from a back room. Unweder called, "Hello?" and a moment later a large, hairy dog came bounding out happily, with a pale, pretty woman behind him.

"Can I help?"

"We're looking for food and drink and a place to stay."

The woman's expression was genuinely puzzled. "A place to stay? Well, then."

Ash crouched to pat the dog, who put his paws up on her knees and tried to lick her nose.

"You have rooms?" Unweder was saying.

"No, sir, we do not. The rooms . . . nobody has stayed here in a long time. Rats ate the beds. Once we were on a trade route. Now . . ."

"Ah."

"We make a modest living serving locals, so there will be food and drink enough for you. And if you're willing to sleep on the hearth tonight, you'd be most welcome to shelter from the rain. Looks like it's set in for a day or so."

Ash stood again, and the dog tried to stretch its paws up and love her some more. As it did, it brushed the purse under her dress, which chinked faintly.

The woman glanced at her, then said to the dog, "Go on with you, Featherfeet."

The dog slid off, the click of its claws on the stone floor at odds with its name.

"Ash? What do you think?" Unweder said to her.

Sleeping inside, by a fire. Yes, she would be in the company of dogs, but after days of walking, the twin hardships of rain and mud would tip her into misery. "Let's stay," she said.

The inn began to fill up a few hours after they arrived. Unweder grew less and less comfortable as more people arrived, shifting in his seat and casting his eye around nervously. Ash sat close to him, close enough to feel the heat from his shoulder, and urged him to be calm. In truth, fewer than twenty people came in and out of the inn that night, but the building was so cramped it felt like many more. The fire seemed too hot and their voices too loud and too sharp.

Ash and Unweder ate their fill of deer stew and drank good beer, and as the last few men and women left for their own homes, they rolled out their blankets next to Featherfeet and her brother Long-belly, and settled for the night. The fire burned low, the candles in the sconces glowed dimly, and silence stole over the room.

Ash woke—unsure how many hours later—to movement behind her. She thought at first it was one of the dogs shifting against her, but then in a blur there were fingers over her mouth and a hand roughly pulling at her clothes. All was dark but for the faint glow of embers.

The gold. Somebody was trying to take the gold.

Ash bit down hard, and when the hand pulled away she shouted for Unweder. Unweder flung back his blanket and struggled into a crouch, but the pretty woman who had served them that afternoon had yanked Ash's head back and positioned the tip of a blade against her throat. Ash's pulse thudded in her ears.

"Just give me the money," she said. "Don't tempt me—I am desperate."

Unweder said, "Give her the purse, Ash."

But Ash, just woken and bent so violently to this woman's will, filled with a rage that swept away sense. She had walked for hundreds of miles over years and years, and this small treasure was her just recompense. It meant the difference between sleeping in dry blankets and sleeping in damp holes. She was tired of sleeping in damp holes.

"No!" she shouted, struggling against the woman.

The blade began to move, drawing behind it a searing, stinging pain. Immediate regret. Her vision clouded. She was sure she could see the walls shaking. She heard a woman's voice shouting in fear; she presumed it was her own.

The pain stopped. The knife clattered to the ground. Ash's vision tunneled. The fire billowed into yellow-bright life and Ash tried to make sense of what was happening. The roof was falling in . . . beams cracking and shards of wood dropping all around her, but not landing on her or Unweder. The walls were also swelling out and out, as though they might at any moment burst and let the night in. The flames shot out of the grate and made orange wings on the walls, and Ash leapt to her feet, grabbed her pack, and turned to Unweder. He stood, horrified, as he watched two fiery hands reach out from the grate and take the woman, screeching, around the throat and ankles. The dogs howled and ran, scratching at the front door as shards of wood continued to rain down. The rushes had caught fire and now the flames were spreading fast around them, but a clear path—so neat it seemed unreal—laid out before them direct to the door.

"Run!" Ash called to Unweder, stumbling toward the door and yanking it open. Cold rushed in; the dogs rushed out. Unweder was behind her. Mighty beams fell as the roof collapsed.

They churned the mud with their feet, stopping only at the top of the hill to turn and watch as the walls of the inn split outward, fire surging into the damp night air.

Ash was struck dumb. Her heart hammered. Her hand went to her throat and came away bloody.

Unweder turned her so he could see her wound by the firelight, and touched her under the chin gently. "It's shallow, just the skin. I can dress it once we . . ." He trailed off, no doubt wondering, as she was, where they would sleep that night.

"They killed her," Ash said. Then she turned and shouted, "I didn't ask you to kill anyone! I don't want you to act without my command!"

Unweder caught her arm and faced her to him. "You would have been dead if your elementals hadn't saved you."

"They burned her alive!" The woman's screech echoed in her mind, amplifying and slapping from one side of her skull to the other. She smacked her forehead with the heel of her palm, a grunt of fear and frustration coming unbidden from her mouth.

Unweder gazed at her with hungry intensity. He licked his lips. "And they say your sister is the unkillable one."

How she hated him in that moment. How revulsed she was by his venal curiosity. She had to look away. Mizzling rain began to fall. Down at the inn, voices and movement as the fire was discovered.

"We should keep moving," Unweder said. "Dawn can't be far away."

"As you wish."

They hugged the edge of the wood to give the burning building a wide berth then rejoined the narrow rut that passed as a road. Ash's heart felt sick and her scalp itched, and the darkness grew upon her soul.

chapter 5

R ose woke to the sound of rain, and groaned before even opening her eyes. Not rain. Not today.

Beside her, Linden stirred. She put her hand on his little shoulder and smiled. She could smell the smoke from Eldra's fire next door and knew that meant there was porridge cooking.

Rose sat up from among the blankets and reached to open the shutter a crack. Gray daylight. "Linden," she said. "Time to get up."

His little brow furrowed, but he didn't open his eyes. He would take his time. He always did.

Rose got to her feet and pinned on her best dress and her gray cloak with amber beads. Today it actually mattered what she wore. Though she liked to think she had left the life of a privileged princess happily behind her, she did miss the fabrics and the beads and the shoes.

Curse the rain.

She made herself ready for the day, then opened the little door that divided her bowerhouse from Eldra's one-room home. Clutter and chaos in the tiny space. For months, Rose had lived in here with her, so close that her stomach couldn't rumble without Eldra hearing. She hadn't admitted at first that another baby was on its way, but when she finally did Bluebell sent money for somebody to build a bowerhouse. Well, Bluebell had first sent many messages demanding she come home and be with her family, but Rose would not. She would be subject to rumor and gossip, as would her new boy. She didn't know how long she could live up here in the wilds of Bradsey with Eldra, but for now she was happy. Not blissful bright-yellow happiness—more of a muted sunset color—but happiness nonetheless. As happy as one could be when apart from the two stars she'd hoped to navigate her life by.

She'd had to give Rowan and Heath up at the same time. While Rowan always seemed close to her thoughts—of course; a mother's thoughts are never far from her child—sometimes whole days would pass without her mind turning to Heath. In the last year or so, she had even wondered if perhaps she had finally stopped loving him. But then she'd remember something small about the way his lips curled when he smiled and it felt like poking a bruise: a dull ache, almost sweet.

"Good morning," Rose said, picking up the ladle and stirring the porridge. "This smells good."

Eldra looked up from where she sat on the little stone bench that ran halfway around the room. She was grinding chalk and herbs and oils together. "We chose a poor day for you to go to town. Would you like to wait until the weather clears?"

"No, no. I have Linden all prepared for my absence now. You know how he can be if his plans are upset." Besides, she wanted to go. She wanted to be out in the world so badly. Once every few months she made this trip, a full day's ride to the nearest village on the border of Littledyke for supplies. She took their aging cart and their equally aging horse and was gone a night, sometimes two.

Linden emerged, dark curls messy, eyes puffy with sleep.

"Good morning, my darling," Eldra said, and Linden made a beeline for the porridge pot.

Linden didn't speak. Ever. Not a single *Mama* or *I want* . . . In every other way he was a normal little boy of nearly four years; if anything, he seemed exceptionally bright. His greatest joy was to help Eldra with her potions and powders, and he knew where every tiny jar of each ingredient was kept, even in the chaos of her cluttered walls. He recognized them by some detail invisible to everyone else. Eldra openly adored her silent little companion. Rose found love easy, of course; he was her son. But his heart was something of a stranger to hers, in a way that Rowan's had never been at this age.

An old pain flared up in her blood. She breathed a moment, then got on.

Rose made Linden a bowl of porridge and sat him down with it, then crouched in front of him, hands on his knees. "Now remember, Mama is going away today."

He nodded solemnly.

"Eldra will take care of you and sleep with you in your bed tonight."

He dipped his spoon in his porridge despondently, hanging his head.

"I'll be back as quick as I can. With honey for your porridge."

This promise failed to cheer him up, but then it was difficult to tell—he did not often smile or laugh. Rather, he had two notable moods: sharply focused, and anxiously distracted. This morning's withdrawn neutrality was normal, and not alarming. It simply told her nothing more about him than the little she already knew.

"We will be fine," Eldra said, rising and limping over to him. "We will keep very busy and I will make your favorite soup for dinner and some new bread, then tell you stories of the old magicians until you fall asleep."

This reassurance must have worked, because he began to eat.

Eldra held out a small rough pouch to Rose. "Here."

"What is it?"

"Blinding powder."

"Why would I need—"

"Better than the sleeping stones," Eldra said with a smirk.

Every time Rose went to town, Eldra made her some new charm or another that was expressly for protection. Last week she'd presented Rose with sleeping stones, meant to be thrown directly at whoever was threatening her. Eldra had her practice in the garden, but when she'd been unable to hit the target with the stone even once, Eldra had harrumphed about trying something different.

"I don't have to get it in their eyes?" Rose asked.

"Just throw a handful of the powder on the ground with as much force as you can. The impact will set it off."

"Will it blind me?"

The corner of Eldra's mouth twisted up. "No. I'm a better magician than that, Rose."

Rose pinned the pouch to the inside of her cloak. She'd never needed one of Eldra's protection spells, but she was grateful all the same. She pulled up her hood and picked up the bag she had packed last night. "I'll go and hitch Sunny to the cart and be on my way, then," she said.

"Ride safe. We will see you tomorrow afternoon."

Rose bent and kissed Linden's cheek. "Goodbye, my love," she said.

He waved goodbye then returned to his porridge.

Out in the stable—bigger than their house—she shooed spiders off the old cart. Up on the ledge, she could see the almost-empty bags of oats and millet. Sunny looked at her mournfully. She didn't like the rain, either, but she was a sturdy mare who had served them well, and would enjoy the exercise once they were on the move.

"Come on, old girl," Rose said, approaching with the bridle. "The weather might be better off the moors."

Then she was away, out into the world—damp and misty as it was—for her small adventure.

As afternoon approached and the clouds lifted, the moors began to gentle and slope downward, and farmland came into view. Rose was cheered by the small signs of civilization. Roofs and chimneys, hedgerows and wide paths, the sound of sheep bleating in fields, blackbirds circling over crops. Sometimes, out in the wilds of Bradsey, it felt as though they were the only three people in the world. On clear nights, she couldn't bear to look at the stars because of the horrible sensation that she lived at the farthest edge of the night sky, and was falling and falling ever backward into it.

Even Sunny's pace lightened as she picked up new scents. They crossed the narrow bridge into Arbury in the full heat of the afternoon. The clang of the smithy swelled and receded on the wind. She took Sunny directly to the stables, and paid a very thin man a coin to unhitch the cart, walk Sunny, and water her. Then she paid his equally thin son—about Rowan's age, she always noticed—another coin to watch her cart, and she straightened her cloak and walked into town to see which merchants had supplies for her. A woman herded a flock of geese ahead of her, and she thought of taking a goose home to roast . . . they hadn't eaten anything so delicate in a long time. They ate wild stringy rabbits or carp from the stream a mile's walk from the house, served with sage and rosemary and roots from their little patch, and flatcakes made with whatever grain was left in the stable. Yes, she would buy a goose. And honey. And cheese. Her mouth watered at the thought of it, and she realized she hadn't eaten since breakfast. She saw the alehouse and decided to treat herself to a cooked dinner and a cup of ale.

Rose shut out the hot sun and stood in the steamy alehouse a moment, waiting for her eyes to adjust. Only two other customers, both men, sat at a rough wooden table by the wall, concentrating on their food, not conversing.

The alehouse wife greeted her merrily. "Is it not a day to sing for?" she said.

"Oh yes," said Rose. "I left the moors behind in mist and drizzle this morning."

A light went on in the woman's eyes and she blinked rapidly. "The moors?"

Rose wasn't sure if the woman was asking this question of Rose or of herself, so she remained silent, curious.

"Is your name Rose?" the woman asked, but she was already bustling past, to the long wooden counter that divided the alehouse from the brewery.

"Yes, it is. Why?"

The woman bent over and pulled out a woven basket, which she tipped onto the counter, spreading objects everywhere—bent spoons and knife handles and bits of broken pottery and objects Rose didn't recognize, but supposed belonged in the brewery.

"Now, where is it?"

Rose was aware her heart had started thudding a little harder.

"Ah, here." The woman's hand closed on a folded piece of parchment. She handed it to Rose. "A young man named Cardew was here, not quite a month past. He said you would come eventually, that he had seen you here before and knew you. Rose. From the moors. With the long dark hair and the hazel eyes." The woman nodded at her. "He left you this message. Said I was to give it to you if I ever saw you."

Rose unfolded the note. It was covered in writing, but she couldn't read. Ash was the only one among her sisters who could read, and she had disappeared four years ago. "What does it say?" she asked.

"I don't know," the alehouse wife said, frowning. "But if you need somebody who can read, there's a trimartyr chapel at the southern end of town. Those preachers can all read."

It was true. In fact, King Wengest's preacher, Nyll, had tried to teach her, a long time ago. She could make out a few of the letters, but one word she was certain of: *Heath*.

"The southern end of town, you say?" The circle of her vision seemed very bright.

The woman nodded and Rose was outside a moment later, hurrying, trying not to run lest she stumble. *Heath*. Who was Cardew, and why was he leaving her a message about Heath?

She pushed her way through the crowds in the market and headed down between crooked timber houses, the smell of nightsoil in her nostrils. She could see the little stone building, its roof a perfect triangle, standing off from the other buildings almost as if it were disdaining them. Low elm branches shaded its front door. Rose knocked loudly, and waited.

In time, the door opened, and she found herself looking at a handsome, clean-shaven, impossibly young man, who smiled at her. "Good day, my lady."

"I . . ." She scoured her mind for trimartyr phrases. "Maava be with you, my lord. I need your help."

He opened the door wide. He was dressed entirely in gray, and his little chapel was as she remembered her own, back in Folkenham when she was a queen. Bare. Stone. Space for nothing except thoughts of Maava. She quickly knelt on the ground as would be expected, and he knelt with her.

She handed him the note. "This bears news of an old friend," she said. "I cannot read it." It occurred to her briefly to wonder if the message would reveal to the preacher some dark truth about her, but her need to know overrode her fear.

He unfolded it and glanced at it briefly, then back at her. "You are Rose?"

"I am."

"I'm Urdi." He smiled.

"Pleased to meet you," she managed, then licked her lips. "The note?"

"For Rose, who comes in from the moors to Arbury, from Cardew, north of Llyr's Hollow. I write to you as somebody who shares love for Heath, who has been in exile in Llyr's Hollow for the last four years."

"Llyr's Hollow?" Rose said. "Llyr's Hollow is only ten miles from here." All the while, he'd been so close. So close!

"More like fifteen," Urdi answered. "I shall continue?"

Rose nodded.

"Our friend is very ill and cannot be expected to live much longer." Here the preacher paused, and said, "I am very sorry. Maava be with you."

Her heart fell like a stone in a cold pond.

"He has not asked me to contact you. In fact, he has asked me expressly not to contact you, but I know from our many long conversations that you are the only woman who has ever had claim on his heart and so I pass

on this news to you, that you may know it and do with it what your own
heart dictates."

Silence followed his words. Rose remained kneeling, the ground
cold through her dress. Outside, birds chirped and peeped in the
elms, and a soft wind sighed through their branches. Inside felt air-
less, cold as a tomb.

"One of the lessons Maava has for us—" the preacher began.

"Maava has nothing for me," she spat, climbing to her feet and
snatching the note. Dimly, she was aware that she was behaving
cruelly, but was unable to stop herself.

The young preacher stood, too, and rather than rise to her anger,
his voice became more quiet, more measured. "Your pain is very
human," he said. "And it will not kill you."

"He's dying," she said, and a sob bubbled out of her.

"But not yet dead, perhaps."

"The letter's been sitting there for nearly a month."

"Perhaps you should go to him. If he has already passed into the
Sunlands, then you and his friend Cardew can pray together, or
maybe simply share some small memories that will bring you
peace."

All along, he had been so close. Would she have already sought
him out, had she known? He hadn't sought her out. His friend
Cardew knew who she was, knew she came to Arbury regularly
enough. Had it been difficult for Heath not to come for her? They
might have been happy together . . .

Go to him. *Go to him.*

The preacher folded the note and grasped her hand, slid it into
her palm, and folded her fingers over it. His touch was warm.
"Maava be with you," he said.

She wondered if he would be so kind if she told him her history
with Heath. Taking him as a lover while married to his uncle, bearing his daughter and passing her off as the king's, then being discovered as unfaithful and making the choice not to name her lover,
and by that choice losing her daughter. No, even this young trimar-

tyr hadn't enough peace and mercy in his heart for someone like Rose.

"May all the gods forgive me," she said under her breath. "I will go to him."

Good sense told her to eat and drink and make sure Sunny was rested before setting out, so she did. Better sense would have made her stay overnight in Arbury, but that she ignored, certain that she could be in Llyr's Hollow by dark. The stable master refused to mind her cart for the night, so she had to hitch Sunny to it again before she headed north. It was only ten miles or so. She could be there in three hours.

After four hours, she wondered if she was lost.

And as the long shadows spread across the fields, she told herself she'd ride for just one more hour.

But then twilight was upon her, and Sunny needed a rest and a walk, and they were near a stream so Rose resigned herself to sleeping in the cart that night and finding Heath's friend Cardew in the morning.

Heath's friend. Not Heath, for surely if he was near death a month ago, he was gone by now. She told herself this over and over again, as she wrapped herself in blankets and curled up in the cart, so that her heart could get used to it. Heath was dead. He must be. It didn't matter; she had already resigned herself to never seeing him again. The folly of her youth was well behind her.

And yet, it *did* matter, because love didn't come to an end. It stretched out toward ever-receding horizons: growing thin, perhaps, but never snapping cleanly. She still loved him, and if he really was dead then grief would storm down on her and nothing she said to herself now could protect her tired heart from that.

At length, she slept, waking a few hours later to the dew of dawn. Sunny was already awake, muzzle in the grass. The sun sat low, gold illuminating the dewfall and outlining Sunny's shining mane. Rose hadn't brought anything to eat, and her stomach rumbled as she took a drink from the stream. She felt mildly nauseous. Expectant and sorrowful. She took her time, hitching up Sunny and climbing into the wooden seat at the front of the cart, then she headed back the way she came, hoping to see a waypoint she may have missed in the dusk. She thought about Linden, waking up without her; about Eldra, expecting her to be on her way with a cartful of food and grain. Rose, the wayward sister, doing the wrong thing again. What would Bluebell say?

In the distance, Rose could see a horse approaching, and she slowed and waved an arm. Perhaps the rider would know where the waypoint to Llyr's Hollow was.

"Stop!" she cried as he was bearing down on her at great speed.

He saw her and slowed. He was an older man, rough-faced but well dressed. Her hand went instinctively to her cloak, pulling it close to hide the pouch Eldra had given her.

"My lady?" he said, with a deep nod of his head.

"I'm trying to get to Llyr's Hollow. I think I may be lost."

He moved his horse closer and Rose leaned back in her seat, but he rode past her and around her cart. "What have you in the cart?" he asked.

"Nothing. As you see." Her senses prickled. She found herself wondering why this traveler was roving around on the edges of the day, cursing herself for not asking that before now. "Walk on," she said to Sunny.

But his horse was unburdened and young, and he was in front of her a moment later, blocking her way. "You must have something," he said.

"I have nothing."

"Empty cart? Have you just sold, or are you about to buy? Either way, you will have coins." He unsheathed a sword and opened her cloak with its point. "What's in there?"

"Please. You don't want this. Just let us be on our way."

He snapped his fingers. "Hand it over, or I'll kill your horse. And then I might kill you, too."

Rose's hands shook as she loosened the purse from her cloak, pulling the ribbon to open it. He leaned eagerly in to take it from her, but she reached in to grab a handful of powder, then threw it with all her might onto the ground in front of him. It made a thunderous cracking sound, then bright white light began to fizz up from the ground, making both the horses rear. Rose held tight to the reins. The man shrieked—an unearthly sound—and when Sunny's hooves were on the ground again, Rose urged her forward.

Sunny didn't need to be prompted; she bolted, the cart bouncing and rattling so hard it shook Rose's bones. She didn't look back, although the man screamed at her, "What have you done? What have you done?" for what seemed like a mile.

She was desperate to be back on a road—a wide road with no bandits roaming it. But Sunny couldn't keep up the fast pace and finally slowed to a walk. Rose continued to glance behind her, feeling exposed and cold between her shoulders. But the bandit hadn't followed, and she had no idea how long the blindness would last.

Then Rose saw a tall, dark shape in the distance that might be a waymark. As they drew closer, she could see two arrows pointing off it in different directions. How had she not seen this the night before? Among flat fields, it was easily apparent.

She gently pulled Sunny's reins and came to a halt. She dismounted, heart quickening as she glanced behind her. But the horizon was clear.

Rose approached the waymark. The post was hewn roughly of wood, ivy growing up it and moss colonizing the damp cracks. But the arrows were blank. She rounded the waymark and looked on both sides. None of the symbols she would expect—birds, acorns, waves, leaves: the language learned by every traveler—were apparent; only uncarved wood.

Rose peered off into the distance. Sun-flooded fields. Smoke from farmhouses. Which way?

A shadow moved at the periphery of her vision and a chill stole over her. She turned back to see the waymark was gone, and in its place stood a man. Six feet tall, angular and bony, his hands spread in precisely the same directions as the arrows. His hair was white and fine, and stirring in the morning breeze. His beard was steely gray.

She shrieked with fright and took a step backward, overbalancing and landing on her backside. She scooted back from him, and he dropped his hands and laughed at her.

"Why so frightened, little witch?"

"I'm not a—"

"I saw what you did to that bandit. Of course you are."

"Please. Don't hurt me."

He offered her a hand to help her up; she eyed it warily. She noticed his long boots were wound about with ivy.

"I don't intend to hurt you," he said. "I was only curious about you, that is all. That was strong magic."

"Not my magic. My aunt made it for me."

"Your aunt?"

"Eldra. We live out on the moors."

"I know of her. I meet a lot of other undermagicians on the border roads out here, making their way in and out of the world." He beckoned that she should give him her hand. "You look lost."

"I am lost." She took his fingers. They were impossibly soft. He pulled her to her feet with surprising strength and grace for his age, keeping her hand in his.

"What is the nature of your . . . lostness?" he asked, his gray gaze burrowing deep.

She blinked rapidly. "I need to find Llyr's Hollow. A man named Cardew."

He closed his eyes and began to hum softly. Rose watched him, all her senses alert.

His eyes snapped open. "Llyr's Hollow is west of here," he said, indicating the mouth of a road a hundred yards away. "The farms are all north of the village, so turn at the inn. You'll know Cardew's farm by the two houses, side by side."

"You know him?"

"No," he said. "But you said you were lost, and I find people who are lost."

"Thank you." She looked down at their interlocked hands and tried to pull away, keen to be in the cart again.

He tightened his grip. "Are you still lost?"

"I—no."

"Are you certain?" His eyes were like storm clouds. She could swear she caught the scent of rain, even though the sky was clear.

"I'm certain."

He released her hand, and Rose felt something that was almost like sadness at letting him go.

"It's not quite an hour from here," he said. "Go."

"Thank you." She turned and ran back to her horse and cart.

"You have many more roads to travel in times ahead," he called after her. "You will be lost again."

She barely heard him over the sound of Sunny's hooves.

The twin houses were identical: lime-washed, thatch-roofed, morning sunlight making them glow against the pale-blue sky. The door to the second one was open, so Rose hurried up the hill from the road, where Sunny waited patiently.

From the bright morning, she peered into the shadowy house. Two men—neither of them Heath. One sat at the side of a bed of straw and blankets, bright-eyed and round-cheeked and ginger-haired. The other, lying under the blankets, was thin and sunken and—

It *was* Heath. The shock kicked Rose's heart.

"Heath!" she cried, sinking to her knees on the rushes next to him.

He opened his eyes a crack. Sea blue. Then they closed again, and his thin hand flopped out toward her and she caught it in her fingers. Alive, he was still alive.

"You must be Rose." This was Cardew, the man with the bright-copper hair. She recognized him instantly as First Folk, the race of original inhabitants of Thyrsland before her people had come across the sea many generations ago. Most of them lived on the margins of society now, hidden away near the magicians in the wilds of Bradsey. Heath was half First Folk on his unknown father's side. His hair was golden, but his beard, if he grew it, was flaming red.

"I am," she said. "I got your message. How long has he been like this?"

"Since the start of summer. I have tried my best to tend him, but he is wasting before my eyes."

Rose touched Heath's forehead, trying to match the person in the bed with the strong, hearty man she had once loved so fiercely it threatened to break her in two. "Can he hear me? Does he know I'm here?" she asked.

As if in answer, Heath gave her hand a feeble squeeze. She could see the bones of his wrist. There was no doubt that he was close to death.

Unless . . .

"My aunt can heal him," she said.

Heath's grip tightened.

"We have tried every village witch and even a physician from the Great School."

"She's a powerful undermagician. Look, he's squeezing my hand. He wants it, too."

Cardew looked skeptical. "Would she come here? How long would that take?"

Rose was already shaking her head. "I will take him to her. Today. I have my horse here, and a cart."

Cardew glanced at Heath, then back to Rose. "Very well, but I will ride with you. There are things you should know about Heath."

She gazed at Heath's face, the first silver hairs among the gold. "I once knew every secret of his heart," she said.

"Many things have changed for him. Many years among the First Folk. He is . . . more important than you can imagine."

Rose considered Cardew by the light coming through the door. She realized he was much younger than Heath, perhaps not yet twenty, and she wondered at their relationship, how they had come to be living here together.

"I should like to know everything," she said. "Let's not delay."

chapter 6

Willow hated the hill up from the market to Bramble Court. Not because her legs weren't strong enough for the steep, winding ascent. Far from it. It was because Avaarni always whined. How she hated the whining; it demeaned both of them.

"Mama, slow down." The little voice was plaintive.

Willow never slowed down. The child was too soft. These small hardships were necessary.

"Mama!" Now Avaarni was sobbing, and Willow turned around to see the child had dropped the bag of wheat and it had split open, its contents spilling onto the road.

An elderly woman who was making her way, crookbacked, up the hill behind them, hurried forward to comfort Avaarni. Willow, who was several yards ahead, pulled her headscarf carefully around her face and started back down the hill.

"Leave my son be," she called to the old woman sternly. "He has to learn to correct his own mistakes. The third book of Maava tells us that to make amends for our errors is godly."

But the woman didn't seem to hear her. She knelt next to Avaarni and put an arm around the child's shoulders. "There, little one. I have a sugar mouse in my bag. Would you like it?"

Avaarni was instantly placated, putting out a hand to receive the treat. Willow stood over them, her shadow falling on the spill of wheat on the ground. Avaarni gobbled the sugar mouse quickly, knowing Willow would take it away.

The woman looked up and tsked. "That bag was far too heavy for your boy to carry."

"He'll never get strong if he doesn't carry things."

"The poor little lad must only be two."

"He's nearly four. He's small for his age." Willow hauled Avaarni up by the shoulder.

"And such a sweet face. Why, he almost looks like a little girl with those long, long lashes."

Willow's blood flamed. "I'll thank you to leave us alone," she said, careful to keep her face turned away. "Avaarni, pick up what wheat you can and put it back in the bag. Don't disappoint me."

The woman struggled to her feet and went on her way. No doubt she thought she knew better than Willow how to raise a child. But Willow had long since refused to take advice from anyone but her Lord, Maava. *May His name be praised.*

When they had mostly refilled the grain bag, and Avaarni was holding it flat with both arms, the tear at the top, Willow crouched low to look the child in the face. "You smiled at that woman too much," she said. "She thought you were a girl. Don't smile so much."

Avaarni nodded solemnly, lips deliberately sucked against each other.

"Come. Home now."

Willow slowed her steps a little, but not so much that Avaarni would know she was making the walk easier so more grain would not be spilled. The child simply had to become harder, stronger. All had been foreseen by Maava, and Willow was not about to let Him down.

Throughout her pregnancy, the angels had told her over and over she was having a son. When the baby had been born a girl, doubt had pierced Willow all the way to her center. But then she'd realized it was a test: Would she succumb to the doubt? No. Maava's work was not to be comprehended by somebody as inconsequential and humble as Willow. One day, Avaarni would wake up and be a boy. A miracle. Willow knew it would happen, as confidently as she knew every mossy stone step up through the gardens to Bramble Court. She opened the gate, ushered Avaarni through, and then closed it behind her. Given Avaarni's fate, it would be wrong to raise her as a girl. And so Willow raised her as a son.

Once away from the public road, Willow pushed back her scarf to feel the sunlight in her pale-brown hair as they crossed the garden. Gudrun's gray-and-white cat Parsley miaowed at them from among the foxgloves, and Avaarni stopped to say hello to him.

"No smiling," Willow said, firmly but patiently. "Get the supplies to the kitchen, then you can come and find the cat again."

Avaarni looked up at her with big gray eyes. The woman was right. Her lashes were too long. Willow wondered if it would be possible to trim them.

"Work first, pleasure later," Willow said. "It's the way of our faith. You don't want to go to the Blacklands when you die, do you? To be tortured forever in the caverns of ice? With all the bad people and the spiders?"

The child shook her head urgently. "No, Mama." Avaarni hated spiders.

"Then hurry up and get that wheat to Cook. Go on."

She scurried off. Parsley had left his spot and was now chasing a grasshopper around the garden. Willow watched for a while. She'd always hated grasshoppers, ever since one got stuck in her hair as a child. More lately, they reminded her of her sister Bluebell—long-legged and hard-bodied, with monstrous faces. Parsley chased the grasshopper right in front of her, where it stopped. Parsley laid both front paws down and raised his backside, ready for the kill.

Willow stomped on the grasshopper, hearing the satisfying wet crack under her shoe.

"Sorry, Parsley," she said, wiping her shoe on the grass, and went inside.

❖ ❖ ❖

Willow was always happy when her knees ached from kneeling and praying in the chapel. Aching knees meant she had done enough to keep Maava happy, and He wouldn't send His angry angels, the ones who snarled and spit ugly words at her. Her entire existence was based on this fact: enough prayer to keep away the awful voices; enough prayer to connect deep and strong with Maava and not be afraid or confused anymore.

Nobody prayed as much as Willow, and she didn't expect them to. However, she did expect Avaarni to join her quietly in the chapel on holy days. Even if the child could not kneel for long, she had certainly learned how to be still and quiet and pray for up to an hour at a time. Willow had been stern enough with her. No child of Avaarni's heritage could plead an ordinary character: She had to behave better than everyone else because she *was* better than everyone else. She would become Maava's chosen king on earth, to bring trimartyrs together in Thyrsland under the holy triangle. She wasn't some sniveling brat from the market, hiding chickens under her shirt.

Willow rose, stretching her legs. Aching knees. She turned. Avaarni lay on her side in the recess under the shutter, eyes closed.

"Avaarni!" Willow roared.

Avaarni's eyes flickered open. "Only praying, Mama. I was only praying, not sleeping."

Willow wasn't sure if she believed the child, but then reminded herself that Avaarni knew well enough what happened to children who lied. Willow had told her dozens of times.

Willow extended her hand for Avaarni to take, helping her to her feet. The child was small, even for a girl. The boys' clothes she wore were little more than baby clothes. Willow often wondered if, on the morning she became a boy, she might also become tall and strong. The thought made her smile. Avaarni smiled back, cautiously.

"Everything I do is as our Lord tells me," Willow said gently.

"I really wasn't asleep. I promise. I was praying that Olaf's dog gets better."

"You can pray for more important things than animals." Willow opened the door of the chapel and led Avaarni across the garden to the house. The house, the chapel, all of Bramble Hill had been paid for by Willow's father, Athelrick, the heathen king of neighboring Almissia. Once he had been married to Gudrun, but put her aside in shameful circumstances, under threats from Bluebell. Athelrick's guilt bought Gudrun a modest life on the hill outside of Winecombe. Athelrick didn't know that Willow and Avaarni shared in that modest life. As far as Willow understood, her family had given her up for dead years ago.

Willow was very, very far from dead.

The door to the house was pinned open to let a breeze in. Avaarni carefully removed her shoes then skipped to the sitting room where Gudrun stood at her loom, weaving in the sunlight that fell through the open shutters. She looked around when she heard Willow and Avaarni enter.

"Avaarni!" she said, dropping her shuttle and scooping the child up in a hug.

Avaarni covered Gudrun's face with kisses and giggles, and Willow stood slightly outside it all, as she ever did. Avaarni had no kisses and giggles for her, but that was because Willow took the business of raising the child seriously. Gudrun was weak, soft. That's why Avaarni loved her.

But Gudrun had treated Willow well, and she owed her a debt of gratitude. Together, they got along somehow. Willow had brought Maava more forcefully to Gudrun's life, and watched Him heal Gudrun's sorrow. Gudrun had helped Willow through the horrors of birth—she would sooner die than do that again—and with mothercraft in the early months, tending her ravaged body and showing her how to feed the child without it stinging her breasts so hard that she cried.

Gudrun placed Avaarni on the floor, and Avaarni picked up the shuttle. "Can I?" she asked.

Gudrun shook her head. "Weaving and spinning are for other little girls, my darling, not for you."

"You can go and sit with Olaf in the kitchen and do some wood carving," Willow suggested. "Or you can practice reading with Penda."

But Avaarni clung to Gudrun's side. "I want Gudrun."

Gudrun patted Avaarni's pale curls, cropped short over her ears. "Leave her with me, Willow. She can make up stories for me. I love your stories, little one."

"She should be telling stories of our faith," Willow said grudgingly. "Liava, her doomed twins, the coming of the triangle."

"There's no harm in having an imagination," Gudrun said. "Let her be a child for the afternoon."

Willow relented. Somehow between them, Willow and Gudrun managed to avoid conflict. One thing was non-negotiable: that Avaarni would be raised as a boy. Gudrun's protests recurred from time to time, but Willow always had a new reason to give her. Lately, she'd been telling Gudrun that as a girl, what was to stop Bluebell marrying Avaarni off to a rough man and sending her somewhere far away? Gudrun had never really recovered from the loss of her only son, Wylm, who had died at Bluebell's hand before his child was born. Ever the protective grandmother, she was so horrified at the thought of Avaarni married off that she had actually cried.

Perhaps Willow had told that story with too much detail and relish.

"Very well," she said, looking at Avaarni and Gudrun, both shining with love for each other. "I'm off for training."

Gudrun nodded, eyes averting almost imperceptibly. Gudrun most definitely did *not* like Willow's trainer—whether for his ugly face or his rough manners, she didn't know—but that was immaterial. Maava had sent him to her, and Maava didn't make mistakes.

Willow went to the bower she shared with Avaarni, and from under the mattress—a trick she had learned from Bluebell—she pulled her sword. Well, Wylm's sword and, because he was dead, Avaarni's sword. But for now Willow wielded it, and she wielded it well.

She left the house and made her way down the hill to the flat area where she trained, every afternoon, without fail. For the first few years, it had been Gudrun's guardsmen, Olaf and Penda, who had shown her how to lift a sword, how to move it around, which body parts to aim for and which of her own to protect. At first, wooden swords. She had taken a wooden blow to the head so many times in the first year that she'd had a permanent lump on her crown.

But she had become good at it. Not just competent—good. First she beat Olaf, but he was old so perhaps that wasn't such a surprise. The day she knew she could have easily taken Penda's right arm off, and held her blow, was the day she knew she needed somebody better to train her.

She prayed to Maava for somebody. Somebody who was battle-hard, who knew how to fight the heathens. And who should turn up, just seven months ago, looking for her by name, but a dirty, desperate heathen warrior. He said Maava hadn't brought him, that his own god had sent him, but Willow knew the truth. They had trained every day since, except for holy days.

So she sat in the glade waiting for him now. Whatever his low reputation, that was less important than what she was becoming: a soldier for Maava, ready to do battle for the souls of Thyrsland. Even if that meant shedding the blood of her heathen sister.

Ivy rode hard.

The stallion beneath her dug its hooves into the sand then sprang away fiercely, as Ivy goaded it forward recklessly.

"Come on," she shouted over the sea wind. "Come on, you bastard!" Whether she was shouting at the horse or the fetus that she believed clung to the inside of her womb, she couldn't be sure. But it felt good to release her frustration nonetheless.

Around the curve she could see the path up to Seacaster. Time to return. Despondent, she reined the horse in and headed up the path at a walk. She paid close attention to her womb. Was that a twinge?

Another visit to the old witch in the Tanglewood, then. The horse-riding trick never seemed to work. Was this the third or fourth time since the boys were born? Curse her ridiculous husband who, though old and sick, had some kind of nightmare seed that managed to embed itself in her successfully time and time again. This one, like the others, would bleed out of her with Dritta's help.

Back on level ground, Ivy sped across the field toward the stables. Summer was the only time of year out here on the coast that the whole world wasn't gray and being flayed by grim northeasterly winds. The fields all bloomed with wildflowers and the days were long and sunny, unless they were long and foggy. She dismounted and handed her horse to the stableboy, Durwin, who never managed to get her riding gear as clean and organized as she'd like. The years of his incompetence had worn her down, though, and she had grown fond of his wide, friendly smile, his simple humility.

"And you have a good day, my lady," he said.

"You too, Durwin," she said.

In fact, years of life in Seacaster had worn her down, just as the relentless sea wore down the gravel on the shore, turning it smooth. What a snappy, silly girl she had been when she'd first come here; always complaining about one thing or another. Ivy stopped and gazed out at the gray sea from the highest point outside her husband's hall. The city of Seacaster was more than just the city square and the duke's hall: Beyond the east gate, crooked, narrow lanes wound up and down the sloping cliffs to the dark harbor. On all sides, little houses, people moving between them, donkeys with carts, chickens loose across the mossy pavings, long lines of washed clothes or drying fish, baskets piled loosely outside doors, the flap of market stall covers along the wharf, ships roped to jetties, traders rolling barrels and crates. Seacaster was the largest shorefort in Thyrsland, and her husband, Gunther, controlled the port. His family had been dukes of Seacaster since the time of the giants, or so it was said, which gave them the longest family history of any noble people in Thyrsland, along with Ivy's own father. Gunther had so much power in his frail old hands. And Ivy's hands were on his.

She let herself into her bowerhouse. The walls were decorated with tapestries Gunther had had specially made. In all of them, she was the central figure, a smiling blond woman who bent to feed a hart by hand, or who stood wistfully in a garden of flowers and trees (all her sisters were represented: bluebells, roses, willow and ash trees), or who reclined daintily on the shore, with the gray sea behind her. The room smelled perpetually of lavender from the dried flowers hung on roof beams. In here, too, were chests full of dresses and pretty shoes, endless trinkets that her husband had bought for her—beads and combs and mirrors and ribbons—and there were her two most prized possessions, playing quietly on the woven rug with Hilla, their nurse.

"Hello, my darling boys," Ivy said, crouching and opening her arms.

Eadric and Edmund ran toward her, squeaking and squealing. She breathed in the raw scent of them: milky and agreeable. Such little, soft things, full of sweet breath and life. She kissed them then handed them back to Hilla.

"Mama has to go see Papa, but I will be back after supper. Be good boys, now."

"We will," said Eadric. And Edmund, much younger, made a noise in echo that might have been agreement.

Ivy untied the scarf from her hair and brushed it loose and golden, then moved to the door that connected her bower to her husband's. He'd been quite clear: Babies made too much noise for him to sleep. Sour old prune.

Ivy closed the door behind her, put on her most honeyed tone. "Gunther, my love?"

"Is that my Ivy?"

She approached and sat on the bed, making a show of tossing her long fair hair. He reached up with his weathered fingers and caressed a curl. She tried not to look directly at his face. His skin was almost gray, his eyes sunken. This long illness unfolded so slowly, increment by increment. She had learned patience.

Life in Seacaster had confounded her expectations in so many ways. She had cried all through the first summer, sniveled through the first autumn. The brooding darkness of the first winter had been laden with the extra dread of approaching childbirth. But then, a small pink person had come into her world and charmed her utterly and completely. His total, unconcealed, unrestrained adoration of her was like a spell. She fell deeply in love. The second baby had doubled the feeling.

Then she had looked down at her breasts and belly and decided two was enough—especially since she had met Crispin. Gorgeous, tall, hard-bodied Crispin, who was half her husband's age and whose smile could make her clothes fall off. How they loved to make moony eyes at each other and fumble about in the hayloft; she didn't want him having to search around her waist for her nipples. Besides, every subsequent child increased the risk of her having a girl, who might grow up to be gorgeous at the same time as Ivy lost her looks. A beautiful daughter wasn't a fate she'd wish on her worst enemy.

In all, life as the wife of a duke was not as bad as she'd feared. Except for the duke himself, that was.

The door to his bower opened and Elgith, his serving woman, stood there. In her hands was a tray with Gunther's supper on it.

Ivy leapt up. "I'll take it," she said.

Elgith, who had always been silently hostile to Ivy, held tight to the tray. "I've brought this from the kitchen and it's my job to serve—"

"I said I'll take it," Ivy repeated, a little more steel in her voice. "I like to feed him."

Gunther chuckled from his bed. "Dear ladies, don't fight over me."

Ivy smiled at him, but inside her head she called him savage names. *Fight over me.* She knew Elgith had once been his lover—still was, for all Ivy knew or cared; it wasn't as if her old womb could quicken. If the fight was over who got to sit on his ancient, crinkly cock, then Ivy was happy to let Elgith win.

"Darling, I love being your wife, and I love serving you," Ivy said to him. "Now sit up and let me give you some soup."

She helped Gunther to sit, propping him with pillows. Elgith still stood in the doorway, eyeing her carefully. Ordinarily, Ivy would tell Elgith to get out, but today she was happy to let the older woman see her tend to her husband, all pretty and young and glowing with her golden hair, spooning the soup directly into his gray mouth. *Slowly does it. Slowly, slowly.*

Elgith, satisfied that Ivy was not up to no good, left, closing the door behind her.

"You are good to me," Gunther said, leaning back and sighing with exhaustion. "Sometimes I think I'll never be well again. I am so tired. Even eating makes me tired."

"Hush, now. You'll be fine after a little more rest. Come along, eat your soup."

Slowly, slowly. If he declined any quicker, it would raise suspicion. Give them time to get used to having a sick leader, a leader who hadn't been out of bed in months. Then his death would look perfectly natural and expected, and nobody would suspect Ivy of anything.

chapter 7

N orth Hall was remote, reputedly Blackstan's favorite hunting location. He was known throughout Thyrsland as the Bear King of Littledyke, because he had killed so many bears on his expeditions. Bluebell remembered many years ago, when her father had married that traitorous ninny Gudrun, Blackstan had sent a huge bear's claw preserved in wax as a wedding gift. It was mounted on the wall in the king's stateroom and Bluebell couldn't stand being near it, with its greasy, faintly rotten smell. When Gudrun was sent back to Tweening—after enchanting Athelrick and almost costing his life—Bluebell had the claw packaged up and sent with her.

They had been on the road a day and a half before they approached the foothills below North Hall. From here, the road was narrow, steep, and gravelly, so they left the packhorses behind to graze on the grassy slopes and took the warhorses up. As they approached the top of the road, Thrymm began to sniff the air and whine softly. Rooks circled above them.

Bluebell inhaled deeply and caught the first whiff of the sweet-rotten scent of corrupted flesh.

"I can smell death," Sighere said at the same moment.

Bluebell nodded. She knew then that Blackstan was dead, probably along with his family. She steeled herself for what she would see.

The fields opened out in front of them, grassy fields where horses roamed peacefully. North Hall sat on a rise two hundred yards north. But in the middle of one of the fields, there was a pile of bodies. They had been set on fire, but had only half burned, hence the smell. Bluebell only glanced at it, but she saw the long fair plait of Blackstan's wife in among the blackened limbs.

She indicated that her hearthband should stop so she could think it through, make sense of what had happened. Had the stronghold fallen?

Lofric rode to the front. "My lord," he said. "The standard. Look."

Bluebell peered toward North Hall again. He was right. Blackstan's flag, the bear on a gold background, was not flying over the hall. Instead, there was the sign of the raven.

"Then Hakon has done this," she said. Was he back in the favor of his brother, the Ice King? Her first instinct was to ride to Merkhinton to secure the stronghold there, but her heart surged with excitement at the idea of facing her old foe. "Do you think the bastard's still inside?"

"They have killed the residents and fly their standard over the hall," Sighere said.

"The hall is small and raiders travel light. Hakon will have perhaps twenty men in there. We have eleven." But they were good men. Raiders tended to be reckless rather than skilled; they always left themselves open. She dismounted and urged her hearthband to do the same.

"We'll approach quietly," she told them, "and take back North Hall for Wulfgar, who will be the new king of Littledyke if, as I fear, the Bear King is among those bodies." She could imagine it all too well: Blackstan and his family enjoying their remote break from kingly duties, a minimal retinue, feeling safe from raiders given their proximity to the standing guard at Merkhinton. She even wondered if Blackstan allowed himself the fiction that he, killer of bears, could protect his family if bandits had come.

"Fight back-to-back if you can," she continued. "Raiders think nothing of burying an ax between your shoulder blades."

She surveyed the area. "We'll stay close to that hedge to the west," she said, turning to face them. "And if you see Hakon, slay him first. You'll recognize him by his face—he's missing half of it. I took it off him with an ax." She smiled, and there was general laughter and excitement, and the rush of blood to their faces that told her they were as hungry for battle as she was.

"Remember," she said, "they are strong, but we are stronger and smarter. Come with me."

There was a chorus of "my lord" and they were away, hurrying past the funeral pyre and hugging the high hawthorn hedge. Their mail clinked softly and they bristled with spears and axes and swords.

Twenty yards from the hall, all plans were discarded as the front door opened and one of Hakon's men emerged. He saw them, shouted, and then Gytha's spear went whistling past Bluebell's ear on its way to the man's heart, silencing him mid-warning.

"Forward!" Bluebell shouted, and they all began to run, just as raiders started to pour out of the hall. There were more than she'd expected, but they were taken by surprise. Most had no armor on, and their unawareness made them vulnerable.

Then the skirmish was upon them all, and the quiet moments of before, where hearts beat surely, vanished. Limbs and shouts and blood, and the fire in her insides that made Bluebell feel as though the pit of her stomach glowed bright hot. The Horse God's favor flowed in her veins. It gave her power and strength beyond the imagining of ordinary men. The movements she made with her arms and shoulders should be tearing her muscles and tissues to pieces, and yet with the battle fire upon her she was able to do anything. Here, a man rushed upon her while his companion tried to spear her in the side. In one movement her sword, the Widowsmith, had broken the spear and opened up the shoulder of the first man, making him fall to his knees so she could deliver the killing blow to his head; a twist back and she knocked the spear-wielder over with her shield and Thrymm tore out his throat. Then a hot voice behind had her spinning and ducking in one swift move, slashing him across both thighs so he fell and Gytha could finish him with a spear through his back, which found his heart with practiced precision. Her other men fought back-to-back as she'd instructed and one by one, the raiders fell.

None of them were Hakon. She couldn't see him anywhere.

"Sighere," she called, "you finish up out here. I'm looking for the Crow King."

As she stalked away from the battle, Thrymm at her heels, another man tried to attack her but she bashed him off with her free hand then stuck him into the ground with the Widowsmith. Some of them, she knew, died at her hand on purpose. It had once been considered an honorable death among raiders to die at the point of her father's blade, but now it was Bluebell they spoke of in those terms.

She didn't care either way, as long as they died.

Bluebell put a foot on his chest and retrieved her sword, then carefully pushed open the door to the hall. Quiet. The soft *drip-drip* of blood from the tip of her sword onto the wooden boards.

North Hall had been built to keep the warm in, so a series of doors led off the hall, presumably to bowers. A fire was burning in the hearth, something savory bubbling in an iron pot over it. Clothes and freshly oiled byrnies and knives and spoons and combs lay on the long benches that lined the walls. The raiders had moved in, almost as though they intended to stay. But why? What purpose had it served to kill a whole family?

No Hakon.

Thrymm growled low in her throat.

"Which door?" she said to the dog.

Thrymm padded forward, sniffing under each door, stopping at the fourth one and sitting to wait for Bluebell.

Bluebell strode across, kicked the door in. Again, no Hakon. Hiding behind a bed was a man, smaller and younger than the others, maybe the son of one of the seasoned warriors who probably lay dead outside. Too much of a coward to try his arm in real battle.

Bluebell loved cowards. Cowards always talked.

"Where's Hakon?" she asked, the tip of her sword at his throat.

"Not here Hakon!" he cried.

"Then where?"

He didn't answer.

"Where are you from? Why are you here?"

He pressed his lips together, but the glaze to his eyes told her he loved life more than he loved staying silent. There were men at Merkhinton who knew how to make cowards talk. Bluebell knew she didn't have the patience or the cunning for it; she withdrew her sword.

"Thrymm, if he moves, kill him."

Thrymm barked and snapped at the man's face, and he cowered, pressing himself against the wall as though he wanted to become part of it. Thrymm stood guard, her eyes never leaving his face.

Bluebell quickly checked in the other rooms but found them empty. Each room made her unhappier. Blackstan's family possessions—soft embroidered blankets and finely carved chests— were strewn about, overturned and defiled by the rough fingers of the interlopers.

Satisfied that the rooms were all empty, she rejoined her hearth-band outside. All the raiders were dead, and Ricbert had sustained a shocking injury to his left arm—a chunk of him was missing. He sat on the ground, panic rising in his face as Sighere tried to calm him and wrap the wound.

Bluebell knelt before Ricbert, taking his chin in her hands and holding it until he made sustained eye contact with her. "You fought well," she said. "You honored your ancestors and the Horse God. We ride now for Merkhinton. Would you ride with me or with Sighere?"

He swallowed over a dry throat. "With you, my lord," he said.

"This wound will not kill you," she said. Her own body was starting to ache now, reminding her of the impossible feats she had performed. "If you lose the use of the arm, my father will compensate you richly: gold and amber and silver and precious red gems from the long-away south. A long and happy life awaits you, Ricbert." She stood, turning to Sighere. "There's a young fellow cowering in one of the bowers; Thrymm's with him. Tie him up and we'll throw him over one of the packhorses. We ride straight away for Merkhinton. I need to see with my own eyes that the stronghold still stands."

"Hakon, my lord?" Sighere said.

"Not here." She glanced over her shoulder back at the house. "Not fucking here."

The long summer evening gave them time to reach Merkhinton before nightfall. Nobody questioned Bluebell's decision to push on. They could see with their own eyes Ricbert slumping lower and lower in the saddle in front of her. Ricbert was the son of one of the powerful southern earls; she didn't want to lose him.

The first glimpse of Merkhinton—whole and unburnt, nestled into the foothills of the mountains—showed that her worst fears were unfounded. No raiders had been here, Hakon was not in league with King Gisli of the Iceheart, and help for Ricbert was at hand. Their banner was spotted from the guard tower, and the huge iron gates were already grinding open before they approached the earthworks that made up the flanking ditch and ramparts of the stronghold. A squad was sent out to lower a bridge over the ditch. The strike of hoof on ground changed from grass to wood to stone, and then her hearthband was swarmed by stewards and stable hands. She barked orders to get Ricbert to a physician and handed down his limp body to five pairs of hands that laid him on the stones. Bluebell removed her helm, handed it to a steward, and shook out her fair hair, striding toward the back of the retinue where the coward raider was bound across a packhorse. She undid the leather straps that had kept him in place and slung him over her shoulders.

"Where is Wybert?" she asked of one of the guardsmen.

"In the keep, my lord," he answered, too in awe of her to meet her eyes.

She took a moment in the twilit courtyard to orient herself. The gates clanged shut behind her. Wooden living quarters and storerooms, an alehouse, a rough hall. There was the keep, a stone funnel built into the side of the mountain. Above it, a cliff rose steeply, and a rocky overhang cast a pointed shadow. The young raider over her shoulders wriggled pointlessly against her. Somebody had bound his mouth, but she could hear he was shouting against the thick gag.

"Shut up," she muttered. Her body ached. Battle, riding with Ricbert, carrying an angry raider. "Just shut the fuck up."

Bluebell made her way across the courtyard to the keep, and kicked twice firmly at the door. The sound of footsteps, bars being slid out of place, and then a woman in brown robes opened the door.

"I'm looking for Wybert," Bluebell said.

"This way."

Bluebell didn't like stone buildings; they were always cold, dark, and hollow, making sounds echo and refusing to absorb warmth from the hearth. She followed the woman down a hallway to a bare room with only a thin rug on the ground and two wooden chairs.

"Wait here," the woman said, and disappeared, closing the door behind her.

Bluebell dumped the man on the rug and put a foot on him to keep him in place. She noticed that the chairs had iron clamps on the legs and arms, and decided not to sit down.

Wybert was at the door a few moments later.

"My lord, what a pleasure to see you," he said. He was a portly man under his gray robes, which Bluebell always thought shameful for one so young. He had been an average soldier, but truly excelled at languages and diplomacy. Bluebell didn't like him. He had wet lips like a frog, and his eyes gleamed too brightly at the thought of extracting information from someone.

"This is one of Hakon's men. I want to know what they were doing at North Hall, where they came from and how, but most of all, I want to know where Hakon is so I can kill him. Got it?"

"Of course, my lord." Wybert knelt next to the man and gently pushed Bluebell's foot off him. "Come on now, friend. I should like to get to know you a little better." Then he spoke to the man in the singsong gutter voice of the raiders.

Bluebell stepped back. "I will meet with you in the morning. For now, I need strong drink and a mountain of food."

"Enjoy your revels, my lord." He turned once again to the man on the floor, gave a small smile. "I shall enjoy mine."

The alehouse was full and hot, music and laughter and fine mead flowing. Bluebell left behind thoughts of the day and of Hakon. She grew weary of company, and wandered away from the alehouse around midnight to find a place to sleep for the night. She remembered a wooden building—it looked like all the other wooden buildings—that functioned as a guesthouse for visiting commanders. The faintest glow of light had stayed in the sky, and probably would until morning. It robbed the stars of their brilliance, but Bluebell could still see a million of them. She stopped a moment, head spinning drunkenly, and gazed up at them.

A voice came to her on the wind. "Southlander. Woman."

She turned and peered off into the dark.

"Southlander." The voice was heavily accented. She took a few steps in the direction it came from. Could see a white face at the window of the keep, behind iron bars. It was the raider, the coward she had handed to Wybert this evening.

"What do you want, dog?" she asked him.

"You die." His grip on her language was clearly limited.

She spread her palms. "We all die."

"You die. Hakon kill you. Randerman kill you. Sword of your doom."

Randerman. She recognized the word. Some tribes of raiders kept among themselves an elder who functioned as both healer and magician.

"Is that right? Well, you enjoy your time locked up in there, won't you?" she said, threw in a few Iceheart curse words she knew, then stumbled off in search of a warm bed.

Sword of your doom.

Bluebell didn't like the idea of magic; she didn't like anything she couldn't see and smash. When she found Hakon, she'd find this randerman, too, and make sure he died first.

❖ ❖ ❖

In the end, the coward told Wybert everything. Wybert won some of the information with threats, and some with promises that would be delivered only when Bluebell and the army she commandeered from Merkhinton had stomped out Hakon's nest. Hakon's settlement was out on an island, reached by a ship down the Gema River then out into the gray sea. Not quite an army; more an angry warband of eighty or ninety men who longed to depose Gisli and take over the Iceheart first, then all of Thyrsland. Grandiose, overweening ambitions that relied on cunning, stealth, and wishful thinking more than grounded war strategy and strength. Still, Bluebell knew never to underestimate a raider. They were born gnashing their gums, eager for battle.

Days on the river and then on the sea. Bluebell's native environment was not water, but she refused to succumb to the seasickness that drove many of her men to the side to vomit themselves inside out. Every time her stomach lurched, she thought about slaying Hakon and crushing his ridiculous ambitions, and it made her stand strong and tall again.

They landed on the far side of the island at dawn. Archers had been ready to take out the night watch, but there was no night watch. Bluebell wondered if Hakon thought the island so well fortified naturally from the west. As she and her army found their way around rocks and cliff faces in armor, she started to wonder if he was right.

And still they met no resistance. A gravel path, obviously built by human hands, led straight up to the encampment and was entirely undefended. Was Hakon so delusional that he thought nobody would tell the secret of his island stronghold?

At the top of the path, the sun cracked the horizon, bathing the scene in orange light. Bluebell's heart thudded from the climb uphill. The morning breeze caught the ends of her hair. Through the slit in her helm she found herself looking at a collection of rough buildings in a hollow, the raven-gabled hall sitting in the middle of them.

"My lord?" Sighere was at her shoulder. She looked behind her and saw the army had stopped, tightly packed together along the gravel path.

"Destroy the buildings and everyone in them!" she shouted.

Stampeding feet churned up the ground. Bluebell called for Sighere, and her own hearthband followed her directly to the hall. She kicked in the doors, then pulled up as she saw what was inside.

Old men. Stewards. Shipbuilders. Fishermen. The weak, the lame. Not a soldier in sight. All of them, sleeping together on blankets on the floor. They began to wake, shocked and scared, scrambling back into one another.

"Hold your swords!" Bluebell called as her hearthband readied themselves to start the slaughter. "There's nobody here who can hurt us." She turned to Sighere. "Go back outside. See what's happening."

"We are the only ones here!" one of the old men called in a thick accent. "Hakon and his army are long gone."

Disappointment swirled down on her. She was ready for war, not for slaughtering old men. Their sagging eyes reminded her of her father.

Bluebell turned and stalked out.

Sighere jogged to meet her. "All the buildings are empty, my lord."

"This one isn't!" This was a stocky soldier, emerging from one of the huts dragging an old man by the collar of his shirt.

Bluebell was about to shout at him to let the old man go when she noticed his clothes covered in feathers and shells. *Randerman.*

He was laughing and laughing as though being dragged from his hut by an army was the funniest thing that had ever happened to him. The soldier dragged him forward and threw him at Bluebell's feet in the dirt.

"Mighty Bluebell," he laughed.

"You speak our tongue?"

"I speak all tongues."

"Where is Hakon?"

"Flown the nest." He shook his head. "It's no point asking any of us where he is. He didn't say. He packed up his army and left, months ago."

"Months ago? Then why are you all hiding out in here?"

"I sensed you coming. You're *loud*."

Bluebell crouched next to him, pinning his shoulder to the ground with one hand and holding her blade across his throat with the other. How she hated magic, especially when it was used against her. "Did you sense I would do this, too?"

He chuckled slowly. "It's not Hakon you should fear; nor me. I'm but an old man with knees that no longer work. You should fear your sister. She is the one who has the sword." He grinned. Most of his teeth were missing.

"What do you mean? Which sword? Which sister?"

"*Grithbani*. A sword forged to kill you. The steel won't rest until it has tasted your blood, Princess."

His words made a light flicker in her memory. Wylm, her stepbrother, had tried to kill her with a strange runic sword four years ago. "It already tried and failed, randerman," she said. "It tasted my stepbrother's death instead."

"You oughtn't have let it go, once you had your hand on it," he said, laughing.

"Which sister has it?" She found it impossible to think that any of her sisters would have a trollblade, let alone intend to use it on her. None of them were fighters. And yet the Horse God himself had once told her to beware her sister.

"I don't feel like telling you."

The old trickster wouldn't give her anything and she knew it. But if he was strong enough to have sensed her coming and he was in league with Hakon, then she didn't want him in the world anymore. She stood and plunged the Widowsmith into his throat. "Then I don't feel like letting you breathe."

He gurgled blood as she stalked away from him, leaving her blade nailed into the ground for now. The army was reassembling around her. She could see that Sighere had placed a guard around the hall where the unarmed men were. Her brain was clouded. She wasn't sure what to do. She had been expecting Hakon, a battle, to capture this enchanted sword and melt it down with her own hands at the forge. She certainly didn't expect to hear that one of her sisters held the means of killing her. But which sister?

And where was Hakon?

Willow had been ill for two days, and could not afford to miss another day of training. She dragged herself from her bed in the cold dawn, Avaarni trailing sleepily behind her, for morning prayers. Then she took the child back to Gudrun and made her way down the hill on dewy grass. She batted away angel voices, the hissing ones who told her she hadn't been so ill as she thought, that she was simply lazy and didn't burn hot enough to fight for Maava. Instead of torturing herself with guilt, she would make it her aim to impress her rough-faced trainer.

She'd offered him gold, but he'd said he'd had enough of gold. He'd asked for payment in two other ways. First, a roof over his head; Gudrun had been happy to find him an outbuilding at Bramble Hill a long way from the family bowerhouse. Second, he wanted to learn the language and laws of Thyrsland, so Willow had been teaching him good manners and trimartyr ways. He acquired language and religious knowledge as quickly as she acquired skill with a blade. She was almost proud of him. For a famous heathen.

He stood, patiently leaning on his sword, waiting for her. When he saw her approach, he straightened, nodded his grim head, and said in his rough musical accent, "Good morning, Willow."

"Good morning, Hakon," she replied. "Shall we begin?"

chapter 8

I t was a sunny, windy day when Ash first glimpsed the sea. Wide green moors choked with gorse and bracken gave way to plunging cliffs and a rough expanse of gray-blue that slurred into the gray clouds collecting on the horizon. The blast of salt and seaweed in her nostrils was sharp and fresh. Here and there, trees twisted by the endless gusting winds bent over them. For most of the journey, she and Unweder had followed the path of a narrow river down toward the sea. Only in the last mile had they veered off to the southwest, away from distant fields and livestock that spoke of civilization too close by for Unweder's comfort.

Where they stood now, the ground was rocky and salt-soaked: not appealing for a farmer.

"Remote enough for you?" Ash said as Unweder caught up with her.

"Ah, doesn't the sea stir the soul?" He gazed at the water for a while. Ash noticed that his nose and cheeks were pink from the sun, and assumed hers would be the same. Then he turned and nodded toward the west. "No, not remote enough."

Ash turned and saw, on an exposed headland, a roof.

"Who on earth would live out here?" she asked, her words snatched away on the wind.

"A trimartyr, by the looks. It's a chapel."

As soon as he said it, Ash recognized the distinctive triangular shape of the roof. They walked a few hundred yards closer. Yes, she could see it was built of roughly hewn stone.

"Well, they really are everywhere," she mused. "If my father knew . . ."

But Unweder had begun to walk briskly toward the chapel, his magpie eye having spotted something she hadn't. She hurried to catch up to him; Unweder could be alarmingly fast when he wanted. Over rocks and bracken, striding out toward the headland with her in his wake.

When she was about twenty yards away, she saw a pair of legs outside the chapel. Human, clearly, though not much left but bones and stringy clothes. The body lay half in and half out of the open threshold, his cloak thrown up over his head. Unweder knelt next to him.

"Has he been murdered?" Ash asked.

"There's no sign of it. No blood. And look, nobody has taken his gold chain." Unweder snapped it off and held it up, the gold trimartyr symbol glinting in the sun. "Perhaps he died of illness, or age, or accident." Unweder peered into the chapel. "Ash, I think we've found a house to live in."

"We can't live here. If it's a chapel, trimartyrs will turn up."

"Well, none have turned up for a long time," Unweder said, indicating the body. "Perhaps he built the chapel then had no time to convert anyone. We're in Almissia, after all. Has your father made it illegal to be a trimartyr yet?"

"He wouldn't think to make laws to govern people's souls."

Unweder turned his face up and smiled. "You really do idealize him, you know."

"He is my father. I am his daughter." Her father. She hadn't seen him in years, and last time he'd been unconscious, in the grip of bad magic. She knew he had recovered because she heard his name from time to time if they stayed in an inn. Bluebell was not yet the king, though she would be one day.

"Come on, Princess," Unweder said, wryly. "Help me with this body."

Ash unloaded her pack from her shoulders and ducked under the doorway. Inside, she found the trimartyr's bed. "Here," she said. "We can wrap him in this. If he died of illness it might still be clinging to his bedding."

They tried to roll the body onto the blankets but bones dropped out of sleeves and the whole process was much more gruesome than Ash had wished for. Finally, they had the body on the blanket. Unweder strode away to stand on the edge of the headland and determine a good place to inter the trimartyr. Ash gathered up the ragged remains of his clothes, pausing momentarily when she noticed that the side of the man's cloak appeared to have been burned away. Her heart sped a little. In fact, what she had taken for black patterns all over his clothes appeared to be scorch marks. She quickly bundled it all away from Unweder's eyes and folded the blanket over everything tightly. Scorch marks. A dead body. She glanced at the chapel and saw no evidence of fire here. He had run back here for shelter, and something had burned him from behind.

"Let's just drop him off the cliff there," Unweder said, his arm extended to the south. "The tide will take him out."

Ash picked up one end of the load and Unweder the other. Together they carried it to a sheer promontory. Crouching, they positioned it ready to drop into the crashing waves below.

"Should we say a trimartyr prayer?" she asked.

"Do you know one?"

"I could make one up. I know all the common faith prayers."

"Go on, then. If you must."

So she said one of the prayers she had learned back at the study halls of Thridstow, in what seemed like another life from the one she was leading now, and substituted trimartyr names for the Great Mother and the Horse God, and asked his god to receive him with love. Then they flung him over the cliff and the blanket half unfolded as he spun down toward the ocean, landing with a splash that was inaudible over the sound of the wind and the sea.

"We will clean the chapel out with salt water and light a fire,"

Unweder said, already leaving the cliff's edge. "Our new home. But not for long. This time, I'm sure we'll find the dragon."

The same words he ever said. But Ash admitted to herself that, this time, he might be right.

Ash woke to a mournful moaning sound. Her eyes flickered open and she took a moment to remember where she was. The stone chapel, the headland, the sea. The wind outside was immense, wuthering over the roof, rattling the shutters. She turned on her side. The moaning was coming from Unweder, who slept on the opposite side of the chapel. She flicked back her blanket and crawled across to him, shaking him gently awake.

"Unweder," she said. "It's just a dream. Wake up."

His eye popped open. A huge intake of breath rushed into his lungs, and Ash thought he might scream. But then he came to his senses, saw her in the dark, and offered a little smile.

"Thank you."

"Are you all right?"

"Nasty dream." He sat up.

Her scalp prickled lightly. "Not an omen?"

"No. Too confused and labyrinthine for that. When you have lived as long as I have, in so many bodies, the dreams are different. Flashes from childhood, memories of people long in their graves. My mother."

Unweder had spoken rarely of his past. Though she'd presumed he must have had a childhood, as everyone did, it was still strange to hear him acknowledge it.

A mighty gust passed over the chapel, seeming to shake the whole building.

Unweder turned his eye up to the roof. "Is it any wonder I wasn't sleeping peacefully?" he said.

"At least it's weathertight," Ash said. "Good night. I wish you more peaceful dreams."

His gaze fixed on her thoughtfully, then he said, "You know, I think I dreamed about you. About your blood."

Ash recoiled. "It's not time again."

"No, not yet," he said, then quieter, "Soon though."

"I will have none left to keep me warm," Ash said, trying to joke but sounding brittle. How she hated him then, hated the way he looked at her with his hungry eye.

He smiled. "It's only a little." At this, he lay back down. "Good night, Ash."

Ash watched him become still again, in the gloom. Resentment was hard in her guts. It would be difficult to get to sleep. She scratched her scalp and rolled over and, as she did, noticed something hard poking her hip. She reached down to pull it out of her blankets. Although she couldn't see it clearly in the dark, her fingertips told her it was a small seahorse, no bigger than her palm, and dried hard as though it had been left for weeks in the sun.

Ash was about to ask Unweder if he had put it in her bed, but of course he hadn't. Why would he? If he wanted to give her something—which was unlikely anyway—he'd hand it to her directly.

Ash lay back, holding the little seahorse in her fist. She would have known if it had been there before: It had been right in the middle of her bed. Almost as though left there on purpose.

Like a gift.

As the days went by, so the gifts accrued. Pretty shells and flat stones with holes worn through the middle, sea beans, a lobster claw, and a spiny fish skeleton, which poked her so hard in the thigh when she found it that she bled. Unweder was intrigued but not concerned.

"Perhaps the sea spirits are friendlier than the oak spirits," he said, and there was truth in what he said. Of all the elementals Ash had sought to command, the tree elementals were the most resistant (especially proud oak), the rocks and river the most indifferent. But none had ever been friendly. Yet she had always felt an affinity with the sea; perhaps this was why she was being given tiny, spiny gifts.

They spent their days picking down vertical paths to the gray shore, in and out of caves that reeked of brine and dead fish. Unweder was methodical, working north, covering a few miles every morning, then spending the afternoon fishing while Ash collected seaweed for their supper. At night, they cooked in the chapel, shutters open to release the smoke and let the wild ocean wind hurl through. Unweder slept dreamless across from Ash while she lay her head on a rolled-up blanket, under which all her little sea gifts were stored. She knew instinctively they were items for her protection, even though she hadn't yet seen who left the gifts and how. Nor had she demanded the spirit show itself. She didn't want to frighten it or turn it against her, and besides, she never practiced her magic unless it was necessary. Unweder took blood from her another time, then asked for more just days later. Ash refused, and he sulked for hours.

One afternoon, a week and a day after they had taken up residence in the chapel, Ash decided to stay in after dinner while Unweder went fishing. She needed to rehem her cloak, and had decided to sew all her little treasures inside it. The day was sunny and still, and the to–fro rush of the sea was soothing to her soul. Patiently, with the shutter open to let in light, she folded her sea gifts one by one inside the hem and stitched it securely. This cloak had once been emerald green, but it had faded to the color of dry grass in winter. More than once she had darned holes torn by brambles or sharp rocks. She sometimes wondered if she would ever have a new cloak again, then told herself that, surely, the end of this journey with Unweder was not far off.

Ash finished her task and packed away her needle and thread. The weather had been unforgiving, but had cleared to a calm warm day. She chose to leave the chapel and picked her way down over steep rocks and slippery gravel to the shore. Her cloak now rattled softly, all the little bony, spiny gifts rubbing against one another. The tide was halfway out, and the gray sand and rocks crunched under her feet. Long veins of rock, smooth and hollowed out, had been revealed by the sea's retreat. Ash pulled off her shoes and tiptoed out along one of the veins. She crouched down to study a rock pool. The sun shone into it, illuminating a miniature forest of algae. Tiny fish darted in it. Small curled shells clung to its smooth walls. A light breeze fanned across the beach, making ripples on the surface of the pool, and she watched it a long time, a sense of lazy calm spreading through her.

At length, she stood and walked a little farther, around a rock wall to a cove where she could see Unweder's wooden bucket, his fishing net, and his cloak on the beach. Unweder himself was nowhere to be seen. Ash made her way around a mountain of orange seaweed, and went to his cloak. Had he gone swimming? The sun was warm on her back and her scalp, and she wondered if the water would be warm, too.

In the bucket was a single fish—bream by the look of it—staring dead-eyed at the sky. Ash walked down to the shoreline, hitched her skirts, and stood ankle-deep in the ocean for a while. It sucked and swirled around her feet, burrowing under the gravelly sand then pushing it back up. Still no sign of Unweder.

She looked back toward the bucket. The fish. It wasn't for their supper; it was the form that Unweder had stolen. He was out there, under the water, looking for the dragon in the caves and rock shelves.

How foolish he had been to leave it out in the open. A seagull might come and take it. She might have mistaken it for food and cut its head off. The idea sat in her heart darkly, temptingly. No, she couldn't kill him. With him would die the secret of the last location, and besides, she could not imagine taking anyone's life. But she imagined it anyway, because she was tired of the way he preyed on her blood. If she'd severed the fish's head, he would have never come up for air again. The spell would be broken and he would die as the fish died. Would his human body have washed ashore later, headless? Ash tried to stop her mind going down that path. How tired she was of this, of him.

With his advantage of shapeshifting, he was more likely to find the dragon than she was. Ash could no longer sit at home darning; she had to get out in the world and find the beast before he did.

The next morning, she was woken by a faint scratching at the shutter over her bed. She sat up, bleary, listening hard. Unweder slept on across from her.

There it was again. A soft rasping, almost as though somebody were running rough fingers over the wood. Ash stood and warily opened the shutter a crack to peer out.

About twenty yards away was a small figure, the size of a child but slender and composed. Ash realized immediately it was an elemental, and the seaweed hair and strange scaly appearance of the skin suggested this might be the sea spirit who had been giving her gifts.

She opened the shutter wide; the spirit saw her and lifted a hand to beckon her.

Ash closed the shutter quietly, pulled on her shoes and cloak, and crept out of the chapel. She looked around, saw the sea spirit disappearing over the cliff, where the gravelly slope that took them to the shore lay. She hurried after it, then carefully went down the slope. Once on the gritty beach, she saw it, bent over the same rock pool she had been bent over yesterday. The tide was significantly higher, about to swallow the rock pools. Ash slipped off her shoes and made her way out to it. Usually she saw elementals with her inner eye—maybe a flash here or a flash there in her real vision—but this one was perfectly apparent. As she drew closer, she could see the uneven details of the coral necklace it wore, could see the way the early-morning sun gleamed on its seaweed hair, could even see its muscles working under the strange silvery skin on its back.

"Hello," she said as she approached.

It beckoned, pointing at the rock pool. She knelt next to it and watched as it pulled out one of the tiny swirling shells. She stole a glance at its face, its odd flat eyes. It held the shell between long, slightly webbed fingers, and blew on it gently. A silvery mist rose from between its parted lips, wrapping around the shell and then evaporating. The sea spirit offered the shell to her.

"For me?"

It nodded.

"I will sew it into my cloak with the others. It makes a lovely sound. Comforting."

Another nod. A toothless smile.

"Can you speak?" she asked.

More nods. "Speeeeak," it said in a raspy voice.

"Why do you give me gifts?"

It pointed at her. "Sea witch."

"I am?"

"Strong sea witch."

"Well, thank you. Do you have a name?"

It said a word, but it was impossible to pronounce. It sounded like the draw of the ocean across gravel, long and sibilant.

"I am pleased to meet you."

It stood, touched her cloak, and began to move away. "I know what you seek," it said.

She followed, but it was fast, clambering over rocks and ducking in and out of the water, never looking back. They headed south a mile, then another, Ash never quite catching up. Then it rounded a rocky outcrop and disappeared.

Ash approached the outcrop. The rock was higher than her head. She flopped her shoes onto it and began to struggle up it, using other rocks as steps. The tide was coming in, and when she finally reached the top of the rock, she couldn't see the sea spirit anywhere. Maybe it hadn't intended her to follow it. Shoes in her hand, she went a little farther now, around the next scatter of big rocks, and saw a cave in the distance.

Unweder hadn't been here yet; he had been working his way

north. The mouth of the cave was ragged, dark. She wondered if the sea spirit had gone inside it.

Over rocks and seaweed, she made her way to the opening and went inside.

"Hello?"

The sound of the water moving echoed in the cave, muffling and amplifying it all at once. There was an exit as well as an entrance, and Ash walked through to the other side, only to find the tide there was up to her ankles.

Time to make her way home.

But the ocean was coming in too fast. It had come in behind her, swirling between the rocks, cutting off the base of the cliff. She could go and stand out on a rock, but had no idea how high the water would come.

She stood there, skirts in her hands, then ran back to the cave. A series of ledges had worn into the rock. She climbed to the first and then the second, slimy and slippery with algae, still not sure how high the tide would come. Then up to the third ledge, which seemed drier, safer. Ash hugged her knees and watched the tide come in.

It was dark and damp, and she was cold, but none of these things troubled her so much as the realization that she'd lost the swirly shell the sea spirit had given her. She had been holding it in her hand the whole time, or so she thought. She felt about on the ledge beside her, but there were many unseeable bits and pieces of rock and shell around her, so she balled up her fist and gently released it, promising only to keep the light on a little while, just to find the shell.

Something else caught the light. Ash pounced on it and held it up, her heart hammering. It glittered iridescently: pearlescent white shot with gold. As big as her thumb, hard as forged steel but so light it was almost transparent. A scale.

A dragon's scale.

chapter 9

Sister Julian always arrived directly after breakfast, but
today she was late. Rowan didn't seem to have noticed.
She was happily playing with Strike and Stranger on the floor, pretending to be a cat and getting them to chase her. Skalmir hovered
near the open front door, watching the road. It had been a week of
foul weather and, today being a fine day, he hoped to get out to the
far side of the wood to do some hedge trimming and mending. He
had his scythe and his crook on his belt, his oak-and-iron shovel
waiting by the door, his ax on his back, his handsaw, tools, and food
in his pack. Ten miles of dense woodland lay between his house and
the far side of the wood, and the later Sister Julian arrived, the more
time he would lose.

As soon as he heard hoofbeats, he kissed Rowan goodbye and
picked up his shovel. But when he walked down to the road, the
dogs at his heels, he saw it wasn't Sister Julian at all, but the son of
the innkeeper from Nether Weald.

"Morning, sir," the young man said, reining the horse in.

"I wasn't expecting to see you."

"No, sir. Sister Julian . . . she's sick. She won't be coming today.
Maybe not for the rest of the week. She sends her apologies."

Skalmir hid his frustration. If Sister Julian was unwell, there was
nothing to be done.

Rowan had emerged from the house and was standing on the front path watching curiously.

"Hello, missy!" called the innkeeper's son.

She waved happily.

"You're Julian's neighbor, aren't you?" Skalmir said.

"That I am."

Skalmir fished in his pocket for a coin and handed it up to the lad. "Here. Take this and visit her twice a day, see if she needs anything, and let me know if there's aught we can do. Tell her we hope she's well again soon."

The lad took the coin. "Will do, sir."

Skalmir watched him go, then turned to see Rowan standing directly behind him.

"Can I come into the forest with you?"

"No, Rowan."

"But you aren't hunting today. You said so last night. You said you are mending the hedge. I can help."

He considered her request. He certainly didn't want to waste a day, let alone the rest of the week, inside with Rowan. She wouldn't be much help, but he could show her how to cast up more soil on the hedge, nip the twigs before burying them to take root, shore up weaknesses, and plug gaps. The more she learned about the way her father's lands were managed, the better.

"It's a very long walk," he said finally. "Three hours, and it will be muddy."

"Then we'd better set off straightaway," she said. "I'll put on my oldest shoes so my new ones don't get ruined." She raced inside.

Strike ran around in a circle barking, picking up on the child's jubilant mood. Stranger, always the more still and circumspect of the dogs, stood close to Skalmir's ankle and waited.

Moments later she returned, shutting the door firmly, then, with her spine straight and queenly, she strode down the path. He noticed she had her bow and quiver.

"Come along, then."

They set out down the main path but soon headed east into the forest. Skalmir knew the Howling Wood well but could never claim to know it intimately. Over the many years he had lived here, he had marked paths in and out and kept a rough map of it in his head. He knew the places where the streams bisected it, where the ridges and vales were. But his work meant he was constantly learning new areas and forgetting others, as populations of deer and boar moved around and his tracks through the woods grew over.

The woodland here was ancient and almost sunless, with towering oaks, birch, elms, and sycamore fighting for the light. Fallen trees, taller on their sides than Rowan standing, lay hollow and crumbling next to boulders so furred with bright moss they had forgotten their original color. The musky, damp smell of centuries of rotting leaves, mud, and cold rushing water pervaded. The quiet of the wood always affected him deeply. His own footfalls, which he was never aware of outside the wood, now sounded like the footfalls of a two-legged animal, as much part of the primal ambience of the forest as the weasels and stoats in the undergrowth or the birds that rustled and twittered between the branches. Today there were extra footfalls—Rowan, his young charge, trotting after him—and her chatter as she pointed out insects and animals, shouted angrily at flies, and repeatedly alerted Skalmir to the presence of brambles and nettles, as though he had never traversed the forest before.

They stopped to eat and drink after two hours, alongside a stream that crashed over boulders at a sudden drop. When they started off again, Skalmir climbed down first and then helped Rowan, and he could see she was limping.

"What's wrong?" he asked.

"It turns out my old shoes are a little small for me."

Skalmir was at once annoyed and admiring. He bent down and put her on his back, telling her to be careful of his ax blade, and she wrapped her strong little legs around his waist. They kept going.

By the time they made it to the far hedge, he was exhausted. He plopped Rowan down on a flat rock under a huge sweet chestnut tree, and she sat there gazing up at the splinters of blue summer sky visible through the canopy, shoes cast aside and head cocked almost as though she was listening to music.

The hedge was a head higher than Skalmir, so first he had to climb up on it and walk a few yards in each direction. On the other side was unused pastureland, overgrown with long yellow grass and nettles, and a few straggling saplings. He carefully picked his way over the growth on top of the hedge, some of it very healthy and stubborn, nipping and trimming with his hook, estimating where to cast up more soil, and trying not to slip into a bank of nettles. In all, it wasn't in too bad a state for its year of neglect. It had stood here for nearly fifty years already, built by the man who had raised him but had never allowed Skalmir to call him Father. They had lived on land outside Nether Weald then. Wengest had not allowed him to inherit his un-father's land and, besides, he wasn't a farmer. He was a hunter, all the way into his soul. The woods spoke to him.

About fifty yards from where he had left Rowan, Skalmir found a breach in the base of the hedge where a tree root had erupted from the ground, cracking it open. He climbed down and returned to Rowan.

"I need to do some work a little farther in, but it's not anything you can help with. Do you want to stay here? There's nowhere as nice to sit closer by."

"I'll stay here," she said, happily. "I'm just listening."

"Well, you'll hear my ax and know where I am if you need me," he said.

She drew her knees up under her chin. Her pale feet poked out from under her dress. "I'm fine. Really, I am."

Skalmir returned to his work. Despite the shade, he grew warm as he hacked at the root with his ax, then bent the broken branch-weave into place, shoring it up with boulders and earth. Soil stuck to his sweat. The sounds of the wood enveloped him. Soft movements, the chirp of birds and bugs, the shushing of leaves in the breeze. He was absorbed in his labors and in the familiar calm of the wood, and he did not know how much time had passed. Then a butterfly flew over the fence and landed on the handle of his shovel. Its wings were pale blue, Rowan's favorite color this month, so he called out to her, "Rowan, come and look at this."

No answer. The butterfly took to the air.

"Too late. You missed it."

Still no answer.

Skalmir put down his ax. The rhythm of his heart sped a little. "Rowan?" he called, tramping back to where he had left her.

The flat rock was empty but for her discarded shoes. "Rowan!" he called, blundering back to the path. "Rowan, where are you?"

"Over here, Snowy!" Her little voice seemed impossibly distant. He slogged through bracken toward it, up a steep rocky incline—how had she managed this herself, barefoot?—and into a dense section of wood where two trees had tangled together and grown bent and impenetrable. Through branches, he saw Rowan. She wasn't alone.

"Stop!" he cried. "Where are you taking her?"

"It's fine, Snowy," Rowan replied, a giggle in her voice. He was around the other side of the twisted tree now and could see she was flanked by two strangers: a slight man and a meaty woman, both with pale-copper hair. Both were shirtless, their upper bodies covered in swirling blue tattoos.

"Step away from her!" Skalmir commanded, striding toward them, his voice booming so loud in the forest that it was followed by a flurry of bird wings.

"Snowy, don't be cross with them. They're taking me to see the singing tree. They know where it is."

But Skalmir snatched Rowan away and held her tightly against him. "This forest belongs to Wengest, king of Nettlechester," he told them. "Poachers are punishable by imprisonment and heavy fines."

"We aren't poachers," the woman said, in a soft, sibilant voice. A circular tattoo covered her cheek. "We are woodlanders."

Even as she said this, Skalmir noted that they had no hunting equipment, just the knives at their waistbands.

"Don't be angry with them, Snowy," Rowan said. "I asked them to take me to the singing tree. They're the only other people I've met who can hear it. I thought I'd be there and back before you knew I was gone. They say it's not far from here . . ."

"A hidden path," said the man. "We would have brought her back."

"We mean her no harm," the woman concurred. "We would not harm one so precious."

Skalmir was never quick to anger, but his own guilt and shock at Rowan's disappearance made him raw, and something about the woman's choice of words fired him up. "She is not yours to judge as precious or otherwise," he spat. "Leave the Howling Wood and don't come back. If I see you again . . . you will regret it." Skalmir limped to the end of his threat, anger ebbing away. He had killed many animals over the years, but had never shed the blood of a man and didn't truly believe he could.

"The Howling Wood is not your king's," the woman said, her voice heated. "It never has been."

The man touched her shoulder and beckoned her away. The woman stood her ground awhile, glaring, then turned and followed him deeper into the woods.

When they were gone, Rowan turned to him angrily. "You were mean to them."

"You cannot go with people you don't know, Rowan. I'm baffled. You are a princess. You know better."

"But the singing tree—"

"Enough of the singing tree. There is no singing tree. They might have been pretending to know of it to lure you away." His anger bubbled up again.

"Then how could they hum the *exact* tune it sings?"

"You're imagining it. They're First Folk. Not to be trusted."

"Bluebell says the First Folk aren't—"

"Enough!" he roared. "I care nothing for what anyone else has said to you. I am your protector. My word goes. And we are going home. I should never have brought you out here."

Rowan burst into tears but followed close behind Skalmir as he went to fetch his tools.

Three nights later, they came. The weather had turned rainy again, and unseasonably cool. The long twilight had extinguished and Rowan had been asleep for hours. Skalmir sat by the hearth sharpening arrowheads. Strike and Stranger dozed nearby, Strike's little legs twitching in a dream. The fire popped softly. Water dripped off the gables.

Skalmir heard movement outside, and at first he thought it might be a wild boar, so he fetched his bow and arrow before he opened the door.

Six of them stood there, the First Folk. What had they called themselves? The woodlanders? It was dark, the only light falling out of his threshold, from the fire and the tallow candles in the sconces. The woodlanders were very still, and said nothing. One of the men, he noted, stood at the head of the group. He had a long tangled beard and wore a headdress of blackberry thorns that had been fashioned into antlers, and in the dim light Skalmir thought he could see that the swirling tattoos covered his face as well as his chest and arms.

"What do you want?" Skalmir demanded.

"To see the little queen," the horned man said. "I have been told she is real and she lives in this house."

"The child sleeps and you will stay far away from her, on pain of death."

To Skalmir's surprise, the man chuckled. "It is she who comes to us."

A woman spoke. "We see her in the sky."

Skalmir shook his head. "Go away. Consider this your last warning."

He went inside and closed the door, paced the house while the dogs watched, curious. When he checked again half an hour later, they were gone.

They'd called her the little queen. Rowan's hiding place had been found out. Would Wengest take her away from him? But he couldn't keep news of this danger from Wengest. Skalmir was trained only in basic combat and hadn't practiced it in years; Rowan needed protection armed with more than a hunter's bow.

We see her in the sky.

What did that mean? First Folk were noted for being odd, otherworldly, even capricious. They weren't to be trusted; everyone knew that.

Skalmir slipped into Rowan's room and sat on the floor next to her bed. She breathed quietly, lying very still on her back. How he loved her in that moment; the child of his heart if not of his body. But it wasn't forever; it had never been forever. He folded his arms on the end of her bed and put his head down. Tomorrow, the moment the sun was up, he and Rowan would ride to town to send a message to her father.

Sister Julian was well again by the end of the week, and Skalmir worked two very long days on the hedges to make up for lost time, no matter that it rained intermittently the whole time. Julian was under strict orders to stay inside with the doors bolted, and not to open them to anyone. Rowan, much chastened by her encounter in the woods, promised Skalmir solemnly not to leave the house unless he was with her.

Arriving home on the second night, cold and soaked, he saw two white horses grazing in the long grass along the front path. Their saddles wore Wengest's insignia, so he picked up his pace.

He burst into the house to see them there: Wengest and a very tall warrior with a scar across his neck. Rowan was sitting, perfectly straight, reading scripture aloud while Julian looked on proudly.

"Ah, here's the man himself!" Wengest said, interrupting Rowan, who put the rolled sheets of vellum aside and maintained her posture with little more than a nod and a smile for Skalmir.

"My lord, you do us great honor."

Wengest stood and came to grasp Skalmir's hand. He was dressed richly, in gold and emerald green, his beard waxed to gleaming, looking every inch the king. "Look at my Rowan," he said to Skalmir. "Look how she grows and how clever and poised she is. You and Sister Julian are doing a fine job. A fine job indeed."

Strike tried to jump into Rowan's lap, but Rowan cautioned him back down onto the floor.

"Thank you, my lord," Skalmir said. "We have good raw material to work with."

Sister Julian rose. "If it's well with you, my lords, I will make my way home."

"Let Lang accompany you," Wengest said, tapping the tall warrior's chest with his knuckles.

"I will be fine," she said.

"But I insist. Rowan, would you like to go riding with Lang on his horse?"

Rowan shook her head, but something about the expression her father gave her made her change her mind swiftly. "Of course, Papa." She looked up at the big warrior and smiled nervously.

"Ride slow, bring her back safe," Wengest said to Lang.

In a flurry of gathering cloaks and scarves and shoes they were gone, leaving Wengest and Skalmir alone. Skalmir wanted nothing more than to change into dry clothes and rest awhile, but Wengest was his king and he indicated they should sit together on the bench by the hearth, so he did, dripping slowly on the floor.

"Your message said you had fears for my daughter's safety?"

"She met some First Folk in the woods. Then they traced her back to here."

"They intend her harm?"

"I don't know. They said not. And they didn't seem hostile, they seemed . . . curious."

"Curious?"

Skalmir took a deep breath. "I will understand if you want to take her from here, but I hope you'd consider letting me continue as her guardian, I—"

Wengest waved his index finger. "I'm not moving her. She's well hidden here. These people, these First Folk, shouldn't be on my land. It is they who will move."

The Howling Wood is not your king's. It never has been.

"My lord, I would do anything to secure Rowan's happiness and health, but I have only basic training in arms."

"That's what Lang is for. He will stay. He will hunt them down and make them . . . go." Wengest gave a tight smile. "And he will make sure Rowan is safe."

"Stay? Here?"

"He has equipment to camp, right out the front. Close enough to make her feel safe, not so close as to intrude on her lessons. You will be expected to feed him, as you feed yourself, from what you catch and what you grow here."

Skalmir realized knots in his back were unraveling; he had been hunched with anticipation since the encounter with the First Folk. "My lord, we are so grateful."

Wengest sighed, pulled himself to his feet, and began to pace slowly. "I want her to have an easy childhood. I didn't want guardsmen around. I wonder what these First Folk are thinking."

"They called her the little queen," Skalmir admitted.

"Rowan won't be a queen," Wengest said. "Not unless she marries another king. We are trimartyrs in Nettlechester, remember; women can't rule."

Skalmir thought of Bluebell, and it made the corner of his mouth twitch in a smile that Wengest didn't see.

Wengest went to the door and stood there, looking out toward the road. "She grows up away from me," he said softly. "I would have had her near me, if I could."

Skalmir had only an incomplete understanding of why Rowan had to spend her childhood away from court, and knew better than to question Wengest. "She speaks of you often," he lied.

Wengest turned, barely able to hide his smile. "She does?"

"Most fondly, my lord. Most fondly."

Wengest turned back to the door. "I think of her fondly, too. And her mother, sometimes." He shook his head. "Well. That's in the past. I am marrying again."

Skalmir was unsurprised. All of Nettlechester had been speculating on when Wengest might try for a male heir.

"I'm very pleased for you, my lord."

"My new wife is a silly young thing, but one can't always marry for love. There's a little too much gray in my beard to be so idealistic." He thumped the threshold twice, as though to emphasize the point. "As soon as Rowan's back with Lang, I'll return to Nether Weald. I've had a lovely day with my daughter, but affairs of state wait for no king." He turned and seemed to look at Skalmir closely for the first time. "Good grief, man, you're sodden. Go and change into something dry."

With relief, Skalmir left the room.

The big soldier, Lang, slept inside by the hearth the first night, but spent the second day setting up a tent by their front path. Skalmir was reassured by his presence, while Rowan was puzzled by it.

"Why is that soldier staying?" she asked as she idly watched through the shutter while he hung an oilskin over his camp.

"To make sure you are safe."

She turned to Skalmir and bit her lip. "Is this my fault? For talking to the woodlanders? They wouldn't hurt me, you know. They liked me."

He moved over to her and rubbed her shoulder. "It's not your fault, no."

"I hope he won't hurt them," she said wistfully.

Skalmir didn't answer. He wanted them gone from the Howling Wood, but it was better not to think about what that might involve. All he knew was that he slept easier once Lang was there.

It was a fine morning, unremarkable in any other way. Skalmir woke before Rowan, ground some wheat, and cooked some breadcakes in a pan for their breakfast. She came out of her room, rubbing her eyes, still in the warm dress she wore to bed. Strands of her fine dark hair had escaped her plait and she sat by the fire and brushed her hair loose then rebound it while he cooked. He made a plate for her, one for himself, and one for Lang.

"Let me take it to him," Rowan said. She was growing fond of Lang; she eventually grew fond of everyone. She had about her such a personal charm that people found themselves wanting to do things for her. In the few weeks that Lang had been with them, he'd carved her poppets, helped her put a baby bird back in a tree, and gotten down on all fours to let her ride on his back like a pony.

Skalmir handed her the plate. He felt the breeze on his back as she opened the door.

Rowan screamed.

Skalmir turned, dropping his plate, and was across the room in two strides to reach for her. She turned, burying her face in his side.

Lang lay across their front path, dead, an arrow protruding from each of his eyes.

CHAPTER 10

Rose passed five long days sitting by Heath's wordless, sick body. Steam filled Eldra's tiny house. The older woman said that bloody shadows had pooled in Heath's lungs and the only way to get them out was time and moisture. The steam was infused with hyssop, hollyhock, and burdock root, lending the room an unpleasantly sweet organic smell, like broken roots and mud and crushed flowers. Eldra had brought his fever down with a potion of snapdragon and bugloss that she mixed into wine with mashed garlic. Heath could only manage a sip or two at a time, in between long sleeps punctuated by violent coughing fits that left him blue with breathlessness.

"He hasn't died yet, so he probably won't," Eldra had said in an abrupt tone that morning before she took Linden walking out on the moors, looking for a particular kind of moss that only grew at high altitudes.

Keeping Linden away from the sickroom had proved challenging. Once Rose had found him standing over Heath, looking at him with an expression that was curious but not empathetic, as Heath slept on with rattling breaths, and she wondered how she could explain who this thin man was to her son. After what Cardew had told her, she could hardly explain him to herself. But warm pleasant weather had been on Rose's side, and Linden had been happy enough to accompany her or Eldra on expeditions that left his little legs aching so much that he slept long and hard from early evening right through until morning.

Rose sat in the quiet room and watched and waited. Cardew had headed home after eliciting a promise from her to send word if Heath recovered. Hours passed. Rose brought more water for the pot, emptied more of Eldra's infusion into it, watched him sleep, then watched him wake racked by coughs. Felt his hand creep out to flop weakly onto her knee. She rubbed his wrist. "I'm here," she said, over and over. And although he couldn't speak, she knew he was comforted by her words.

Sometime around the middle of the fifth day, when Rose's stomach was starting to rumble with hunger and she considered how she might get some mashed stew into Heath's mouth without making him cough himself inside out, his weak hand on her knee became a more insistent tap.

"Heath?" she asked, pulling herself back from the thoughts she was lost in to regard his sunken face.

He pawed at his mouth.

"Water?" she asked.

"Water," he managed, the first word he had said whole since she had first found him at Cardew's. To hear his voice electrified her heart. Despite its frailty, it sounded like him: a voice she hadn't heard in nearly four years. Memories and sadness tumbled through her.

She rose and fetched him a cup of water and helped him half sit so that he could sip it. The first gulp set off a violent coughing fit, and most of it ended up in Rose's lap. He said sorry with his fingers against her sleeve, and indicated she should try again.

He drank. Stopped and breathed. Drank.

"Your medicine," she said, when he had managed the whole cup of water.

He nodded and lay back down as he waited for her to find the right potion from Eldra's shelves, then rested in her arms again—so thin—while he took a deep draught of it. Then he nodded and settled on his back, looking at her.

Rose returned the cork to the little stone bottle and put it aside, fixing him with her gaze. "You spoke," she said.

He nodded, then said breathily, "My Rose."

A smile overtook her face and warmth flushed her cheeks. "How wonderful it is to hear your voice. But you must continue to rest. Eldra says you are getting better, but very slowly. Do you feel better?"

He nodded once, then the coughs racked him again and she stroked his hair away from his forehead and settled him once again among the blankets and told him he mustn't try to communicate more. He lay, gazing up at her, a great sadness in his eyes.

"You . . ." he said, gesturing weakly with his hands. "You talk. How is Rose?"

"Rose is . . . I'm well and happy, all things considered, and . . ." She couldn't bring herself to tell him about Linden. Not yet. "I see Rowan sometimes in the seeing-loop. She has grown. She's beautiful. Some days I don't look. It makes me too sad." The only contact Rose had with Rowan was via the magic eye that a witch had given her. Once a day, at dawn, she could see her daughter upon waking. But now that she had thought of Rowan, she couldn't resist asking Heath for confirmation of what Cardew had said. "Is it true?" she asked softly. "The story Cardew told?"

He nodded, sighed, and opened his mouth to speak.

"No, no, don't speak," she said. "Rest. When you are well again . . . we will talk at length then."

He hadn't the strength to nod again, but closed his eyes and tried to breathe over the shadows in his chest. Rose watched him awhile, then closed her own eyes to sift through what Cardew had told her.

Heath's provenance had always been a mystery. Wengest's sister had taken a First Folk lover. "It was the kind of thing she would do, just to annoy my father," Wengest had always said. Now she was long dead, but Heath's father remained unknown. According to Cardew, though, he had not been a servant of no consequence, as Wengest had suspected. He had been the Wood King, Connacht of the West, warlord druid of a First Folk tribe in southern Bradsey, who had been working for many years to unite all of the First Folk under one banner in order to take back some of the land that had once belonged to them. When illness had fallen upon him, he charged his followers to look for his heir.

"Connacht was both strong in battle and strong in the sight. He could have been an undermagician, but he loved the company of his kinsfolk too dearly," Cardew had explained. "Six feet tall he stood, and broad of brow. Often he wore the antlers of the great hunter and told mysteries and prophecies at the full moon. He declared that his heir, blood of his blood, would be marked by the same combination of war and magic as he was.

"I was part of the band that sought out Heath. We took with us an old seeress who found him on a farm on the northern border. He looked as surprised as you, Rose, when we told him of his great lineage. It took us many weeks to convince him to accompany us to Connacht's encampment. But finally he did.

"Father and son were reunited in the grim little wooden hut where Connacht was weakening daily. This is how low our people have been brought, when our great chieftains die in dark places. Heath sat by his side and reminded Connacht of his mother, by name and description. Connacht remembered her fondly, remembered a love affair as passionate as it was doomed, for she was of Nettlechester and he was of the woods. With his dying breaths, Connacht declared Heath his son and heir."

Here Cardew had fallen silent a few moments as they made their way slowly up onto the moors via overgrown roads, passing rocky formations that looked as though they had been built by giants.

"You know Heath," he'd said at last. "He is strong in battle, but he has no sight. He worked hard to understand his dead father's plans, to continue bringing the tribes together at council, but it took only a few months for the tribes to look to him and find him wanting. No horns at the full moon. No mysteries and prophecies. A good man, yes, but ultimately only a man.

"For my own part, and that of my kinsfolk, we were prepared to wait to see if those other aspects would develop. But the tribes began to splinter again, until the same old seer who had found him dreamed that Heath had a daughter of war and magic, and that she was Connacht's true heir. Heath reluctantly admitted she existed but that he didn't know where, and she had no idea he was her father. But excitement grew among the First Folk, and they have been looking for her ever since, despite Heath's pleas to leave her be. Blood of the First Folk, granddaughter of the most powerful kingdom in Thyrsland, Almissia. They call her the little queen."

Rose's daughter. Rowan.

Rose sat quietly as the afternoon light changed, sending yellow splinters through the shutters so that the steam in the room was visible and ghostly. Rowan was too young to be a warrior, but she suspected Bluebell had long hoped she would become one. And did Rowan have the sight? Rose had seen no evidence of it, but Rose hadn't been in the company of her child in four years. Rowan's aunt Ash and great-aunt Eldra had both taken the path of undermagic; even Rose herself had sometimes felt glimmers of something that couldn't be explained with the senses most people used to ground themselves in the world.

And most persuasively, sometimes, late at night, Rose woke and was sure she felt Rowan in the bed with her, breathing soft and warm against her back. She would turn and see nothing, but still the strong sense her daughter was close—had always been close—persisted.

The door flew open, and Eldra and Linden entered. Linden held a large basket of plants and Eldra limped along beside him, her hand on his shoulder as it often was, either for added support or protectively or both. Nobody had to tell Linden to be quiet because he was always quiet. He placed the basket by the hearth and approached Rose to give her a kiss. Then he stood a little while looking down at Heath, that same look of passive curiosity on his face.

"How is our patient?" Eldra said in a soft voice, joining them.

"He spoke," Rose said. "Not much, but he said he is starting to feel better."

"Of course he is," Eldra said with a prideful sniff. "Come on, Linden. Let's fetch more water for the steam pot."

Eldra moved away, but Linden stayed a moment, looking at Heath. Then Heath opened his eyes and saw the boy, saw Rose's hand around his soft wrist, and his eyes flickered with understanding. Tears pricked at Rose's eyes.

"Linden, come," Eldra repeated.

Linden turned and walked away. The door closed behind them.

"The boy," Heath managed.

Rose's tears fell freely. "I'm sorry."

"Wengest," he said. "The boy is his."

Rose nodded. The likeness was unmistakable. When he was clean-shaven, which was rarely, Wengest had a distinctive cleft to his chin. Linden also. "I must have been pregnant last time you and I were . . . together. I didn't know. I wasn't sick . . . I didn't count my courses because we were traveling. We were—"

Heath tapped her knee with his fingers. "Nothing to explain," he said breathlessly, then began to cough.

Rose had believed Wengest infertile, and perhaps he was most of the time. But somehow one tenacious seed had survived its journey to her womb. Somehow she had done in exile what she could never do while living the life of queen of Nettlechester: produce a true, male heir to the kingdom.

"He can't ever know," Rose whispered. "Wengest will take him from me."

Heath tried to talk but couldn't. Still, Rose knew what he would say. *Wengest might have you back.* Wengest needed a male heir almost as much as he needed to breathe. He had ambitious kin; his grip on Nettlechester was not as firm as he would wish. A son, especially a son by the bloodline of Almissia, was the end of all his troubles.

The troubles of kings, always circumscribing her. Rose knew her true destiny was never to *be* anyone special, but to continue to produce special children for other special people. Little more than a broodmare.

"He's not taking my son and he's not taking me," Rose said, under her breath.

Heath didn't reply, but she knew he understood by the brush of his knuckles across her hand. She grasped his fingers and pressed her face against them, and told herself to breathe.

Skalmir knew it was too late, that Rowan had already seen the grim corpse of Lang on their front path, but he still covered her eyes with his hand as he carried her past the body and down to the road. Rowan wore a little moleskin backpack that he had hastily stuffed with clothes for her. She clutched in her right hand her bow and quiver; she had refused to leave Skalmir's house without it. But leave she must, and immediately.

As he reached the road, he noticed the drag marks through leaves and mud. Lang had not died on their front path. He had been killed in the forest then dragged back there, as a warning to Skalmir, no doubt. Lang hadn't died on watch: He'd died while hunting the woodlanders.

Rowan began to squirm. "I can walk myself," she said.

He set her down, facing her shoulders firmly forward. "Walk fast, don't look back," he said.

She did as she was told. The morning was still cool and dewy. Birdcalls in the trees sounded too ordinary and too sweet. Skalmir's field of vision seemed bright with fierce vigilance. Every movement, every sound was a potential threat. He kept a hand on Rowan's shoulder, even when she tried to shrug it off.

"Who did that to him?" she kept saying. "Who would kill Lang? Lang was a nice man. I know he looked fierce, but he saved that baby bird with me. Why would anyone kill him?"

Skalmir didn't answer, just kept urging her on. To the village, to Sister Julian and safety.

"Snowy, why aren't you answering me?"

"Because I don't know, Rowan. And that's why you have to go stay with Sister Julian until I can find out, and make sure you are safe."

"How long will I have to stay?"

"I don't know."

"Sister Julian is very boring. She won't let me shoot my bow."

"Rowan!" he boomed. "Keep walking."

She dissolved into tears, but kept walking nonetheless. The road curved away from the house, and he was glad. The grisly sight was behind them for now. The farther out of the forest they drew, the more his shoulders relaxed. Rowan sniffled and dragged her feet, but it would be all right. She was out of the woods, and the woodlanders wouldn't dare to go to the village. Would they?

Should he take her farther south, all the way to Withing? Or even back to Folkenham so her father's full retinue could keep her safe? How was he to make that decision with his head and not his heart?

"Skalmir?" Rowan said in a little voice, disrupting his thoughts.

"Yes?"

"Are you angry?"

"I'm angry at whoever did that to Lang."

"Are you angry with me?"

"No."

"Is it my fault? Is it my fault he died?"

"How could it be your fault?"

"Because I talked to those people . . . were they bad people?"

Skalmir didn't know how to answer. In all likelihood, they were protecting themselves when they killed Lang. Wengest had radically underestimated them. "All I know is I need to keep you a long way away from them."

"Will I have to stay a long way away from *you*?"

His heart squeezed. "Perhaps, Rowan. I can't make that decision. I have to send a message to your father."

"They knew about the singing tree," she said, setting her little jaw. "I'm sure the singing tree isn't bad."

He stopped and pulled her in front of him, bending so his eyes were level with hers, a hand firmly on each arm. "You must put the singing tree out of your mind. It would be dangerous for you to try to find it, do you understand?"

"Ow, Snowy, you're hurting my arms."

"Tell me you understand. Rowan, tell me."

She nodded. "Yes, I understand. Then it *was* my fault. I went with them that day and they came back and Lang got arrows in his eyes." Her bottom lip began to shake and he pulled her against him and held her and inhaled her sweet scent, wondering if it would be the last time.

Then he stood. "Let's keep moving," he said.

"Whoever killed him was a good shot," she said, and the words seemed so cold after the warm embrace that he shivered.

"Yes," he replied. "They were."

He had never been so grateful to see the village. They met Sister Julian just outside her painted front door, as she was leaving to come to the woods.

"Rowan?" she said, startled, as the little girl ran to her and started crying into her skirt.

Skalmir approached. As always, Julian looked slightly alarmed by his presence.

"Can Rowan stay with you?" he asked.

"Of course. Why? What has happened?"

"Lang is dead!" Rowan cried.

"Murdered and left on our doorstep," Skalmir muttered. "It's not safe for Rowan there."

"What makes you think it's safe for her here?" Julian asked.

"I don't think they'll come to the village."

"And what if you think wrong?"

He nodded. "I understand. I'll hire a standing guard for a few days, until I hear from Wengest."

"More guardsmen?" Rowan asked, turning her tearstained face to him. "They'll get arrows in their eyes too!"

Sister Julian's face went white.

Skalmir put a hand on Rowan's shoulder but addressed his words to Julian. "They didn't come for him," he said. "They killed him in the woods. He went after them first."

"Do you intend that to give me comfort?"

"Sister Julian, you know she can't stay in the woods with me."

Julian nodded, her eyes falling on Rowan. "You'll have to share my bed," she said with a little smile. "I have terribly cold feet, I should warn you."

Rowan blinked back tears. "Then we will have to make you some socks."

Julian indicated her bow and arrow. "You go on in, but leave those dirty things outside the back window. I'll be inside in a few moments."

Rowan went inside and Julian pulled the door closed so she and Skalmir could speak without her hearing.

"What do they want?" she asked him.

"Rowan," he said simply. "But they aren't going to get her. I'll send a message to Wengest and—"

Sister Julian was shaking her head. "I love and honor my king," she said, her voice low and urgent, "but you have told him once of this threat and he went about resolving it the wrong way. You and I both know who you should send that message to." Her mouth turned down at the corners, as though the words tasted sour.

Sister Julian was right. He needed to summon Bluebell.

Skalmir spent the day in the village, settling Rowan in, finding and employing two watchmen to alternate shifts, sending an express message to Bluebell. He had no idea where she was so he scattered it out to Blickstow, Fifelham, and Merkhinton. Somebody somewhere would bump it along to where she had last been seen. It was a simple message: *Snowy. Nether Weald. Urgent.*

He ate his supper with Rowan and Sister Julian then took his leave. Rowan cried a little, but he said he'd be back to see her in a day or so, and Sister Julian saw him off.

"If anything troubles you, anything at all . . ." he said.

"I'll send for you immediately." Her eyes darted to the watchman who stood at the outside corner of her little house, his dark hood pulled over his head.

Skalmir tried to smile reassuringly. "They won't come to the village."

"I hope you are right."

Long shadows striped the road on his way home, and he dragged his feet because he knew what awaited him: a body to burn.

Strike and Stranger came pounding out of the undergrowth when they heard his footfalls draw near. They were hunting dogs so he never had to worry about them going hungry, and in fact he saw the telltale splash of feathers and blood on the road that assured him they had already eaten. Still, he walked right past Lang's body— grown stiff and gray now—and through the house to freshen their water and take a moment to rub their heads.

He was putting off the inevitable.

Skalmir was not a superstitious man, but he did not want to burn Lang's body so close to his house. In a chest by his bed, he found the sword Wengest had given him when Rowan had first come to live with him. Its edge was dull so he took his time sharpening it, then hunting for a belt to hang it on. In the same chest he found an old cloak that he hadn't worn for many years, and set about his bleak business.

He knelt beside Lang, forced himself to look. First he snapped off the arrows and threw the flights into the hedges. Then he lay out the cloak and rolled Lang into it. Blood had run down the man's face and dried black in his hair. Skalmir folded the cloak around his face and upper body. It wasn't long enough to cover his calves and feet, where Skalmir grasped Lang's body and began to drag him into the woods. He knew of a rocky clearing a few hundred yards in where he could build a pyre. Slowly, as the afternoon deepened to twilight, he made his way into the woods with his grim burden. Birds watched from their perches in the oaks and lindens. The quiet of the forest enveloped him. The body bounced behind him up a rocky slope. Finally, he was there.

Skalmir left Lang crumpled on his side while he collected dead-fall and built an ankle-high pyre. Night was falling before he wrangled the big soldier's body onto it, splashed it with fire oil, then used a flint to light it.

He stood back, said a prayer to the Horse God. *Take this brave man into your train.* Sparks spiraled up into the sky. The firelight lit the leaves and branches in soft orange tones. The heat flushed his face and he stood back a little, head bowed, as the fire rushed up and over Lang to turn his mortal remains to ashes.

A noise.

Skalmir whirled around and saw them—the man with the thorn headdress and the tattooed woman, both dressed in skins. He fumbled at his hip for the sword but the woman already had a bow and arrow trained on him, so he put up his empty hands.

"I am a hunter," he said. "Not a soldier."

The man stepped forward, touched the woman's shoulder, and said, "Down, Dardru." She lowered the bow.

"He tried to kill us," the man said, pointing at the pyre.

"I guessed that," Skalmir said. "I won't try to kill you, but you should know that Rowan has gone. I have sent her far away. Don't come looking for her anymore."

The man smiled. His face was almost pleasant, and the lines around his eyes told Skalmir that he had seen many summers. "What is your name, hunter?"

"Skalmir."

"You are from the Iceheart?"

"I am a son of Nettlechester. I don't know the source from which my blood runs. I am a foundling."

"My name is Rathcruick. My daughter's name is Dardru. They were her arrows that took down this . . . cutthroat." He spat the last word as he indicated the pyre with a dismissive gesture. "Our war is not with you. He sought us out in the hope of killing us on our land, in our homes."

Skalmir shook his head. "I have lived and worked in this forest for many years and never seen evidence that anyone lives here, let alone could call the Howling Wood 'our land.'"

"And yet it is," Dardru said, her face defiant by the firelight. She was a meaty woman, a circular tattoo of intricate swirls on her left cheek. "Who are you to gainsay us?"

"The keeper of the wood."

"You see only a sliver of the wood," Rathcruick said with a small laugh. "My people have been here since the time of the giants."

Skalmir wanted to disagree, to tell them that he knew the woods better than anyone, but despite their reassurance that they meant him no harm, he didn't want to anger them. "Very well," he said. "Perhaps we can go on avoiding each other, now that Rowan is gone."

"She isn't gone," Rathcruick said. "She will fly over us tonight, as she so often does, on her way to other places."

"As long as she's in her own bed in the morning, I don't care what she dreams," Skalmir said firmly. "I repeat: Don't go looking for her. Your people aren't wanted in our towns and villages."

Dardru snorted. "The feeling is mutual."

Rathcruick smiled again, the pleasant, open-faced smile that was so at odds with the foreboding bramble-horns upon his head. "We don't need to go looking for her," he said. "She will come to us in her own time. We can wait."

Skalmir said nothing. They didn't know Rowan as well as he did. She was strong-willed but ultimately obedient, and her guilt over possibly contributing to Lang's death would make her very cautious now.

"Come, Dardru," he said to his daughter. "Let's leave the hunter to burn the dog."

They turned and disappeared back into the forest. Skalmir watched the place where they had stood, tensed, half expecting them to change their minds and come back to kill him. Everyone knew First Folk weren't to be trusted.

But they didn't return, and the fire's first burst of heat and light had diminished, so it was time to leave Lang to fall into embers and head to his own bed, to his empty house, without Rowan.

chapter 11

luebell's task was as straightforward as Torr's steady stride and as crooked as Thrymm's hind legs. One of her sisters had a sword forged with troll magic and designed to kill her. She had four sisters. Therefore, all she had to do was find and ask each one of them.

But she had no idea where Ash was, no idea where Willow was (in fact, had many times wondered if she was dead), would be risking her life to return to Bradsey where Rose lived among undermagicians, which left Ivy, who was the last person in the world who would know what to do with a magic sword unless that was her new favorite word for a cock.

Bluebell didn't imagine that any of them would knowingly harbor an instrument of her death or seek to use one against her. Rather, she supposed the trollblade—the randerman had called it *Grithbani*—had fallen into a sister's hands without her knowing its significance. The work ahead of her ought to be a simple seek-and-destroy mission, but the seeking was going to be anything but simple.

She pondered this as she sat, hugging her knees, under a moleskin tent by the Gema River. A thunderstorm had split the dark sky overhead and tipped an ocean of rain upon her and her army. The summer days had been long and hot since leaving Hakon's nest, and the sea breezes all too soon behind them. This storm had been brewing for days, and not a single man or woman minded it. Some had even gone out in the rain to wash the stink of sweat and traveling grime off their bodies. Bluebell hadn't. She had been imagining scrubbing it off in a warm bath, and once an idea was fixed in her head she almost never let it go. A fast leak in the tent ran along the inside seam and dripped hurriedly in the corner, creating mud among the grass. Bluebell stuck to the dry corner, not yet ready to lie down and sleep. Perhaps she would when the storm passed. Travel made her weary, but not so weary she could sleep through booming thunder. Thrymm was already asleep, pressed hard against her hip. Not for the first time, she envied the life of a dog. Bright, brief, simple.

Just across the river was Bradsey, the least populated kingdom in Thyrsland. The land was mostly moors and fens, ridges and rocks. Lean hunting, wretched farming. Undermagicians lived there, drawn by the isolation. Also First Folk, the strange, red-haired first inhabitants of Thyrsland whose tribes had been driven west by her own ancestors, generations ago. Towns were spread a long way from one another, and were often poor and half empty. The king, Renward, was barely a king. He was the head of the wealthiest family, yes, but the army he commanded was thin and toothless. Bradsey could have been her father's years ago, had he a mind to take it. But taxing the people's resources wouldn't have raised enough to pay for administering their levies, so he left them alone. Almissia and Nettlechester had heavy joint defenses stationed on Bradsey's northern border against ice-men, and in the past Bluebell had traveled through the rough countryside many times.

No more, though. Last time, she had upset the undermagicians. Most of them. They said she stank of horse magic and now it was too dangerous for her to travel there. They could smell her for miles. And yet Bradsey was where Rose lived and she needed to see her, to ask her about the sword.

A dark thought slithered in behind that one. What if Rose knew it was a trollblade? What if Rose was angry at her for not doing more to reunite her with Rowan? For taking Wengest's side? For exiling Heath?

Bluebell dismissed it. No matter how angry her sisters might be with her, they surely knew all she did was for the good of her family, her kingdom.

So ought she assemble her hearthband, boldly cross the river, and march through Bradsey, arms and armor ringing proudly? Ought she brave the undermagicians and their jealousy of her good favor with the Horse God? No undermagician could compete with swords and spears and axes if surprised, but undermagicians were notoriously unsurprisable. Even the randerman had said he knew she was coming. She wondered if he had an inkling she was going to kill him, too, or if the limit of one's own life was always unseeable, by the nature of one's perspective inside it.

No. Rose was close in miles, but unreachable nonetheless. Bluebell wouldn't enter Bradsey, and certainly wouldn't risk the lives and minds of her best fighters among the sly whispers of undermagicians.

That left only one course of action: pay a visit to Ivy in Seacaster. Ivy may have heard from Willow, who was her twin and closest to her since Bluebell had last been to the busy port town—how long ago was that? She remembered Ivy had a belly full of her second baby that time and seemed to have outgrown the worst of her childish faults. Ivy was also surrounded by a court that largely saw Bluebell as the enemy. The northern earls of Nettlechester had most reluctantly come to the peace deal with Almissia, and Bluebell and her father had a particularly well-earned reputation for having killed many friends and relatives before the peace. Perhaps one of them had left *Grithbani* in Ivy's possession, waiting for an opportunity to strike.

The rain began to ease. Bluebell rose and pulled out a raincloak, threw it over her head, and passed once around the encampment, offering murmured words of encouragement to the night watch, sharing jokes and jibes with starstruck young men who knew they wanted to be like her one day but couldn't see how it would ever be possible. She dropped in on Sighere's tent, found him awake, and told him of her plan to get their horses—sent to Fifelham to await their return—and head with her hearthband to Seacaster.

"Do you think it a wise course of action?" she asked him.

"They say Gunther is very ill."

"I don't care about Gunther. You understand I need to find and talk to every one of my sisters?"

The corners of Sighere's mouth turned up. "I find it impossible to believe any sword can kill you, my lord. Especially one made in a raider's forge." Ice-men were known for the poor quality of their steel compared with Southlanders and especially Bluebell's hometown of Blickstow, where the smiths' guild was powerful and disciplined. "Especially wielded by one of your sisters," he continued with a chuckle.

"Never underestimate magic," Bluebell said. "Besides, I am tired of this army. I can't wait to divest myself of its command and head east. A trip to the seaside, Sighere?"

He nodded. "As you wish, my lord. Always, as you wish."

Bluebell had been traveling for six—or was it seven?—days when she finally rode into Seacaster with her hearthband. A messenger had been sent ahead, and so they entered the town with full honors, the city guard arrayed along the bridge and a small crowd of young men and women—those not old enough to brew on old troubles—cheering and throwing flowers at them. A soft bouquet of meadowsweet hit the cheek of her helm and slid down her armored right arm, but not before she caught its sweet smell. It was such a stark contrast with her own dank odor that she almost laughed: They may as well throw petals on a turd.

She raised her hand in greeting, Torr's muscular body strutting beneath her as though he believed the cheers for him. Seacaster was a very old town, and the buildings had been built close together for warmth. Its gray narrowness made the town seem unwelcoming, even on a fine shining afternoon like this when the sea was a silver-blue expanse gleaming beyond the jettied houses and Gunther's smoke-stained hall. But Seacaster was perhaps the most important port town in all of Thyrsland. Its docks heaved with imports from faraway places, and were lined with traders' ships, sitting deep in the water with their own hulls full. Its position—part of Nettleches-ter but close to Littledyke and the hump of the high-cliffed shoreline of Thridstow—was also crucial in maintaining peace, especially from Almissia's perspective, as it was so far from Athelrick's hall, beyond their ceaseless watch.

At the end of the procession, under the jutting eaves of Gunther's hall, stood Ivy. Her golden hair—the same color as Bluebell's—fell in two braids over the shoulders of a rich emerald gown. Ivy was beautiful, full-bodied, smiling but clearly nervous: Bluebell didn't visit often. She thought of taking off her grim helm so Ivy could see her face and know she wasn't in any trouble, but decided against it. On either side of Ivy, her tiny sons clutched her hands and looked up at Bluebell's hearthband with awe.

Bluebell rode up to Ivy, towering over her on Torr, and said, "Sister."

"Welcome, my lord, to Seacaster," Ivy said with practiced grace. "We have a feast laid out in—"

"I need a bath before anything else."

The smallest little boy pressed his face into Ivy's thigh and began to cry with fear.

"Hush now, Edmund, it's just your aunt." But this affirmation of kinship seemed to make him cry harder.

Ivy turned her face up to Bluebell. "The stable hands and stewards will take your horses, and your men can use the guest quarters behind the hall. Come with me, Bluebell. I have a bower prepared for you, and can have a bath drawn for you in quick order."

"Thank you." Bluebell dismounted. A steward ran forward and

she removed her helmet and her byrnie, but took back her sword-belt and refixed it around her hips. Ivy instructed the two children to walk close behind them, and led Bluebell by the arm away from the crowd and through a high guarded gate, then into a compound of bowerhouses bordered by flowering gardens. Bluebell could hear the sea in the distance, over Ivy's nervous chatter.

"I put all these gardens in," she said. "The boys love being outside and they love flowers and the summer has been so lovely. The rest of the year has been a bit bleak. Not that I'm complaining. Poor Gunther can't even rise from his bed and—"

"It's all right," Bluebell interrupted. "I'm not here to make your life difficult in any way. I just need a bath and some fresh clothes, then we can talk."

Ivy indicated a small bowerhouse at the end of the path. "I'll send Elgith to tend to you."

Bluebell had to duck under the doorway of the little round-roofed bowerhouse. The fire had been lit and the bed made and there were fresh flowers in a brass cup on the dresser, a polished mirror, and a warm nightdress and cloak laid on the end of the bed. Bluebell sat on the bed and eased off her shoes, wrinkling her nose at her own stinking feet. The door opened and an older woman with a sour face came in, rolling a tub.

"Over there," Bluebell said, indicating a space by the hearth.

Elgith righted the tub then left for water. Bluebell continued to undress down to her shirt while Elgith and two helpers moved in and out of the bowerhouse, filling the bath with steaming-hot water brought from the kitchen. Finally, when the tub was full, the helpers left and Elgith stayed to sprinkle the water with lavender leaves.

Then Elgith turned to her and said, "Would you like me to sponge you, my lady?"

Bluebell shook her head and took the scratchy sea sponge from her. "I can do that myself."

"As you wish."

The woman stood there a little longer than was polite, so Bluebell asked, "Is there something wrong?"

"My lord Gunther is very ill. He ought to be here."

"To bathe me?" Bluebell said, with a wry smile.

Elgith blushed so rapidly, it was as though her skin changed color in an eyeblink. "To welcome you. To—whatever king's business you have, it is with Gunther, not your sister."

"You speak very plainly for your station."

"My station has been brought low. But I have heard tell that you will listen to even the lowest people, that your spirit is fierce but that your heart is great."

"It's really not," Bluebell said. "But it's true that I believe all people under the sun have something to say, so perhaps you should say it. Your name is Elgith?"

She nodded. "I was once Gunther's closest companion. Now I am your sister's maid."

Bluebell understood the situation immediately. Elgith loved Gunther. "You must feel his illness very heavily, then," she said.

"Very heavily." She stared at Bluebell, and the intensity of her gaze was unreadable. Was it hostility? "And if he should die . . ." She trailed off, and Bluebell was almost certain an unvoiced threat had been made.

Bluebell was tired, dying to get in the bath. Perhaps Elgith was descended from one of the old families who hated her. "Well. Perhaps he'll get better," she said lightly. "Now please leave me to my bath. Even I can't stand the smell of myself. I'm surprised you're still breathing."

Elgith, stony-faced, backed out and closed the door behind her. Bluebell stripped naked and stepped into the tub, sighing with joy as her body was swallowed by the hot water. Her hair floated around her. She made a note to tell Ivy to get rid of Elgith the moment Gunther died. She couldn't be trusted around Athelrick's grandchildren.

Bluebell was the last to join the feast. Underneath the clothes she had borrowed until hers were washed, her skin was still pink and puckered from the long soak. She wore ill-fitting trousers that she'd had to rope in around the waist, and a green and gold-trimmed tunic of Gunther's that was inches too short. Her hair was damp and loose, her sword-belt a familiar weight around her hips. The hall was warm and crowded. Music played and a drunk soldier danced to it out of time. Her hearthband sat at the head table, being served by two pretty First Folk twins, but it was Ivy that Bluebell sought. She found her with her boys and their nurse in a quieter back corner.

"Hello, boys," Bluebell said, crouching down.

"That's Papa's shirt," the older boy said.

"Why, you have the eye of a hunter," Bluebell replied.

The child grinned stupidly.

"Eadric," Ivy said. "This is your aunt Bluebell. You've met her before when you were a baby."

"I remember," he said, though it couldn't have been true.

"And this is Edmund," she said, presenting the younger one, who sucked on his fingers and looked at Bluebell with round eyes.

"I'm not so scary now, am I?" Bluebell said to him, reaching out a big hand to ruffle his curls. "What a fine young lad you are."

Edmund's facial expression didn't change, but at least he wasn't crying.

Bluebell stood and nodded at Ivy. "I need to speak with you alone about a matter of great importance. Is there somewhere we can go?"

Ivy glanced around the room, and Bluebell wondered whose eyes she was hoping to avoid. "Perhaps it would be best to take a walk in the garden behind the guest quarters? We could take in the view of the sea."

"I'll follow you."

Ivy left instructions for Hilla, kissed her boys, and led the way out of the hall, down the side, then around the roughly built house where Bluebell's hearthband would all be staying. She debated whether she should move in there with them tonight, but days on the road sleeping by them in tents had been enough. She wanted a warm bed in a quiet room, a long way from anyone else's snores.

Behind the house was a round, overgrown garden with a wooden seat in the middle, angled so it could look down over the city walls and toward the sea. Ivy sat and Bluebell sat with her, but side-on so that she could see if anyone approached them from the direction of the hall.

"Why did you check the room before you left it?" Bluebell asked her.

"You have enemies here. If you and I were to slip away into Gunther's hall tower together, they would become my enemies, too." Ivy shook her head lightly and smiled bitterly. "More so than they are now."

"You underestimate your power. Mother of the heirs to Seacaster. And what a bonny pair of lads they are."

Ivy's eyes lit up. "Are they not just so?"

"I have come to ask you a question that is both simple and terrifyingly complex. Do you own a magic sword that can kill me?"

Ivy snorted a laugh. "What? No."

"Such a thing exists in our world, and I'm told that one of my sisters has it. Think hard. Has anyone—perhaps one of your enemies—made to you or to Gunther a gift of a weapon? Told you it was ceremonial or something to pass on to your sons?"

But Ivy kept shaking her head. "No, absolutely not."

"Are you certain?"

"I am certain."

"If such a thing should fall into your hands, promise me you will destroy it immediately. Take it straight to the forge. Have them turn it into a puddle. Do you understand?"

Ivy nodded. "Of course."

Bluebell sighed, turned her eyes to the sea. "I don't suppose you've heard from Willow."

"You think Willow has the sword?"

"I don't know. Perhaps. She's mad but not a murderer. Maava would surely stop her from skewering her own sister."

"I haven't heard from her. She'll have found some trimartyrs somewhere. Be living a simple life in a chapel, trying to pretend she was never one of us."

Bluebell clenched and unclenched her hands. "She will always be one of us," she said. "I must find her, and I must find Ash. Perhaps you could go to Rose for me?"

"I haven't seen Rose in years," Ivy said. "I will go if you like, but my husband is very ill and I oughtn't travel too far for too long. As it is, I must go to Wengest's wedding without him soon."

"Father will be there. He'll be glad to see you."

Ivy lowered her eyes. "It's always so awkward with Wengest."

"You're a daughter of Almissia. Daughter of the Storm King. You can manage a little awkwardness, can't you?"

"I'm not what I once was," Ivy said quickly. "I want you to know that."

"I can see that with my own eyes, Ivy." Bluebell tried an encouraging smile, and hoped it didn't look like a baring of her teeth. "Who is Elgith?"

"Gunther's lover. He ought to have married her, I suspect, but she is too old for babies."

"When he dies, you need to get her away from Seacaster. She has hate in her heart for us."

"I know. I will."

"Is he going to die?"

Ivy began to twirl and untwirl one of her braids around her hand. "I think it very likely, though perhaps not very soon."

"You'll be vulnerable. Send to Father or me the moment it happens."

"I shan't be vulnerable. Nobody would think to take the town from the sons of Gunther."

Bluebell shook her head at Ivy's naïveté. "They are little more than infants. You need to make a clear ruling that you are in charge until they come of age."

"Me? But . . . we are trimartyr in Nettlechester. Women can't rule."

"Fucking trimartyrs," Bluebell spat. "Then close all the chapels. Do it quickly and quietly, get the preachers out, and take control of the standing guard."

"I'm sure he won't die soon," Ivy said, but the expression in her eyes was distant, as though she was thinking about something too large and complicated to be articulated.

Bluebell slapped her shoulder comfortingly.

Ivy laughed. "Ouch."

A shape moved from behind them and Bluebell turned, hand going to her sword. It was only Sighere.

"My lord," he said. "A messenger came for you."

"For me? How did they know we were here?"

"They didn't. It has been waiting here two days with the town guard, in case you came to your sister. Someone calling himself Snowy has sent for you from Nether Weald. He says it's urgent."

Bluebell frowned. Snowy had never sent for her, let alone urgently. Was Rowan in danger? She stood, her loose pants nearly falling off her hips.

"You can't go tonight," Ivy said. "Nether Weald is nearly fifty miles away."

"We can have the hearthband ready by dawn," Sighere said.

"Ivy is right. I'll stay here tonight, and head off in the morning, but I'll go alone. It's . . . private business."

Bluebell was aware that Sighere and Ivy exchanged glances. Her love life had always been the subject of amused speculation, and the fact that Skalmir Hunter had chosen to call himself by the pet name Snowy in the message had clearly pricked their interest. Of course he had done it to protect his identity and Rowan's hiding place. Snowy was a smart man. One of the best. Though it was unhelpful for her to think that way. She had seen her father and her sister Rose both make bad decisions when their hearts went soft. Love clouded judgment.

Ivy stood and grasped her sister's hand. "Come inside my hall, Bluebell. You have been traveling for days, I hear, and you need food and mead and a long slumber in a soft bed. Let me be the one who gives you all those things, and tomorrow you can make your journey with a full belly and a rested mind."

Bluebell allowed herself to be led inside, wondering what Snowy needed from her, and hoping she would get to him before it was too late to help.

CHAPTER 12

The fog came, so thick that Ash and Unweder were pinned inside for nearly a week. On the first two days, Ash was grateful. The dragon scale weighed heavily on her mind. She could never allow Unweder to see it, so she had sewn it into the hem of her cloak with the treasures her sea spirit friend had left her, and it rattled and rasped in there among them. After four years as Unweder's companion, when her destiny seemed an abstract thing situated beyond the veil of the everyday, it was finally present—bright and hot—and she found herself paralyzed by the weight of fear in her limbs.

Ash had to kill a dragon, and she had to do it before Unweder found out.

As the days inside wore on, her nerves began to fray and her scalp itched furiously, even though she had practiced no new magic. Her low-level deception, the inaudible murmur of intentions counter to her companion's, now threatened to burble to the surface noisily and messily. Unweder had some sight—all undermagicians had a little—but they all knew how to hide their thoughts from one another, too. If Unweder suspected her of anything, it might be because she evaded his gaze or was too often lost in her own thoughts: the ordinary ways people knew they were being lied to. Ash held herself together outwardly, but her heart and mind pulled in all directions. Scheme after scheme formed and failed in her imagination. She knew only that if she could keep Unweder hunting to the north, the south—and the dragon cave—was hers. She imagined that if she could find and destroy the beast without his knowledge, he would never find his quarry and they could part company at last and she might return home.

These imaginings seemed too precious and perfect to be in any way possible.

With the fog came rain, of course, and unseasonable cold. They lived inside a cloud, eating the dried fish that hung over the hearth-pit, immersed in long stretches of unpunctuated silence as Unweder mixed his potions and Ash sewed or ground grain for bread.

Then the fog passed, as everything good or bad eventually does.

Ash woke to the cry of gulls, opened her eyes, and saw that the light was different. Unweder had opened the shutter and a wedge of sunshine had fallen on her feet. The sliver of sky she could see was pale morning blue. The wind was gusty, cold. The shutter creaked with its inhalations and exhalations.

She turned on her side. Unweder sat on the bench, pulling on his shoes.

"Off already?" she asked, her heart speeding a little. "Back toward the north?"

"Back toward the north," he affirmed. "I am being led there by some lodestone inside me."

She was too relieved to ask further.

"Will you come with me today, Ash?" he asked.

Her mind scrambled for an excuse. "One of us will need to stay and catch some fish or collect some seaweed."

"Very well. Then I will fly." He stood. "If I skim along the coast for a few miles, I may see something that can't be seen from the beach or the cliff."

Another gull's cry. He cocked his head. "A gull will do."

He left the door open, and she watched him. Outside, the sky was perfectly clear. The fog had all been chased away by the gusting wind. She could hear the sea now, the tide full and roaring. The sun was a yellow-white glare behind them, making their shadows long on the dewy ground. Flocks of gulls swept back and forth above them. The world was all air and movement and light, high contrast to the still, stuffy days they had lately spent indoors.

Ash hoped he would try to find a lame bird, or an old bird, then cursed herself for a hypocrite; she ate the flesh of animals, why should she care so much for a bird? *It's what they go through.*

She watched as Unweder stood very still on a rocky protrusion. Then with a few words on the wind and a pulling gesture, one of the birds began to draw down toward him. The bird fought, flapping its wings madly, but was no match for the charm Unweder possessed over animals. He slammed the bird down at his feet. It struggled and flapped and cawed, and Unweder bent over it, placed his magic fingers upon it, and slowly—unbearably slowly—squeezed the life out of it.

Almost all the life, and therein was the necessity of the slowness. The creature needed to be suspended upon the moment of death for Unweder to steal its form, and so minutes passed, the bird black-eyed and crazed with shock and pain. Its caws echoed in Ash's mind sharply. It fought Unweder down to the last beat of its heart.

Then stillness, silence. Unweder, crouched by the bird's body, un-corked the little jar he kept hanging inside the sleeve of his cloak and, using his forefinger and thumb, made a minute pulling motion from the bird to the jar. "Pouring its soul inside," as he liked to call it. In that jar was her blood, a binding agent for the magic.

When he was done, he turned and gave her the uneven smile she so rarely saw. "Farewell, Ash. I will be back in the evening."

A whole day without him. She breathed.

"Take the bird's body inside for me?"

Ash emerged from the chapel and scooped up the bird—impossibly light—and went inside. She laid it by the door, but couldn't stand its deathly stillness, its uncanny warmth, one of its legs crooked as though still fighting Unweder, so she covered it with a cheesecloth, hating him for his cruelty. The shutter was still swing-ing to and fro on the wind, so she stood to close it. Out the window, she could see Unweder making his transformation. It was as fast as the bird's death had been slow: a blur of color and shape, and then Unweder had vanished and a white seagull took to its wings. She watched awhile as it cruised away, and she thought about how strong the wind was, and wouldn't it be convenient if he simply slammed into that rocky outcrop and never came back?

And it happened. It happened upon her thought and as it happened the shock of her power and guilt cracked through her like lightning because the white bird was caught on a gust and hit the rocks, but it was a man all in black who fell out of the sky.

Ash ran, leaving the door wide open behind her.

"Unweder! No!" she cried, heedless of the rocky ground as she sped over it. At the edge of the cliff she pulled up sharply and looked down.

His crumpled body limp on the tide, his clothes swelling and swishing around him. He couldn't possibly still be alive, could he? A fall like that . . . But how much of him was man and how much still bird—weightless and hollow-boned—when he fell?

Ash couldn't leave him to drown, especially given it was her fault—*is it my fault?*—that he had fallen. "I didn't ask you to do this!" she shrieked at the wind, but the wind did not answer and Unweder would soon run out of breath. If he was still breathing.

Down the path she went, commanding the water ungently, harshly, to turn him over, and so he flipped on the waves as if he had flipped himself but she could see now the enormous gash across his left temple and the blood that oozed from it. She stumbled and ran, ran and stumbled, then waded into the water, which raged and swirled around her thighs.

"Unweder," she gasped, desperately. She got her arms around his upper body and leaned close. And despite the noise and movement around her, she became very still and held him, waiting, listening.

The tickle of his breath upon her ear.

She began to pull him out of the water, falling on her backside and dropping him, swallowing sea. She stood again, and saw unexpected movement from the corner of her eye. It was the sea spirit, standing on a vein of rock that jutted out into the sea a few hundred yards away. It signaled to her with both its hands.

"Not now," she mumbled, getting a grip on Unweder again, and she saw the sea spirit dive into the water and disappear.

One hand around his chest. His arms bobbed on the water uselessly. She pushed the sea out of her way with her free arm, kicked against the rocks and sand.

Then the sea spirit popped up in the water directly in front of her and spoke from its mind to hers.

"Let me."

Ash was puzzled a moment, then let Unweder go. The sea spirit grasped Unweder's foot and eased him through the water as though he were nothing more than a poppet made of rags. Ash stumbled out of the water, drenched and panting, as the sea spirit hoisted Unweder onto its shoulder and began to carry him up the cliff path.

Ash hurried after it. "Thank you, thank you," she said. "I think I hurt him. I didn't mean to hurt him." Did she mean to hurt him? "I don't know what happened, I had a thought and—"

"Your thoughts are loud as bells to us," it said.

Loud as bells.

At the chapel, the sea spirit stopped, gently lowered Unweder to the ground, then turned and gave Ash its full face. Its strange scales shimmered in the morning light.

"How can I make it so my thoughts aren't as loud as bells?" she asked.

"Why would you want them to be quiet?"

Before she could answer, it vanished, leaving her alone with Unweder. She opened the door of the chapel and dragged him inside. She stripped him and rubbed him dry, neither surprised nor embarrassed by his naked body. Then she wrapped him warmly and cleaned and dressed his wound, performing the tasks with single-minded focus, so that the larger, more difficult questions would stay at bay. His face was slack and his skin looked bloodless, but he breathed yet and his heart ticked softly under her searching hand. Her eyes kept returning to the wound on his head, where he had taken the full force of the accident. How could he hope to survive after such a blow to his head, such a great, grinding rattle of his brain?

She gathered his wet clothes and took them outside to hang in the sun, boldly stripped out of her own to leave on the rocks as well, and returned inside to dress and tend her patient.

As she sat next to him, she became aware of noise and movement near the door. Her heart started, and she turned to see the seagull flopping against the cheesecloth. She reached over and plucked the cloth off it. The bird lurched this way and that a few moments, then righted itself, cawed at her, and spread its wings. In a flash it was airborne, flapping past her to the window and out beyond into the world, alive and perfectly well.

Ash turned to Unweder. His chest rose and fell softly, almost as though he was sleeping. Blood had seeped through the bandage already. She returned to her seat beside him, took his hand, and prepared herself for the fact that he would die. As she did so, a lump at his wrist caught her attention. It was the little jar of her blood, full and unbroken, tied in a strip of material. Hopes and regrets played across her mind. She imagined her life stretching out before her with the stain of her betrayal of him, her unintended murder of him, upon her conscience. But she also imagined being free of him and his demands and his ambiguous nature.

And she half hoped he would live, and she half hoped he would die.

Neither living nor dead, Unweder continued day after day in his strange, still sleep. Ash could not feed him, and the few drops of water she squeezed from a rag into his mouth would not sustain him for long. He was withering before her eyes.

Each morning when she left to hunt in the southern caves for more evidence of the dragon, she expected to come home to find him dead. Each night, when the sun had finally disappeared into the sea and she rolled out her blankets to sleep, she expected she would wake up beside a corpse. Somehow, he did not die, and she wondered if it was an effect of his magic. Perhaps he had lived so long that he was now incapable of death—only this still, cold barely living that echoed the fates of all the animals and people whose spirits he had stolen to shift his shape.

The solitariness was hard for Ash to bear. She hadn't realized how much she relied on Unweder's company. The evenings seemed to linger forever, and she found herself yearning for the short afternoons of winter, for early dark and long sleep so she wouldn't see him there, a breathing corpse. Sometimes she spoke to him, just to hear the sound of a human voice, and to feel not quite so alone and abandoned on the edge of a vast and empty world.

On the fourth day, she dressed and went out in the morning as usual. The ocean was green and cold, stretching out toward measureless horizons. The sun was behind her, her shadow preceding her along the cliff path. She walked resolutely down the beach, trying not to think about how alone she was, how far from everything. But this morning loneliness and distance had gotten inside her somehow, made the lining of her veins cold. Even the hot summer sun, as it climbed in the sky, couldn't warm her. Her feet crunched over shell grit, and she wished that she would see the sea spirit so she didn't feel as though she were the last being on earth.

Ash stopped, pondered, eyes toward the sea. She could simply command it to come. She had avoided doing so until now, wary of damaging its trust in her. But now that the thought had formed in her mind—*loud as bells*—it only took a beat of her heart for that thought to become a command and moments later, she heard little footsteps behind her.

She turned, the sea wind whipping her cloak against her ankles.

"I'm sorry," she said.

The creature looked at her curiously. "Why are you sorry?"

"For making you come to me."

"Do you need me?"

"I . . . No. Unless you know where the dragon lives?"

Its gray, translucent skin seemed too thin, and its eyes widened in fear. "You ought not seek dragons."

"Have you seen one around here?"

"Not with my own eyes. But you ought not seek dragons, for they are made of fire and talons." It shook its head sadly. "Please don't make me go with you to find one."

"No. No, that is my own challenge, my own risk."

The sea spirit brightened, lifting its head. "I can show you something even more wondrous, though."

"What is it?"

"Come with me." It began to hurry along the shoreline, just as it had the first time she had followed it. She called out for it to slow down, which it did for a few minutes, but then it was off again. Ash kept up as best she could, scrambling over rocks and picking around huge clumps of seaweed washed up on the beach. Eventually, they came to a cave with an entrance so low she had to duck to get under it. Once inside, the roof of the cave was two feet higher than her head, with rocky formations jutting all around. The ground was gritty sand, so wet that it sucked at her shoes. The sea spirit climbed onto one of the outcrops so she followed, head low, until they settled on a rough rock together, Ash with her shoulders hunched so her head wouldn't touch the roof of the cave.

"What are you showing me?" she asked.

"Look, the tide is coming in," it said.

Seawater swirled into the mouth of the cave then out again. "I can see that."

"Let me sing to you," it said. "Close your eyes."

Ash was amused but closed her eyes. The sea spirit started a tuneless song, filled with repetitive melodies and strange percussive noises. At first it jarred, but after a few moments it began to settle into her body and bones calmly, and she found herself drifting on the sounds as one might drift on water. Rhythms seemed as haphazard and mutable as waves, with currents underneath that were strong and predictable. Time blurred away from her, the way it did if she napped in the daytime; then she shook herself and opened her eyes and realized the song had finished. The light had changed in the cave. More important, the water had come up—all the way up, over her ankles and knees—and she hadn't noticed.

"What—was I sleeping?"

"Did you like my song?"

"The tide's come in. I can't swim." She looked around frantically. There was nowhere higher to go. Barnacles on the roof told her the cave went underwater completely. "I'll drown here."

"You will not drown."

"Help me get out, please." But now her heart was beating hot and fast, because for the first time she entertained the idea that the sea spirit was not friendly, that it did not want to protect her or keep her safe. That it wanted, in fact, quite the opposite.

"No," it said.

"I command you to—"

"Don't command me." It gestured to the water. "Command the tide."

"What do you mean?"

"I can feel your power. Tell the water to go back." It nodded, its strange fishlike eyes blinking roundly.

Ash looked at the seawater around her knees, then eased herself off the rock ledge so it sloshed around her hips.

"Take off your cloak," it said. "Sometimes the protection charms mute the magic."

Ash slid off the cloak and it dropped at her feet. She tried to grasp the tide in her mind, but it was mighty, a complex and supple matrix of pushing and pulling; she couldn't find its edges and had to cast her thoughts out wide and wider and wider still toward impossible horizons, and all the while the water was rising.

This is going to hurt me, she thought, but she caught the tide in her mind and raised her hands and already the water was draining from the cave, being pulled out with a great guttural roar of shale and rasping waves. Down, lower and lower, until only her ankles were covered and she could hold it no more. Ash let it go with her mind and ran from the cave, blood thundering, out to the shore and up onto rocks. The ocean stalled, gathered its sovereignty once again, and came roaring back. It engulfed the shore, thundered into the cave she had just left, and split so hard over the rock she stood on that it broke ten feet above her. Salt water rained down on her, drenching her from head to foot. She grasped at a rock outcrop to stop herself from being knocked into the water. Then the water settled, and the waves took on their usual shape.

Ash's body felt as though it had been beaten from the inside. Her cramping stomach forced her to her knees, where she threw up vigorously, seawater pouring out of her along with her breakfast. When she finished, she wiped her mouth with the back of her hand and stood, glanced around, wondering where her sea spirit had gone.

"Ash!" it called from behind her, higher up the cliff.

She turned, her head still spinning so violently that she thought she might fall or faint.

It waved, its creaking voice carried on the wind. "You are as strong as the moon!"

Ash turned her eyes back to the sea. As strong as the moon. And now, as weak as a kitten. She sat down heavily, waiting for the illness to pass, breathless at what she had done.

Ash trudged up the cliff path toward home, sodden cloak in her arms, intending to change out of her wet clothes and spend the remainder of the day resting. In one small mercy, her scalp wasn't itching at all. She kept imagining it might start at any moment, but it didn't, and that tiny comfort buoyed her spirits. But as she approached the chapel, she noticed immediately the door was open. She knew she had closed it, as she did every morning, to keep Unweder safe. Had the trimartyrs returned to the chapel? She broke into a run, thundering over the tough grass. She grasped the threshold, dreading what she might see inside the dark room.

No trimartyrs. No signs of disturbance. Everything was just as she'd left it except for one detail: Unweder was gone.

chapter 13

Ivy could hear the sea's melancholy roar as she quietly closed the door to her bowerhouse behind her and stepped out into the night. Inside, in their warm bed, her boys slept on. If Hilla noticed Ivy leaving, she said nothing about it. She was a woman who knew when to keep her mouth shut.

The moon was bright, outlining the clouds. Ivy pulled her cloak closer against the cold and hurried across the garden and down toward the stables. Durwin was on duty tonight, so it was safe for her and Crispin to meet. A coin in the stableboy's warm hand and he gave her his broad smile and slipped outside to wait in the cool night air.

Crispin was already inside, up high in the hayloft, waiting for her. Sconces burned on the walls, giving the space a warm glow. The smell of horses and hay, comforting and raw in her nostrils.

"He's a good lad, is our Durwin," Crispin said as she reached the top of the ladder and fell into his arms.

"Come here," she said, fingers already at his belt.

Ivy had seen, too close for comfort, the misery an illegitimate child could cause a mother, a family, a kingdom. She and Crispin had their fun carefully but no less passionately. The cold outside was immediately forgotten in his warm embrace. As he unpinned the front of her dress, her fingers and lips traced over his broad shoulders and big arms, his hot skin, so different from Gunther's withered limbs. With Crispin, she embraced life and youth, not age and death. She couldn't be blamed for seeking him out again and again.

Nearly a year now. The longest she had ever chosen to stay with anyone. Of course it helped that he was captain of Gunther's city guard, and was stationed right here in the duke's compound at Seacaster.

Crispin's lips were on her breast now, his thick dark curls under her fingertips. Slowly he ran a hand under her skirt, up her thigh, and then he began to massage that soft, hot place where all her pleasure seemed to condense and catch fire. Steady, steady, the pressure growing under his expert touch. Gasping, she arched her spine and he pinned her down hard against his hand, making sure she took every last drop of bliss.

By this stage he was so hard with desire that it took only a minute to pleasure him, too, and then they curled, half naked, around each other, nose-to-nose in the warm stable as the sea wind thundered over the roof.

"You are beautiful," he said.

"I love being with you," she sighed.

"Love won't help us," he said.

"I know." Neither of them ever mentioned what would happen after Gunther died. Crispin had no suspicions that she was the cause of her husband's illness, and she never spoke to him about how desperately she wanted to be free of her marriage. To mention Gunther was to ruin all the fun.

She wasn't without guilt about her husband's long illness. When she'd started, she'd only wanted to make him sick. She couldn't remember now what small slight she'd wanted to punish, as it had been over a year ago. But then his illness had given her the space and freedom to imagine a future without him. Almost without meaning to, she had kept going, until his death was inevitable and she had grown used to the idea that she would cause it. Soldiers killed all the time; Bluebell had probably killed hundreds of men.

That's what families of kings did. Her one little killing—of an old man who had hardly any time left anyway—barely rated a mention.

"I have to go to Folkenham tomorrow," Ivy said, fingers twining with Crispin's. "King Wengest is remarrying, and Gunther cannot go."

His thumb stroked her palm softly. "I shall miss you."

"I wish you could come. Could we make some excuse why I might need the captain of the city guard to accompany me?"

"They'll send you with some younger fellows. I will have to stay."

"I won't feel as safe without you."

"You're safe on the road between here and Folkenham," he said, laughing. "It's the busiest trade route in Thyrsland after the Giant Road."

"I won't feel as *happy* without you," she said, with an exaggerated pout.

He kissed her bottom lip. "I saw your sister when she came yesterday."

Bluebell had raced off that morning. "She's ugly, isn't she?"

"There's no doubt she hasn't your beauty, my love, but if you took away the scars, the broken nose, she would have been a handsome woman."

"Her tits are made of iron," Ivy said, stupidly jealous.

Crispin laughed loudly and then pinched her bottom and called her a naughty, silly thing, and they fell to kissing a little more. Then Crispin lay on his back and Ivy propped herself up on her elbow and took a piece of straw and drew soft patterns on his forehead and cheeks with it.

"I used to hate her, you know, in my youth," she said.

"Your sister?"

"Bluebell. Yes. I hated all my sisters really. Except Ash. And Willow was tolerable before she found Maava and lost her mind."

"There's a lot to admire about a leader like Bluebell," he said. "There isn't a warrior in Thyrsland who is her equal, and we all know it and love her for it, and hate her for it with the same hearts."

"I don't hate her anymore," Ivy said. "I see now that she simply does what she thinks is right for our kingdom. She said something to me just before she left . . ." Ivy trailed off, not wanting to talk about Gunther's impending death openly.

"Go on."

"When Gunther . . ."

He nodded, indicating he understood.

"She wants me to take control of Seacaster immediately. She says I have to secure it for the boys."

Crispin considered this carefully. "It's good advice. Your husband has a cousin south of Withing who might make a claim, and I can think of at least two of the thanes that come to every feast night who might think they can take charge because Gunther's sons are so young."

Ivy felt the first thrill of her potential power. "So I would simply say—"

"You are ruling in your sons' names."

"And to those who say women can't rule?"

"Ivy," he said, his eyes intense, his hand reaching up to touch her cheek. "You have me. And while you have me, you have control of the city guard."

"And together we could have control of the most important harbor in Thyrsland."

He dropped his hand, his eyes rounding as though he was momentarily afraid of his own ambition, just as she was of her own. Then she smiled at him, and they both laughed and kissed again.

"Who knows the future?" she said, lightly. "All I know is poor cold Durwin is going to be most unhappy if I don't let him back inside soon."

"Good night, my beauty," Crispin said.

Ivy pulled her clothes together and descended the ladder while Crispin stayed to dress himself. Outside, she whispered a soft good night to Durwin, who smiled at her in his simple way and wished her a peaceful night's sleep.

But Ivy had too much to dream about.

❖   ❖   ❖

Every inn in Folkenham was full to overflowing with people who had come from all over Nettlechester in the hope of glimpsing the king and his new bride. This was all terribly inconvenient for Ivy, who'd had to take a room half a mile's walk from Wengest's hall and then carefully keep the hem of her new midnight-blue dress from becoming mud-spattered on the way across town to the celebration.

Wherever she went, she turned heads. Women admired her gown, and men admired her figure. But she found she didn't take the pleasure in their interest she ordinarily would. What did it matter if a man passing on the street found her pretty? It was really only Crispin's opinion she was interested in, and that thought sent her into smiling remembrances of their times together. She wondered, not for the first time, if she might be falling in love.

It was still broad daylight when she arrived and was ushered in. She answered many questions about Gunther's health and feigned sad optimism to them all, finding she quite enjoyed the compliments about her courage and her kindness. As the hall filled and grew hot, she saw her father arrive with his full retinue and hurried over to bow to him and take his arm.

Her greeting died on her lips as a barrel-chested man of about forty approached, wiping mead from his beard and pointing an accusing finger at Athelrick.

"You have a thick hide, showing yourself here," the man slurred. Obviously, he had already been partaking heavily of the celebratory mead.

Athelrick drew Ivy protectively close while his retinue closed around him, some reaching for their swords. But Athelrick waved them down with a calm hand. "No, no. It is a king's business to hear how he has failed. Tell me, sir, what is it I have done to upset you?"

The barrel-chested man was taken aback by Athelrick's calm demeanor. He stumbled over his words. "They say Blackstan has fallen to Hakon. They say his raiders have been in every quiet corner of

Littledyke, moving southward. Will you do nothing? Will you sit on your hands while we fall victim to those fiends?"

"Our garrisons at Merkhinton and Harrow's Fell are—"

"They go around the garrisons. In tiny bands or in their dragonhead ships. If they are in Littledyke, then Nettlechester and Tweening are in danger. Your realm is farthest from them. Will you sacrifice all of us before you act? You must raise an army with Nettlechester and you must go after them."

"An army? For a small band of raiders?" Athelrick smiled blandly. Ivy could tell he thought the man a drunken fool. "Well, that is a good suggestion and I will talk to King Wengest about it. But for today, I think I shall let him marry in peace."

"You are not—"

Athelrick gave a subtle nod to his second-in-command and stepped aside, drawing Ivy with him. His retinue blocked the drunken man's access to him, and they slipped toward the tables.

"Is it true, Father?" Ivy said. "Are Hakon's raiders on the move?" She thought about Seacaster, so far north in Nettlechester.

"It's true that some men, with Hakon's flag, killed Blackstan's family. But they were easily dispatched by your sister and were few in number."

His eyes flickered in a way that told her his calm words were at odds with an unquiet mind. She didn't want to think about it, not today, so instead she said, "Sit by me, Father, for I haven't a husband here and you haven't a wife."

"Soon Wengest will have two," Athelrick said in a low, disdainful tone, but allowed himself to be led to one of the highest mead benches.

It was true that Wengest now had two wives, but the first—her sister, Rose—had been put aside after her infidelities had been revealed. Unfortunately, it had been Ivy who had revealed these infidelities, but she'd been very young and could surely be forgiven by now. She'd forgiven herself, at least. Though she had no idea if Rose ever would.

The chatter in the hall grew louder and the smells of cooking filled the thick air. Ivy talked gently with her father about nothing important: weather, travel, who brewed the best mead in Blickstow. She and her twin, Willow, had been raised apart from the rest of the family, on the warm south coast with their maternal uncle. Athelrick had always intimidated her, with his stature and his kingly gaze, but today he seemed mellow, happy to talk to her. And Ivy was happy, too: As Athelrick's companion, she was seated near the front of the room, and not all the way at the back with the random cousins and half-remembered friends.

Finally, Wengest entered with his new bride, trailed by the portly preacher. Ivy stifled a laugh, then glanced at her father, who was doing the same. The new bride, a princess of Tweening named Marjory, was a pinch-browed girl no older than sixteen with a complexion so spotted her face glowed pink. Greasy strands of straight hair escaped her headscarf. Her dress—undyed wool as was the trimartyr fashion for weddings—hung on a body that looked as though it had been fashioned from ropes: skinny and boneless. Her hunched shoulders under Wengest's strong hand told of her reluctance for this union.

"She's no Rose," Ivy said, close to Athelrick's ear, and he had to suppress his laughter.

The ceremony was very boring and pious, as were most things to do with trimartyrs, and then the music started and the revels were on. Heat and noise, slabs of meat in thick gravies and plates piled high with turnips and carrots and bread pudding and flowing mead. Ivy's stomach was bursting and her head was spinning, but she allowed herself to be carried along on the joyous atmosphere in the firelit room.

"Come along, Ivy," Athelrick said as the evening grew dark outside the shutters. "Let us go and pay our respects to the new queen of Nettlechester." The quirk at the corner of his mouth told her he took delight at the new wife being so inferior to Rose. She placed a hand on his arm and approached Wengest's table with him.

She had managed to avoid Wengest since that awful day when she had exposed Rose's infidelity, but with her father on her arm she wasn't so afraid of him saying something cruel. Indeed, he seemed to be in quite a merry mood and welcomed them to his table, introducing his bride with a flourish.

"Queen Marjory of Nettlechester," he said, "I present you to King Athelrick of Almissia and his daughter Ivy, who is also the Duchess of Seacaster."

The girl stared at them sullenly and Wengest grew impatient with her. "Come along, Marjory. One doesn't fulfill the duties of a queen with scowls. Smile, girl." He poked her in the ribs and Marjory curled her lip so Ivy could see her teeth.

"How is Gunther?" Wengest asked, seeming to remember him for the first time.

"He is still unwell, but I hope for improvement soon. I will tell him you asked after him. I am sure it will cheer him, King Wengest."

Now Wengest turned to Athelrick and said, "And how are all your other daughters, Athelrick?"

"All well," Athelrick said cautiously. "Those that are accounted for."

Wengest held his gaze a moment too long, and a challenge passed between them. Almissia and Nettlechester had traditionally been enemies, and perhaps would be again if they didn't share blood now in the form of little Rowan. Ivy, frankly, had her doubts that Rowan was Wengest's, but she seemed to be the only one who'd noticed. King Wengest was known as a man with a large heart and large passions. He loved his daughter and he had loved Rose. He didn't love Marjory; that was clear enough.

"How is Princess Bluebell?" Marjory chimed in, with an expression of superiority and distaste on her face.

Ivy felt her father stiffen: Had his favorite daughter been insulted?

"Why, I saw her just recently," Ivy answered smoothly and sweetly. "She looked very well, and very tall and very fierce as she always does. I'm sure she would have stayed but she had to race off at the request of a person named Snowy—though with a name like that, perhaps it was a horse."

"Snowy?" Wengest asked urgently, his brows twitching.

Ivy felt that familiar sinking feeling. "You know Snowy?"

Wengest smiled to cover whatever he was feeling. "Your sister and I have many mutual acquaintances."

Athelrick had grasped her arm. "Let's return to our seats, Ivy," he said.

They made their farewells and her father chastised her softly for talking about Bluebell's business to Wengest, but he didn't know who Snowy was, either, so perhaps it would all be fine.

And then, in the midst of the clatter and chatter, the door opened and a messenger stood there and Ivy knew—she *knew*—it was for her. One of the thanes hurried over to the messenger but Ivy was already standing up. The messenger and the thane conversed, she was duly pointed out, and the messenger approached with his head bowed.

"Yes?" she asked, and could barely hear her voice over the crowd.

Athelrick grasped her hand and squeezed it firmly.

"I am sorry, my lady. Your husband, Gunther, Duke of Seacaster, is dead."

Wengest was making his way toward her through the crowd. Her head felt light. She fell back onto her seat and Athelrick caught her, and the thought crossed her mind that she was probably very convincing as a new young widow; nobody knew that her head spun because the weight of her actions had struck her with full force.

"Bring her some water!" This was Wengest, supporting her from behind, while she leaned unsteadily on her father.

"I will be . . . I will be fine," she managed. "But I need to go home."

"Of course, Ivy," Wengest said. "Return to your boys."

"At first light I will return to Seacaster," she said, her voice growing stronger. And once there, she would advise Crispin to empty the chapels and form a standing guard around Gunther's hall, while she took control of the city. The weight of what she had done must have its counterweight in what she did next.

Ivy hadn't poisoned her husband for nothing.

❖   ❖   ❖

More people came to visit Gunther dead than ever had alive. To Ivy, they seemed like wolves closing in, sniffing the breeze, searching for prey.

Gunther looked very old lying there, his white hair scant on the pillow, his bony body folded into a noble pose on the rich red fabric that had been laid across his bed. Elgith had dressed him while Ivy was on her way back from Folkenham, and he wore a deep-green tunic and breeches, bordered all around with gold thread. It seemed a waste to bury him in it, but Ivy had no desire to redress him. *I will never see him naked again*, she said clearly in her mind, and the thought cheered her immensely.

Though that brooch was certainly not going into the ground. Garnet and gold, two birds gripping each other. She knew he had it from his grandfather, and that it was his favorite piece. Maybe he had even told Elgith he wanted to be buried with it, but it was far too beautiful and precious to abandon in the mud. Ivy searched about quickly on his dresser, found a plain silver brooch instead, and swapped them over. She pinned the garnet-and-gold brooch inside her sleeve and straightened Gunther's tunic. The door to his bower opened, and Ivy tensed. Who would it be this time?

She turned. His face was familiar; his name escaped her: a second cousin of Gunther's who owned seven hides of land outside the city walls. He was round in the middle, gray at the temples, ambitious to his marrow.

"My dear Ivy," he said, advancing, taking her hand. "My sorrow at the passing of my cousin is only exceeded by my pity for his widow."

She offered a little smile. It was the third time today she had been oiled with false sympathy. "You are too kind, though forgive me. In my grief and distress I have forgotten your name."

"Garrat, your departed husband's second cousin. We met at your wedding and I was at both your sons' devotions to Maava. What a shame the boys are not older and cannot take over from their father.

A heavy responsibility, indeed. And yet Gunther's family should retain the leadership of Seacaster. It is too important a town to entrust to . . . just anyone." He fixed her with his dark gaze, and she tried to hide her open loathing for him.

"You'll forgive me," she said, turning away. "But such discussions . . . my husband is not yet in his grave. Decisions will be made in due course."

"Of course, of course," he muttered, but remained standing there behind her for a long minute before finally slipping out.

Ivy took a deep breath. All of them—not just Garrat but the other distant cousins, counselors, thanes, who had already come to offer their sympathy with hunger in their eyes—would soon know how little their words meant to her. If she was strong enough.

"You are strong enough," she said out loud, softly. Then louder, "You are strong enough."

The door opened again, and she knew by the smell of cheese and incense that it was the young preacher, Albus.

"It's time, Ivy," he said gently.

She stood aside, and a group of men walked in and picked up the pallet that Gunther lay upon. She followed them out into a blustery, sun-drenched afternoon. Hilla, the nurse, was outside with her boys, and Ivy took them by their little hands and began their solemn procession.

The people of Seacaster lined the streets. Some had bowed heads; some made jokes among themselves. Children fidgeted and made noise while their mothers shushed them, and Ivy was so proud of her boys—dressed so beautifully in yellow and blue—who seemed to understand the gravity of the occasion and stayed serious and silent the entire route.

The mighty city gates opened ahead of them, and Gunther was carried out of the city and down the earthworks, out toward the burial grounds of his ancestors. Albus had made no objections about the funeral adhering so close to the common faith. He'd said as long as he could pray to Maava, he didn't mind if Gunther was buried in his ship as his father and grandfather had been. Gunther had always been a reluctant trimartyr, going along because of his loyalty to Wengest.

The large pit had been dug the day before, the ship already lowered into it, filled with pots and plates and weapons and armor. Somebody had strewn flowers into his grave and Ivy wondered if it had been Elgith and why she had loved Gunther, who seemed to Ivy a slightly foolish, perpetually irritated old man with nothing interesting to say.

They lined the edge of the grave as Gunther's body was carried to its final resting place in the prow of the ship. Ivy surveyed those who had gathered. Her hair whipped across her face. From down in the harbor, she could hear the gulls calling. The city guard stood by on the other side of the pit, Crispin armed but helmless amid them. He didn't meet her eye, and she was gripped by a powerful feeling of being lost, swamped by troubles too big for her.

"Why is Papa going in that ship?" Eadric asked in a clear, bell-like voice.

Ivy intended to crouch by him and hug him, but overbalanced and fell onto her bottom. A gasp ran through the crowd, and people rushed to help her, assuming she had collapsed. Ivy waved them away, crying, aware that she was playing the role of the heartbroken widow to perfection.

CHAPTER 14

The village of Nether Weald came into view in the late afternoon. Bluebell let Torr walk the last half mile and then handed him to the stableboy, careful to unhook her shield and hoist it onto her shoulder. She wore her helm and mail byrnie despite the heat of the day. She stopped long enough to drink from the village well and give Thrymm a rest, then she fitted her helm back on her head and began the walk to Snowy's. As she passed a small cottage on the last street of the village, she heard the door open behind her and a little voice call out, "Bluebell?"

Bluebell glanced over her shoulder and saw Rowan. She immediately turned back. "Rowan?"

The girl held her finger to her lips. "I'm not supposed to be outside." She looked at her position in the doorway and said, "I'm not really outside though, am I?"

"Hardly at all. But why are you here? Is Snowy with you?"

Thrymm stuck her nose through the narrow space between the door and its frame and sniffed Rowan's hands. Rowan patted her absently. "This is Sister Julian's house. She's gone to the village but I mustn't be seen. Snowy is back at home. I want to go home so badly, but I can't. Papa left a guardsman named Lang because of the woodlanders and then he got shot in both eyes with arrows and died on our front path and Snowy was beside himself and now I'm here and I think we're all waiting for you." This all came out on one long, teary breath.

"Go back . . . shot in both eyes?"

"By the woodlanders. Whoever did it was a good shot, Bluebell! I think it was the big woman, the one called Dardru. She told me she was the best archer in Thyrsland." She dropped her eyes. "That was the day I said they could take me to the singing tree. I think I'm to blame for all this happening."

Bluebell gave Rowan a rub on the head. "If you are, then you'll have to learn to live with it. Kings and queens always have heavy consciences."

"You look so fierce in that helm. I can only see the bottom of your face and your eyes are in shadows."

"It's my job to look fierce."

Rowan glanced up the street. "I'd better go inside before Julian sees me. Tell Snowy I love him. Tell him I'm so very bored inside and I can't wait to come home. You'll fix everything, won't you? That's why you're here?"

"Once I've talked to Snowy, I'll fix what I can, little chicken. Off you go inside, and mind you stay away from the shutters and don't watch people walking by."

Rowan ducked inside and the door closed. Bluebell heard the latch fall into place and headed back to the path that wound into the woods. Every sense was on high alert. She didn't like arrows; they were hard to hear coming, and whoever had killed Wengest's guardsman was obviously a highly skilled archer. Her hand rested on the pommel of her sword, palm itching to kill something. Thrymm sensed Bluebell's vigilance and was similarly alert, her ears pricked up, her nose raised to catch a scent.

Into the woods, Bluebell and her war dog went. The afternoon breeze didn't quite reach underneath Bluebell's helm to cool the sweat in her hair. She trod as quietly as she could, still aware that she was tall and big and armed, and the things that lived in the woods could probably hear her loud as thunder. She would have made a terrible hunter. From time to time a sound among the trees had her turning, sword half drawn. But the sounds were only branches falling, or hares bounding away, or ground birds scratching in their nests. When Skalmir's house came into view, she relaxed a little.

Strike and Stranger came tearing out barking, and Skalmir's deep voice boomed after them, "Heel!" He followed them and saw her, his shoulders slumping. She could see in his face that he was exhausted, worried. His golden beard, usually neatly trimmed, was ragged.

"Thank the Horse God you are here," he said.

She bounded up the path. "I saw Rowan in the village. She told me what happened."

His eyes went to the trees around them. "Let us go inside. I don't feel safe out here anymore."

Leaving Thrymm outside to guard the door, they went into the house. Bluebell removed her helm and shook out her hair, grateful to have the weight and heat off her head. Skalmir sat at the side of the hearth, his knees spread wide, elbows resting on them, head in his hands.

"It's not safe for Rowan here anymore."

Bluebell didn't sit. She paced. "Have you told Wengest?"

"Wengest left the guardsman. The one who got killed."

"Rowan said the woodlanders had killed him. Who are they?"

"First Folk. They say they live in the Howling Wood but I have never seen them before now."

"And Rowan had met them?"

"Yes. She believes there's a tree in the wood that sings—"

"She told me about that. I thought she was imagining things."

"They found her one day and lured her off. I got to her just in time." He ran his hand over his beard. "They call her the little queen. At first I thought they meant that they knew she was Wengest's daughter, but now I'm not so sure . . ."

"You did well to get her out of the wood, but she must leave Nether Weald. I will take her with me to Blickstow and we will find safe haven for her in Almissia. Maybe she can go to my uncle Robert, who raised Ivy and Willow." That thought gave Bluebell pause: Neither Ivy nor Willow had turned out particularly well. Though her old horse, Isern, who was pastured there, seemed happy enough.

"Wengest won't allow that."

"Let me worry about Wengest."

"I will miss her." He pressed his lips together after he spoke, as though he wished he hadn't said it.

"Then come with her. You can remain her caretaker. We don't have a remote wildwood the size of this for you to hunt in, but we can find something for you to do . . ."

Skalmir smiled up at her. "And will you come to visit us more often if we are closer to Blickstow?"

She kicked him lightly in the ankle, exasperated with him pushing his affection on her. "Whether I visit you or not is hardly worth thinking about now."

"If I'm going to give up my home, my livelihood, the graves of my wife and children . . ." He trailed off and Bluebell turned away and let him be.

"For now, all that's important is that I take Rowan with me to Blickstow," she said. "Tomorrow. You can join us or not. Come later or not. I swear to protect you but cannot swear to comfort you. I am not built for comfort." She turned and spread her arms. "As you see."

He laughed, but whatever he was about to say next was drowned out by the sound of Thrymm barking loudly, tearing off and growling, then yelping.

Bluebell had the door open in half a moment. Thrymm lay on the path ten yards away, an arrow protruding from her back. Bluebell's heart seized.

"No!" she cried, hurrying down the path and skidding to her knees next to her dog.

Thrymm was still breathing, whimpering softly, licking her lips.

"Ah, there, my girl. There," Bluebell said softly, feeling around the arrow. Her fingers came away bloody, but the small volume of blood told her the arrow had not penetrated an artery. She cracked off the shaft.

Skalmir was on his knees next to her. "The poor girl."

Bluebell stood and drew her sword. "Take my dog inside and remove the arrow cleanly."

"Bluebell, no. The woodlanders are sharp shots."

"I am fast on my feet. As was Thrymm. She isn't dead."

"They won't hurt us unless we hurt them. Thrymm must have attacked one of them. Maybe they've been watching the house to see if Rowan returns."

"Fetch me my helm."

He put his hand on her arm to stay her. "They won't hurt you if you don't—"

She shook him off violently, boiling over with rage. "I said fetch my helm! Whoever attacks Thrymm attacks *me*. I go now to defend myself, my kingdom, my people, of whom I am the guardian!"

Skalmir took a step back, a wounded expression on his face.

"Oh, for fuck's sake," she said. "Just tend to Thrymm and let me deal with this."

Within a few seconds he had her helm and she jammed it on her head. She stalked off into the woods, heart thundering, pulling all the anger out of her fingers and toes and limbs and banking it. She needed her thoughts to be clear and vivid, not overheated. Blood drops on the ground. Thrymm had wounded whomever had hit her, and the path led into the trees.

Bluebell heard a whispering split the air and in an instant had her shield up. The arrow thunked into it, and the next, and the next, as Bluebell crouched behind it. The archer stopped to grab more arrows and Bluebell advanced over the undergrowth toward a thickset woman, twenty yards away, with coppery hair and a round tattoo on her cheek. *The one called Dardru.* She had her bow loaded and pointed at Bluebell and Bluebell could see the ragged tear in her right forearm from Thrymm's jaws. It made her arm tremble.

"Stop!" Bluebell commanded.

Dardru didn't stop. Here came the next arrows, but her arm was wounded and tired and they whizzed past Bluebell, who batted them away easily with her shield as she ran forward, knocking the woman to the ground. Dardru was still trying to fit another arrow to her bow so Bluebell stomped on her bow arm and she cried out in pain. Bluebell felt bones crack under her shoes.

Foot on the woman's arm, Bluebell lifted her sword. But Dardru raised the arrow clenched in her hand and drove it hard into her own heart before Bluebell could deal the killing blow.

"*Our* woods," Dardru said, as blood started bubbling out of the wound, so dark it was almost black.

"No," Bluebell replied, lowering her sword. "We fought a war with your people and we won."

"*Our* woods," she said again, closing her eyes.

Bluebell stood by and waited for her to die, then sheathed her unused sword and headed back to the house. She slammed the door behind her and pushed a bench up against it, then went to the back door and heaved a barrel inside to bar that as well. Only then did she turn to Skalmir, tending to Thrymm on the floor by the hearth. His hands were bloody and his hunting knife lay on the ground next to the broken arrow.

"We have to get out of here quickly," she said. "Can she travel?"

"No. If you want Thrymm to live, we need to keep her still for a while."

Bluebell stroked Thrymm's muzzle. "There, girl. Good girl."

"I've gotten the arrow out. It seems to have missed her lungs. We just wait to see if the bleeding stops now."

"You're a good girl," Bluebell said again, and Thrymm cautiously licked her hand. "No, no, you stay still."

Skalmir's dogs sat back and watched, as though especially reverent at the idea that one of their own was terribly injured.

"Did you find who did this?" Skalmir asked, pressing a cloth into the wound.

"A woman."

"With the circular tattoo on her cheek?"

"Yes."

"Dardru," he said.

"She's dead now."

"Her father will be angry," Skalmir said. "Rathcruick."

"He can be as angry as he likes. I didn't kill her. She pierced her own heart rather than die at my hand, and he'll see that when he comes to take away her body." Adrenaline was dragging its way out of her veins now, her heart slowing, her breathing returning to normal.

As Skalmir lifted away the cloth, she could see the tidy job he had done cutting out the arrow. He was a hunter: He knew where skin and gristle and bone were in animals.

"Thank you," she said to him. "Do you think she will live?"

"The bleeding is slowing. I'll pack the wound with angelica and thyme to stave off infection, but I think we should stay here tonight and head off in the morning. The pain and shock of moving her might kill her."

"Very well," Bluebell said, and gave Thrymm one last gentle head rub before standing and stretching her legs, pulling off her helm and beginning to pace the room.

"Don't pace, Bluebell," he said. "You make me nervous."

"Why do you think you can speak to me that way?" she snapped.

He looked up. He had a smear of Thrymm's blood across his cheek. His clear blue eyes met hers in challenge.

"Forget I said that," she mumbled.

He stood, bloody hands at his side, and moved close to her. Kissed her hard. All the anger, the frustration, the strong currents of feeling she was perpetually managing and holding down, sensed an outlet, a clear path toward light and freedom.

"Clean off your hands," she said on a rasping breath. "Let's go."

The long evening had turned to dark and Skalmir was asleep beside her, but Bluebell didn't sleep. She lay for hours, her brain ticking over, making plans. Then she heard Thrymm whimpering from the next room and rose to look in on her.

By soft firelight, Bluebell could see the dog was dreaming. Bluebell stroked her ears and she opened her eyes but didn't try to move under the blankets Skalmir had carefully laid on her. The fire was low, so Bluebell added more wood and stoked it. Thrymm closed her eyes again.

What was that noise?

Bluebell's body sprang to alert, but as she listened more closely she realized the sound was distant. Singing. She went to the shutter and unlatched it, opened it an inch, and listened out into the dark wood. Voices, singing a melancholy song that rose and fell on the breeze. They were singing for Dardru, their fallen companion. Bluebell listened for a while, then closed the shutter and latched it again. She sat by Thrymm, hugging her knees to her chest. The singing continued, faint and mournful, long into the night.

Skalmir opened his eyes to morning light. He could feel the warmth of another body behind him and smiled as he remembered Bluebell was here. Their second morning together, the longest she had ever stayed. The rest of his troubles tumbled into his mind only after he had smiled, but the first feel of her—now he rolled over—and sight of her, long fair hair falling over her face, made troubles easier to bear. Sometime during the night Thrymm had joined them, and Bluebell lay asleep, curled on her side, with the dog pressed against her. Thrymm's eyes were open, and she looked at Skalmir guiltily, not sure if she was allowed in the bed. The fresh bandage he had applied last night was unspotted by blood. Skalmir reached across Bluebell's body and rubbed the dog's head, and she closed her eyes and huddled closer to her mistress.

Bluebell didn't sleep through more than a few seconds of being watched. Her eyes opened and her body filled with its usual intensity and power.

"What is it?" were her first words to him.

"Thrymm's better."

Bluebell shifted her head, saw Thrymm against her, and patted her gingerly. "Is that right?"

Thrymm licked her softly.

"Ah, she'll live, but I don't know if she'll do battle anytime soon," Bluebell said. "If ever again. War dogs often grow timid after an injury like this one. Curses. I don't want to have to train a new one."

Even though she spoke practically, Skalmir could see by the light in her eyes that Bluebell was happy her companion had survived.

"I expect we have to move on today, then," Skalmir said. He had enjoyed the last two nights, playing house with Bluebell even though she had been armed (when she wasn't naked or sleeping) and had likely been playing siege, checking the doors and shutters, accompanying him outside with her sword and shield when he went to get food or water or firewood.

The sound of approaching horses ended their morning cheer. Bluebell was out of bed in a heartbeat, reaching for her clothes. "Is it Sister Julian?" she asked. "Your woodlanders aren't horsed, are they?"

"Must be someone from the village," Skalmir said. His first thought was that it was ill news from Rowan and he, too, scrambled out of bed and into clothes.

A thundering on the door. "In the name of King Wengest, unbar this door!"

"Did you send to Wengest?" Bluebell asked him.

"No."

She pulled her brows down, strode out and across the room, pulling her sword free and throwing the door open. Skalmir saw the expression on the men's faces and nearly laughed. The last thing they had expected was to be confronted by Bluebell the Fierce.

"Who are you?" she demanded.

Skalmir approached, more congenial. "What do you want of us?"

"I am Harack and this is Ned. The king sent us," the elder of the two men said. He was florid and plump, while his companion was tall and wiry. "We're to take the little girl home to Folkenham."

"She's not here," Skalmir said, pulse thudding at his throat. "I moved her for her own safety. She's in Nether Weald. I can take you to her."

"As you wish."

"Did Wengest not come with you?" Skalmir asked. "Is Rowan to travel with strangers?" His heart felt tight. Rowan was unhappy about being decamped to Sister Julian's; how was she going to feel about spending two days on the road with two unknown men? Had that thought never crossed Wengest's mind?

"The king is lately married, hunter. He has no time for travel. His new wife will be the child's custodian."

Bluebell turned to Skalmir. He read in her face that she understood how he felt. "You will travel with them," she said.

"The king has not asked for—"

Bluebell silenced them with one irritated glare. "This hunter stays with the girl," she said. "Go back to Nether Weald and wait at the mouth of the wood. Skalmir will join you within an hour, and he will accompany you all the way to Folkenham, and you will provide him with food and shelter along the way. If Wengest has a problem with any of that, you tell him Bluebell commanded it."

"Yes, my lord," the younger man, Ned, said.

Harack was more grudging in his compliance, but he agreed nonetheless. As soon as they were gone, Skalmir hurried to Rowan's bedroom.

"She'll be safe with Wengest," Bluebell called after him.

"I'd rather she was going to Blickstow," Skalmir replied. "I'd rather she was going with you. She'd be safer."

"They may look like half-wits but I'm sure they are high up in Wengest's retinue," Bluebell said. She was in the doorway now. "What are you doing?"

"Packing her dresses and dolls." He threw things on Rowan's bed, rolled them up tightly. Concentrating on the task at hand stopped him from feeling too helpless and bereft. He didn't know what the future held for him and Rowan, but at least he would be with her the next few days.

"Wengest will have plenty of dresses and dolls ready for her."

"But these will be familiar to her," Skalmir said. He grabbed the leather bag that hung on the back of Rowan's chair, and began to push the things into it. "Everything is about to change for her." He stood. "I don't know how long I'll be away."

"I'll make sure everything is in order here. I'll stay another night with Thrymm."

"What shall I do with Strike and Stranger?"

"I'm on my way south soon, and Thrymm isn't well enough to travel with me. I intended to leave her with a very kind woman who looks after Torr in Nether Weald. I can take your dogs, too."

"Thank you."

He grabbed his traveling pack and shoved some clothes in it, then found himself standing in the center of the house he had built with his own hands, about to leave. "The Horse God willing, I will be back here one day soon," he said. Without Rowan.

"The house will still be standing," Bluebell said. "Don't look so lost."

"I'm not lost." He reached across and took a strand of her fair hair between his fingers. "Where are you headed?"

"I need to continue hunting for my sisters. I'll collect my hearth-band at Withing and head deep into trimartyr country to see if Willow has taken up refuge there."

"Tweening?"

"Yes. Last fucking place in the world I want to visit, to be honest." She brushed away his hand. "Send me a message when you're safe in Folkenham. Let me know how it goes."

"I will." He wanted to tell her he loved her, but last time he did that she ignored him for a few months. "It was good to see you," he said instead.

"I agree," she replied with a twist of the lips that could have been a smile.

Skalmir gave Strike and Stranger a last affectionate pat and was on his way.

By midafternoon, Rowan had traveled as far as she was able. Skalmir reminded Harack and Ned that she was a child and couldn't spend any longer in the saddle, and they made for the nearest village, a tiny lakeside community fifteen miles out of their final destination, Folkenham.

Rowan had not taken the news that she was leaving the Howling Wood, Snowy's house, the life she knew, with any kind of good grace. It had pained Skalmir to see her face fall, her brow turn pink just as it had when she cried as a tiny girl. He was uncomprehending that Wengest could have expected her to travel so far and so sadly with strangers, which made him wonder what kind of father Wengest would be to her once she was with him again. As he rode on a borrowed horse with Rowan sitting in front of him, between his arms, he wondered who would love her as much as she needed to be loved.

Around ten miles outside of Nether Weald, she'd appeared to accept her fate. By the time they stopped for the day, she seemed her usual self.

"Come on, Snowy," she said, grasping his hand while Ned and Harack waited at the stable for somebody to take their horses. "Let's go and look at that lake."

He allowed himself to be led away from the stables and along the dirt road, where the smithy clanged and the market stalls hung with hares and waterfowl. As they approached the grassy bank of the lake, Rowan kicked off her shoes, lifted her skirt, and began to run, sloshing out into the water until it was up to her thighs. Her legs looked impossibly thin and white in the afternoon sunshine. Skalmir slipped off his own shoes and rolled up his pants to join her. The sky was cloudless, blue. Dragonflies darted across the water weed and lilies. He could feel the sun on his back, a light breeze moving the cloth of his shirt. He reached for her hand and squeezed it. She looked up at him, the sunlight in her hair, and, fixing him with her clear gaze, said, "I will always love you, Snowy, even though we are apart. I am used to being apart from people I love, though, so I know I will be all right."

"Perhaps we won't be that far apart," he said lightly. "I will come to Folkenham to see you."

She wrinkled up her nose. "I don't like the sound of Papa's new wife."

"You don't know anything about her."

She shrugged. "I know that she's not my mother. Or you. Or Bluebell or even Julian. She is nobody I love."

"You may come to love her."

"My heart is already full enough, Snowy." She leaned against him. "You're not to worry about me. I'm big enough to look after myself."

"If you say so, my darling girl," he said, rubbing her shoulder. "And I will do my best not to worry."

Dawn broke on a grim, wet day. Skalmir lay a few minutes listening to the rain outside the inn. Traveling to Folkenham was going to be a miserable affair. He turned to see if Rowan was awake.

Rowan wasn't there.

He sat up, called her name. No answer. That's when he saw the trunk pulled up against the wall, directly under the shutter, which had been left open.

I'm big enough to look after myself.

"No, no," he said, running to the window and looking out. The street, the lake beyond. Dreary, gray, hammering rain. How had he not heard her slip out? Where had she gone?

But he knew already. She had gone where her heart and spirit were always drawing her, back to the Howling Wood.

Rowan had gone to find the singing tree.

chapter 15

Ivy knew the wolves would be meeting in secret, making plans, so she wasted no time. That afternoon, while the workmen were still filling in Gunther's grave, she summoned Crispin to the hall tower, a stone tower attached to the hall by a wooden staircase. In all these years, she had only visited this room one other time; it was used to hear and settle civil disputes. Once, it had been Gunther who managed these disputes, but increasingly it had been one or more of his thanes, the very men who now sought to step in as ruler of the city while her sons were too small to protest. Maps and deeds were kept here, sorted into wooden shelves that lined the walls. As the tower and the room were made of stone, Gunther believed the documents to be safe from fire here.

Crispin arrived, in his byrnie and sash, just as the smith was leaving. She'd had a metal bolt and box padlock installed on the inside of the hall tower door; the key hung on Ivy's waist along with the keys to the hall and the bowerhouses. Her first small step toward shutting out the wolves.

"Smart girl," Crispin said admiringly as she closed the door behind the smith and drew the bolt.

She smiled and felt her face flushing as it always did when Crispin was around. "Well, Crispin, captain-defender of Seacaster, do you swear to me your allegiance?"

"I do, my lady."

"I don't believe you," she teased.

"But I promise," he said, falling to his knees in front of her, grabbing her around the hips and burying his face in her skirt.

Ivy laughed and tried to bat him away, but he held her bruisingly firm.

"I swear, my lady," he said, his voice so muffled by her skirt that she could barely hear it.

"Swear again," she said. "But closer to my skin."

He ruched up her skirt, running his hands over her white thighs, and placed his face against her pubic bone. "I swear my lady," he said, his warm breath setting her senses alight.

"Closer and deeper," she said, not laughing anymore.

He kissed her hotly, wetly, between her legs, then his tongue slid into her, between the folds of her flesh, insistently. She gasped, leaned her head back on the tapestry, one hand in his hair, the other steadying herself on the wall. His hands kneaded her buttocks. Her ears began to ring as her blood thundered past them. The pleasure lifted her up, higher and higher . . .

Then somebody tried the door. Found it locked. Banged on it loudly.

"My lady, are you in there?"

Crispin stopped, looked up at her uncertainly.

"Keep going," she said softly.

"My lady, it is Garrat again. I had hoped to speak to you before I left. Could you open the door, please?"

But Crispin was making love to her with his tongue again, and she shut out everything but the spinning, weaving pleasure that crashed through her, leaving her gasping, sagging against the cool stone wall.

Crispin stood, pressed his lips hard against hers so she could taste her own salty sweetness.

"I love you," he said.

Ivy's head spun. He had never said that before.

"Don't listen to any of them," he said in a quiet voice, taking her face gently in his right hand. "Listen only to me. I will keep you from harm. Do you understand?"

"I do," she said.

He shook his head, fought with something, then said, "I don't think you *do* understand. I love you, Ivy. I love you freely now, because your husband, my lord, is dead. And even though we must love in secret, you and I are each other's futures." He fell silent.

Ivy gazed at him, pulse flicking at her throat. "I love you, too," she managed, wanting to say so much more that there weren't words for.

He nodded, released her. "Don't let him in. This evening at dusk, you will address the city elders, the thanes, the various cousins and preachers and other interferers. I have sent the guard around to gather them in the hall downstairs. I will tell you what to say." And when he saw she looked frightened, he forced a smile and added, "We will make your sister Bluebell proud."

Ivy nodded. Bluebell's good favor had never been important to her, but at this moment, Crispin's was.

"My lady?" This was Garrat, still at the door. "Are you well? I thought I heard you cry out."

"Leave me be," she said sharply. "I will speak to you all as one this evening."

A pause, then, "As you wish, my lady."

She gave Crispin an uncertain smile.

"Are you frightened, my love?" he asked.

She nodded. "Everything is about to change."

"Yes, and they will all have to do precisely as you say. Imagine that. All of them. The thanes who feast in your hall. The farmers who pay you port tax. The traders who rent a berth at the docks, and the sailors who come across the sea with a full half of Thyrsland's imported goods. You, just as Gunther did, will stand at the head of it all, and nothing will happen but by your say-so, and their gold will flow to you and your sons."

Ivy smiled. "Well, now you say it, it doesn't sound so frightening after all."

"And of course, I will be by your side the whole time." He chucked her under the chin. "You can lean on me."

She grasped his hand and squeezed it tightly. "Thank you, my love. I will."

Ivy strode into the hall at dusk, Crispin by her side. She had taken care to braid and pin her hair, to wear the richest cloak she could find, embroidered with gold and silver and secured with the brooch Gunther had almost worn into his grave. Crispin's dark curls shone in the firelight from the sconces. His byrnie was oiled and gleaming. Together, they must have looked impressive, because as the crowd parted around them, quite a few people openly gaped.

Ivy climbed up onto the dais where her husband's table would ordinarily be set up. But this wasn't a feast, this was a meeting, and she doubted many of the three dozen or so here would feel like feasting after she said what she had to say.

Hilla brought her boys forward and she held them still under steely hands in front of her. The mutterings of her audience tailed off. Quiet reigned.

She took a deep breath, made her voice even and forceful, and spoke.

"I have brought you all here for important reasons. I have discussed the fate of Seacaster with many of you in the days since my husband died. As his wife, the Duchess of Seacaster, and as the mother of his sons and heirs, I have made my decision."

A few whispers passed through the crowd, and Ivy looked out over them and was struck that they were all men. Every last one of them. Even though it was not surprising, something about this realization lit a fire inside her. It was *always* men.

"I am taking over the running of the city—"

The sentence wasn't out before the crowd erupted into protests and sounds of suspicion. She held up her hand for them to be quiet, but they were not, so Crispin stepped forward and boomed, "Quiet!" at the top of his lungs.

The crowd came to order, though open hostility was now readable on their faces.

"As I said," Ivy continued, her voice sounding very young and female to her own ears. Once again, that flare of anger. If she was Bluebell, they'd all be listening to her. She drew her spine up straight. "I am taking control of Seacaster and I am aided by the city guard, who have promised to support me loyally. My beloved husband was sick for a long time and neglectful of his duties, but I will be taking them over so that I can one day teach his sons of their responsibilities. All of the thanes who helped during Gunther's long illness, I thank you for your kindness and advise you that you may now step down and go on with your lives as they were before."

"Wait!" shouted a voice from the back, and she was unsurprised to see the insistent Garrat make his way to the front. He pulled his beard thoughtfully. "Are we not trimartyrs here?" he said. "Do we not follow King Wengest's example and believe in the dictates of Maava?"

A murmur of assent, including from men Ivy knew still sacrificed their old oxen to the Mother in blood month.

Garrat addressed his next speech to the gathered crowd. "Does it not say in the second book of Maava that a woman can bear no authority over a man?" He gestured around him. Firelight bathed their faces. "And here we are, all men. Does not Maava say women should submit in silence unless they are magnifying the name of the One Lord?" He turned to her again, his face screwing up in disdain. "Why are you even speaking?"

A ripple of laughter.

Ivy's hatred made her voice roar out of her like fire. "All the chapels will be closed!" she thundered. "Closed . . . and burned! My family are not trimartyrs and Seacaster is, from this moment, abandoning that faith. Crispin . . ." She turned to him, saw him nod once, softly. "Make it so. All of you, leave and do not come back here unless it is to promise me your allegiance, under threat of the city guard."

Crispin raised his arms and began to shoo them. "The duchess

SISTERS OF THE FIRE 169

has spoken. Leave quietly, please. There will be penalties for any groups of three or more caught meeting together in the city. Seacaster is safely in the hands of Gunther's family, as is right and proper."

Ivy watched, pulse thudding fast, while Crispin shepherded them out. There were threats and protests and shaking heads. There were also several thanes who came immediately to stand before her and congratulate her and offer their blessing, though Ivy wasn't sure whether to believe them. Finally, the hall was empty and Ivy stood there with her boys, still in the quiet.

Crispin came back in and held up his hands to help the boys down.

"That went well," she said, though it was more of a question than a statement.

"It went well enough for now. When they see what a competent ruler you are, they will come around."

Little Edmund began to whine, so she picked him up and squeezed him hard against her. "Mama has been so brave for you," she said, smooshing his impossibly plump cheek against hers. "Crispin, can you organize somebody to send a message to Bluebell, telling her what I've done? I need to get the boys back to Hilla."

"As you wish, my lady," he said, with a sweeping bow and a sparkle in his eyes.

She watched him go, a smile on her lips, then put Edmund down on his chubby little legs and led her sons toward the door.

Standing just outside was Elgith.

"Elgith," Ivy said lightly. "I haven't seen you all day."

"I went by Gunther's grave to pay my own respects quietly, alone," she said, and her eyes landed on the brooch Ivy wore.

"Is there something wrong?" Ivy asked, her voice a challenge.

Elgith met her eyes. Her gaze said everything. *I know what you are really like.* "Now Gunther is dead," she said, "I will be happy to serve his sons. What task would you have me perform for them?"

"They already have a nurse," Ivy said quickly. "There is no place for you in the duke's compound anymore."

Elgith didn't break her gaze.

"Perhaps you should go to Folkenham. I could recommend you to Wengest."

"There is nothing for me in Folkenham," Elgith said evenly.

"There is nothing for you here," Ivy countered.

Elgith fell silent. Whatever she was thinking of saying, she ultimately kept to herself.

"Good evening," Ivy said. "These boys need to be fed and put to bed." She left Elgith standing there, wordless in the long shadows. Something about the older woman's stoic silence made Ivy more nervous than all of those men shouting at her. She fervently wished Elgith would go as she'd asked, and not hang about Seacaster like a shadow.

Ivy woke to the smell of smoke the next morning, pulled on her gown, and hurried to the door. A pall hung over the city, and her pulse flicked hard at her throat. She checked that the boys were still sleeping then closed the door behind her and headed into the dewy outside air. Shouts rose on the wind. She hurried to the gate and stopped on the edge of the city square. The nearest chapel, a little gray-roofed place, was being consumed by flames. Four members of the city guard stood around it, roughly keeping back a small but vocal group of protesters. "Maava will see you burn!" cried a dowdy woman wearing a gray scarf.

Ivy's hand went thoughtfully to her own hair. She hadn't worn a scarf since Gunther died, but the trimartyrs believed a woman's flowing hair was immodest.

"There's the duchess," one of the protesters called, spotting her.

Ivy backed toward the gate but in seconds they had surrounded her, were shouting and spitting at her.

"Leave me be!" she shrieked.

The guards descended and in seconds the protest became violent. The dowdy woman was on the ground, a guard's foot holding her head down, while an elderly man took four punches to his gut before keeling over and lying groaning on the earth.

"Stop it! Stop it!" Ivy cried. "I am your duchess. I rule this city. All of you stop behaving so awfully."

Nobody heard her. A gust of wind sent the smoke into her lungs, and she coughed and turned away, making her way back through the gate and back to her bower. She could hear shouting and crying, so put her hands over her ears to block them. She wrenched the door open and hurried inside, closing it firmly behind her, went to the bed, and lay down next to her sleeping babies.

Curled on her side, her heart slowed. Had it been a mistake to order the chapels burned? Surely not. No more a mistake than building them and forcing a conversion in the first place. Only a few had protested after all. But there were many chapels burning this morning, and Ivy knew there were others who would take a dark view of her actions. She put an arm over Eadric, who was closest to her, and breathed in the warm, milky smell of him. She was doing this for him, after all, was she not? So that he may be the Duke of Seacaster when the time came?

And a little for herself. A very little.

Whenever Willow felt she couldn't go on, when her arms ached and her back roared with hot pain and her lungs were raw and her heart hammered like galloping hooves, she reminded herself that Maava needed her to be His warrior in Thyrsland and she pushed back harder and harder. In the small circular garden, surrounded by a colorful abundance of snapdragons, sweet peas, and roses, Hakon loomed over her. She had long ago grown used to his hideous face: the sunken pit where his eye should have been, the jagged-edged hole in his cheek through which she could see his teeth. It was his physical strength she struggled to grow used to. His height, his reach, his power. And she knew he was not fighting her as hard as he could, that he could crush her easily with only a little more force.

Churning clouds choked the sky, but rain had held off during their drills. The grass was wet and it was a constant challenge for

Willow not to slip, but she held firm, blocking Hakon's blows and even getting a few good strikes in against him.

But as always, she was glad when it was over. Then guilty that she was glad. She sent up a prayer of apology to Maava, and one of His angels hissed in her ear and told her she was weak.

"I'm not weak," she said aloud.

"You are far from it," Hakon agreed in his rough but musical accent, not realizing the remark was addressed to invisible angels, and not to him. "One day you may be the equal of your sister." He touched the wound on his cheek, and Willow knew he was remembering his last encounter with Bluebell.

Willow didn't want to be like Bluebell, but she had to admit that her body was changing under the demands of learning to wield a sword and shield. Skinny limbs were growing thick with sinewy muscle. Just a week ago she had scratched an insect bite on her leg, only to feel unfamiliar steel in her once soft thigh. Transformation. The kind that cracked open seeds and ripped them apart, sending tenacious shoots out of the earth. That was what was needed to take her from naïve girl to Maava's warrior.

Hakon sat on a wooden bench and cleaned and oiled his weapon. Willow fixed her scarf on and joined him, and they sat side by side in silence a moment before she said, "Did you think over our lesson from yesterday?"

He grunted. She thought it might be a yes.

Willow was not easily discouraged. "The first book of Maava is very clear on this."

"The Horse God has served me well."

"There is only one god, and that god is Maava," she said patiently.

"The Horse God brought me to you. My randerman prayed to him, and saw you in a vision."

"Yes, so you've said, but I'm telling you it was Maava who sent the vision. The Horse God has no such power because he's a heathen fiction."

"Maybe your god is the fiction."

Willow felt the flame of indignation. "How can He be, when I feel His power inside me as mighty as an ancient tree?"

Hakon shrugged. "Maybe they are all the same gods but with different names."

But Willow was already shaking her head.

Hakon snorted a laugh. "You are as stubborn as your sister, too."

"It's not stubbornness, it's faith."

"Maava is a good idea for rulers," Hakon said. "Kings would like him because the second book says that kings rule by divine right. He's not so useful to people like me."

It annoyed Willow when anyone mentioned the political expedience of the trimartyr faith. But she told herself to bank her anger, and concentrate instead on finding a way to convince Hakon to convert.

They sat in silence a little longer, then Hakon said, "If you help make me a king, perhaps . . ."

She raised an eyebrow. "What do you mean?"

"My brother Gisli. My twin. He has the throne of Iceheart. He knows I have a greater claim on it, and that's why he had me imprisoned and spread rumors I was dead. But one day . . . I would like to return to Iceheart and reclaim what is mine. I have many followers. They have grown to the size of an army and even now are bringing fear and fire in my name."

Willow looked at him dubiously. "An army?"

"Yes. They are scattered but I have a plan. All is falling into place."

"How could I possibly help?"

"I don't know yet, but you are strong and canny and a daughter of Athelrick. If you helped to make me king, I would convert and so would all of the Iceheart."

A kingdom. A *whole kingdom* to convert. Angels began to sing and snarl and argue in her head. *You cannot do it. You are too weak. You must do it. It is the only way to show Maava your love.* Willow resolved to make it come true somehow. She only had to turn her focus to it wholly and solely. Perhaps if she did that, Maava would reward her with Avaarni's rebirth as a son.

"It will happen," she said, in a clear cold voice. "I don't know when, but I am young. Do you swear you will convert if I help make you king of Iceheart?"

He spat in his hand and offered it to her. She did not recoil. She spat in her own hand and they slapped their hands together and held them firmly. His fingers were big and rough.

"But first," Hakon said, "your sister."

"My sister," Willow said. "I will be ready for her soon. Maybe by next summer."

"Before then." He sniffed. "You do not know your strength. I see it."

And with Almissia in disarray, King Hakon of Iceheart could take it and from there all of Thyrsland would resonate with Maava's great name. The thought popped into her head, a ringing song of joy and praise. She began to laugh.

"What is funny?" Hakon asked, smiling his awful smile.

"The angels love us. You should hear them singing!"

He shrugged, pulling thoughtfully on his long plaited beard.

"But you would take Maava as your soul's Lord for the sake of power," she chided him. "I will show you. I will show you His might and you will come to your knees for Him. I promise you."

Hakon sheathed his sword and stood. "We will see," he said dubiously. "Same time tomorrow."

"Yes, same time tomorrow," she said. And in her head she said, *Yes, you will see. You will see.*

CHAPTER 16

Skalmir pulled on his shoes and slammed out of the room, through the empty drinking area that smelled of stale beer and cold ash, and into the rain. He almost ran into Ned, the younger of the king's guardsmen, standing under the shelter of the eaves, pissing against the wall.

"Have you seen her?" Skalmir demanded. "How long have you been out here? Did you see Rowan?"

Ned refastened his trousers and gave Skalmir a quizzical look. "She's with you."

"She's not. She climbed out the window. She's gone."

"Gone?" He blinked back at Skalmir, the significance of what he was saying starting to sink in. "The king's daughter is gone?"

"Yes, and we need to go after her. I don't know how long ago she left, but on horseback we should catch her." Was that true? Wouldn't she stay off the road, trying to avoid them? But how would she find her way? How long had she already wandered in the dark? The thought was like a punch in his stomach. Rowan. So young and small, somewhere alone and unprotected in the wide world.

But then it occurred to him: Perhaps she wasn't alone at all. And although she had gone willingly, that didn't mean she had gone without assistance.

"Wake your friend," Skalmir demanded of Ned. "We have to get after her."

But Ned was peering at him darkly, his hand on the pommel of his sword. "Go back inside," he commanded. "Show me the room where you both slept."

Of course suspicion would fall on him. He'd insisted on coming, insisted on staying at an inn and sharing a room with Rowan.

"Yes, yes, this way," Skalmir said, deciding the safest strategy was to go along with Ned. As soon as he saw the evidence, he would know Skalmir wasn't lying, and he would get on with trying to find Rowan.

Skalmir led the man inside, opened the door and gestured to the trunk, the open window. But the door slammed behind him, with Ned on the other side.

Skalmir tried the handle, but it was being held firm from the outside, jammed by something hard and unbreakable. He heard Ned calling for Harack, people's voices as others woke, footsteps, a dog barking; and he pushed against the handle with all his might until he heard the innkeeper's voice and the jangle of keys and knew he'd been locked in.

He looked around desperately. The more time they wasted imprisoning him, calling for help from Folkenham, the farther away Rowan was. He went to the window, but while it had been big enough to let a small girl through, he would never be able to get his shoulder and hips through the space.

His eyes lit on his pack, by the side of the bed. He fell to his knees beside it, pulling out clothes and old tools. His handsaw, the one he used to cut through branches, was there in the bottom, as was his chisel. Skalmir climbed quickly up onto the trunk, applied the chisel to the frame of the shutter, and pushed hard. Nails split away from wood. A gust of wind carried a blast of rain into his face. He pulled away the window frame and let it drop to the floor. Now with the handsaw he quickly and roughly widened the hole, pulling out pieces of wooden plank as quietly as he could and casting them on the blankets on the floor. As soon as the opening was wide enough, he grabbed his pack and dropped it out ahead of him, then let himself down quietly. He slipped in the mud and saw Rowan's small footprints; fear clutched his heart. Her tracks led to the road, where he could see two sets of adult footprints.

At least she had gone with them willingly.

Skalmir knew better than to go to the stables looking for a horse. He had to disappear, and quickly. He ran for it, his pack jangling on his back, as the rain hammered down. A stand of woodland lay on the other side of the road. He could make out prints, evidence of people walking . . . here Rowan's little feet disappeared while the other set became deeper. Someone had carried her into the woodland. Up the hill—the bracken was crushed. Clear tracks among the oaks, through the leaf litter and toward a moss-furred stone dolmen then . . .

They stopped. Skalmir had been hunting and tracking nearly his whole life. If he read these tracks properly, they told him that those who made them were exactly here, on this spot. He spun around, peering at the ground. Ran his hand over the table stone. His fingers came away dirty. There was nothing.

It was as though they had vanished.

Heath could now sit for a few hours every day. The coughs were still awful to Rose's ears, but racked him less often. Color returned to his cheeks, even though neither fat nor muscle had yet returned to his bones. He was still ill: Nobody could be in doubt if they looked at him. But he was not dying from it. Slowly and gently, her feelings for him rekindled day by day. Now that he spoke and smiled and moved, she remembered him. His familiarity caught her and carried her. Lightness and air seemed to come to Eldra's little hut in the middle of nowhere. Rose had the distinct feeling that a long period of darkness had come to an end; the same feeling she had seeing the first shoots of spring once the frosts had fled.

Still, the newly woken emotions left her feeling a bit foolish as well. Heath, she saw now, was only a man: flesh and blood. Four years ago, he had been more than that: He had embodied all her searing passions and dim-lit dreams. To love Heath was to love her own cravings, her own resistance to being satisfied with what she had been given. And she had been given so much: a powerful, handsome husband, the queenship of Nettlechester, a life of comfort and plenty. Now Rose felt embarrassed by that youthful, heedless flame that had engulfed her good sense. She could still love Heath, but she would have to love him as a man. As flesh and blood, even if that flesh and that blood were ill and weak. The real Heath, not the Heath made of starlight and embers.

One morning, when Heath's voice was growing surer and his lungs stronger, Rose was early to the main room to light the fire and start the steam for his lungs. Heath was awake already, sitting up but with his eyes closed.

"I am here," she said softly, so he didn't get surprised. Eldra said his heart would be weak for some time.

"I heard you," he said, opening his eyes. "You are early this morning."

She came to sit next to his bedding, drawing her knees up under her chin. "I slept badly. In the end, it seemed easier to get up."

"Bad dreams?"

"No, I . . . it's going to sound mad, but I was cold all night. Cold in my heart."

He reached for her hand and took it in his, rubbing her palm with his thumb. "Do you know why?"

"I'm always missing someone," she said with a rueful smile.

"As am I," he said. "But it's dawn. Can we look together to see Rowan in the magic eye?"

"Yes, of course," she said, feeling on her belt for the little loop of ice and gold. She settled next to him, breathed her daughter's name over the magic eye, and waited for the image to resolve.

"Ah, she is so big now," he said.

But something wasn't right. Why was she sleeping on rough wood? Where was the bed Rose normally saw? The little white dogs that were sometimes with her? "She's not at home," Rose said with a frown.

Heath glanced at her sharply. "What do you mean?"

"It's probably nothing. I've long ago given up wondering where she is and with whom, but I—" Here, Rowan turned in her sleep, and Rose caught her breath.

On her daughter's soft, poreless left cheek was a rough, round tattoo.

"Rose?" Heath said. "How long has that mark been on her?"

"I have never seen it before." The idea of blades and ink so near to her daughter's face made her skin flinch.

"That's the mark of Rathcruick," Heath said, his voice grave. "He's one of the most powerful First Folk chieftains."

"What is she doing with him?"

"I don't know," Heath said, "but there are few people in the world I'd trust less than him."

Rose's heart thumped hard, and she felt helplessly, desolately distant from her daughter.

"Rose," Heath said urgently. "You can't leave her with him. He has a black heart."

"But how am I supposed to find her? How will I—"

"You don't understand," Heath said. "If she's with Rathcruick, I *know* where she is."

"You do?"

"The Howling Wood," he said. "And you have to go after her."

A hundred scenarios played out in Skalmir's head as he made his way north. Some of them were comforting: Bluebell had not yet left the house, she'd intercepted the woodlanders and had Rowan safely at home. Some were too awful to contemplate: When the First Folk chose to live a woodland life rather than a life among Thyrslanders, the rumors grew that they sacrificed children for blood rituals. Skalmir tried to cling to hope, even as he slept rough in the rain for one night, unable to walk another step. Fitfully, he slipped in and out of anxious dreams, cold and wet. When dawn came and the rain eased, he kept walking, arriving back at the Howling Wood many hours later, when all hope must surely be extinguished.

"Bluebell?" he called as he let himself into the house. But Bluebell wasn't there, and she had made good on her word to take his dogs to town. Not another living heart beat in the house. "Rowan?" he called anyway.

No answer.

Skalmir changed his clothes, leaving his wet ones in a heap on the floor by the cold hearth. He gathered an oilskin cloak, a flint and fire oil, his hunting knife, and his bow and arrow. Wengest's men would come looking for him and Rowan here, and he had to get out and find her.

No matter what the woodlanders said, nobody knew the Howling Wood better than him.

The soft rolling hills of Thyrsland's central downs characterized the small kingdom of Tweening, the first kingdom to take the trimartyr faith. Once they'd been ruled by a queen. Bluebell still remembered her: She had visited Blickstow when Bluebell was a child. Dystro had been a tall, full-bodied woman past her youth but not yet white-haired, with a gaze like lightning and a laugh that shook the room. Dystro's cousin, Tolan, a silver-tongued orator, had taken Maava's faith and converted the most powerful thanes in the country with him. Dystro was put to the blade—famously, by taking off her head—and Tolan remained the king of Tweening to this day.

He and Bluebell didn't always see eye-to-eye.

She and her hearthband were stopped on top of a hill. The road wound down toward chapels with chiming bells, streets with jettied houses, the sound of horses and carts. Stretching away on either side from the town were acres of the finest, richest farmland in Thyrsland. The sun was high and dazzling, the sky a blue arch that made her eyes ache. Streaky clouds up high were being driven by the wind.

"The only thing this place is good for," she said to her hearth-band, "is roast beef."

They all laughed behind her.

"Come on, then," she said, urging her horse forward. "And stay close about me. I quite like my head where it is. If anyone makes a move on it, slice off their hands."

More laughter, this time not so lighthearted.

They wound down the hill toward the town, three abreast on the dry dirt road. Elm branches arched over the path, turning it into a tunnel of green. She could hear ground birds in the undergrowth, and thought about Thrymm with a pang. How she would love to tear into the bracken and catch one. But it would be weeks before Thrymm recovered enough to run the long roads with Bluebell and Torr again, if ever—it depended on how the wound healed and scarred. Dogs of war were hard to train, priceless. Bluebell had hoped for four or five more good years with Thrymm.

As they were ascending another hill toward Tolan's hall, Gytha called from the back of the band, "My lord! Wait!"

Bluebell reined Torr and turned. Gytha had stopped outside a lofty wooden gate between high hedges.

"What is it? Sighere, go and see."

Sighere dismounted and hurried down to Gytha. They conversed a moment, inaudible, then Sighere returned.

"The insignia on the gate," he said. "We missed it."

"Whose is it?"

"It's Gudrun's. King Athelrick's . . ." He felt about for the right words, and settled on, "last wife."

So Bluebell had found the bitch. She turned Torr around and her band cleared the way. Soon she was standing outside that gate and she knew—she *knew*—that her father had given Gudrun this land, these well-kept hedges, this impressive gate. Gudrun had lost her first husband, a wealthy merchant, and had means of her own, but

not for this kind of estate. Gudrun's goal had always been to turn
Father against Bluebell, and in the process she had nearly killed
him, sent Willow out of her wits, and forced her own son Wylm to
take up arms against Bluebell. The thought that Gudrun had not just
gotten away with what she'd done to Athelrick, but even been re-
warded by him, made Bluebell's guts squirm.

"Well, then," she said. "Maybe I will call on her. She is just as
likely to have seen my sister Willow, more likely to have remembered her if she did. Somebody get that gate open."

Sighere tried the gate, but said it was barred. Gytha offered to
climb over and, at Bluebell's word, she shinnied up a tree and onto
the hedge, then picked her way over it carefully to the gate, which
she scaled while the rest of the hearthband clapped and cheered her
on. She disappeared from view, then moments later the gate swung
slowly inward.

"My lord," she said to Bluebell with an exaggerated bow.

Bluebell laughed. "I am much obliged by your hospitality," she
said. "Follow."

Bluebell was aware that the thundering horses had probably already alerted Gudrun and her guardsmen, that the woman was
probably even now peering through shutters and wondering if
Bluebell had finally come to settle an old score. She tried not to relish Gudrun's fear too much. She ordered her hearthband to remain
mounted in the garden outside the house, but climbed down from
Torr herself and handed Sighere his reins.

"I won't be long," she said.

"As you wish, my lord."

Bluebell approached the front door. Dogs were already barking.
A tall man opened the door, his shoulders squared against her.
"What do you want?"

"I need to see Gudrun. King Athelrick has sent me." It wasn't
entirely untrue. Athelrick had certainly expressed a desire to have
all his daughters home, and Gudrun might know what cold chapel
Willow was skulking in.

The guardsman opened his mouth to order her away, but then

Gudrun appeared behind his shoulder. She seemed very small and frail beside him, her little face pale.

"What do you want?" she asked. Her eyes went past Bluebell to the armed retinue, and she visibly quaked.

"Athelrick is looking for Willow. Willow has become a trimartyr and we had hoped to find her in Tweening. Have you seen her or heard of her?"

Gudrun shook her head. "I haven't seen any of you since—"

"I ask not for myself, but for my father," Bluebell said again. "A man who was at one time your husband." She paused, let the blow sink in. "If you know of Willow's whereabouts, you owe it to him and all of Almissia to tell me. It won't go well for you if you know something and keep it from us."

"I know nothing. I wish you would go away." Gudrun began to sob, and the guardsman looked at her and offered her a kind word.

This game wasn't fun anymore.

"If you see her," Bluebell said, taking a step back, "let Athelrick know. He will be grateful."

A small child appeared at Gudrun's side. A boy with curly pale hair and huge round eyes. He looked up at Bluebell in awe. Something didn't look quite right about him, but Bluebell couldn't put a finger on it. She crouched, her light mail ringing.

"Hello, young sir," she said.

"Avaarni, this is Bluebell," Gudrun managed.

"Maava be with you," the child said. He had no eyelashes. Not a single one.

"And may the mighty Horse God be with you, little one," Bluebell answered, standing again and stretching her back.

"Go inside now, Avaarni," Gudrun said, pushing the boy away, but he stayed, gazing up at Bluebell with his round, lashless eyes, transfixed.

"I will leave you be," Bluebell said, wondering whose the boy was. Gudrun was far too old to be his mother. "I go now to King Tolan's hall to ask him the same questions. We are determined to find her."

"Good luck," Gudrun said. Then, "Give my best to Athelrick."

Bluebell bit back the dark joke that leapt onto her tongue. "I might," she said instead, and returned to Torr. The door closed behind her, but the guardsman now stood outside watching, making sure she left. Did he really think he would be any defense against Bluebell and her entire hearthband?

"Back to the road," she told them. "Nothing for us here."

"Did that scratch an itch?" Sighere asked her in a low voice as they passed once again through the gates.

"That's an itch that will need an amputation," she joked grimly.

Cramped up in a kitchen cupboard with the mold and rat droppings, her knees under her chin, Willow cursed her sister for causing this loss of dignity. Also for the fear, the gut-churning, vein-burning fear that soon the cupboard door would open and Bluebell would be standing there outlined by fire as she always was in Willow's imagination, the Widowsmith raised for the kill.

But then, in the dark, she told herself that Maava would love her specially now, for look how she was prepared to suffer for Him. And the angels roared in her head then, because *this* wasn't suffering. This wasn't being burned alive with her babies as the good widow Liava had been, leaving only their bones to form the triangle that now showed the path to the wayfarers of the world. Willow put her hands over her ears and tried not to whimper as their deafening shouts clanged through her skull. *You are weak! You are a coward! You are a cringing disappointment to Maava!* She crushed her teeth against one another and hated herself so violently that she was sure it would make her bones bleed.

Quick footsteps, then the door opened. Gudrun and Avaarni stood there.

"She's gone," Gudrun said softly.

"Mama, why are you in the cupboard?" Avaarni asked.

Willow tumbled out, gasping for air. A pot hung on a chain over the fire, and it smelled like boiling animal flesh. She grasped Avaarni around the shoulders. "Now you have met her. That is your aunt, and you must never trust her, for her soul is doomed."

"I know," Avaarni said, outraged. "She blessed me with the Horse God."

Willow burned with indignation. She would have to scrub the child with the wire brush tonight, make sure she was cleansed of the insult.

Willow looked up at Gudrun. "What did she want?"

Gudrun trembled, pale in the low firelight. "You," she said simply. "They are riding even now to the king's hall to ask everyone if they've seen you." Gudrun's hands covered Avaarni's ears. "Willow, she says she's determined to find you. It's not safe for you in Tweening anymore. You must leave."

"But where will I . . . ?" The question hadn't left her lips before the angels supplied the answer: *The Iceheart. Show your courage. Show you are worthy. Show you are willing to carry Maava's name into dark places.*

Willow began to stride toward the door.

"Where are you going?" Gudrun asked.

"I need to speak to Hakon."

Willow slipped out of the house, across the garden, and climbed the low hedge that separated the main building of Bramble Court from the outhouses. The neat buildings where Penda and Olaf and the serving girls lived caught the sun at their windows; even the stable looked bright and well kept. Hakon's house was at the back, nearest the forest, engulfed in the shadows of crooked oaks, the wood stained black with mold.

Willow lifted her hand and knocked, calling out, "It's me. It's urgent."

"Come in," he said, and she opened the door.

She had never been inside before. He lived roughly. Skins on the floor for a bed, a hearth made of stones of different sizes that she presumed he'd collected from the woods. A faint rotting smell under the smoke. He sat on the bench that ran the length of the room, cutting bread and layering it with cheese. The shutter on the forest side of the room was open and let in the sound of wind moving in branches. Willow shivered, even though it wasn't cold.

"Bluebell came by," she said. "She is in Tweening."

Hakon continued eating the dark bread and cheese. He didn't blink. "Did you kill her with *Grithbani*?"

"You know I didn't. You know I can't. Not yet."

"I know," he said, giving her his nightmarish grin. "But part of me hoped."

"I need to leave Tweening. She will set spies upon me, I will be discovered . . . I don't know what she intends for me. You must take me to Iceheart."

"Must I?"

"Yes. Maava's angels told me."

"So it's their decision?"

"It's my decision. If Bluebell is looking for me in Tweening, she is looking for me everywhere else. But not in Iceheart." She fell to her knees in front of him. "My life does not unfold at random, Hakon. My life is carefully planned by Maava. It is time for us to go to Iceheart, and it is time for you to return to face your brother."

Hakon shrugged. "I'd rather not see his face. His back will do nicely."

"Will you take me?"

"We will need to get to a port, and we will need a ship."

Willow thought quickly, then said, "My sister is the Duchess of Seacaster. She will help us." It had been many years since she had seen Ivy, but she had never borne any great love for Bluebell, either. Just as they had shared a womb, they had also shared a childhood a long way from Blickstow. Willow was certain she could trust Ivy. Almost certain.

"Seacaster it is, then," Hakon said. "When do you want to go?"

"In the morning. At dawn before everyone is awake, looking for me. I will speak to the stable hands now and have it all ready." She offered him her hand and he took it firmly.

"We have a saying in Iceheart," he said, and then turned to his own language, with its strange, rough sibilance.

"And what does that mean?" she asked.

"Although the sky is cold in the Heart of Ice, the blood is fiery in the hearts of the bold. My blood is on fire, Willow. It tells me our Becoming is upon us."

Willow didn't believe in the heathen idea of "Becoming," but she did believe in Maava's grand plan.

"My blood is on fire, too," she said. "I am burning up."

Tolan met Bluebell and Sighere in his famous gardens. High on a hill above the narrow-laned town of Winecombe, he had planted and grown fruits and flowers brought from the wider, sunnier parts of the world. The stories held that he tended the gardens himself, though they were too large for this to be entirely true. The hill and the slope down to the gates was covered in a profusion of color, and the smell was sweet and heady. She had left the rest of the retinue at a tavern in town, and the horses were being tended in the royal stable.

Bluebell and Sighere found Tolan crouched next to a hedge, pruning it with a sickle knife. He rose languorously on their arrival, an easy six and a half feet tall, with a bald head and long fingers.

"Princess Bluebell," he said with a slow smile. "And Lord Sighere. My pleasure to welcome you. Though I do not know if the weather will hold." He turned his eyes skyward at the heavy gray clouds rolling overhead.

"We need not stay long," Bluebell said, unpersuaded by his charming manner. "I need only to know if you have heard word of my sister Willow."

"Lost a sister, have you?" he said, curving one of those long fingers thoughtfully over his pointed chin. "Inconvenient."

"I take it you have not seen her, then?" she said impatiently.

"No, I have not. I am curious, though. Why would you believe a princess of Almissia lingered in Tweening?"

Bluebell smiled tightly. "She is a trimartyr."

Tolan could not contain his laughter. Bluebell and Sighere exchanged glances.

"Well," he said, theatrically wiping a fake tear from his eye. "You must be very proud."

"If you hear from her," Sighere said, as though he had not offered Bluebell such ridiculous insult, "could you let King Athelrick know?"

"Of course. And I will ask around for you, really I will. I am not so callous as my laughter might make you think. Family is important to you, yes? Famously so. If I can help you find your sister, I will. Now," he continued, folding his arms across his body, "perhaps you can help me with something."

"What is it?" she asked cautiously.

"Is it true old Blackstan was seen off by raiders?"

She nodded. "His wife and some of the children, too. Wulfgar and Annis remain."

"Hakon's raiders?"

Her face felt like stone. "Yes, it would appear. Though Hakon himself was not there."

"So is Hakon dead, or is he not?"

"He is not dead."

Tolan pursed his lips. "Two villages on the border of Littledyke were this week burned to the ground. None survived. Do you suppose this was also the work of Hakon's raiders?"

Two more villages. "Did they raise the raven flag?"

"Nothing survived the fires. If they did, they would have been incinerated along with the thirty dead in each village. Women and children, too."

"That sounds like Hakon." A light spit of rain landed on her hand. She looked down at it, keenly aware of her mortal flesh.

"Then Gisli has failed to contain him and soon we will be at war," Tolan said.

"I am not afraid of war," Bluebell said, raising her head.

"That is widely known," Tolan said with a smile.

Another raindrop and another, and suddenly the heavens opened.

Tolan pulled up his hood. "Come, let me bring you inside for bread and mead."

"No," Bluebell said firmly. "We have stayed here long enough. I must get home to my father in Blickstow."

"Ask your father what he intends to do about Hakon," Tolan called after her. "If he has the courage to do anything."

Bluebell stalked back toward the stables, Sighere hurrying to keep up.

chapter 17

Ash stood at the end of a narrow finger of rock that pointed out into the green-blue ocean under the warm sun and a moist, salty breeze. She traveled along the coast a little farther every day, hunting in caves, and when she could no longer stand their lightless dank she would come out and stand here at the ocean and practice pushing the water in and out.

The place where she stood had been underwater just ten minutes before. She clutched it with the fist of her mind—a feat that made her eyes and nose sting as though she had inhaled seawater. Ash was tiring now, and was starting to loosen her grip when the wind rippled over the rock pool at her feet, making the sun catch an iridescent object.

Another dragon scale?

Ash ducked to pick it up, lost the tide, and managed to close her fingertips over the scale just as the water came thundering back over her, choking and blinding her.

Bubbles rushing past her ears as, in green darkness, she struggled to work out which way was up. In panic, she forgot she could call for aid, but the little hands reached for her nonetheless, pushing her toward the surface, where she grabbed a breath and found the shore with her eyes before she plunged under again. She half paddled, half walked until her head was above the water, then waded out, pushed in the back repeatedly by waves, onto the gray beach.

She sat, sand crusting her skirt, and caught her breath. Even with the warm sun on her, she was cold and dripping and it was a long walk back to the chapel.

But she opened her fist and there was the dragon scale, identical to the first. Pearly white if looked at directly, with a sheen of gold appearing if she turned it toward the sun. While it didn't tell her where the dragon was, it did reassure her that her strategy of searching to the south was justified. Now here she was, sodden and three miles of coastline from the chapel. She started walking.

And the thought came to her: She didn't have to stay in the chapel. She could collect her things and leave and make her way farther and farther south until she found the dragon. Unweder had been gone for days, and she assumed now that he had died and his borrowed body, with no spirit to hold it together, had simply vanished.

Many times she had imagined being free of Unweder, but she had never imagined it would happen so suddenly and mysteriously. Nor had she imagined how alone she would feel, here at the quiet edge of Thyrsland.

Once back at the chapel, she changed into dry clothes and hung her wet ones outside in the sun. The prickling scalp was back, and this was a terrible disappointment since she'd thought perhaps it had stopped forever. Ash sat on her blankets to study the dragon scale in the sunshine that fell through the open shutter. The light passed through it and made a tiny rainbow on the gray cloth. She turned it this way and that, then gathered up her cloak and picked open the hem—heavy now with the weight of softly clattering sea gifts—and inserted the new scale.

Ash was sewing, head bent over the hem, finishing off the last stitch, when the door to the chapel slammed open.

She looked up, shrieked, scrambled back on her hands. A stocky man stood there, broad across the shoulders and forehead, thick black hair and eyebrows, all dressed in black. He had huge hands with black hair springing rudely from the knuckles.

"Who are you?" she gasped.

"Don't you recognize me, Ash?" he said, in a gruff voice.

No, she didn't recognize him, but at the same time she did, because she already knew before he said, "It's me, Unweder."

He stepped into the chapel in his new body, and she noticed he was unsteady on his feet. His skin was gray and mottled.

"Are you well?" she asked, climbing to her feet. "You look—"

"Like a new man!" he bellowed. "A new man at last. I cast off that broken body you demanded I stay in. It got me as far as the road, then collapsed. A kind fellow rode past and . . . now I am he." He spread his arms. The smell of decay overwhelmed her.

"No," she said.

"Yes," he replied, with a cruel smile. "And I need your blood."

Ash's veins cooled. Her scalp and skull felt as though lightning were zigzagging across them and she realized in an instant that the sensation had always been Unweder. Of course it had: a weasel in among her thoughts. It had started at precisely the same time that she had become reluctant to give him blood, when his demands had become too frequent for comfort. With an effort she shook him out of her head. "Old friend, remember yourself. I will help you again if I can," she said, frightened now, because the way he was staring at her told her she was not a human to him, but an object.

He leapt on her and, unlike the old Unweder, with his palsied hand and ruined eye, he was strong and vigorous and he sat across her ribs and grasped her wrists with one huge hand, withdrawing a knife from his belt with the other. This close, she could see contusions flowering around his neck, as though he had been strangled.

"No, Unweder. Not like this."

Her sleeves had fallen toward her elbows and she saw with horror that he was about to slash her right wrist. She twisted her arm in the hope that he would miss the thick vein. During her studies, she had seen how quickly someone could bleed to death if that vein was cut.

"Help me!" she called to her elementals. Instantly, the wind picked up, banged the shutter closed, began to tear at his clothes and hair.

"Too late!" he cried, slicing out, and blood began to pulse out of her and run down her arm. His knife clattered to the ground and he caught some of her blood in a stone jar. It flowed over his hands. The wind tore through the chapel, lifting the wood of the roof, but Unweder was right: It was too late. He had what he wanted and now blood was pouring from her.

Unweder stood and the wind instantly knocked him off his feet, slammed the door open, and picked up the corner of her cloak. Ash seized the cloak, wrapped it hard around her wrist, and stumbled from the chapel.

She ran. He tried to run after her but the wind kept pushing him back. She half slid down the cliff path and crunched along the beach, great spurts of blood leaving a trail behind her. Her eyes grew dim. She looked up at the sky, willing herself not to faint. If she fainted she wouldn't be able to help herself. On the wind, she could hear Unweder calling her name, over and over again . . .

Dark. Cold. Wet.

Alive. Ash was alive. She sat up, looked at her wrist. It was tightly bound in seaweed. She was on a cave ledge, on her blanket from the chapel. And beside her, her pack. She opened it, wincing at the pain in her wrist. Here was food, fire oil, a flint, the not-quite-dry clothes she had been wearing when she found the dragon scale. Her blood-soaked cloak was neatly folded next to her.

She was alone, but she knew her sea spirit friend had saved her, most likely with some help. Ash lay back down, staring at the roof of the cave. No going back to the chapel now; no going back to Unweder, if he had survived the lethal winds that had come for him. Just an hour more lying down, gathering her strength, then she had to move. She had to get as far away from this newly dangerous Unweder as she could.

❖ ❖ ❖

Ash walked for miles and miles, fearful that Unweder was behind her. Wherever she went, she willed her tracks to be hidden: Long grass strands stood again unbroken, footprints in mud filled out, crushed leaves crumbled to unreadable dust and were blown away with the high winds. She slept outside under glittering constellations and bright hurtling stars; and when the rain came she sheltered in dank sea caves, waking up to find small gifts of food and trinkets. Hot day after hot day passed, the west of Thyrsland in the grip of sticky warmth that drove her to remove all but her shirt, and carry the rest of her clothes in her pack. Her forearms grew tanned from the sun, and the stinging cut across her wrist scabbed over. The cliffs grew taller and the shoreline narrower until she was forced to climb—hand over hand, grappling with rocks and roots—up to the grassy cliff face. She stood awhile, heart pounding from the climb. From here, she looked out in both directions across the restless sea. The way she had come was fading into misted distance; the way ahead was lofty gray cliffs and white seagulls and hazy sea spray. About a mile away, she could see rock formations, one almost resembling the giants' ruins behind her father's hall in Blickstow. But this was made by nature, the tumbling procession of rocks far less carefully placed, the sharp ridges and valleys formed of the same pale-gray rock. Ash began to walk along the edge of the cliff. The bracken and gorse were thick and from time to time she passed wild goats, standing in the sun at impossible angles on the steep cliff slopes, staring at her with their strange square pupils.

As she drew closer to the rock formations, she noticed that the bracken on the slopes was brown, as though winter had come already.

Ash stopped. No. It was black. As if it had been burned.

Now her heart was thudding again. Part of her wanted to run away, never find the dragon, live her life in a cave somewhere until her mind dissolved and she didn't ache so intensely for those she loved. But then she steeled herself. Her fate. In her hands.

She quickened her step, looking down on the blackened slope from the clifftop. About ten yards below her, the back half of a goat, charred and bloody, lay rotting in the sunshine amid the burnt bracken. Ash knelt, crept as close to the cliff edge as she dared, and saw deep claw marks in the goat's rump.

Then a shadow moved over the sun.

Ash glanced up, saw the wings, heard its shriek. She scrambled— half on her feet, half on her knees—to the shelter of a rock. The dragon plummeted past her, wings half folded, toward the shore-line. It hadn't seen Ash.

She peered out from behind the rock, inched toward the cliff edge again. The dragon skimmed over the water, rich red wings spread and dazzling with sunlight. Ash's breath caught in her throat. The most beautiful thing she had ever seen, with its craggy head, its tough membranous wings, its rosy colors shot through with gold and blue, its underbelly white. And red; red like the creature in her Becoming. It dived, claws plunging under water, coming up with a wriggling porpoise, which it flung onto the stony shore. Then it landed beside its prey, bent its head, and began to eat.

Ash stood, her heart thundering. If she destroyed it now, she would take back her fate. She raised her tanned wrists, saw them shaking, and reached out for the tide. No time for being gentle. She pulled the water in hard, frothing white thundering over rocks and stones and swamping the dragon, who realized too late and spread its wings only to have them crushed. It tumbled over and over, dis-appearing under the gray sea.

Ash held it, held the sea over its head. The pain was splitting her in two, but she held and held and held and—

With a vast crash that echoed all around the cliffs, the dragon shot out of the water forty yards farther out, spiraling and screeching and perfectly unharmed, spewing angry fire. It seemed the dragon could swim. Ash backed away, looked for an escape.

The beast flapped its mighty wings and came for her, shooting up the cliff like a deadly arrow of fire. Ash dropped her pack and ran for the rock formation, hoping to find a cave. The heat was on her heels. She saw a crevice and dashed into it, wedging herself as far between the rocks as she dared, and the dragon flayed the rocks with flames while Ash tried to hold up some kind of elemental barrier with her exhausted mind. Her skin turned red from the waves of heat surrounding her, and blooms of black spread across the rocks toward her, but they didn't reach her.

Finally, after what seemed like minutes but was probably only seconds, the fire stopped and Ash heard the great wings flapping away to the south. It rounded a large, humpbacked rock out to sea, and dived away from sight.

She collapsed to the ground, arms over her head, teeth chattering and legs shaking. It hadn't killed her but neither had she killed it. And yet kill it she must, if she was ever to be free to return home.

Late-afternoon sun speared through the shutters and fell on the heavy wooden table where Bluebell sat. Her father's stateroom, hung with gold-thread tapestries and cluttered with war booty, seemed to glow in the slanted sunlight. As she waited for Athelrick, she knocked her knuckles fast and light on the table. She didn't like to sit still and wait, not when she had somewhere to be.

The sea. That was all she knew. On arrival back in Blickstow that morning, she had dismissed her hearthband, gone to her bowerhouse—musty from being closed up so long—and laid her long body down on her bed. With her eyes closed, she reached out for Ash with her mind. Bluebell knew that she was a blunt object, with none of her sister's subtle and mystical nuance, but Ash had heard her before. Ash, always with part of her heart turned toward her family, might still be listening for her.

Bluebell had experienced a rush of sound, then all had closed down in less than a moment. But it was enough. She had heard the sea. Ash was near the sea.

Unfortunately, Thyrsland was an island. The sea was everywhere.

The door opened and Athelrick entered. He had been on king's business in town all day and wore his mail and sash, a gold circlet on his head.

"Hello, Bluebell. I thought I heard you ride into town," he said, removing his crown and placing it on a shelf beside a collection of gold cups. "Have you been waiting for me long?"

"Long enough," she said.

"All your mother's patience went to your sisters," he replied with a smile. "Where is Sighere?"

"I've sent my hearthband north under his command, to help Wulfgar organize his guard, then to Withing to keep an eye out for Hakon's men. They have been raiding and burning in southern Littledyke and the north of Tweening."

"So I have heard." Athelrick sat opposite her, the sun flaring in his long wavy hair.

"Withing is well placed between them. If anything happens, Sighere will move on them."

"I thought you'd be keen to hunt Hakon yourself."

She smiled tightly. "I need Ash," she said simply. "You told me you'd been tracking her. Have you had any luck?"

"We believe she's in Almissia," he said. "She was last seen just a few weeks ago, in the company of a half-blind man dressed in black. I can show you on a map."

So she was still with Unweder.

"Will you bring her back to me?" he asked.

"If she'll come."

"Then why go after her? You could drive her farther away."

"That's why I'm leaving my hearthband behind. I'll go quietly and softly. Don't laugh, I can be quiet and soft, you know." She leaned back in her chair. "Father, a sword has been forged by Hakon. It has troll magic welded into its steel, and it is designed to kill me. All I know is one of my sisters has it."

"And you believe this?"

"I'd be foolish not to take the threat seriously, especially with Hakon's raiders on the move. He intends to destroy me, one way or another."

"Destroy *us*," Athelrick said. "You think Ash has this sword?"

"If she doesn't, she will at least be able to see who does. And perhaps even what they intend."

Athelrick stood and rounded the table, coming to kneel next to Bluebell. He took her hand, and she noticed how rough and swollen his knuckles had become with age. "Must you travel alone? I don't want to lose you as well. I don't want to lose you above all. Not only will my army have nobody strong to lead them, but I will be a lonely old man."

He smiled weakly at his joke, even though Bluebell knew it was not entirely a joke. She remembered bullying Gudrun and felt a pang of guilt.

"Promise me, no more than a month," he said. "If you can't find her, come home."

"I promise you. I'll be back before holy month."

"I don't like Hakon being back from the dead. Ill-favored and slippery as a fish. His brother, King Gisli, is bad enough, but at least I know where he is, what he stands for. Take all care, my daughter. Almissia is nothing without you."

"Almissia has you," she said, squeezing his fingers.

"I am old. I am our kingdom's past. You are its future. Take all care."

"I will," she said. "And I will find my sister."

Ash woke from a dream as sharp as it was sweet.

She had been home at her father's hall with her sisters Rose and Bluebell. She was twelve years old again, before any of the stirrings of the sight had begun to trouble her, and they were rolling apples to one another beside the hearth as a feast whirled around them. Her face grew hot and shiny from being so close to the fire as they rolled the apples back and forth. Bluebell rolled four at a time, laughing, knowing Ash couldn't catch them all. Rose chided her for being mean but Ash was laughing too, the bellyaching laughter of childhood. She caught the apples and rolled them back, but when she looked up, Bluebell and Rose were moving farther and farther from her, and the apples were running under people's feet. Then the music faded and the hearth went cold and her sisters were nowhere to be seen and she was alone and it was dark.

She opened her eyes. Cool dawn, the sky palest pink beyond the treetops. Ash sat up, hugged her knees to her chest, and refused to cry. In the distance, the sea sat mute under sunlight, lonely and gray-green. She had set up a camp in a wooded valley that plunged dramatically down to the sea, scored into the land by a swift stream that had its source many miles away on the southwest moors of Almissia, the remotest and least populated part of her father's kingdom. She knew of only one town there, Stanstowe, a mining town that she would find if she followed the river toward its source. Knowing her camp lay in a direct line to some kind of civilization had given her a little comfort yesterday, but after the dream that comfort was dwindling to scraps.

Ash knew why she'd dreamed of home, and especially of her sisters: Bluebell had tried to contact her. Ash, feeling her sister's spirit on the air around her skin, had tuned in hungrily, but only for half a moment before she remembered that allowing that connection did nobody any good, least of all Bluebell. So Ash had shut herself down. Bluebell would never find her that way. Nobody would ever find her if she didn't want to be found. She knew Unweder was looking for her; she could feel his insistent attention pressing around her, like ghostly fingers against a membrane, sending her scalp prickling. There was always the chance that one of them would happen across her in person, but the chance was so remote it made her feel hopeless. Thyrsland was big and she was small.

Her stomach rumbled, reminding her that she hadn't eaten since she found some mushrooms yesterday morning. She was tired of boiled seaweed. She had nothing to catch a rabbit or a pheasant with. She held her hands up in front of her. Her bones and tendons were visible, the scar across her wrist still angry red.

The morning was dewy and soft, and she rose and drank from the stream and wandered a little way into the woods in the hope of finding more mushrooms. After she had eaten and the sun had risen enough to warm her skin, she followed the rocky path down the valley to the beach. The trees—walnuts and sycamore—led all the way down to the stones and sand, where they stopped abruptly on either side of the gully the stream had carved on its path into the sea. It ran not in a mighty waterfall, but in a series of falls and trickles all across the rock face. Ash climbed down over boulders, her shoes crunching on shells, then jumped the last two feet onto the damp sand. The sea was morning-gentle, a high tide that seemed too full for waves to gather themselves into the crested rolls she ordinarily saw. As she cast her eyes and mind out over the ocean, she saw and felt instead colder currents moving at profound depths, swift and dangerous, belying the pretty, sun-starred surface. She closed her eyes, reached beneath the ocean, felt the current flow through her fingers, pushing them until they bent backward. Snapped her eyes open. Her hands, of course, were not in the water, not being broken by the weight of the ocean, but she had felt its power.

Ash walked out as far as the rocks would take her until she was surrounded by water. She no longer feared the rise of the tide, the crush of the waves. With her mind she felt for fish. Slippery, silvery, fast. She had no net, but perhaps she could trap one with her mind.

The thought formed. The sea closed its strangling grasp around a squirming flounder, then spat it up so it landed on the rocks at her feet, flapping and flipping.

She pulled out her knife and killed it quickly, filleting it clumsily and throwing its non-edible remains into the sea. A shadow caught the corner of her vision, and her heart knew what it was before her eyes saw. Cruising high on the thermal currents around a rock half a mile off shore, its gold-shot crimson wings dazzling in the morning sun.

Her first thought: *I know where it lives.*

Her second: *Why is it coming this way?*

Ash's heart swelled against her ribs. It was coming for her. It remembered her and it was coming for revenge. Her caught fish forgotten, she ran. She scrambled to her feet, nearly tripping and falling in the water. Climbed over rocks, banging elbows and shins on rough edges in her haste, the taste of her thundering pulse bitter and dry in her mouth. She could hear its wings, tough leathery billows behind her, heard the sharp intake of breath.

Ash hit the cover of the trees just as the dragon unleashed its first gout of fire. Two tall walnuts behind her instantly combusted. She ran farther into the forest, higher up among the stones, then jumped in the stream and crouched so only her head was above the water. The dragon circled, blocking the sun from the east, but too large to fit between trees. Instead, it ignited the canopy above her, so that burning leaves and twigs rained down, sizzled to damp black in the water. Then Ash remembered: She had controlled fire back in the little village where the inn burned down. She grasped the fire with her mind, expected to be able to extinguish it with the fist of her will, but a searing pressure in her head startled her and she had to let go, hands to her temples, in agony.

Unnatural fire. Her command of the elements was no use to her against this beast.

The dragon circled a little longer, setting fire to treetops and roaring belly-deep in its frustration. Then, as if realizing it was fruitless, it flew two last circles above her, making the light come and go, before taking off back toward the sea.

Ash submerged herself under the cool, dark water, releasing her held breath. It bubbled around her and she emerged again, then walked back toward her camp, stamping out burning debris. As she trod on a blue-gold ember, a flash of color caught her eye. She bent to pick up another dragon scale. This one was not the same pearlescent white, like the ones on its underbelly, but crimson like its back and tail. She tried to bend it, couldn't. At her camp, she placed it carefully by her pack, then stripped naked and hung her clothes over low branches to dry. She rarely saw herself naked, but today her jutting ribs and hips, her hollowed stomach, alarmed her. Nothing could convince her to return to the seaside to retrieve her fish or collect seaweed. Today she would stay under cover of the wood, find more mushrooms, some berries perhaps, even if they were green. Unweder had always hunted their food. He could charm prey right into his hands.

The thought of town came to her again. An inn—she still had gold left from the dragon's barrow—a meal. Ale. Other people's voices. Human hearts beating around her. Of course, the closer she drew to civilization, the closer she drew to discovery, especially now she knew Bluebell was looking for her.

She fetched her cloak from her pack and shook it out, heard the charms rubbing against one another, and pulled it around her naked body. Then she sat down, and her thoughts turned sad and dark, and she realized she was missing Unweder. Not that awful, aggressive man who had pinned her down to forcibly take her blood, but the old, familiar Unweder with his blind eye and crooked arm, who was at the very least made of the same substance as her: undermagic and exile.

He was gone now. She wondered if he was still exploring the northern caves, hoping to find his dragon. Ash knew precisely where his quarry was, and the old tired desperation washed over her. She had to kill it before he found it, but she didn't know how to. She couldn't drown it; she couldn't put out its fire. There were other things to try, she supposed: rain down stones and trees upon it. It seemed to Ash, though, that all of those things would simply make it angrier. She had felt its scales. They were tougher than steel.

She needed to know more about dragons. Unweder had been custodian of that information, and had deflected any of her questions. And she hadn't pushed, afraid he would discover that her purpose was counter to his.

To defeat this enemy, she had to know it better.

Her eyes turned toward the rock out at sea where the dragon lived. She couldn't see it through the trees, but she knew it was there, encircled by sea mist. And she told herself there were more ways to travel than in person.

❖   ❖   ❖

It took a long part of the day and many miles of wandering between trees and rocks in the woods, but Ash eventually gathered everything she needed. Greenwood, angelica, and one god-eye toadstool—the last being dangerous poison, so she only handled it by rolling it up in a thick chestnut leaf and shaking a few spores onto the fire.

The weather had turned wild, and that troubled her. The smoke would dissipate too quickly. Traveling on undermagic to the dragon's bower required her to be immersed in the smoke, so she put her cloak carefully around her shoulders, extending her arms as close as she dared to the sides of the fire pit she had dug, and leaned over the smoldering twigs. The smoke scratched the back of her throat, and the strong, organic smell of the ingredients burning on the fire made all the cavities in her face throb and sting. The wind whipped overhead; spitting rain iced her back, then was gone. The light was leaving the sky.

Ash focused, then dropped the dragon scale on the fire. It flared, fizzed. She closed her eyes.

With a barely audible pop, Ash separated from her physical body in the wood and rose above it, looking down on herself, a thin hunched figure in a stained cloak. She felt pity seeing herself there—a depleted, shrunken thing—and a pang of sorrow zigzagged through her subtle body, almost returning her to the physical.

But then she remembered her purpose and shot up and up, above the high treetops, until she could discern in the distance—not with her eyes, but with an ineffable sense between sight and feeling that she recognized from a lifetime of dreams—the narrow crooked hump of the rock out at sea where the dragon lived. She arrowed toward it through glittering rain and mist like spun silver, buffeted by the sea winds but true to her path.

Over waves silently slamming rocks.

Over sea spray and gleaming whorls of seaweed.

Above the gulls' nests.

Down and around to the jagged mouth of a cave hidden under an overhang.

I would never have found this, she said in her head, the words too articulate, making her again teeter on the brink of falling back into her body. She balanced herself again and, slower now, moved inside.

A labyrinth of black rock and barnacle led her to a softly gleaming chamber with a high vault of ceiling above it. Gold coins and brooches and cups tangled among thick ribbons of seaweed, old fishing nets that had washed away, and bones. So many bones. A collection of skulls that looked almost to have been arranged in an arrow, pointing to the center of the cave.

Curled at the point of the arrow was the dragon. She (for somehow in her subtle body, Ash could tell it was female) had her eyes closed; her ribs rose and fell softly. Ash reached out to touch her, feeling only tough scales like the ones she had found. All the way down her back, on her ribs and flanks, no ingress for spears, no soft gaps for clubs. Ash even felt around to the side of her tummy, but the scales were doubly thick here, to protect from attack as she flew overhead.

She frowned. She had assumed the pearlescent-white scales came from the dragon's underbelly, but here in the cave with her, they looked more of a pale pink. She tried to pull herself closer to examine them, but then the dragon stirred, let out a long breath. A faint curl of smoke rose from her nostrils. Ash moved herself around to the dragon's head, feeling the rough procession of leathery horns that ran from crown to snout. Even her nostrils were lined with the impenetrable scales. Gingerly, Ash reached with her mind's hands for the creature's eyes.

One snapped open. Ash rebalanced; she didn't want to startle and end up back in the wood just yet. The other eye opened. Had the dragon become aware that something was in here with her?

She lifted her head, nostrils twitching, sniffed the air, then dropped her head again and half rolled on her back, putting Ash in mind of a dog. Ash waited until she was sure the dragon was sleeping again, then continued her exploration. Each eyelid was crusted with steely scales, but here . . . just *here* . . . Ash stopped and slowed herself, wishing she had her physical fingers to prod with, because she was almost sure she could feel . . .

Yes, in the exact midpoint between the dragon's eyes, where the leathery horns ended but before the double scaling of the snout and nostrils began, in a place where too much armor would impede the creature's vision, there was a soft spot that was simply leathery skin. A heart-shaped gap in the skull and the shell, about two inches across.

So small, she said, and again the words tipped her back to herself but this time she let it happen, retracting toward the woods swiftly and lightly, then down and down, feeling the density and pressure of her body closing around her once more.

Ash gasped and sat up, coughing and coughing, nausea thundering through her. She climbed to unsteady legs and stumbled to the stream, falling to her knees and vomiting until she was sure she would turn herself inside out.

Throat burning, eyes stinging, she sat back. Rain started to fall in earnest. She crawled to her campsite. The seeing fire had been extinguished by the rain; it was just a mess of black with one shining red dragon scale in it, perfectly intact. Ash curled on her side, pulling her cloak over herself. Usually, in heavy rain, she might send up a command for the drops to run either side of her, but she was weak and tired. She closed her eyes and let the misery roll over her.

Tomorrow, raining or not, at the first glimmer of gray light she would head upstream toward Stanstowe. She needed a weapon— a sharp one.

chapter 18

S kalmir woke with a start. At first he was disoriented, thinking it must be morning. But the streaky light above the trees told him it was still night, perhaps a few hours before midnight, and he had only been asleep a few minutes. Something had woken him. He listened hard, heard footsteps. Just one set. He reached for his bow and arrow, climbed into a crouch, and silently, silently, pulled himself behind a sturdy chestnut tree. The footsteps were coming toward him. Whoever it was, they would see his blankets, the remains of his fire, and they would know he was nearby. He loaded an arrow into the bowstring, pulled it taut, waited.

A woman emerged between two oaks, dressed in a dark-red cloak, her long dark hair flowing over her shoulders. This was no woodlander. She saw his camp and froze.

Skalmir stepped out from behind cover, his arrow still trained on her. "Who are you?" he asked.

She reached under her cloak and a moment later a blinding flash overwhelmed his senses, sending him reeling into the trunk of the tree behind him. His sight had fled, leaving behind only swirling patterns of black on black. He dropped his bow, fell to his knees, and began to rub at his eyes. He felt her close by, her soft hands at his waistband, taking his knives. He tried to fight her off, but was dizzy and disoriented.

Then the point of a blade was pressed against his ribs. "Don't move," she said.

He raised his arms. "Please, don't kill me," he said.

"I won't if I don't have to," she said in a steely voice that was at odds with her shaking hand. "I have no mercy for raiders."

"I'm not a raider," he protested. "I'm a hunter."

She ignored him, pressing the point a little more firmly, forcing the shaking away. "Have you seen a little girl?" she asked. "Dark-haired, around seven years old? She may be in the company of the First Folk."

The first glimmer of understanding. "You mean Rowan?"

She was silent, but it was a silence born of surprise, not anger.

"You're Rose of Almissia, aren't you?" he said. "You resemble your daughter. I am no raider, my lady, and I am not your enemy."

She dropped the knife. "Do you know where she is?" she said in a breathy rush.

"I'm looking for her. I have been her guardian these last four years. My name is Skalmir Hunter." He lowered his arms. "How long will this blindness last?"

"I don't know," she admitted. "A matter of hours, perhaps. I'm sorry, I saw you and I panicked. One doesn't grow up in Thyrsland without a healthy fear of very tall, fair-haired men."

"I have lived in the Southlands my entire life," he said. "I have been a faithful servant to King Wengest."

"I should have known you weren't a raider," she said. "Your beard is far too short and tidy."

He laughed. "Give me a few more days away from home."

Her hand slid under his elbow. "Here, let me help you back to your blankets. I will stay with you until your sight returns."

He stood, leaning on her.

"Lift your foot here," she said. "There's a hot, burnt space where the powder went off." She led him across the unseen forest, then helped him to sit on his blanket. "I'll fetch your weapons," she said. "Wait there. I kicked them into the undergrowth."

He waited, heard her brushing around in leaves. Her warm body returned and sat next to him, took his hand, and one by one handed him his knives, his bow. "I couldn't find the arrow, sorry," she said.

"I have more."

"Is your sight returning?"

"Not even a little bit. Why are you in the Howling Wood?"

"I came to find Rowan."

"I know that, but why are you *here*? How did you know? I understood that nobody knew where Rowan was, least of all . . ." He couldn't bring himself to say, *least of all you;* it sounded cruel.

"It's more complicated than I can explain," she said. Then there was a long silence.

Skalmir wondered if perhaps Bluebell had told her, but that couldn't be right. Bluebell had always instructed him that, should Rose ever discover Rowan's hiding place, she wasn't ever to know that Bluebell had been privy to its location all along. "Rose is forgiving by her nature," Bluebell had said, "but this she would not forgive. She may have settled to a new life with her boy, but she has never stopped pining for Rowan."

"Perhaps I'll explain another time," Rose said at last. "But we are both in pursuit of the same quarry, Skalmir Hunter, and after a day where I have been lost twice, dropped my pack in a stream and soaked my blankets, and accidentally blinded a man who looked like a raider but tidier, I find myself hoping with all my heart that we may help each other." She paused, and when she spoke again her voice was less certain. "Or at least, that you may help me."

Her uncertainty, her soft, feminine voice, stirred protective feelings in him. He had only glimpsed her for a moment before she'd blinded him, and now he was reconstructing her appearance from that brief glimpse and from his intimate knowledge of Rowan's face. "Of course. We will search for her together. I'd be honored to serve your family this way, my lady."

"Call me Rose," she said lightly.

"Well, Rose, there are enough blankets here for you to borrow so you will be comfortable tonight. You may sleep, if you please."

"You can't see," she said. "I'll stay awake and watch. You may sleep."

"I don't want to sleep until my sight is restored," he said.

"Then sit with me and tell me about my daughter," she said, a note of strained desperation touching her voice. "Is she well? Clever? How tall does she grow? Please, I have been so far away from her, and now I fear for her life. Let me at least know her a little, for she has been so long denied to me."

So Skalmir sat with her in the dark and told her everything he could, careful to keep Bluebell's name out of it. He spoke about his own wife and her death, about Wengest's regular visits, about Sister Julian's lessons, about Rowan's aptitude with the bow. Rose asked a thousand questions, needy for more specific detail, as though she wanted to crawl inside Skalmir's head and press his memories against herself.

After more than an hour of this, she seemed to lapse into quiet sadness, so he asked her, "What about you? What do you remember most about her?"

"Her poreless skin and liquid eyes," she said. "The sweet softness of her cheek. And now they've marked her and carved ink into her beloved face."

"What do you mean?"

"That's how I knew to leave home and come for her: a vision of her with Rathcruick's tribe, with a tattoo like a circle of knotwork carved into her cheek. She's only a child! It must have hurt her terribly . . ."

"She is stoic in the presence of pain," Skalmir said in a comforting tone. The circle of knotwork—that was the tattoo Dardru had worn. Was Rathcruick making some fatherly claim on her? Was her kidnapping—if it could be called a kidnapping when she went willingly—a way of Rathcruick seeking restitution for the loss of his own daughter? Rowan already had too many fathers.

"I will tell you this," he said to Rose, "I am almost certain your daughter went willingly to Rathcruick. She has heard a tree singing in the woods. Nobody else can hear it, but Rathcruick promised to take her there."

"Will they hurt her?"

"I don't believe they will. But neither do I think they will willingly return her to us." A fluttering gray light passed over his field of vision and he said, "Rose, I think my sight may be returning."

"Really? I'm so glad. I honestly didn't know how long it lasted. It might have been weeks."

"I'm glad you didn't tell me that," he said, holding his fingers close to his eyes and wiggling them. He thought he could see them faintly. "We must be wise. It's after midnight and we need to start hunting at dawn. Sleep now, if you can. By morning, my sight will be restored and we can track them to their camp. Nobody knows the Howling Wood like I do. We will find her."

"I have lived so long without her that finding her doesn't seem possible," Rose said. "But I'm glad you are with me, Skalmir Hunter."

"Your daughter calls me Snowy," he offered.

"I am glad you are with me, Snowy," she said with a smile in her voice.

Rose was awake before the hunter, and she lay for a while on the other side of the cold fire pit looking at him. This man had been Rowan's only parent for four years, longer than Rose herself had looked after the girl. The way he spoke about Rowan made it clear that he loved her deeply, and the stories he had related showed Rowan loved him, too. She was at once fascinated by him and filled with raging jealousy. All those years that should have been hers were his instead, and she could never take them back.

Yet she was so grateful to him. For being kind to Rowan, for giving her love and making her safe. For protecting her as long as he could, and for coming after her when that protection had failed.

He sighed in his sleep, shifted, then opened his eyes.

"Can you see?" she asked him.

"I can, though my eyes are sore." He rubbed them vigorously.

Morning light made them unsure of each other. He had an intensity to his blue gaze that was unsettling, and he kept stealing glances at her as they ate and prepared themselves for the walk ahead.

"You are so much like Rowan," he said at last. "And nothing like Bluebell."

"You know Bluebell?" she asked.

"I have met her once or twice, yes. My adoptive father was one of Wengest's thanes."

At Wengest's name, her face flushed: anger and embarrassment. No doubt Skalmir would have an opinion based on Wengest's version of events.

"Well. I don't think there is anyone quite like Bluebell," she said. "But I am glad to know my daughter is like me."

"Not just in appearance," he continued. "In mannerisms. The way you hold your mouth when you are concentrating is identical."

"Really?" The thought pleased her; she couldn't hide her smile.

"Really." Then he laughed at himself. "You have to excuse me, my lady, I don't mean to sound as though I have been examining you too closely or strangely."

"No, no. I am pleased to know such things. You can tell them to me anytime."

They continued rolling up blankets and sorting their packs, then Skalmir covered the fire and gestured to the east. "I hunt mostly in the west corner," he said. "If Rathcruick and his company have moved in, it would be the farthest from there."

"Lead the way."

They began to walk, Rose just behind Skalmir's shoulder. The forest was full of sounds—cracks and pops and squeaks and birdcalls—and each one startled her, but nothing seemed to worry Skalmir. She took her lead from his broad, quiet shoulders. The terrain was easy at first, growing rougher as the morning wore on and they had to climb over a rocky ridge and cross the stream she had crossed yesterday. They sat on the other side after, letting their legs dry, and ate some bread and dried rabbit meat.

"Do you think we are getting anywhere?" she asked him after drinking from the stream and pulling her shoes back on.

He shook a pebble out of one shoe and carefully examined the other. "Oh yes."

"How do you know?"

"Rowan has left waymarks behind her. Little stones balanced on rocks and logs. She learned it from me. I noticed them about an hour ago. She intended to find her way back out." He pulled on his shoes and picked up his pack again. "We are about to take a different course. The markers are leading toward the old stone barrow in the northeast of the Howling Wood. First Folk love their old barrows, so I assume Rathcruick has set up camp there. I know a way we can come around by following the stream on this side for a couple of hours. If they are expecting us, they will be expecting us from the other direction. If they are not expecting us . . . all the better."

Rose took comfort in his knowledge, in his height and skill. She imagined herself wandering in the wood for days, finding nothing. Skalmir made it sound as though they would find Rowan today, though Heath had also warned her that Rathcruick might not be willing to part with her easily.

Well, she had still more blinding powder; Eldra had insisted on it. Thinking of Eldra made her think of Linden, and she sighed heavily as she made ready to move again.

"What is wrong, Rose?" Skalmir asked.

"I'm missing those I love," she said.

"Me too."

She didn't ask for further detail and offered none herself. Once more, they began their trek through the Howling Wood. Strange electricity traversed Rose's body: the thrill of knowing she would see Rowan soon; the terror of coming face-to-face with Rathcruick. Time seemed to crawl. Her feet began to ache.

The trees thinned ahead. Skalmir turned to her, put a finger to his lips, then grasped her hand and pulled her close against him.

"Be perfectly quiet," he said, his breath warm against her cheek.

She nodded. He withdrew his bow, nocked an arrow, and they crept forward.

Rose caught a glimpse of the spotted stone barrow at the end of a narrow way between a procession of lindens, so riotously decked in green leaves that their branches seemed to heave. She hunched down behind Skalmir, expecting at any moment an arrow to come whizzing toward them, or a rough hand to grab her around the neck, but no such thing happened.

The procession of trees ended, the clearing opened out in front of them with the stone barrow standing at the center of it. And nothing else.

Skalmir lowered his bow, frowning.

"Have they set traps?" Rose asked.

"I'll see," he said. "Wait here."

He moved into the clearing, carefully brushing leaf-fall aside with his feet. He circled the edge, moving in and out of the trees and wild vines that surrounded them. This space was man-made, too perfectly circular, with the linden procession too perfectly straight to have been anything but planned.

Skalmir came back to her and shrugged. "They aren't here."

"Any markers?"

"Nothing."

Rose walked down to the barrow. Ancient First Folk burial sites like this dotted Thyrsland. This one was long and narrow, with two enormous menhirs at the entrance, crossed with a heavy stone lintel. She went inside. It smelled dank and muddy.

Skalmir came in behind her. "These places make my skin crawl," he said. He crouched, touched the ground. "This stone."

The stone was balanced on a small, carved rock. "Rowan's?" she asked.

"Yes, a marker. She's been in here."

"Alone?" The thought made Rose's heart clench. She crouched, too; touched the same place as Skalmir. Their fingers brushed.

"It seems so," he said.

They looked at each other. The sunlight, filtered through thick trees and falling through a stone opening, was grim and gray. But then warmth infused his cheek and caught in his yellow hair.

A puzzled expression came over his face at the same moment. "What just happened?" he asked.

She turned her face toward the entrance to the barrow. Her heart stammered. She stood and raced out.

"Snowy!" she cried, but he was directly behind her. The clearing was gone. The linden procession was gone. They were in a crowded wood and it was sunset, the amber sunlight shining horizontally through the trees, making long spindly shadows.

"Where are we?" he gasped.

Rose turned in a slow circle, took in the entirely different place and time. "Lost," she said. "We are lost."

chapter 19

In Almissia, her father's kingdom—the land she would one day rule—Bluebell was known by all. On the first night of her journey, at a large inn fifteen miles from Blickstow where the long summer sunshine streamed in through windows thrown open to the breeze, mutters had started the moment she opened the door. Some had come over to touch the hem of her cloak, ask her business, express their love for her or their suspicion of kings and politics. She realized she would have to travel far less conspicuously. Despite the summer heat, she left the next morning in her heavy riding cloak, the hood pulled up over her head and throwing her face into shadows. On the second night, her hood still drawn forward, she sat close to an unlit wall in a dingy inn that smelled of mice droppings, and managed to eat and drink without attracting a single pair of eyes. Then she rode out of town a few miles in the dusk and set up camp off the road, pulling an oilskin over herself against a light drizzle.

On the third day, she parted company with the main road, taking Torr out over damp grass. Ash had last been seen coming down off the moors and heading toward the remote southwestern coastal regions by a small retinue belonging to one of Athelrick's old thanes, a man Bluebell had always known as Uncle Elder. The retinue had been out searching for an aging mare who had wandered, and at first Elder had not recognized the face of the "thin woman" who passed with the man in black. It was much later that her face triggered the glow of recognition in his memory, and he had sent a message to Athelrick the next morning. Ash and her companion were miles from the main road, sticking to the unpaved, overgrown tracks of the dead, the lost, the lawless, and the exiled. These were the low roads Bluebell had to follow to find her sister.

Bluebell oriented herself by the sun, and rode Torr off into the southwest. It was strange traveling alone. Without her hearthband and the packhorses, she was forced to travel lightly. She wore her thinnest mail under the riding cloak, and had just one change of clothes to make more room for her oilskin, blankets, dried food, and water containers. She traveled without helm and spear and ax. Just her sword and a knife at her waistband, her shield on Torr's flank, with her family's royal insignia—the three-toed dragon—turned away from the eyes of passersby.

Not that there were many passersby. The track was rough and ill defined, winding in and out of groves and over rocky hills, plunging down into a valley to meet a stream Torr had to swim through, soaking Bluebell's legs in the process. The rhythm of the day played out around riding, resting, adjusting her route by the sun, then riding again, until she came in the afternoon to an abandoned village surrounded by stands of hazel and fields overgrown by nettles. The architecture of the houses—the rounder gable finishings and smaller doors and shutters—told her that they had been built more than a generation ago. Seven houses and two stables stood around a rectangular stone well. The earthworks around the well had partly washed away, meaning the stream now ran through the village and had crumbled walls on two of the houses. Not one roof was intact. Decades of mud and leaf litter had layered and hardened over the cobbled road. Bluebell reined Torr in and dismounted, and led him around the village twice to cool down. While he drank at the stream, she went to the nearest house and pushed open the door.

Creeping vines had grown through the roof, and the house smelled of animal droppings. The sound of frantic scurrying told her rats had nested here. She eyed the hole in the ceiling. The sun lined up with it almost perfectly, its fierce brightness making her squint. She returned her gaze to the house, the hot flash of the sun still on her vision. The collection of looms told her this had once been a weaver's cottage, and as she went from house to house, looking for somewhere bearable to stay the night, she found more looms among the dusty benches and chests. This had once been a village of clothmakers, probably an extended family. Perhaps they'd kept sheep in the fields beyond the stream. Their dynasty's end might be blamed on their distance from viable port towns, or perhaps something as simple as an illness that took them one by one. Bluebell unlatched an ancient chest and flipped it open, found rotted cloth and tarnished bronze cups inside.

Bluebell chose the house with the least damaged roof. Clouds moved over the sun and then fanned apart again, and she couldn't predict whether rain would come. She tended to Torr and shut him in the old stable, then came back inside to spread her oilskin on the floor with a blanket layered over it. Although it wasn't cold, she longed for the comfort of a fire in the hearthpit. Around the house were enough broken twigs and wood-fall to build a measly fire, and she dribbled fire oil on it to make it crackle and roar. She pulled food from her pack and settled down to eat. The only sounds she could hear were birds and the wind in the trees. She missed Thrymm. The dog was a good hunter who could catch her a rabbit or a pheasant to roast, but, more important, she was another beating heart, a pair of ears to listen.

The afternoon seemed too long and hollow. She ate disconsolately, the hard bread dry in her mouth. Bluebell wasn't ordinarily given to melancholy, but this strange, empty village seemed to have a dismal pall hanging over it. Her father's words from Byrta's funeral feast came back to her. *Death will come to you, too, one day.* Out there somewhere was a weapon forged with magic to kill her. The sword of her doom. So here she was far from company and comfort, wandering the low roads and sleeping in rain or ruins, in the faint hope she could find Ash and the fainter hope Ash could help her.

Bluebell grew angry with herself. She should be hunting for Hakon with her men; she should simply put the trollblade out of her mind and if or when it came to her, in a traitor's hands, then she should fight bravely and win. But she was afraid. Not of losing such a fight, although the idea that the sword was magic niggled in her guts. No, she was afraid that if it was one of her sisters wielding the weapon, as the randerman suggested, Bluebell would have to kill her. Bluebell did not want stories of her deeds, when told over fires in halls all over Thyrsland, to remember her as a sister-killer.

With these thoughts, Bluebell passed the long afternoon before taking Torr on one last walk around the village and into the edge of the woods to eat in the long grass. Bluebell took a drink from the well, then returned him to the stable and made her way to her own bed. She curled on her side and promptly fell asleep.

She woke in the dark, only it wasn't quite dark. A half-moon in the clear sky shone through the crack in the ceiling, casting a soft blue-silver light against her half-closed eyelids. Bluebell became aware of sound and movement, opened her eyes fully, and felt her heart go cold.

A woman stood by the hearth, winding thread onto a spindle. Another woman stood at the loom by the window with her back to Bluebell, humming softly and expertly moving the shuttle through the thread. Both women were translucent, the same blue-silver as the moonlight. They didn't seem to have noticed Bluebell, who sat up in her bed and reached for the Widowsmith, even though she knew a sword was no use against ghouls.

From outside, Bluebell could hear footfalls, voices. She scrambled to her feet, stood uncertainly. The spinning woman ought to be looking directly at her, but her eyes were fixed beyond Bluebell, through the other side of her. Bluebell waved her sword. The woman didn't notice. She lifted it and slammed it down into the woman's skull in a killing blow. The woman didn't flinch; nor was she injured. She was as immaterial as smoke.

Bluebell went to the door and opened it, gazed out at the street with her skin creeping. The village was bustling with movement. Ghostly men having conversations with one another by the well. Ghostly horses pulling translucent carts laden with folded bundles of cloth. Ghostly children calling to one another as they chased a ghostly duck, quacking down the dark street.

Bluebell heard snorting and neighing, and turned to the stable. Had Torr been joined by a band of ghostly horses? She returned to the house, pulling up sharply as a little boy of about nine walked into her and directly through her on his way inside. Bluebell experienced a sensation like frost creeping around in her stomach. She quickly gathered her things and ran to the stable, where Torr was kicking against the door.

"I'm coming, I'm coming," she called to him, unlatching the stable door and grasping him firmly around the neck with her free arm. She pressed her cheek against his, eyes on the ghostly stable hands waxing saddles in the corner, and said softly, "I know. I know. They frighten me, too."

Torr snorted, more softly now, and allowed himself to be led back into the stable. Bluebell picked her way around ghost horses and ghost dogs, keen to avoid a return of that creeping-frost sensation, to find the bridle and saddle, and the two sturdy leather packs Torr wore on his rump. Despite her care, one of the ghost horses bolted for the unlatched door, directly through her. Cold nausea. She prepared Torr for the road as quickly as she could, then led him out of the village and onto the dark, rutted road. She did not mount him; she felt the way ahead with her feet and led him around rocks and ruts that he wouldn't see in the dark.

An hour or two out of the ghost village, she heard little footfalls behind her. At first she thought them a deer or some other innocuous creature, because they didn't run to gain on her. But then she noticed that if she slowed, so did the footfalls. If she stopped, her pursuer stopped.

Clutching Torr's reins in her hand, she slowly turned to look behind her.

The ghostly child who had run through her held up a hand to her. Bluebell's skin rose in gooseflesh. None of the other ghosts had been aware of her presence.

"Leave me be!" she called. Torr whinnied anxiously.

The child approached, its hands spread out as if asking for a hug. Bluebell itched to draw her sword, even though it wouldn't help. "Go away!" she cried instead, making a shooing motion.

The child abruptly stopped. Bluebell could see his curly hair and his too-big tunic. "I saw them all die," he said in a tiny, lisping voice. "I am the last alive."

"You are not alive," she said.

"The well made us sick. None of us knew."

Alarm prickled under Bluebell's skin. The well made them sick? She had drunk from that well, and Torr had drunk from the stream that ran from it.

"What do you mean?" she demanded.

"The earth was full of poison. It got in the water. They all died, except me."

"Oh, you are dead. You are very, very fucking dead," she said.

The ghost child paid no heed. "Will you take me back to the village?" he said. "I am so lonely."

Bluebell cast her eyes at the horizon. Light was beginning to break. Impulsively, she turned and vaulted onto Torr's back and drove him forward, fast, away from the child, who ran along behind them for a dozen yards but then fell too far back. Sight of him was lost around the next bend.

She slowed Torr. In the dawn half-light they made their way carefully down the rutted track. Bluebell's pulse flicked hard at her throat. A whole village dead. A poisoned well. She had drunk from it, and so had her horse. But she felt fine and he seemed to be fine also. They had only drunk a little and anyway, at least fifty years had passed since the villagers had died. As light came to the land and the horrors of the dark faded, Bluebell reassured herself that all would be well.

In her hurry to leave, she hadn't thrown on her heavy cloak. The sun was soft and warm on her face and wrists as it rose and shone down upon her, lifting her mood. Around midmorning they entered an ancient holloway, a tunnel of green where the track had been worn down so far that roots were visible. Gnarled trees that looked as though they had never been coppiced bent overhead, overgrown with brambles and vines and blocking out the sun. The sound of Torr's hooves and the sound of birds and nothing else, not even a breath of wind, as the sun climbed beyond the shadowy tunnel on a still, hot day.

Because of the quiet, she heard the hoofbeats long before they approached. Bluebell remembered her cloak, her desire to remain unrecognized, and pulled Torr to a halt. She climbed down, untied the pack, and pulled the cloak out, accidentally pulling out her roughly rolled-up blanket. It landed in a muddy puddle. She bent to pick it up, hung it for now on Torr's rump, and pulled on her cloak, lifting the hood over her head just as two riders came into view around the bend. Bluebell took her time folding the blanket and storing it, hoping they would simply ride past her and on their way.

"Well, what have we here?" one said to the other. "A woman traveling alone."

"It doesn't matter how far you pull down your hood, my darling," the other said to her directly, "we saw your hair. We saw you were a woman."

They laughed.

Bluebell swore under her breath. They pulled up, of course, and she studiously ignored them. They were voices, not faces. She concentrated on organizing the things in her pack, tying it and tightening it, hoping her silence would embarrass them and make them go away.

She heard one of them dismount.

"Do you need any help, my flower?" he said. "Is there anything in that pack that we can carry for you?"

"Leave me be," she said. "I need no help and I want no trouble."

The other dismounted. Bluebell pulled her hood around her face and stole a glance at them. Both were young; perhaps not even in their twenties. Both were handsome with strong bodies, one blond and one of sandy, freckly coloring. Clearly brothers. What made men with such gifts—youth, health, vitality—turn to a life on the low roads, thieving for a living? Or were they simply opportunists? Did they ride out this morning for quite some other purpose and see a lone woman and believe that their very youth and health and vital masculinity gave them the right to exercise their will on her?

They advanced with a casual saunter.

Red mist. "I said to leave me be," she said again. "I meant it."

They laughed, kept coming.

Bluebell pushed back her hood, had her sword in front of her in a moment. "All right, fuckers. Come on, then."

Both froze.

One brother, the sandy one, grasped the other's shoulder and said, "Let's go."

"No," the blond one replied, and she saw in his face the stubborn anger of a man who was frightened and embarrassed at the same time. "She may be ugly but she's just a woman. I don't frighten that easily."

"I am more than a woman," Bluebell said. "I am your king's eldest daughter. You know my name and you know my reputation. Now back on your horses and be on your way."

Bluebell could see his face working, could almost read his thoughts. She was without her shield, without her helm, without her hearthband, without her dog. They were a long way from anywhere, and she was outnumbered.

"You know who she is, brother," the sandy one said. "Don't be a fool."

The blond man reluctantly turned away. His brother was already at his horse.

" 'I don't frighten that easily,' " Bluebell said, repeating his words in a mocking, girlish voice. " 'She's just a woman.' "

The blond man spun back toward her, and her heart thudded because whether she liked it or not about herself, she thrilled to the fight.

"No!" his brother called to him.

His jaw visibly trembled, but then he turned and they rode away.

"You don't own the world or anyone in it," she called after them. "Remember that always."

She climbed back on Torr and took off into the morning sunshine.

In and out of woods and glades, with only Torr and her own heartbeat for company. From time to time, she thought she heard an echo of hoofbeats. Would those brothers come after her? But when she slowed Torr and stopped to listen, all she heard was the wind in the trees, distant sheep bleating. Three times she stopped and listened for the phantom hoofbeats. Three times she heard only silence.

The cramps started that afternoon. Low in her gut. At first Bluebell dismissed them as the familiar herald of her monthly courses, but by morning she was in the grip of the heaving shits and knew it was the well water.

Torr, for his part, seemed tired but otherwise fit, so she kept riding. She stopped frequently to relieve herself, thanked the Horse God she didn't have the vomits as well, and steered herself inexorably back toward civilization in the hope of finding an inn where she could rest in comfort.

She was still a long way from the high roads when she smelled peat smoke and followed her nose down to a collection of houses surrounding a tiny inn. Just in time—she couldn't ride another mile on her stinging arse and perhaps somebody would have a remedy on hand for stomach flux. She had only drunk from the well once. She wouldn't die. Or so she told herself over and over through gritted teeth.

But as she rode down toward the inn, she saw that the roof had fallen and all but the front façade was scorched. It was little more than a burnt-out ruin, and she pulled Torr up in front of it and sat there staring, sweating, blinking back tears of exhaustion and pain.

"It's all burned down." A voice behind her.

She didn't turn, pulled her cloak over her head. "I can see that."

"I knew your father."

Bluebell peered sideways at the man, who had come to stand next to her and was gazing up at her with a smile.

"You did?"

"I fought proudly alongside King Athelrick at the Battle of Withing. Before you were born, I believe, Princess Bluebell."

"Bluebell," she said. "Or my lord."

"As you wish, my lord," he said sheepishly.

"That's better."

"If you need a place to stay, my lord Princess Bluebell," he fumbled, "my home is just here." He indicated the little hut next to the inn, where the peat-smoke smell came from.

She considered him. He was tall, stooped, gray; perhaps a few years older than her father. He'd been a good soldier in the Almissian army and she really couldn't go farther without rest and help.

"What is your name?" she asked him.

"My name is Grimbald the humble. My home has very few comforts since my wife died, but it would be an honor to host you."

"Grimbald, I have drunk bad water and have stomach flux. I am ill." She blinked back the heat behind her eyes, and for a moment her vision swam. "I am very ill."

His face crinkled with concern. "Let me help you, my lord Bluebell," he said, offering his hand to help her down. She dismounted unsteadily, her stomach lurching. "Go inside. Lie down. The chamber pot is beside the bed. I will see to your horse and fetch you some ale. Can you eat?"

Bluebell shook her head, her stomach flipping over at the thought. She pushed open the door of his house—neat as a pin, whitewashed, brass sconces for tallow candles—and launched herself out full-length on her front on his bed. The straw ticking of the mattress poked her through the thin blankets. She lay with her eyes closed a long time, heard him come and go, leaving a cup beside her. Finally she sat up and drank the ale, but it decided to go straight through her.

Grimbald pulled the curtains around the bed and she spent the afternoon behind those gray curtains, shitting hot liquid into the chamber pot that he duly and uncomplainingly emptied for her every time. She had never been more grateful for a person's help in her life, never been more humbled by quiet kindness. When the cramping slowed and stopped for a few hours of reprieve, she was keen for distraction. He offered her food once again, but the thought of it made her stomach shiver.

"What happened to the inn?" she asked. "Why haven't they re-built it or pulled it down? Do you not worry it will fall over onto your house?"

Bluebell sat up on the bed, having drunk a mixture of bayberry and comfrey to help settle the flux. She was hopeful that the worst was over but still feeling sick and weak. He sat by the hearth, stooped over, an elongated shadow on the dark wooden wall.

"It only happened recently," he said. "A matter of weeks ago. The owner . . . she perished in the fire. We are still waiting to see if her brother will come up from Fengard to claim what's left."

A shadow crossed his brow and Bluebell grew curious.

"What is it?" she asked.

"It was a terrifying night. None of us around here will forget it."

"Lightning strike?"

"Worse. Undermagic. A powerful sorceress . . ." He shook his head.

"Go on," she said. "I'm in need of distraction. Tell me."

He pulled his knees up, his long hands resting over them. Out-side, the sun had begun its slow descent. The candles were not yet lit, and a little soft light was admitted through the slats of the shut-ters.

"She came with a companion, a small slight man with an eye patch. He was dressed all in black, but his hand . . ." Grimbald mimed a hand curled over on itself, useless, and Bluebell's skin began to prickle. "She was small, pretty, but all her hair shorn off like a sheep in spring. I saw them coming down the hill. I see every-one. I saw you." He indicated the window over her head. "They disappeared into the inn and all was well. I saw them there that night when I went in to drink. He was hunched up around himself like a wounded cat, and she sat next to him as though she was protecting him. Alert as a fox. Watching us all as though she was hungry. As though she hadn't seen people or heard laughter in a hundred years. There was something haunted about her face. For such a young lass, I'd say she'd seen more dark affairs than any of us can imagine. They say it's the way with the undermagicians."

"How do you know they were undermagicians?"

"It was what she did, my lord Princess. Though I wasn't there to see with my own eyes. What we know is young Marigold who owned the inn told her friends that the undermagicians had upon them a large sum of money, and that she was going to . . . ask for a little extra. Marigold was a sly one, and we all knew it. Who knows? Perhaps she tried to steal it or extort it. But the sorceress, she was having none of it. They say that she set fire to the inn with the power of her mind. Marigold didn't survive, though her dogs lived and now hang about the village relying on everyone's kindness."

"But if she didn't survive, how does anyone know that's what happened? Why do you blame a sorceress? Undermagic? It might have simply been an accidental fire."

He was already shaking his head. "I was there when the villagers ran out to help. The first bucket of water on Marigold doused the flames, but they sprang back immediately. Six times we doused her, in the rain. Six times the flames returned, angrier than before. Determined to burn her to cinders. This wasn't just a fire; it was fire of rage and vengeance."

Bluebell digested all of this. This powerful sorceress could only be Ash; the description of Unweder was unmistakable. Bluebell knew that Ash had turned to undermagic, but when had she become the kind of undermagician who would set a woman on fire and keep her burning for revenge? If this was Ash, then did Bluebell have cause to be afraid?

Did Ash have the trollblade?

"How is your stomach, my lord?"

"It seems settled for now."

"You are very pale. If I cannot tempt you to eat, perhaps I can suggest you sleep."

Bluebell looked around. "You would give me your bed for the night?"

"I would do all that I could to serve my king and his family."

"Then, thank you. I am . . . very tired." Achingly tired. So tired her bones weighed like granite.

"Go on, then. I shall keep watch."

Bluebell stripped down to her undershirt and lay down, was most comfortable on her front. For a long time she didn't think she would get any rest. The pain in her guts, while no longer acute, throbbed and cramped. She felt hot, shut in.

Late in the deepest part of the morning, she heard the hoofbeats again. She kicked off her covers and stood, opening the shutter. Listening hard into the dark. They drew closer. This time she knew she wasn't mistaken, and she was about to turn and pick up her sword when the beast burst from the trees and she saw what had been following her.

A horse made of thin moonlight. A handsome mount, but a ghost nonetheless, saddled and alert, waiting at the top of the road. Like the village boy whose ghostly form had touched her, this horse had followed her, too. Now it waited for her, as if it knew she would soon die.

Bluebell closed the shutter. The heat in her body had turned to chattering cold. She curled among the blankets and closed her eyes, fell in and out of half dreams about ghosts. Finally, just before dawn, she drifted to darker, quieter realms.

Bluebell woke and had trouble clearing her vision. Her head throbbed.

I am very ill.

She sat up, found her clothes and began to pull them on.

"My lord, you cannot be thinking of leaving." This was Grimbald, slipping back into the house on his return from some errand. She hoped it was tending to her horse. "You are pale, shaking."

"I just need to wake up."

"Eat something at least."

"I have no appetite. I have to keep going."

"But my lord—"

She put up a hand to silence him. "Tell me, how many miles to the sea from here?"

"Five direct, ten by the road. But do use the road, my lord Bluebell."

She climbed to her feet, bent to pick up her byrnie, and nearly fell back down. He caught her elbow, held out her mail and helped her slip it on. Its familiar weight settled across her shoulders.

"How is Torr this morning?"

"The destrier? He is well."

Then perhaps Torr had escaped poisoning. Bluebell remembered the ghostly horse she had seen the night before. She forced her teeth to stop chattering. If Grimbald saw how ill she really was, he would find a way to stop her leaving.

"Let me help you—"

"I want no more help." She pulled herself up to her full height, despite shaking knees. "Grimbald the humble, I will remember you and I will tell of your kindness to my father when the Horse God wills that I see him again."

Grimbald beamed, making him look thirty years old again.

"Now, goodbye," she said. And strode out as if there were nothing at all wrong.

Vision swimming, perspiration prickling her top lip, she mounted Torr and turned him toward the sea. The morning breeze caught her hair and cleared her head a little.

"See?" she said to nobody. "A touch of fresh air and . . ." She didn't finish the sentence. She had nobody else to convince, and she certainly couldn't convince herself.

chapter 20

U p in the hall tower, Ivy sat on the carved wooden seat where Gunther had always heard the civil business for the week. Crispin stood behind her right shoulder, watching but neutral, as Ivy ran through the day's business with one of the thanes. Rain fell outside the window now, heavy and mournful. The room was chill.

"I don't understand," Ivy said, for the fourth time that morning. "How is it that we have lost so much in taxes this week?"

The thane—why couldn't she remember his name? Gunther always remembered their names—dipped his head and explained again patiently. "The taxes come in when the ships leave. We have had some difficulties getting ships away, which means other ships cannot make land. This is why the harbor is filling up, and why some are sailing directly past us to Brimheath."

"When you say, some difficulties getting ships away . . ."

He exchanged a glance with Crispin over her shoulder. "Half of the wharfmen are trimartyr, my lady."

"So? Is there a holy day I am not aware of?"

"I think what Torsten is trying to say, Duchess," Crispin offered, "is that they are protesting the chapels being . . . closed."

Ivy sagged in her chair. Every day, protesters gathered at the sites of the burnt-out chapels to pray. Every day, guards were sent to

move them on. Ivy had assumed they would all get tired of protesting soon, but they were piously dogged. "Can we not force them to
work, if they are being paid?"

"We have threatened to stop paying them, my lady," Torsten offered. "They hold that Maava is more important than coin."

Ivy blinked rapidly. "Then throw them out of the city," she said.
"Seacaster does not want such citizens."

"Madam—" started Crispin.

"What? Why should they be allowed to stay if they are causing
such strife? Hire some new wharfmen."

"It may take some time to . . . Of course. Of course, my lady."
Torsten bowed. "I will have the protesters removed from the city
and new workers hired."

"And in the meantime, increase the taxes on shop owners to cover
the gap. Just for a month or two."

He spread his palms and smiled tightly. "If my lady wishes it."

"Good. Then that is solved." She forced a bright smile. "See, this
governing is not so difficult, is it?"

He lifted the corners of his mouth weakly. "As you say, Duchess
Ivy. Now, one final piece of business before I let the rabble in." He
indicated the door to the room with a slight incline of his head.
"Could you please look over this latest correspondence from Wulfgar of Fifelham?"

Torsten had withdrawn a sheet of fine vellum, inked with neat
letters.

"What does it say?" she asked.

The expression on Torsten's face was clear. "You can't read this?"

Heat came to Ivy's face. "I never needed to. Bluebell can't read.
Nobody says she is a bad leader."

"I did not mean to suggest anything of the sort," Torsten said, but
a strange gleam had come to his eye nonetheless. Was it a veiled
expression of triumph?

"What does it say?" she repeated.

"Wulfgar is requesting forty men to help form a temporary standing guard. Given that his family members have been slaughtered by

raiders, he's understandably fearful of their return in these difficult months while he establishes his own rule."

"Wulfgar? That cat's paw? They should put his sister Annis in charge," Ivy harrumphed. She had met Blackstan and his children several times since coming to Seacaster.

"Your answer, my lady? I would advise—"

"No. If there are raiders about, we might need our own soldiers."

"Our diplomatic links with Fifelham are long standing."

"I said no." Ivy was tired of Torsten and his smug face. "Now away with you."

Torsten backed out of the room, bowing. Ivy glanced at Crispin and offered him a smile, but he looked straight ahead, face stony. Ivy turned toward the first face at the door and took a deep breath. "Come in," she said.

The boys slept in their beds, Hilla dozed while sitting up by the fire, and Ivy pushed her brain against the marks on the bound vellum pages in front of her, determined to understand the lines and shapes that made up words. Albus, the preacher, sat beside her, bent forward to catch her words as she said them. He had been encouraging her to read for years; she had always found reasons not to, but now she was determined to learn. It wasn't as though Albus had much to do now that she had emptied the chapels.

"Come along, Ivy. Just two more lines."

"It's grown so dark. The candlelight hurts my eyes."

"One more line. You know this." He tapped the page. "This word. You've read it a hundred times."

"King!" she said as recognition came. "Oh, yes. King. *If the king should arrive . . .*" The rest of the sentence weighed too much for her eyes and her mind. She closed the book. "I'm sorry, I really can't go on. I'm tired and worried."

Albus smiled at her gently. "Maava would give you great comfort."

"Maava was never my god," she said curtly. "And you will do

well to remember that now you're a teacher. It would be better for Seacaster if I can read laws and accounts. I'm relying on you."

His smile never left his face. He really was irritatingly patient. "As long as it's no crime for me to believe what I believe," he said.

"Of course not. I don't care what people think as long as they do what I say." Here she laughed, even though she had only been half joking. "You may go. I will see you after dinner tomorrow."

Albus stood, laid his hand flat on the front of the book. "Practice," he said. "You have a good brain. This will be easy for you."

She glowed at his compliment and saw him off at the door to the bowerhouse. Hilla woke at the swirl of cool sea air that entered the bower, blinking and glancing around.

"Go to bed," Ivy said. "The boys are fast asleep." Hilla had a small bed in an alcove off the main room. Ivy usually slept between her boys. She had been considering moving into Gunther's bed, but the mattress still bore his impression, the room his smell. Perhaps she was being superstitious.

"As you wish, my lady."

A loud knock on the door made them both jump. Ivy wondered if Albus had forgotten something and returned for it, but when she opened the door it was Crispin, who ordinarily came nowhere near her bower.

"My lady," he said, anxious eyes glancing over her shoulder and seeing Hilla. "A woman has come who says she is your sister."

"My sister?" Ivy immediately thought of Bluebell, but then realized Crispin would have named Bluebell. "Which one?"

"I don't know," he said. "I came straight here. She is tall but not so tall as Bluebell, and traveling with a man who is hidden by his cloak."

Ivy was already reaching for her own cloak, which hung on a hook by the door. "Dark-haired?"

He shook his head. "She wears a scarf, but I think she is not dark."

Ivy gasped. "Then it's Willow." *Willow.* Her twin, whom she hadn't seen in many years. Whom her family had lost contact with, considered lost or dead. It couldn't be Willow. It must be Ash or

Rose. "Hilla, I don't know how long I will be. Kindly sleep with the door open so you can hear if the boys wake."

"Yes, my lady."

Ivy closed the door behind her. The night air was cold and heavy with the smell of salt. Mist gathered over the ocean. The torches on the southern side of the hall were lit, and by their light she could see the tall figure of a man, a dark cloak pulled over his face. He leaned his back against the outside wall, one knee bent. Her curiosity prickled. Crispin led her into the hall, where a strong, sullen-faced woman waited for her.

Willow. She was all in gray, a scarf tied over her hair in the trimartyr style, but wisps of her pale-brown hair had escaped. Much changed by time and circumstance, but unmistakably her twin sister. She looked tired, harried.

"I never thought I'd see you again," Ivy said as the door to the hall closed and they were plunged into near-dark.

Crispin lit a row of candles as they spoke, gradually adding an amber glow.

"I have come because I need your help."

Ivy stepped close, held out her arms. "You don't have a hug for your sister?"

"I don't have a hug for anyone who burns Maava's chapels," Willow said, a disdainful sneer pulling up the corner of her mouth.

"You speak plainly for somebody who wants a favor," Ivy said, dropping her arms. Her eyes ran over Willow's body. She had once been a skinny thing, but she appeared to be developing the gristle and dense power of Bluebell in her limbs. Her wrists were ropy.

"I need to go far away," Willow said. "I need a small boat. My companion and I will row it and work the sail."

Ivy thought of the tall cloaked man. "And who is your companion? Is it your husband? Your lover?"

"He is neither of those things. I have no need for a husband or a lover. I have Maava in my heart and a high purpose beyond your imagining, on other shores."

While it was like Willow to say something like this, Ivy could never remember her sister using such a high-handed, condescending tone with her. Willow had often been judgmental, but always spoke gently. More about her was hardening than her wrists and shoulders.

"Why should I help you?" Ivy snapped. "You speak to me so rudely." Crispin was at her side now, and she felt comforted by his presence.

"You will help me because you want me far away, as my whole family does. As you always have."

Ivy considered Willow in the flickering candlelight. "What happened to you?" she asked at last, gently. "Where have you been?"

"I have been wherever Maava wants me to be. I don't answer to anyone other than Him. I certainly do not answer to you after what you have done. When I arrived I went to pray, but there are burntout shells where there ought to be chapels, and crowds of folk who despise you. I have heard them speak of you in the streets of Seacaster this day. Good trimartyr folk who see in your reign only heathen chaos."

It seemed Willow was determined not to share the slenderest shred of information about herself. Ivy thought about Bluebell's visit; she'd wanted to know where Willow was, whether she had the sword. Bluebell would surely be happy if Ivy gave Willow the means to sail far away, sword or no sword. "You can have a boat," Ivy said. "It makes no difference to me. Will I ever see you again?"

"If Maava wills it."

"You know that Maava nonsense is really quite infuriating."

"You don't know fury."

Ivy narrowed her eyes, a soft alarm sounding in her blood. "Do you have a sword? A magic one?"

"I have no weapons and no armor beyond that which Maava has granted me in His wisdom and grace. I am a poor pilgrim who seeks a solitary life away from these filthy cities."

Ivy half turned to Crispin, asked his opinion with her eyes.

"You have enough to concern yourself with," Crispin said. "Send her away if she wants to go away. I can take her and her companion down to the harbor, give her one of the smaller boats."

"It needs to have a sail," Willow interrupted. "We can't row all the way."

"I will find you something suitable from Gunther's fleet," Crispin said to her with respectful courtesy.

"Will you stay the night?" Ivy said. "Head off in the morning?"

For the first time, Willow looked unsure. "I—no. If we can't sail at night, then we can sleep in the vessel." She seemed to gather herself. "Maava rewards those who suffer hardship while doing His work."

"Well, good on Maava and good on you," Ivy muttered.

"This way, my lady," Crispin said to Willow, showing her to the door.

Ivy stood in the threshold. Willow called for her companion, but not by name—just one simple word: "Come." The tall figure began to move; a statue come to life. Ivy watched him closely, trying to catch a glimpse of his face. As he passed under the torchlight, she thought she saw a skull under the cloak and recoiled. But then he said something quietly to Willow and Ivy told herself that skeletons didn't walk and talk. It must have been a trick of the light.

"Goodbye," she called to her sister's departing back. Tomorrow she would send word to Bluebell that Willow had been, that she was gone now, and that she certainly represented no threat to the family while sailing away to distant shores.

It grew late. Hilla was asleep in her little alcove. The boys, curled on their sides to face each other, slept on with their soft eyelashes pressed gently against their plump cheeks. The fire had grown low, but still Ivy was awake, pacing in her nightgown to keep herself from nodding off, listening for Crispin's footsteps returning from the dock.

Finally, deep in the night, she heard him. She dashed to the door and pulled it open. He took a step back, startled, then smiled. All the torches had extinguished, and only starlight and a half-moon lit his face.

"My lady, you are still awake."

"Come into Gunther's bower," she said, grasping his wrist. Quickly and quietly, she led him past the boys to the adjoining room, then closed the door silently behind them.

Crispin sat on Gunther's bed, grinning at her in the dark. "My lady, are you keen for company?"

Gunther's bedding hadn't been freshened since his death, and she recoiled at the idea of lying there naked with Crispin. "Not that kind of company," she said. "Not on the very mattress he died upon."

Crispin leaned forward, elbows on knees. "Your sister and her strange friend are even now sleeping upon one of Gunther's boats. They intend to leave at first light. You say she is your twin? She's nothing like you."

"Her brain is addled," Ivy said. "Full of trimartyr nonsense."

"She was very angry with you about the burning of the chapels."

Ivy shrugged. "She's gone now. Perhaps another four years until I see her. Maybe more, with any luck." She sat on the rushes in front of him, touched his knee. "What a strange evening it has been. I find it tiring, making decisions."

"Let me help you make them," he said, grasping her fingers. "I would ease your burden."

She smiled up at him, heart brimming.

He stood and paced to the shutter, opening it to let a cold sea breeze in. "You are young and soft, Ivy. You know too little of the world."

Ivy, unsure if this was a compliment or rebuke, watched him uncertainly.

He turned. "Your dead husband's cousin, Athmer of Nether Withing, came to see me today."

"Came to see you? What? When?"

"He found me out at the guardhouse, on his way home from visiting for the funeral. He offered me rewards . . . a great deal of gold and land."

"I don't understand. For what?"

"To undermine you. To take away the support of the city guard. He wants Seacaster. He believes it needs to be back in strong hands. Tales of our . . . instability are reaching other parts of Thyrsland. As the closest adult male relative, he believes the city should be his."

Ivy felt at once hollow with panic and too full of rage to speak. "What did you say?" she managed to ask.

"Ivy," Crispin replied, with an expression bordering on sadness. "*Of course* I said no. How could you think otherwise of me?"

"I didn't!" she squeaked.

He came to crouch beside her, took her face gently in his hand. "You know I love you."

She beamed so hard that her cheekbones pushed against his strong fingers, and he released her and leaned to kiss her. Just once. Swiftly.

Then he stood again and said, "You can trust me. I don't know who else you can trust. My feeling is you should trust no one at all. No one but me."

"I will. I do," she said, keen to erase that moment of sadness her doubt had caused him.

"Good," he said. "Next time you wonder, *What did Crispin do?*, know that the answer is always that I do what is best for you and your boys."

"I'm sorry I ever questioned you."

He smiled at her. "You are beautiful."

"I love you," she said, quickly and boldly. "I love you, Crispin."

"Whatever happens next, we will be together," he said.

"Together," she said, and stood to hold him, letting her uncertainty melt away.

chapter 21

After a day of walking uphill, Ash's knees felt as if they could no longer bear the weight of her body. But the uncomfortable cost was repaid when she struggled over a rocky rise and looked down on hazy fields and quarries and a small town huddled in the crook of the hill's arm. Civilization. People.

She crouched, took a moment to catch her breath. Stanstowe. She could already hear the clang of the smithy ringing out, almost as though it were calling her. Ash stood, looked behind her. She had been looking behind her the whole way, wondering if the dragon would follow. Dark imaginings of the beast winging into Stanstowe after her, spewing hate and fire, had preoccupied her restless mind the whole way.

Ash stood and made her way down the grassy slope, around rocks and gorse, toward the town. Her feet met the road at the bottom of the valley, and she crossed a wood and stone bridge into Stanstowe. A woman with three young children passed, and Ash once again checked over her shoulder, looked to the sky for red wings, but saw only white clouds.

The town had more stone buildings than most other places in Almissia. As a consequence, the predominant colors were gray stone and green moss. She followed her ears toward the smithy, and found it soon after: an open-fronted building where blasts of heat and noise kept passersby on the other side of the road. Ash waited awhile near the thick wooden columns that served as a shopfront, because the smith—a hulking woman who looked as though she had never denied herself a meal—had her back to Ash. Ash was surprised and curious to see her father's insignia, the three-toed dragon, hung on one of the columns.

Eventually, the woman turned, saw her, and strode over.

"You should have called out to me," she said.

"You were busy."

She shrugged her big shoulders. "What can I do for you?"

"I'm in a hurry and I need a sword."

"You need arms to lift it. How about a knife?"

"No, that won't do. It must be long and sharp."

"I'll make you a spear, then. A light ash haft with a lethal tip. I can do that quicker, too. How much of a hurry?"

"Today?" Ash asked. "I have money." She pulled out her purse and dipped in her hand, withdrew a palmful of gold coins.

The smith shook her head. "Tomorrow morning. I would love your money, but I have long-standing customers who mean more to me."

Ash didn't want to stay in town overnight; her conscience wouldn't allow it. Her eyes went to the royal insignia. "Why do you have Athelrick's insignia hanging on this column?"

The woman's chest puffed out proudly. "I am Gartrude Smith. This business has forged weapons for Athelrick and his family for twenty years. First my husband, then me when he . . . passed."

Dared Ash tell the smithy who she was, in the hope that she could get her spear sooner and leave town? But no. In four years, nobody had ever found her. She was determined to keep it that way.

"A great honor," Ash said.

"Princess Bluebell's famous sword, the Widowsmith, was forged right here in Stanstowe, by my husband's hand. It was the last thing he made before he died. He kept working through his illness because he wanted to make the greatest sword in Thyrsland. She wields it well. Long may she live."

At Bluebell's name, Ash felt piercing melancholy. "Yes, long may she live. I have been long out of company, smith. What is the news of Athelrick's family?"

"He is well and visited us not two moons past."

Ash's heart leapt. "Really? Has he remarried? Is he as strong and handsome as he ever was?"

"He is much aged, and unmarried, but yes, still strong and handsome for a man with so many winters on his brow. Now Bluebell leads his army and has secured the great strongholds of Merkhinton and Harrow's Fell, and they say that King Gisli and his raiders dare not approach the border anymore. Only Hakon's men, driven as always by greed and malice, still raid the towns of the north. And news came to me just a day ago that Princess Ivy, Duchess of Seacaster, has lost her husband the duke and now governs the city for her two sons."

Ivy was married? With two sons? Governing a city? Ash couldn't imagine it. She had always been so flighty and thoughtless. Such sweet and bitter comfort came from the smith's words: reminding Ash both of the living, breathing existence of her family, and her cold dislodgement from them.

"Nothing of the other sisters?"

The smith shook her head. "Not that I've heard. They must be living quiet."

"Yes," Ash said. "They must." She opened her fist again and reached for the smith's hand, pouring the gold in. "Tomorrow morning."

"This is far too much money."

"I have little use for gold," Ash said. "I will see you tomorrow morning."

The smith nodded and dropped the money with a resounding chink into her apron. "You shall have my best work."

Ash walked four paces into town, longing to sit in an inn and eat a meal and have a hot bath, but then she turned, one eye on the sky, and walked back out again. She would sleep in the woods and return in the morning, only for long enough to collect her spear.

If she wanted company, if she wanted the warmth and comfort of her family, it would have to wait until she had killed the dragon. Until then, on the other side of that impossible horror, there would be no rest or happiness for Ash.

Torr was sick. He'd bravely kept his head up for miles, but now he grew weak and Bluebell couldn't make him go on. She'd kept hope in her heart that neither she nor her horse had drunk enough of the poison water to kill them—that a few days would pass and their symptoms would improve and they could continue on their journey—but now they were both too ill to travel, and a long way from help.

Bluebell had long ago left roads behind for the meandering cliff paths. There were few trees for shelter in this part of Almissia, but she found a gully of hardy ferns where Torr could fold his legs under him. She gave him water, then stroked his nose as he snorted softly. He, like Bluebell, had no appetite. The phantom hoofbeats were still following them, and Bluebell grew superstitious that the ghost horse knew that she, too, would soon be a ghost.

Despite these cold thoughts, Bluebell was hot. Fiercely hot. The afternoon sun was in part responsible, but she had been fighting a fever for three days and the ocean looked invitingly cool. She found her way down to the shore by a winding, gentle path and stood a moment, scanning the world in all directions. Completely and entirely alone. Why was it always when she was most profoundly alone that death seemed to stalk her? Last time she was injured in battle and the Horse God had come. Now, though, it was illness that threatened to claim her. The gods were notoriously indifferent to the sick.

She stripped naked, leaving her armor and weapons and clothes between two rocks, and waded into the sea.

The water sucked at her skin, cool and bracing. She stood in it up to her breasts, arms floating on the waves, looking back at the land. Ash could be anywhere. Anywhere at all. This journey was fruitless, and would likely end in her destrier's death if not her own. She was confused about how she had thought this plan worth following through. Had her mind been addled by the poison as well?

Bluebell ducked under the water completely, felt her long hair snake about her face, heard the bubbling waves breaking over her head. Yes. If it got too bad, she would not die on the side of the road. She would come here, under the water, where it was cool and dark.

She stood, waded back out to the shore. Almost immediately the heat came back to her face. She looked down and saw that her belly, usually flat and hard, was distended, tender to touch. She sat on a rock for a while, let the air and the sun dry her. Then she picked up her clothes and dressed again, hung her sword across her hips.

A flash at the edge of her vision made her lift her head. Slipping behind a rock was a child, barefoot and wild-haired.

"Hey there! Hey!" she called, speeding her feet toward the child. Her head spun.

The child emerged from behind the rock and Bluebell saw it was not a child at all, but a goblin of some kind with seaweed for hair. It tried to run from her but she picked up a rock and threw it, knocking the creature off-balance. It scrambled to its feet as she stalked toward it, and then her sword was out, the tip resting under its barnacled chin. It froze and stared at her with huge, limpid eyes. In them she could see her own reflection, her wet matted hair, her febrile eyes. Her heart pounded.

Bluebell shook sweat out of her eyes. "I am sick. Can you save me?"

"No."

"Is there another of your . . . kind who can?"

"Yes, there is. A strong sea witch who walks these cliffs." Its voice was raspy, the sound of somebody gargling sand. "She could draw the elements out of your gut and veins, the ones that have poisoned you."

Bluebell's sword arm wavered. "Can you take me to her?"

"You will die before you get there," it said simply. "You are mortally sick."

"I'm not. I didn't have a fatal dose. I'm sure of it." She brought the tip of the sword up again. "Why can I see you?" she demanded.

"Because you are near to death. The veil has grown thin."

"I can't see any other spirits. Only you. Is this a trick?"

The creature blinked its big eyes. "We must have some connection, then."

"I have no connections with goblins."

"Is there one you know who sees the unseen world?"

Bluebell sagged forward, relief and pain making her drop her sword arm. "Ash," she said. "You must know Ash."

The creature's face turned up in a grimace that might have been a smile. "Ash is the sea witch I spoke of. You are her friend?"

"I am her sister. Will you bring her to me?"

The strange smile disappeared. "She wanders alone now. Ash does not want to be found."

"She will want to help me. I promise you," Bluebell said, sitting heavily on a rock, tide lapping at her heels. Even the thought of climbing back up the cliff path was too much for her. If she could rest awhile, just long enough to get a little strength back . . .

"Promise on your bones?"

"On my . . . Yes, I promise on my bones. She will come, if you go to her. Please."

"Then I will go to her and ask. Rest near your mount," the creature said to her. It hurried its steps to the sea. Bluebell watched as it turned to frothing water and dissolved into the waves.

Rest near your mount. The creature was right about that. The tide was coming in. She couldn't collapse here on the beach; she'd be swept away. She wasn't yet prepared to accept that she would die.

Grasping at rocks, half standing, half crawling, she started up the slope. "Torr!" she called, not because she thought the horse would hear her or come, but because she couldn't bear to be alone. Somehow she made it to the top, found her horse lying very still in the bracken. She bent to listen, heard his heart pumping faintly, curled against his body, and closed her eyes. Everything spun and swung about. It reminded her of being a child: she and Rose turning as many circles as they could before lying down with eyes screwed shut. She breathed, and waited, and didn't notice when she slipped away into crushing sleep.

The haft of Ash's spear was made from the wood of the tree that bore her name. It was light and smooth in her palm as she carried it upright, using it like a walking stick, down the rocky river valley back to the sea. Its head was shaped like a pointed leaf, with an iron core and shining steel edges, adorned with swirling welding patterns. It was a pretty thing; the smith had made it well because of the amount of money Ash had given her, not knowing that it was a single-use weapon. One blow, between the dragon's eyes. Or a missed blow, and Ash wouldn't survive to use it again.

The thought loosened her stomach and made her knees weak.

It had been nearly impossible to leave the village behind. She had stood in the market square for many long minutes before a dark flash at the corner of her vision—as it turned out, a colony of rooks making their way overhead—galvanized her to leave. Alone now, she struck out toward the moment for which she had been preparing for four years—a moment she felt completely unequal to.

Ash stayed inside the tree line, noticing everything. Every dappled sunbeam, every birdcall, every pop of a broken twig or rustle of a loose leaf making its way to the ground. Memorized all of it in case it was the last time she ever saw and heard such a thing. One foot in front of the other, down toward the sea.

Many hours later, when her body was weary and her soul wearier, Ash eased off her shoes, took a last drink from the stream, and left the cover of the trees. She made her way down to the gritty sand and stood there, toes working in the sand, with her spear beside her. She expected the dragon to come for her immediately. It did not.

Well, she could wait. And if an hour or two or an afternoon and evening passed and it still didn't come, then she would see if she could part the water and walk out there to the dragon's cave on the wet sand.

An afternoon breeze caught her cloak, lifting it softly and slowly. The sea rose and fell. The sun glinted off the tip of her spear.

In the distance to the north, a wave was coming, frothing and white, cutting sideways across the tide. Ash tightened her grip on her spear. The white wave curled around when directly in front of her, and rushed toward her. Was it coming out of the water? She lifted the spear, said, "Help me, Great Mother," and felt the blast of heat to her heart.

But no dragon emerged from the water. Instead, the little sea spirit, the one who had brought her the gifts, clambered onto the shore.

"What is this?" Ash asked. "I hadn't thought I would see you again."

"Your sister," the sea spirit said. "Bluebell. She lies not twenty miles from here, poisoned and dying. She says you will come."

Ash stared at the sea spirit, struck dumb. Bluebell was nearby? But this was awful. The dragon would come for her, kill her sister . . . the thing she feared most.

"Her blood is poisoned by metal from the ground. Elemental poison," it said. "You command the elements." It reached up and put its sticky hand over hers. "I can take you to her. Why do you hesitate?"

Poisoned and dying. While she knew her sister was capable of defeating any mortal enemy, her weapons and armor were no match against poison. She had no choice but to go to Bluebell. "Show me the way," she said.

Bluebell opened her eyes. Didn't know where she was. Her guts ached. A shadow moved in front of her. She tried to focus on it. The sky was dark blue, streaked with the last pink light of the day. The shadow came closer. A grim face emerged, hollow cheeks.

"It's me," the shadow said, and Bluebell recognized the voice but couldn't place it. Beside it stood a goblin with a hideous face. Fear stirred in her; a half-remembered phrase about promises on her bones. She tried to move her mouth, but she was cold and sweating and everything was stiff. "Not my bones," she managed to say to the shadow. "Don't take my bones."

"You are sick," the shadow said. "Close your eyes. This may hurt."

Rather than comforting her, the familiarity of the voice made her fearful. She had forgotten something. "You're a witch," she said. "You're here to steal my bones." She tried to sit up but couldn't move her limbs. Had her skeleton already been stolen? Bluebell felt hands on her stomach, then grinding, grabbing pain. "You're killing me!" she gasped.

"I'm removing the poison," the shadow said, her head bent so that Bluebell could see how short her dark hair was. "Lie still."

All along her veins, the grinding pain drew its jagged feet, as though her blood had been replaced by shattered steel. The pain was beyond her imagining, and she had suffered a lot of pain in her life. She called out, her voice echoing loudly around.

"I'm so sorry, Bluebell," the voice said, and the feeling of recognition flared again. If only she weren't dying, she'd be able to place the voice.

The shadow drew the pain into Bluebell's stomach, and it gathered like a storm, heavy and grumbling. She was sure she would split in two, but then the shadow threw her hands in the air and the pain evaporated. Bluebell felt a small popping sensation low in her guts. Then nothing.

She lay back, eyes closed, breathing ragged, as she forced herself to overcome the wake of the pain.

"Now your horse," the voice said. The shadow moved off, a soft rattling sound accompanying her steps. Torr made awful noises of pain, and Bluebell said, "Shh," but so quietly she knew the horse couldn't hear. Maybe she was quieting herself. Her head spun. Her thoughts were scattered.

She slipped into a brief blackness.

How much later she woke, Bluebell did not know. She opened her eyes and righted herself slowly. The shadowy witch sat beside

her, face turned away toward the sea. She watched her a moment
and knew who it was. She didn't want it to be Ash. Not this pain-
fully thin woman who had aged twenty years in four, with her bony
shoulders and her raggedly cropped hair. But it was Ash.

"Ash. What has happened to you?" Bluebell asked.

Her sister turned, then lay down, put her head in Bluebell's lap,
and sobbed. Bluebell stroked her hair softly, still gathering her
senses, still disbelieving of how hollow Ash's face had become.

Finally, Ash sat up, palming tears off her face. "You must go and
forget you ever saw me," she said.

"No."

"You couldn't have come at a worse time. I found it. I found the
dragon in my dreams of Becoming. I'm going to kill it . . ." She
trailed off.

Bluebell shook her head. "You can't kill anything. Look at you."

"It will come for me," Ash said, crying, shaking her head. "And if
you're with me, you will die."

"No. If I'm with you, I'll kill the fucker myself. Ash, you are not
up to this fight. I am. Let me help. Then when it is dead, you return
to us in Blickstow. To your family."

This made Ash cry harder.

"I have you now," Bluebell said, gathering her sister in her arms.
"I am not letting you go."

Ash nodded against her shoulder. "Very well," she said. "I'll
show you where the dragon lives."

As Bluebell lay, half dozing, in the dark edge of woodlands, Ash sat
by the softly popping fire. She had said her farewell to the sea spirit,
who warned her away from dragons. As though she didn't know
how dangerous a dragon could be.

In her fingers, she held the two dragon scales she'd originally
found, the ones that had been sewn into her cloak. They were large,
pearlescent white, and the beast's belly *was* pale. In the cave, those
belly scales had looked faintly pink, but perhaps that was only a

trick of the dim light. She tucked them back into her hem, pulled the stitches tight. If Bluebell killed the dragon, it would be still enough to examine its scales. She would find a match, and she would stop worrying. It had long been held there were no dragons left in Thyrsland; ridiculous to suspect there were two.

They sometimes mate, and when they do, it's for life.

She shook her head to clear it of the thought and was about to lie back down when clouds moved over the moon, and she heard movement in the leaf-fall. Her skin prickled in alert. Bluebell must have sensed her body stiffen, for her eyes flickered open and she said, "Ash, what is it?"

"I heard . . ." There it was again.

Bluebell sat, reaching for her sword. At the same moment, a ghostly horse emerged from the shadows and came to stand in front of them, head bowed.

"Not you," Bluebell shouted at it. "Go away! I'm not dying anymore."

Ash rose and approached the horse. "You've seen this apparition before?"

"It followed me from the well where I was poisoned."

Ash considered the horse. It took a few steps forward and pressed itself against her side, whickering softly. "I think it likes me."

"It's dead."

Ash rubbed its ears and grasped its reins.

"How can you touch it?" Bluebell said, leaping to her feet. She tentatively stretched out a hand to the horse. "My fingers go straight through it."

"Perhaps because it is a thing of the shadows. Like me." Ash ran her hand along the horse's flank. It was cold, not quite solid, but her fingers did not grasp the air the way Bluebell's did. She reached for the reins, and the horse stood still as she tentatively mounted. The beast moved under her strangely: fluid, finding its balance as a boat might.

"This is madness," Bluebell harrumphed, returning to the fireside. "I wish you would not."

Ash dismounted, patted the horse's moon-cold rump. "I am not the woman I once was," she said to Bluebell. "Such a creature is not the strangest thing I have seen."

Bluebell's eyes softened.

Ash sat with her, put an arm around her sinewy shoulders. "I'm going to keep him."

CHAPTER 22

"None of this is familiar," Skalmir said, and Rose had heard him say it dozens of times already in the last three days, so she had stopped responding. She recognized it as his way of reconciling his bafflement, their strange dislocation from one place to another, from certainty to incomprehensibility. *None of this is familiar.* Not the forest or the feelings. They wandered in a fugue of enchantment, not knowing who or what had enchanted their way and why.

They suspected Rathcruick, of course, which was why they were still moving, hoping to find him and his encampment, and thus Rowan as well. Skalmir wouldn't admit any other possibility, though Rose supposed that he, like her, feared wandering endlessly and never returning to the Howling Wood, to the real Thyrsland and safety.

Rose followed Skalmir down a rocky gully, balancing by staying low to the ground, steadying herself with her hands when she needed to. Skalmir was much lighter and fleeter of foot, quiet too. At the bottom, the leaf-fall was ankle-deep. She waded through it behind Skalmir, following the line of the gully toward densely growing hazel trees.

"There's lots of hazel in the west side of the forest," Skalmir said, always hopeful.

"We aren't in the Howling Wood anymore," she said, and she knew she sounded dour and sharp, but couldn't help herself.

He shrugged his big shoulders. "If I can just get a fix on where we are . . ."

"We are nowhere!" she said, a wave of panic rising. "And perhaps we will wander here for all our lives and die here." *Please, Great Mother, let me die first.* She didn't want to be old, wandering a forest alone.

Truly alone. Even the warm shape that usually curled against her at night, the one she imagined must be Rowan, did not come. She was colder and more alone for it, no matter how close by Skalmir always was.

"Did you want to return to the barrow, then?" he asked, as though he hadn't heard her lose her composure, his back still turned to her.

She shook her head, realized he couldn't see her, and said, "No." They'd agreed after the first day and a half there was no use waiting there. Hundreds of times they had gone inside the barrow and waited to be transported back. Eyes open. Eyes closed. Standing. Sitting. Touching hands. At sunrise. At sunset. At moonrise. Every time they emerged, they found themselves in the same place. Rose herself had suggested they move, and Skalmir had carefully marked waypoints back to the barrow with patterns of small, stacked stones.

"Then we move forward," he said, and she followed him into the cover of the trees. The sunlight disappeared, the temperature dropped. They crossed a stream and stopped to fill up their water-skins and rest awhile. The wind moved in the branches. Rose sat with her legs stretched out in front of her. She was numb and tired, and struggling to keep up with her companion's long, athletic stride. She felt defeated and hopeless. For once in her life, she had taken bold action, leaving behind the safety of her home with Eldra to find and rescue her daughter. Now she was the one who needed finding, rescuing.

Skalmir stood and hitched his pack back on. "Time to keep moving," he said.

Rose groaned. "I am a woman, and nearly a foot shorter than you. I need to rest a little longer."

He nodded, and his expression was sympathetic, more patient with her complaining than she was with herself.

"I'm sorry," she said, getting to her feet. "You're right, we need to keep moving."

He strode over to her, gently laid a hand on each shoulder. "No. You sit and rest. I will go a little way farther and leave some way-points. I am slowly building a map of this place in my mind. I know where you are, and I will return for you."

She became uncertain, the idea of him disappearing and her being left alone overwhelming her.

He read her expression and smiled. "I will not go far, I promise."

Her aching legs told her to trust him. She sat, wrapped her arms around her knees, and watched the stream flow by, long ribbons of bright-green algae caught in the currents. Skalmir's footsteps were audible farther in among the trees, and he whistled a tune—a folk tune, cheerful and comforting—which she could still hear, sometimes softer, sometimes louder, deeper in the wood. She closed her eyes. The breeze shivered over her. The waves of panic were awful, exhausting. Rose reassured herself that Rowan was here in the wood. She must be. Rose had seen her in the magic eye, sleeping in the shade of huge boughs, all three mornings. Though she hadn't dreamed about her as she usually did.

The whistling abruptly stopped. Rose sat up, listening hard. Rustling leaves. Birds.

"Rose!" Skalmir called, and she climbed to her feet, stood uncertainly.

He burst back through the tree line and beckoned. She grabbed her pack and hurried after him through thick leaf-fall, over rocks and roots. "Just out the other side here," he said, "there's a ring of standing stones."

"Standing stones?"

"Yes. The patterns that the First Folk left, many generations ago.

Like the barrow. Like the dolmen where Rowan's footprints ended. I think Rathcruick's people can use them to move from place to place."

They picked their way between trees, ducking under branches. Rose kicked her toe on a jagged rock and swore under her breath, but then the trees thinned and they stood in a perfectly round clearing—much like the one around the barrow—that contained a perfectly round pattern of ragged, rough-hewn stones half a foot taller than her. The late-afternoon sunlight made their shadows long and thin.

Rose began to move toward them, but Skalmir stopped her, grabbing her hand firmly.

"I don't know how these strange gateways may work," he said, "but I do not want us to become separated."

She nodded, and together they walked into the middle of the stone circle, their feet crunching on leaf litter and twigs blown in by harsh winds. There, they stopped, waited.

Nothing happened.

The skin on Rose's scalp began to prickle.

"Skalmir?" she asked.

"Yes?"

"Can you . . . ?" She looked around, straining her ears.

"What is it?" he asked.

She dropped her voice to a near-whisper. "I feel eyes on me."

Tightening his grip on her hand, he turned, watched behind them awhile, then the other way. "There is nobody here."

"And yet . . . can you not feel it?"

"Let's move into the cover of the woods," he said, pulling her gently out of the stone circle.

The moment they crossed between the big standing stones, the sensation disappeared as quickly as it had come. She said nothing at first, glancing behind her and seeing only stones, dappled in weak sunlight. Relief mixed with embarrassment. When they reached the cover of the trees, she said, "I think I might have imagined it."

"We are safer in the trees," he said. "We can wait here until sunset, then go back among the stones and try everything we can to open the gateway." His eyes went to the sky. "If there is one."

Rose sat on a rock and lifted off her pack. "Perhaps we don't want to go back," she said. "Not yet. Perhaps Rowan is in here with us." She looked around. "Wherever 'here' is."

"Why would Rathcruick bring us to her?"

"We don't know that Rathcruick has enchanted us."

"Who else?"

"Nobody. The forest. Perhaps this is just the way the forest works."

"I have lived in the Howling Wood for—"

"Yes, yes, you have said. But did you ever go into the barrow before?"

He shook his head. "Such places are . . . disquieting. The haunts of First Folk ancestors. Their ghosts." A muscle pulled tight in his jaw, and he reminded her so much of Bluebell in that moment: fearless, unless there was something supernatural afoot.

"So if it is a gateway, as you say," Rose continued, "you have to admit that it's not a gateway you've ever been likely to pass through before."

"Then why couldn't we pass back? There's nobody in this forest but us. No footprints. No signs of life. Where is everyone, if this is their realm?"

"I don't know. I'm not First Folk."

"No, you are much more trustworthy." He nodded. "They say undermagic is derived from the First Folk."

"Then I wish Eldra was here," she said, and she felt it keenly. She had grown used to her aunt's practical warmth and comfort. "If she were here she could probably walk out there and—" Rose's words died on her lips as she turned her gaze back to the stones.

"What is it?" asked Skalmir, reaching for his bow.

She stayed his hand. "Can you not see? The stones? Some of them have changed places."

He shook his head. "Are you certain?"

"The big one, the one that peaks almost to a triangle . . . it was on the other side."

Skalmir locked his eyes on the stones as though trying to make them stay still with the power of his gaze.

"And the one closest to us, the one that's pinched in the middle. It was where the one leaning over is." She rose, moved as close to the circle as she dared.

"How can you be sure, Rose?" Skalmir asked, joining her. "We were only among them for a few moments."

Now she doubted herself. Had her imagination run off the leash again?

She turned around to face him. "Maybe you are right. Sunset. We wait until sunset and try to travel back through the gateway again. That will be our plan."

Rose built the fire and Skalmir climbed a tree and sat in the fork awhile, very still and alert. Sure enough, after twenty minutes or so Rose heard an arrow whiz off, and he jumped out of the tree to collect his game. They spitted the rabbit and took turns holding it over the fire, then ate it with their hands. It tasted intense and wild, like smoke and rain. Rose washed her hands in a puddle gathered in a rock then turned her eyes to the sky.

"It's almost time," she said.

"I have an idea," he replied. "Let's set up camp right in the middle."

Rose remembered the feeling of being watched, and shuddered. "Why?"

"Perhaps we will . . . be transported while we sleep. I keep imagining waking up back where everything is familiar. Could we try?"

"You can. I will stay here."

"We have to stay together," he said. "Rose, we have wandered three days without seeing another soul. We must try something."

Rose opened her mouth to say, *But must it be sleeping among those stones?* The words died on her lips. It was precisely such fearfulness that had made her impatient with herself earlier in the day. Skalmir was right: They had to try something.

"Yes," she said. "Yes. Let's set up there now." Before she lost her nerve. She stood, collecting her pack. "Come."

Careful to stay close, they moved between the stones and dropped their possessions. They sat awhile, arms linked, while sunset came and went and no gateways opened and no unknown woodlands appeared around them. Then they built a fire and laid out their blankets.

Skalmir stopped, looked at her blanket on the other side of the fire from him. "Rose," he said. "We . . . need to be closer. We can't risk being separated."

"Oh. Yes," she said, and stood to drag her bedding across to his. She felt awkward. She knew nothing of him, and to sleep so closely made her feel vulnerable, embarrassed somehow.

He moved her bedding even closer, so it butted up against his. "I'm sorry," he said. "I know this is not comfortable, that our situations should call for different behavior. I can assure you that I have no interest in taking advantage of our proximity and that I love another woman and would not be untrue to her." He said all this in a matter-of-fact tone while pulling the laces out of his shirt and binding their forearms together. He didn't meet her eyes until he had tied them firm. "But the truth is, we cannot afford to lose each other."

She nodded and they lay down side by side on their backs, joined at the arm. Rose was not yet ready to sleep. "Tell me about this woman you love," she said.

He was silent a few moments and then said, "She doesn't love me in return."

"No?"

"It was madness for me to fall in love with her. She is highborn and I am a hunter . . . but perhaps that's not the reason she doesn't love me. I don't know. I would ask her, but she angers easily."

"Are you sure it is wise to be in love with somebody who angers easily?" she asked, keeping her tone light.

"Whenever has love been wise?" he said.

The fire crackled and popped while she lay quietly and thought about his words. She knew better than many how unwise love could be.

"Is she beautiful?" she asked at last.

"Not many would think so," he said with a laugh. "But there is more to a woman than a pretty face." He fell silent again and closed his eyes, and Rose asked him no further questions.

She didn't ordinarily like to sleep on her back, but she had no option. She lay a long time, listening to the fire burn low, the animals moving in the trees. The sensation of being watched had not returned and she eventually drifted off into a light sleep, filled with half dreams and scrambled thoughts. She tried to turn on her side at one point but the bindings held firm and the weight of Skalmir's arm allowed for no movement. Then a deeper sleep came, the dark zone of forgetfulness and blank comfort.

When she woke, it was still dark.

No, not dark. Firelight, as though the fire had sparked back into life. Her eyes struggled to open, the lids gluey, being weighed down by the tide of returning sleep. Shadows moved in the firelight. She wanted to sit up, wake up, but her body felt as immovable as stone; all she could move were her eyes. And she saw them: dancers, around and around they whirled, to music only they could hear. The stones were gone and the strange dancers had taken their place. She tried to say Skalmir's name, but her tongue was frozen in her mouth. Sleep was crushing back down on her, claiming her.

Then she was under again, the stone dancers hazing into dreams about Rowan saying, "All is well, Mother, you are close to me. Please come before I am too much changed." Then a long, dreamless sleep.

Skalmir woke at first light. Rose snored softly beside him. He rolled over as far as he could without waking her to see if it had worked, if the gateway had transported them home. His heart leapt. The stones were gone.

But it took only a few moments to see that the absence of the stones was the only difference. The rim of the woods was identical. He could see that their extinguished cooking fire remained, the bones of the rabbit scattered about it.

"Rose," he said softly.

She woke, eyes moving about fearfully. Then she sat up, wonder and horror on her face. "They're gone."

"But we are still here."

"Rowan is in this forest," she said. "I know it. I don't want to go back to the Howling Wood."

"How do you know it?" he asked, careful to keep any impatience out of his voice.

"Because she came to me in a dream and told me."

Rose hadn't even finished her sentence before he remembered that Rowan had been in his dreams, too. She had said something to him. What was it? Something about how the wood changes those not native to it, but children most quickly.

"She said she was close," Rose said, "and that I should find her before—"

"Before I am too much changed," he finished.

Rose met his eyes, her mouth slightly open in shock.

"Farther into the woods, then," he said, and began to unbind their arms.

"Yes," she said. "Farther into the woods."

Another day in the forest, and another, and then another, and Rose barely kept her despair at bay. She didn't mention it to Skalmir in the evenings when they ate by the fire. Instead, she mined him for stories about Rowan: what they did, what she liked, what she said. Sometimes he answered her readily, other times more guardedly. Rose presumed his reticence had to do with his loyalty to Wengest, who had probably never said a fair word about Rose.

Nor did she mention her worry that they would be lost forever, when they lay down on either side of the fire at night to rest. Instead, the fears bubbled and bounced in her mind, holding sleep at arm's length. She would never find her daughter; she would never see her son again. Eventually, she would drift into fear-dreams until dawn. Tired, she dragged herself to her feet to walk again the next morning.

It was close to midday on the fourth day—midday was the only time of day she could accurately tell, given it was the only time when the sun shone directly down through the thick canopy—when Skalmir stopped walking, and said, "No."

Rose caught up with him. "No? What do you mean?"

He pointed at the ground, and she saw one of the little piles of balanced stones he used as markers. It took a moment for her to catch on.

"We have already been here?" she asked.

"So the marker would say . . . but I have been taking us directly west. Following the sun. It can't be."

She crouched, touched the stone on the top of the pile. It tumbled to the ground. "Sorry," she said.

He was crouching, too. "This is certainly my marker," he said. "I remember this heart-shaped stone. Do you see?" He held up the stone for her to witness.

"Yes," she said. "So we have come around in a loop?"

"I can't see how it is possible, but the evidence is right here." He sat back, knees spread, and put his face in his hands.

It was the first time Rose had seen him adopt any posture of despair, and it unloosed all the nerves in her stomach. If Skalmir was losing hope, then she had nothing stable left to hold on to. She stayed still, waiting for him to raise his head.

Finally, he did. "Rose, we are not in the world we know. I believe the forest is losing us on purpose."

"A forest cannot have 'purpose,'" she said, but even as she said it, she knew he was right; they were not in a world where the usual rules applied. Their experience with the standing stones had proven that. "Are we doomed to wander, then?"

He shook his head. "I still believe Rowan is in here somewhere, with Rathcruick and his tribe. I saw her footprints at the dolmen near the lake where I lost her; I saw them again in the barrow that lost us. The First Folk can transport themselves, and we took the same route . . . though whether they know we are here or not remains a mystery. But more important, Rathcruick and Dardru said they had always lived in the Howling Wood but I had never seen them. That's because there are two Howling Woods, one laid over the top of the other. The real one, the one we know." He looked around, his face drawn and weary. "And this . . . haunted one."

Rose lay down on her back, forearm over her eyes. She tried to breathe away her panic.

"But if this Howling Wood has rules, if it has routes and landmarks, we will eventually learn them," Skalmir said. "So I do not believe we are doomed to wander forever, and I do believe that we will find Rowan."

"How?"

"She spoke of a singing tree. We must just keep listening for it."

"What if we just keep going around in the same loop?"

"We crossed a stream about a mile back. I propose we follow it. Streams don't run in circles."

Rose was about to say, *What if streams running in circles is one of the rules of this place?*, but she didn't. If it were the case, they would find out. For now, she had to hold on to small hope. She climbed to her feet, and they headed back the way they came and found the stream readily enough. By then, they were both hungry so Skalmir went to shoot a bird or a rabbit while Rose started a fire.

The glade was dark, overshadowed by towering oaks and sycamore. The stream bubbled by. She had her back to it as she knelt on the leaf-fall, making a circle of stones and filling it with twigs.

She sensed the movement behind her before she heard or saw anything. A prickle of cold up her spine. Then the soft footfalls. Heart pounding, Rose stood and turned slowly.

By the stream, a woman crouched. She was elderly, her black hair streaked with iron. She didn't seem to have seen Rose, which was impossible as they were only a few yards from each other.

"Hello?" Rose said.

The woman had an armful of clothes and, as Rose watched, she began to wash them in the stream.

"Hello?" Rose said again, louder, still too frightened to approach the woman. Who was to say whether she might grow claws or turn into stone in an eyeblink? "Do you know where we are?" she asked. "Can you help me find my way out of here?"

"There's so much blood," the woman muttered, scrubbing and scrubbing a handful of cloth on one of the rocks. "I'll never get it out."

Rose wasn't sure if the woman was talking to her or to herself. She ventured a few steps closer. "Are these your clothes? Are you hurt?"

"Clothes of the soon-dead," she replied.

Rose's blood turned thin and cold. She dared not look at the clothes and see one of her own dresses, or a small frock the size of Rowan, or Linden's little pants. She covered her eyes, peeked through her fingers at the woman.

"Where am I?" she asked the woman. "Please, you must help me."

The washerwoman slapped the garment against the rock, dunked it, and wrung it out. "That will have to do," she said, and as she spread it over a rock to dry, Rose saw with relief that it was a man's shirt, not a child's. Not her own. Was it Heath's? Skalmir's?

Bolder, she lowered her hands, moved to stand closer to the stream, still out of reach if the woman suddenly lunged. Now she was washing a robe threaded through with gold and crimson, and with a cold sensation in her heart, Rose recognized it immediately.

It was her father's.

"Is that Athelrick's?" she asked, a catch in her voice.

"The soon-dead," the woman said.

"How do you know? How will he die?"

"So much blood on it."

"Stop. Stop and talk to me. Who are you? Where are we?"

"Rose?"

Rose turned as Skalmir emerged from the trees with two pheasants in his hand.

"Who are you talking to?" he asked.

She looked back and the washerwoman was gone, as were the wet clothes.

Skalmir came to stand beside her. "Did you see something?"

"There was a woman here . . . she said she was washing the clothes of the soon-dead. My father's clothes."

They stood together a few moments, both tensed, as if waiting for the woman to return.

"I don't suppose she told you where we are?" he asked.

"She wouldn't say," Rose replied. "I'm afraid for my father now."

"I wouldn't trust anything a ghost said," he said with a reassuring smile. "Put it out of your mind."

But the thought stayed in there, along with all the other shadows.

chapter 23

It was a sunny, blustery afternoon when Ivy took the boys out into the garden for fresh air and space. Hilla had been unwell, and so they had been climbing over Ivy all day, demanding she play with them and tell them stories, and Ivy was weary to her marrow. At least outside, with the yellow light and the salty air, she didn't feel so oppressed.

Ivy sat on the garden bench and watched as the boys spun themselves in dizzy circles, jumped on each other's afternoon shadows, chased ladybugs, and wheeled around pretending to be seagulls. She turned her face to the breeze and closed her eyes. Being a mother after so many days engaged in politics—oh, how clueless she was about everything: where Gunther earned his money; how it flowed to services in the city; how many people had loathed him for his taxes—felt at once terribly easy and terribly hard. Easy, because all she had to do was love the boys and occasionally tell them off for suffocating her with their endless demands and sticky fingers; but terribly hard because it was so unimportant in the grand scheme of things. Whether or not she wiped Edmund's face made no difference to whether kingdoms rose and fell.

A shadow fell over her and she presumed it was one of the boys, was about to say, *What now?*, when she opened her eyes and saw

Elgith standing in front of her. The woman's threadbare brown cloak was drawn up over her head, throwing her face into shadow.

Ivy narrowed her eyes in a way that she hoped looked menacing. "What do you want?"

"To talk."

"Who let you through the gates? I left strict orders about who can come and go from the family compound."

"Everybody knows me, Ivy. I have worked for Gunther since I was a young woman."

"If you want to talk, you apply for an appointment through my captain like everyone else does," Ivy said. "You may go now."

But Elgith didn't go. She sat down, and Ivy was at once both outraged and terrified by her boldness.

"What do you mean by this?"

"I cannot stand by and say nothing. Gunther would approve of nothing you've done."

"Like what? Closing the chapels? He was the most reluctant trimartyr ever converted! Saving the city for his boys rather than portioning it off to his jealous and ungrateful relatives? I think not."

"He would have had his cousin take over until Eadric was of an age to become duke of Seacaster. It cannot have escaped your notice that you are running the city into the ground."

"I am not!"

"Protests every day? Ships unable to dock or leave? Looters in the poor parts of the city?"

"If Gunther wanted his cousin to take charge after his death, he should have told *me* rather than his *lover*," Ivy snarled.

"Perhaps he told me so that I would pass it on. Perhaps he didn't trust you to do so."

"And have you passed it on?"

"I will."

Ivy stared at her.

"Unless . . ."

"Ah, so this is blackmail?"

"If it were blackmail I would ask for riches," Elgith said. "I simply want my old station returned to me. To be housekeeper again, here at the duke's residence."

Ivy was immediately suspicious. "Why would you want that? To spy on me? To turn my staff or my boys against me? For petty revenge?"

Elgith's eyes darted away, and Ivy knew she had hit upon the truth.

"Oh, you can't bear it, can you? That he loved you but wouldn't marry you? Elgith, you were too lowborn for him to marry. He married me because my father is Athelrick of Almissia. Who was your father? A pig farmer? A peat cutter? Did he come home covered in mud and shit every day?" Ivy could tell from Elgith's expression that again she had landed very close to the mark. "No, you cannot have your position back. I want you nowhere near me. Go to his cousin, for all I care. I have an army on my side, you understand. Men who are willing to fight and die for me. That is what it means to be the daughter of a king, the wife of a duke. But you, you are no one. The day you can raise an army, then you might be able to threaten me." Ivy's heart was beating hard after this tirade, but it felt good to have said it. She noticed the boys had stopped playing and were hanging back near the garden beds, watching her curiously.

"Come along, boys," Ivy said, standing and motioning to them. "We are going inside. The weather has turned unpleasant out here."

And in the seconds before they arrived under her wings, Elgith stood and leaned close, and said directly into Ivy's ear, "I know what you did to Gunther, and when I have proof you will lose it all."

Ivy's heart froze over. Elgith strode off, her cloak flapping behind her in the wind, the hood blowing back to reveal her gray hair. She didn't look frightening, she looked aged and uncertain and Ivy tried to comfort herself with that image of her. Just a silly old woman nobody would listen to.

I know what you did to Gunther.

Did she? No, perhaps she suspected, but if she'd known she would have told Gunther while he was still alive, surely? Or did she try to tell him and he dismissed her, so deceived was he by Ivy's feigned adoration?

When I have proof you will lose it all.

But there was no proof. All of the soup bowls were cleaned. Gunther's body was deep in the ground.

Dritta still lived, though. The wise old herbalist who sold Ivy all her potions. Perhaps Ivy would have to pay her a visit and buy some silence, too.

Ivy paced the hall tower, her hip bumping the corner of the large table every time she passed it. She would have a bruise there next time she undressed. The lamps were lit but the room still felt small and dark, the stone flags cold under her feet. The wind had whipped up strongly and was howling over the roof and rattling the shutter on the single window that looked down to the harbor. Ivy felt she had been waiting for hours. As the shadows of the evening grew longer, so did Ivy's fears.

Finally, she heard footsteps on the stairs and the door opened. Crispin was there.

"My lady," he said. "You sent for me?"

"What took so long?" she asked, going to him, grasping his hand.

"I came straight here," he said, with a slight note of irritation in his voice that made her flinch.

"I'm sorry," she said. "I'm just . . ."

"What is wrong, my love?" he said, pulling out a seat and helping her into it. He crouched before her. "You are pale and shaking."

"Elgith threatened me," Ivy said.

"Who is Elgith?"

"Gunther's old housekeeper. Also his lover."

"Ivy, take a deep breath. She's seventy. How could she hurt you?"

Ivy couldn't tell him the truth about what she had done to Gunther; couldn't bear for his opinion of her to be brought so low. "She says she will go to Gunther's cousin and tell him that Gunther had wanted him to take over Seacaster. She says she will tell any lie necessary, including that I am fucking the captain of the guard, that the children aren't even Gunther's." She managed to work herself up to a hysterical pitch with these wild imaginings—anything to make Crispin feel the urgent press upon his heart that she felt upon hers.

"Shh, shh," he said softly, soothingly, stroking her hand. "Look me in the eye . . ." She did so. "Good, now calm down. You've let your silly imagination run away with you."

But he didn't know how bad it really was, so she said, "I'm still afraid."

"Of course you are. Of course you are, my love." He ran his hand over his neatly trimmed beard. "I will take care of this. All of it."

"You will? How?"

"You go back to your bed. Go and be with your boys. Not a word of Elgith's will leave the city. And no foul rumors about our relationship will take us down. I promise you. Silence will follow my actions."

But Ivy wouldn't settle. She shot out of her chair and paced again. "She hates me. She hates me and she won't stop trying to take her revenge on me for marrying the man she loved."

"She will stop."

"How? How will you make her stop?"

He fell silent and she turned. He was very still, gazing at her, dark curls catching the lamplight. She knew then what he intended.

"I will make her stop," he said at length. "I will make it all stop. I will manage all the risks."

But he was waiting. He was waiting for a signal from her, a word of approval, of permission.

Ivy nodded.

Crispin offered her a tight smile, then turned and left. The door banged shut behind him. The wind howled overhead and Ivy sat, head in her hands, and tried to stop herself from trembling.

Ivy woke deep in the night, a shock to her heart. She listened hard into the dark, wondering what had woken her. Slowly her pulse returned to normal. Perhaps she had dreamed something dark that had fled the moment she opened her eyes. She wondered where Crispin was, and then wondered whether Elgith was dead by now.

Of course she was. Ivy knew the old woman's death was the thing that had startled her awake. Her own guilty intentions had circled back on her like ravens coming to roost. Elgith was dead; Crispin had made sure of it.

Sleep didn't return.

Ivy went to the stables early the next morning, before the boys were awake and demanding food. Hilla would simply have to be better today. She called out to Durwin, but he was nowhere to be seen. She checked the little room off the stable where he slept, but his bed was empty. Ivy supposed she would have to saddle her own horse.

She went through the motions, expecting Durwin to turn up, apologizing and bumbling in his friendly way, but he didn't. Ivy mounted the horse and pulled her hood up high. She swept down and away from the duke's compound, then out onto the road around the outskirts of the city, and from there down toward the winding road, five miles along, that took her to the Tanglewood.

She knew the way from here well. Too well. She'd visited Dritta for the first time after she'd had Edmund, for a sea sponge soaked in herbs that she'd popped up her woobly to prevent another pregnancy. Unfortunately, the damned thing had made her itch so much that she'd nearly torn herself in half, so back she'd gone to have it fished out, and to be told that surely her husband couldn't find the mark that often with arrows so bent by age.

How wrong Dritta had been. Luckily, the old woman was also an expert at abortion potions, and luckily, too, she had never blinked when Ivy had asked for something to poison the rats in the stable, something mild that wouldn't do more than make a man sick if he were to take a single dose by accident. "More than a single dose, though," Dritta had said, when handing her the little jar with the rat poison in it, "could make a man very sick over time. Especially if he was old."

Truth be told, Ivy wasn't sure what Dritta suspected about her repeat business. She dispensed her herbals and took Ivy's money and never thought to offer advice or ask for favors. Here in the little house in the woods, Dritta was hidden away from the trimartyr nonsense that went on in Seacaster, and Ivy understood that she did a brisk business from city girls in trouble—Ivy included—or who wanted to stay out of it in the first place.

Take the narrow road after the dead oak, then down the gully and over the stream, past the rock that looked like a bear and . . . there it was. The little lime-washed house. Ivy dismounted and tied her horse to a tree and, keeping her hood close about her face, knocked on the door.

Dritta always took forever to open her door, as though she lived on different time measurements from everyone else. Ivy tapped her foot impatiently. She was nervous, jumpy. The morning air in the wood was damp and cool, the inescapable smell of salt on it even this far from the sea.

Finally, the door opened, and Dritta smiled and gestured her in. "My lady Ivy," she said.

"No," Ivy said. "Never again. I am never coming again and you need to forget you ever saw me here today or any other day."

Dritta nodded with a slight smile, her long silver hair being picked up gently by the breeze. "I forget all my ladies the instant they are gone, whether they be duchesses or whores."

"I need you to forget harder than you ever have before. No matter what happens or who comes knocking." Ivy reached under her cloak and brought out the garnet-and-gold brooch that Gunther had nearly been buried with. "This is to buy you a forgetting potion."

Dritta reached for it tentatively, stared at it in wonder.

"Do we have an understanding?" Ivy asked.

"Yes, we do," the old woman said.

"Thank you," Ivy said, and she meant it. "Thank you for every-thing."

"Take care of yourself, little one," Dritta said as Ivy turned to her horse. "Hard roads call for hard feet. Yours may be too soft."

"I will be fine," Ivy muttered, untying her horse. Without a glance back, she galloped toward home.

Down near the docks she saw a commotion, people gathered, and thought nothing more of it until she was riding back through the city. Two men and a crying woman, bent with age, were carrying an empty stretcher to the sea.

"What is it?" Ivy asked. "Is somebody ill?"

"They've found a body in the water this morning, my lady," one of the men said.

Elgith. It must be. But then the man hooked a thumb toward the crying woman. "It was her grandson."

He was barely audible over the old woman's sobs. "My boy!" she cried. "My boy! My Durwin!"

Durwin. The woman was Durwin's grandmother, whom Ivy knew had raised him when his own mother died. She could do nothing but watch as the trio hurried off. Stiff in her saddle, the one that Durwin always cleaned so cursorily, waves of cold crashed over her. Durwin had known about Crispin and Ivy. Now Durwin was dead.

No foul rumors about our relationship will take us down.

She thought about Durwin's face. His sweet smile. His endearing bumbling.

I will make it all stop. I will manage all the risks.

She'd known he would silence Elgith, but what other horrors had Crispin committed in her name? Ivy urged her horse forward and returned to the unmanned stable.

chapter 24

hey stayed by the fire that afternoon. Skalmir was finding it more and more difficult to know how to help
Rose, who was frightened and pale most of the time, jumpy, superstitious. He hadn't seen the ghost of the washerwoman, but the encounter had gotten under Rose's skin. All afternoon, she watched
the place by the stream where she said the washerwoman had hung
out the clothes, gnawing on her fingernails and softly clearing her
throat. Clouds had come over her eyes. Again, he had the uncanny
feeling that he was looking at Rowan, grown, and it sparked his
protective instincts.

They didn't speak, and even when the sky began to grow dim she
sat there still. He was about to suggest they eat something when
there was a loud rustle in the leaves a little farther into the dark
wood, then confident footfalls.

Rose sat up straight. Skalmir tensed, listening.

"A person?" she asked.

"Four-footed," he said, and thought of wolves, though they were
usually softer on their feet, more cautious and canny.

The footfalls grew faster. Skalmir stood and grasped Rose's hand
to pull her to her feet, his blood sounding an alarm. "Run," he said,
just as an enormous black hound burst from cover and leapt toward
them.

They ran, Skalmir dragging Rose by the hand, leaving their camp with their food and their packs and their fire behind. Rose shrieked as the monstrous dog snapped at their heels. Skalmir kept his head up, searching in the early-evening gloom for just the right tree to climb to escape it. They were being driven into thinning woodland. He could see a mass of sky, the corner of the moon, then a huge ash tree came into view in the center of it all. Some of its mighty branches reached nearly all the way to the ground.

"Rose, the tree," he said, redoubling his speed as the dog barked and snarled.

He propelled her ahead of him, and she climbed up onto a low branch and then from there scaled her way up and up, to sit in a fork high above the ground. He followed. The dog easily reached the lower branch and took a bite out of his foot, piercing through his shoe leather. Skalmir pulled his foot free of his shoe and climbed up next to Rose. The dog mauled the shoe, then stretched its huge paws up on the tree and barked and barked, slavered and sniffed, but could not reach them.

Skalmir had never seen anything like it. Even Bluebell's war dog was less than half the size of this thing. Its gigantic black head was like a boulder, and its eyes shone an uncanny red like embers. Rose shivered on the branch next to him, clinging to the trunk with white fingers.

"We are too high up for it," he said soothingly, then pressed a finger against his lips to quiet her. "It will eventually go."

Eventually. After a few more minutes of barking, the dog curled up at the base of the tree, scratched itself for a time, then went to sleep. Skalmir's foot stung where the dog's tooth had ripped a jagged wound in it. Rose tore a strip of material from the hem of her dress and bound it for him.

"I am afraid it will never leave," Rose said.

He opened his mouth to say something reassuring, but the words "Perhaps it never will" came out. He clamped his mouth shut, shook his head as though addled.

"What? Do you really think not?"

"No, I—"

"I don't know if you're cruel and I oughtn't trust you." This time it was Rose's turn to press her hands over her lips. "I'm sorry," she said. "I don't know why I said that."

Realization dawned slowly on Skalmir. "It's a true tree," he said. "The First Folk legends say that the oldest ash in the forest makes people tell the truth." He gazed down at the dog. "The black hound is another First Folk legend."

"And the washerwoman?" Rose asked.

"Perhaps. I don't know them all." Rathcruick's words came back to him: *You see only a sliver of the wood. My people have been here since the time of the giants.* Skalmir and Rose were wandering somewhere ancient and enchanted, a place made of trees and old legends, where the First Folk reigned. He was more certain than ever that Rowan was in here somewhere.

"So we are constrained to tell truth while we are here?" Rose asked.

"I believe so."

"Then perhaps it is best if we don't talk."

Skalmir looked at her, saw the corners of her lips turn up, and chuckled. "Perhaps, if we want to stay friends, we *should* talk. Is it true, then, that you don't trust me?"

She shook her head while saying, "Yes. I am trying to trust you, but I don't know you and you are a man and stronger and taller than me by miles, so I have wariness in my heart."

He took her hand. "Remember, I have kept Rowan safe these four years."

"You lost her. You lost her to the First Folk. I would not have lost her."

"You already did." Again, the strange sensation of words jumping on to his lips without his permission.

Rose's brows drew together sharply. "Stop talking," she said. "We must stop talking."

So they did. They sat in silence a long time while the dog snored beneath them, but now Skalmir's curiosity was roused and so he asked Rose, "Why did Wengest hide Rowan from you?"

The look that crossed her face hurt him, so he held up his finger to her lips and said, "Forget I asked."

But she spoke anyway, her breath warm against his fingertip. "I loved another. Wengest found out. I was simply lucky that he never suspected Rowan wasn't his."

"Is she his?"

Rose shook her head. "Her father is Wengest's nephew, Heath. I loved him in the way only the young can love: foolishly, burningly. I wanted him because I couldn't have him. I risked and lost everything to grasp at imagined happiness." Her eyes were sad. "I expect you'll tell Wengest."

"I won't," Skalmir said. "Nothing could persuade me to."

She looked at him, and a smile came to her eyes. "I believe you," she said. "Because in the true tree, you couldn't lie to me."

He smiled back. "See? It's not so bad up here. I can say to you that I will protect you because of the love I hold for your daughter and your sister." The last words came out completely unbidden, and he drew a sharp breath.

"My sister?" Rose said, eyes narrowed. "Which sister?"

"Bluebell."

"How well do you know Bluebell?"

"I . . ." *Everyone knows Bluebell. Say it. Say everyone knows her and she's not special to you and she never visited Rowan.* "I am in love with her."

"She is your highborn lover?"

Skalmir nodded and waited for Rose's mind to tick over, to realize—

"She's seen Rowan, hasn't she? She's been to visit you and Rowan? She's known all along where my daughter was and she told me nothing!" Her voice grew wilder, infused with repressed sobs. "Four years! Four years I have been apart from my own child and she swore she knew nothing!"

"She thought it for the best."

"She *always* thinks she knows best. She doesn't." Rose looked down at the dog. "Leave us be, you foul creature. We need to get out of this tree before the whole world shatters with the horrors of the truth."

Skalmir put a hand on her sleeve, aware of how soft she felt beneath it. "Don't, Rose. Bluebell knew how much it would hurt you if you knew. She only wanted to be part of Rowan's life."

"So did I," Rose said, then fell to silence.

Skalmir turned away from his guilt and applied his mind to the problem at hand. The woods were silent and still. The dog had fallen asleep; they couldn't stay up this tree forever.

"I'm going back to the camp to get my bow and arrow," he said.

"You won't get past the dog."

"I have a plan. Of sorts."

"Tell me what I can do."

"You need to do nothing but wait up in this tree for me to kill the dog," he said. "You don't seem much use." Again, he wished for the words to return. "I'm sorry," he said, because that was also true.

Rose gave him a hard look. "Good luck," she said. "I don't want to die in the forest alone."

"We understand each other" was all he could say as he eased off his remaining shoe and threw it with all his might deeper into the forest.

The dog woke, lifted its head and sniffed, then got to its feet and padded off toward where the shoe had landed. Skalmir jumped from the tree, jarring his joints and sending pain shooting up through his injured foot. At once, he heard the dog's footfalls stop, turn . . .

Skalmir ran. He was quick, but he was shoeless, and he was not entirely sure which direction to take to return to the camp. The dog gained on him, hot breath on his heels. Leaves plowed up on either side as they ran. Skalmir heard the stream, reoriented himself and redoubled his speed, broke through the trees and skidded to the ground, reaching for his bow and loading it just as the dog landed with a crushing thump on his chest, knocking all the breath out of him.

Then *crack.*

The dog yelped and turned, snarling. There was Rose, launching another rock at the dog's head, clipping it over the ear.

Skalmir nocked an arrow, shot it.

It slid through the air and into the base of the dog's skull, right into its brain.

It froze, shuddered, and fell over on its side.

Skalmir stood and filled the damned thing with arrows: heart, liver, lungs. Making sure it never got back up.

Then he stood back, catching his breath. He glanced up at Rose. "I'm sorry I said you were no use."

She smiled at him. "It wasn't true."

The feeling of nights and days melting and washing into one another was not simply a trick of time and tiredness, Rose realized. The hours actually passed differently here in the Howling Wood. They would lie down to sleep only to find the sun rising an hour later. This distortion of time grew more skewed every day, until Rose was just as baffled by *when* they were as *where* they were.

"It's because we are drawing closer to Rowan," Skalmir said one evening—or was it early morning?—as they gathered fuel for a fire. "I know it. Closer to where Rathcruick hides his tribe."

"I hope you are right. I am tired all the way into my bones."

"Let's hope it stays dark long enough for us to sleep well," he said, dumping an armful of kindling in the circle of stones she had laid out. "Stand back."

He dribbled fire oil on the kindling and lit it up. Rose watched his face from the other side of the fire, waves of heat blurring the detail. He looked weary, too. Whatever had passed between them in the true tree had not put them at odds with each other; quite the opposite, in fact: It was easier to trust now that they knew each other's shadowy thoughts.

"Are you hungry?" she asked.

He shook his head, sat down. "I don't know. I don't know when I ate, when I slept, when I shit. My body is as confused as my brain."

Rose sat down, too, then lay on her side. "Tell me something I don't know about Rowan," she said. She asked him every night, or at least every time they lay down to rest. It saddened her to think that he would likely never run out of stories.

"Hmm . . . what this time?" he said, leaning forward to drop a log on the fire. In the bright firelight, she noticed for the first time a streak of gray in his blond beard.

"What did she dream about?" Rose asked.

He furrowed his brow, thinking. "Just before her fifth birthday," he said, "she developed a fear of the dark. She'd been utterly fearless until then. Nothing scared her; not spiders or storms or strange noises in the night. Then suddenly, she wouldn't sleep without a candle burning. One night, I smelled smoke and she'd managed to roll on the candle in the night and make her blankets smolder. After that, I would have to put her to bed screaming about the dark, screaming about how her body came apart in the night . . . I think that's how she said it. I remember it being a very difficult time and thinking I might have to send her back to Wengest. I was grieving my wife's death and presumed Rowan was, too, in her own way."

Rose's heart squeezed tight, thinking about Rowan's distress. Remote, yet needling under her skin.

"But then one night, she stopped resisting. And that made me guilty, as though I had broken her spirit somehow, and I said to her the next morning that I was sorry it had been so hard on her. Do you know what she said to me?"

Rose shook her head, realized he couldn't see her, and said, "No. What?"

"She said, *I'm all right now because I found Mama.*"

A rush of feeling crashed over her. Her eyes grew damp. Maybe the feeling she had often experienced, of Rowan curled up against her back, hadn't been just her desperate imaginings after all.

"She never displayed any fear of the dark after that. I was never quite sure what she meant. Perhaps she had a dream . . . I don't know. It was enough that the thought of you gave her comfort."

Rose propped herself on her elbow. "I haven't seen her for so long, Snowy. The idea that I might see her soon . . . it doesn't feel real. And all the while, my other child is without me. Missing me. Maybe crying in the dark." No, not Linden, she reminded herself. He would endure and say nothing.

"You have another child?"

"Yes. A boy." She didn't elaborate, didn't name the father. "He's nothing like Rowan, but I love him with my whole heart. And I often think, which of the gods did I upset so greatly that they won't allow me to have both my children with me at once?"

"The gods don't care so much about any of us," Skalmir said. "I lost two children before they were even born. To me, you seem lucky. Yours are, at the very least, alive somewhere in the world."

Rose fell quiet, chastened. After a while, curiosity got the better of her. "Is that how your wife died, too?"

"Yes. The child was due in the winter, but both died in a torrent of blood in the autumn."

"Did Rowan miss your wife?" she asked gingerly.

"Mildrith? Of course. In her way. She has a . . . hardness about her that I attribute to her losing you so young. She loves, of course, but to her mind love is always bidding farewell."

Hardness. Rowan had grown hard. Whatever happened next, whatever reunion and further separation they had to endure, Rowan was already changed by these years apart, by Rose's own actions and the impossibility she had felt about giving up Heath. The thought weighed heavily on her. Love, now, seemed a gentler thing than it had then. Perhaps, in some bright corner of her heart, she'd kept believing that the Rowan who would return to her would be the little chubby-legged, smiling girl she'd last seen four years ago. But too much time and experience had passed; a river of change had washed through both of them. There would be no return, only reparation.

"She has been happy," Skalmir said. "I promise you, she has been happy."

"But always so far from me . . ."

"I'm sorry to make you sad."

"My life is sad." She took a deep breath. "But so is yours."

"If we live long enough, rough winds will eventually blow our way. But at least we are still out here, with the wind on our faces. Many are not. Many know only the still air of a tomb."

She sat up so that she could look at him, and he was smiling lightly, his eyes turned toward the darkening sky. "Bluebell could do a lot worse than marry a man like you," she said, then instantly felt guilty for bringing it up.

"I don't want to marry her," he said. "I wouldn't dream of making a claim like that on her. I just hope that she will keep wanting to come to visit me and be with me, even when I am old."

Rose didn't ask further questions. For some reason it made her desperately uncomfortable to think about Bluebell making love or being in love or talking about love or even thinking about love. Bluebell and love didn't even belong in the same sentence. Besides, Rose was still monstrously angry with her sister for withholding news and information about Rowan for all this time.

Her own thoughts turned to Heath, to memories of the full-bodied man she had loved, and to the half-bodied invalid she had left behind. And she smiled, too, wondering if there might be a future with him that she had been waiting for all this time, without realizing that was why she was waiting. Living with Eldra, not returning home. The irony of Heath raising Linden while Wengest remained Rowan's father was almost too much for her to bear.

"What was that?" Skalmir asked, but without alarm in his voice.

"What was what?" she asked.

He stood and pointed over her head, and she turned to see a handful of small blue lights darting about between the trees. "Fireflies?" she asked.

"Not blue," he said, transfixed. "Is it a chance they are a sending? From Rowan?"

"Or Rathcruick," Rose replied, her voice cautious.

"Rowan is with Rathcruick," he said. "If we find him, we find her."

Rose climbed to her feet and came to stand next to him. There was something hypnotic about the lights. They ducked and wove among one another, and she thought she could hear a faint musical hum.

"Can you hear . . . ?" she said.

"I keep thinking of the singing tree," he said.

Suddenly, the lights gathered together in a blue ball and shot toward them. They stepped apart and the light arrowed through the air and into the woods.

Skalmir bent to tie the rags back on his feet and started after them. "I'm going to follow," he said.

"We oughtn't—"

"Wait here. I'll whistle so you can hear where I am. I won't go far, I promise."

Then he was limping after the blue ball, which disappeared into the gloom of the forest. Skalmir disappeared too, but she could hear his whistling and she waited, not quite ready to sit down again. She turned her eyes toward the sky, could see it was becoming light again. They hadn't slept.

Skalmir's whistling abruptly stopped.

A shot of heat hit Rose's heart. "Snowy?" she called.

Nothing.

"Snowy?" Louder this time, and she could hear the note of panic in her own voice. She warily edged toward the woods, but it was dark still and the fire was bright. Perhaps he'd start whistling again soon. She waited, every fiber in her body tensed to hear the whistling, to know that she wasn't alone in this place.

Nothing. Silence.

chapter 25

The sky was pale and Willow felt the cold all the way to her bones. As always, she embraced discomfort, proof that she was eager to work Maava's will. Long yellow grass, sea air bristling and alive with salt, and gray clouds on the horizon. The sounds of strange seabirds that she had never heard before. Willow had grown up by the sea, but in the southeast, a delicate pretty part of Thyrsland where apples and berries grew wild and the summer air shimmered with the constant movement of butterflies. Not this barren, yellow-and-gray peninsula off the eastern coast of the Ice-heart, where Hakon had left her with supplies, an oilskin tent, and vague directions to a crater lake with sticky clay sides.

"I will return as soon as I can," he had said, and she had been afraid, frantic angel wings beating in her heart. Afraid to be alone in this strange place, where she knew none of the language, nor any of the routes and landmarks to get herself back home.

Wherever home was now.

But as he had sailed off, the unease in her body began to harden into strength and intensity, just the way that her muscles grew harder the more she made them ache during training. So what if he was abandoning her, never to come back? She would survive. She would build a chapel right here in the remote east of Iceheart and she would send for her son and they would do Maava's good work and all good would grow from there. Because only good grew from her faith, she felt that as surely and strongly as rocks felt sure and strong in their seats in the earth.

It had been two days. She hadn't seen another soul, but she could see the smoke of a village across the shallow gray water, and she had watched the tide seep away from the causeway each day, leaving a gleaming muddy path exposed for several hours before closing over it again.

So this morning, she waited for the water to move out of her way, so that she could walk to the village. Willow had money, of course. Before she'd fled with Hakon, she had gathered her savings and a few trinkets to sell if she needed to. She never wore jewelry—her gray clothes were always fastened with plain iron pins, her long mousy hair always in an unadorned plait tied with yarn under a rough scarf—but she had a good collection of it packed. Some were pieces given to her by her uncle, her father, her sisters, back in the times when she knew her family. She had no need for them anymore, not with Maava's angels as her new kin.

Willow waited an hour after the tide had cleared the causeway so the gray, rippled mud wouldn't be too sloppy to walk on. Still, it sucked at her feet as she crossed. Broken shells and fish skeletons crunched under her shoes from time to time, but she kept her eyes up, fixed on the smoke of the village so she didn't wander her way into more remote places. She was exposed on the causeway, and the wind whipped at her cheeks.

Back on dry land, the same spiky yellow grasses pulling at her skirts, Willow made her way along a rutted track, her fingers chilly. Another mile and she could smell the smoke and the sweet steam that told her somebody was brewing mead. After so many days at sea and then alone on the peninsula, with only sour rainwater and dried beef for sustenance, Willow's mouth watered. She hurried her steps, ascended a steep, slippery slope where stones loosed themselves under her feet, then down again toward the village. The long lines of fish drying under a thatched roof told her what the primary work of the villagers was. She made directly for the alehouse, only remembering as she opened the door that she didn't speak the language here. Her focus had been on teaching Hakon her own language, and she'd picked up nothing from him but the occasional frustrated curse.

She let the door close behind her. The inn was tiny, smoky. The smell of fish was strong. A fire burned and Willow approached it, stretching out her hands to it and feeling the ice leave her fingers. Two old men sat at a table in the middle of the room, playing a game with counters on a wooden board. The alehouse wife called out to Willow in the strange Iceheart language. Willow assumed it was a greeting and waved in return.

She picked her way around a great sleeping hound and stood in front of the alehouse wife. "I don't speak your language," she said.

The woman shrugged.

Willow mimed drinking and eating, and this time the woman nodded and held out her hand, pointing to her palm to ask for money. Willow felt under her cloak for her purse and withdrew a handful of coins. Again the woman nodded and Willow said, "Thank you," before finding a place to sit down.

"Southlander," a sly voice said.

Willow looked up. At a table in a dim corner sat a cloaked man. She hadn't seen him when she'd come in because his clothes blended with the dark. Now he'd pushed back his hood and she could see a pale face with a broad, smooth brow and hooked eyebrows. He might be thirty or he might be forty. She glanced at his hands; the knuckles were knotty. Forty then.

"Good morning to you," she said to him.

"Why are you in Dewthorp?" he asked, with the same musical accent as Hakon.

"That is my own business," she replied.

"I have many fine charms for sale."

Now his stained cloak and sly manner made sense. He was a traveling peddler, and he was selling charms. In her own lands, he would be known as an undermagician. Here in Iceheart, they were called randermen. She knew this because Hakon told her a randerman had forged the sword she could feel reassuringly pressed against her hip. And she knew what an undermagician was because her aunt was one, and possibly her sister Ash. Whatever they all called themselves, they were full of evil and an enemy of the one true god. And the ones who were so pathetic that they sold tricks to strangers were the worst.

Frustration boiled over. She was surrounded by devils. "I have no use for heathen magic," she said imperiously. "Leave me be."

He shrugged and turned his gaze back to his mug of ale.

Willow's meal arrived and she ate it in silence, the proximity of the randerman eroding the edges of her satisfaction. How could she happily enjoy her food and drink when Maava's enemies were so close: breathing, hearts beating, unbelieving?

She pushed her plate away and left without a backward glance. She was better off across the water, on the deserted peninsula where there was nothing between her and her god.

Willow returned to the causeway. Long-legged birds were picking over the mud now, catching tiny crustaceans and fat worms that had gone to ground too shallow. Mud splattered her hem, and she felt her profound and unshakable abjectness in the eyes of Maava. She was just a worm in the mud, in a land determined to shun the trimartyr faith. She cried as she walked, huge heaving sobs, and shouted at the sky, "I'm sorry! I am sorry, Maava, that I am so low! How dare I even take your name on my tongue, Maava, Lord of all kingdoms, on earth and in the Sunlands?" She stopped, wiped her nose on her sleeve, then lay down on her back in the mud and looked at the sky.

I will show you, I will show you, she said in her head. *I shall raise your name high above these heathen dogs. I pray to you, Maava, and all your angels, that you return Hakon to me only if he is able to be converted to our faith. I would rather be here alone, among the mud and the mute animals, than surround myself yet longer with heathens. Send him back to me only if it means we can take the Iceheart and dedicate it to magnifying the name of Maava.*

And angels began to sing to her in clanging, overlapping voices that buzzed against the inside of her skull. The sound obliterated everything but her prayer, as she repeated it: *I will show you, I will show you.*

She must have entered some kind of trance, because when she became aware of her surroundings again, seawater was lapping around her face and lifting her hair. She stood, saw that the tide was returning, and waded across, ankle-deep, to her little tent.

Willow's body was racked by shivers, from the cold and from the trance. She made a fire and stripped off her muddy clothes, then sat naked close to the flames. Her skin turned pink. The triangle on the chain around her neck grew hot. She unclasped it and dug it hard into her inner thigh, harder until she felt the skin give, puncture. A bubble of blood squeezed out. She smeared it with her thumb, drew a triangle, and stared at it a long time.

When she finally looked up, the shadows had grown long and her fingers and toes were icy. She dressed and combed the mud out of her hair, then washed her muddy clothes and strung up a line of rope to hang them on. Just as she was tying the rope, she glanced out and saw ships in the distance. She counted them with her eyes. Seven ships. And among them she recognized the small vessel that she and Hakon had taken from Seacaster, from her chapel-burning sister.

Willow could tell from the sails and the prows carved like dragons that these were raider ships, and she had grown up with a healthy fear of raiders. Hakon's presence among them didn't reassure her, so she went inside the tent and tied the entrance together. She held her triangle between her fingers to wait. But he had returned, and that meant that she and the angels—no, she and Maava Himself—had an agreement. She would now do everything in her power to convert Hakon. Though she hadn't reckoned on him being surrounded by hundreds of raiders . . .

She heard them. She heard the ships sliding onto the gravel and mud, she heard them calling to one another in their strange language, she heard Hakon's voice above them all.

Finally, he came, calling her. "Willow! Willow!"

Hands shaking, she unpicked the knots on the tent. He put his hand out to help her to her feet, and she emerged into late-afternoon sunshine and wild sea wind to see 350 ragged, hairy men setting up an encampment.

"I told you I'd return," Hakon said, a merry glint in his eye. "And look: I brought us some company."

Willow's tent became her refuge from the noise and commotion of the raider encampment. These men had been followers of Hakon for many years, traveling from place to place—islands and remote peninsulas like this—always believing that he should be the true king of the Iceheart. The current king, Gisli, was Hakon's twin, and Hakon's followers despised him for what they saw as his betrayals and for his caution about raiding in the south. If Hakon was to be believed, there were plenty more back home in Marvik who would follow him if he had the chance to take the throne again. Hakon explained that when he had come to find her, he'd sent his followers off in small bands to raid where they could cause the most chaos with the least risk of capture or engagement. "All of Thyrsland quivers before us," he said with a horrible grin.

Willow listened to their musical chatter as she traveled to the lake to fetch water for her porridge, and wondered what they were saying. Perhaps they were talking about how all the riches of the south could be theirs. The ports and the mines and the farming soil that wasn't mixed with ice. Willow had never thought about her homeland as a lucky place, but to these folk from the meager, permafrozen north, it had been a place to envy for generations.

That afternoon, Hakon took her out past the encampment, which was growing by the hour, to train on the causeway mud.

"You won't always have trimmed grass beneath your feet," he said, crunching his linden shield against a blow from her sword. "You might be slipping on the guts of your fallen companions."

She shut out all but the force of Maava in her body and soul, and let Him guide her movements, swift and strong. She battled with Hakon until her shoulders burned and then went at him harder through the burn. Too hard. Lost her footing. Fell to her knees in the mud, bringing her shield up too late.

Hakon's blade fell to the curve between her shoulder and neck and then stopped.

Willow panted, gazing up at him.

He smiled. "You are almost ready."

"How can you say that? I just died."

"I am one of the mightiest swordsmen in all of Thyrsland." He lifted his sword, twirled it in a flourish, and sheathed it. "And I said 'almost.'"

Willow climbed to her feet. Her heart still thudded. She sheathed *Grithbani* and pressed the shield against her stomach, arms folded over it. "Why did you bring your army to me?"

"Because I am thinking of doing something . . ." He ran out of words, said a word in his own language, then tried again. "Wild? Unexpected?"

"And what is it?"

"Invading Seacaster." He looked at her closely, the wind whipping his long hair across the ragged wound in his cheek.

"Why?"

"Because it would give me control of the port, but mostly because I saw with my own eye it is in disarray." He pointed to his remaining eye. "Your sister can barely hold it. It's ripe for the taking if somebody is bold enough to take it."

Willow thought of the chapels across Seacaster, all hollowed out and burning. The books of Maava scorched and disfigured. Willow felt her destiny rushing upon her. It was *perfect*. It was *right*. Ivy couldn't go unpunished for burning the chapels. "Hakon," she said, her voice trembling with the significance of what she had to ask. "What miracle would prove to you that Maava is real and is in favor of your plan?"

"I don't need Maava's permission," he said with a laugh. "I do as I please."

"Name it," she said. "Name your miracle. I will ensure you get it, if you promise to convert yourself and all of your army."

His smile dropped away and he tilted his head curiously. "You seem very sure of yourself."

"I feel the surge of destiny in my blood." And in her teeth and toenails.

"Whether one god or another," he said thoughtfully. "No man knows."

"I know."

His hand moved to his face, to the hole in his cheek through which she could see his gums, the yellow outline of his back teeth, and she knew—even though he was too embarrassed to say it—that this was the miracle he hoped for. To have his face restored. The lost sight in his missing eye he had learned to compensate for, could cover with a patch readily enough, but this most ugly of wounds still stung him.

"I will make it so," she said softly.

He looked away diffidently. "You are almost ready," he said again. "Keep working."

Willow walked back across the mud to her tent and began to pray.

She prayed all afternoon. She prayed through supper and didn't eat, instead cherishing the pangs of hunger as signs that she was in Maava's good favor. She prayed as the long shadows and low light came, for night did not come this far north in summer.

But as she fell asleep, still praying, the angels kept showing her the same image over and over again.

Can you not see? they said. *Can you not see?*

The peddler in the alehouse, selling his charms.

❖ ❖ ❖

Maava, give me the strength to do what I must in your name.

Willow crept from her own tent. A huddle of raiders sat around the fire, talking in soft voices. She had to walk right past them to get to Hakon.

Light of foot, chin raised high.

They said something to her. Ragnar, Hakon's second-in-command, laughed. She ignored them, kept moving toward Hakon's tent. As she lifted the flap and peered in, she heard more laughter. She knew what they were joking about.

Hakon was asleep on his side, wearing only a pair of trousers. He slept on a bearskin, with a wool blanket kicked off beside him. Willow had two shirts on and was still cold. These raiders had skin like seals.

His head rested on a rolled-up blanket, his wounded cheek pressed against it. She could see a dark patch of drool. In her palm, she could feel the weight of the charm she had bought.

"I knew you'd be back," the peddler had said.

Willow hadn't made conversation with him. She had merely stated what she needed and given him a gold coin. She could not wait to be rid of the charm. It looked just like a shiny stone, unless she peered very close. Then she could see the soft swirling mist inside it. She knelt next to Hakon.

His eye opened. He asked her a question in his own language. She presumed it was something like, "What are you doing here?" She had never come to his tent before.

"I have come to pray," she said quickly, so he didn't think she was offering her body to him.

"I don't want to be prayed over."

"I will be silent."

Hakon rolled onto his other side, pulled up his blanket. Willow began to pray in her head—long rambling prayers to Maava for forgiveness, for help, for reassurance that she was doing the right thing. All for His name. All that He might be the king of Iceheart and then all of Thyrsland after. Of course she was doing the right thing. The angels had sent her to the peddler. They had all but screamed at her to go, and they had rejoiced and sung the whole way across the causeway.

When she was certain Hakon had gone back to sleep, she quickly and silently slid the charm under his pillow. Softly, she muttered the words the peddler had told her: "You are healed." Then she sat down and grasped her knees and kept praying, long into the night.

Willow woke, disoriented. She could hear heavy snoring, and realized she had fallen asleep next to Hakon. She blinked sleep out of her eyes and turned to look at him. The hideous wound was still there. She slid her hand under his pillow. The charm was gone.

Disappointment's sharp edge pressed her heart. She ought to have known that rough magic wouldn't work, not in Maava's name. She had brought her god low by trying the stupid trick. She got to her feet and left silently. The raiders on watch snickered at her again as she walked past, heading to the lake to splash her face and drink some water.

She sat by the lake a long time as the sun rose and the camp woke up. At length, Hakon came, grunted a greeting at her, and then knelt next to the lake's edge to drink.

He froze, his hand halfway to the water, looking at his reflection. He turned his face this way and that, and his body flexed so that she could see the muscles between his ribs bulge.

He turned his face to her, eyes round. And then he smiled, the death's-head grimace that made him so fearsome to all. "I am healed," he said.

Willow scrambled to understand. He was most decidedly *not* healed.

He turned back to his reflection, ran his thumb over the wound, and even though he must have felt the gum and the teeth through the tear, he laughed wildly. "Look at me. My face is whole again!" He leapt to his feet and grabbed her, pulling her against his sweat-stinking body to garble something in his own language.

Now she understood. The charm had made Hakon think he was

healed, even though he was not. But this wouldn't work. Everybody could see with their own eyes that his face was still a mutilated mess. He stood back and dragged her by the hand toward the encampment. What happened next was a blur, and Willow understood none of what was said.

There was shouting, mostly Hakon. He tore the triangle from around Willow's neck and held it up and she heard him say "Maava" several times and turned his cheek for the gathered army to see.

Ragnar fixed Willow with a frosty gaze as Hakon raised her floppy hand with his hard fingers. The men looked at one another, then to Hakon. One by one they started to kneel and, clear as a bird's call, she heard them say Maava's name. It rippled over the crowd and Hakon gave her a broad grin and shook her arm again.

Then one young soldier called out, to say that Hakon looked as he ever had, Willow presumed.

Hakon dropped Willow's arm. Handed her back the triangle. He marched directly to the young man and snatched his ax from his hand. With a swift, brutal blow, he buried the ax in the young man's head. Willow heard the crack, saw the splatter, then closed her eyes and prayed and prayed.

When she opened her eyes again, they were all on their knees. Hakon took her fingers once again in his bloody hand and said, "Here is your trimartyr army."

And even though a small, thin voice at the back of her mind told her it couldn't last, it wasn't real, the charm would wear off and Hakon would eventually see sense, she silenced that voice and swelled with pride and godly fervor. Because hundreds of rough men now knelt before her, with Maava's name on their lips.

Hakon came to Willow's tent late that afternoon. She had found a rocky part of the ground to kneel on so that her prayers were more than usually painful, and she dedicated herself heart and mind to her Lord. She felt unaccountably guilty and fearful, despite the morning's triumph. The conclusion proved the method was just. No angels had told her differently. Perhaps she had been hoping for more of a sign from Maava. Perhaps it was just her own innate wisdom telling her that Hakon's army could never truly trust her.

She looked up from her prayers to see Hakon smiling down on her. He sat, crossing his long legs so that his knees seemed to sit up around his ears. "You need to come to training," he said.

"I was praying," she said.

"You can't kill somebody with prayers." He smoothed his hand over his face again, his fingers not noticing that he had pulled down the corner of the tear. It popped back into place with a wet sound that he didn't hear. The charm had him utterly convinced. Her guts clenched, thinking about how evil heathen magic was.

"I need you to use steel," he continued. "You and I have to go north to Marvik. To my brother."

"Marvik? I thought we were returning to Seacaster."

"In good time. Ragnar is taking the ships and will position them so they can be deployed the moment we are returned from Gisli's mountain hall. I haven't told them yet what I intend. I have been thinking over my next steps . . ." He trailed off, then leaned forward suddenly and urgently, grasping her wrist hard. "Could you heal my eye?"

Willow shook her head. "That is between you and Maava now," she said. "If you pray well and do as He would wish, He may reward you." She was about to tell him that now he should cherish his hardships, but stopped herself. Instead she said, "The more souls you bring into His fold, the greater His debt to you."

"I just converted three hundred men," he said impatiently, letting her go.

"All in the Lord's good time," she said, caution tapping at her heart. Her wrist felt bruised. "Why don't you pray with me, Hakon? We could—"

"We go north," he said, "so that you can kill my brother."

"What?" Angel shrieks bloomed in her brain then evaporated, leaving stinging echoes.

"I'll never get near him. But you, a princess of Almissia . . . he probably won't even be armed."

"And I'm to kill him? He'll be surrounded by guardsmen."

"You'll conspire to get him alone. One blow. Willow, you are more than ready to take on an unarmed man. Then I take Iceheart, and you will be my queen, and our first act will be to invade Seacaster." He laughed. "Is it not . . . ?" He said a native word, then looked at her curiously. "What is the word I seek? The height of knowledge?"

"Cunning?"

"Godly knowledge."

"Genius," she said.

"Is it not genius?" he said. "A plain woman, all dressed in pilgrim's gray, lost daughter of Athelrick . . . he'll suspect nothing."

"What did you mean about me being your queen?"

"Why would you say no?"

She merely stared back at him, her head too full of voices shouting at her to answer.

He took her silence for assent. "We leave in the morning. I will let Ragnar know."

"Wait," she said, recovering her senses. "Let me tell him. Let me tell all of them."

"Why?"

"So that they trust me. So that they see I am willing to sacrifice my sister Ivy, willing to risk my own life in battle with Gisli. There will be some who will cling to their heathen ways otherwise."

He shrugged. "If you must. I will translate. Come."

They emerged from the tent together, and soon enough the cohort was assembled. Willow cleared her throat and gathered all of the Lord's strength into her lungs. "My friends," she began.

Hakon translated. There were sidelong glances exchanged.

"My sister, my twin, with whom I shared my mother's womb, has lately taken control of Seacaster and burned all the chapels. This affront against Maava must be avenged. We must take Seacaster back . . ." She let Hakon translate, let the idea sink in. "And when we have, we will have control of one of the richest ports in Thyrsland. We will adorn ourselves in the gold of the Southlanders."

Grudging assent. Her heart hammered. *Forgive me, angels, for appealing to their baseness.*

"Ragnar will take the army thence. Hakon will provide detailed orders. In the meantime, I will go north to test my blade against Gisli himself, to magnify the name of the Lord and to take Iceheart for Hakon, who is rightfully its king."

As Hakon translated this last line, there was a whoop. There was no doubt at all that they loved him and would follow him devotedly. Hakon kept speaking, and turned to take her hand and press it against her lips. A perfunctory clap went around the camp, and she presumed he had just told them they would be married. Very well, she thought. Whatever it took to spread the word of the Lord.

Willow smiled at him, nodded, tried not to see the terrible gash in his cheek. Tried not to think about what a dangerous game she was playing.

chapter 26

After a night of good sleep and a slow start in the morning, Bluebell could readily declare herself fit for duty once more. No trace of the nausea and bloating and brain fog of the last few days remained. And if Torr's vigorous step was an indicator, he, too, was recovered.

Yet in the hard light of noon, looking at Ash was more alarming than the night before. Deep shadows circled her eyes. The apples of her cheeks had become points. But it was the expression in her eyes that Bluebell flinched from the most. Something had died inside her, something young and sunny. Bluebell had seen that expression before: a young soldier she had taken into a skirmish during the building of the stronghold at Harrow's Fell. He had frozen in battle, watched companions die in horrific and unimaginable ways. He was too sensitive for war, and he never recovered. Last time she had seen him, he had been wandering the low streets of Blickstow, cringing at loud laughter and pulling at threads on his clothes.

Bluebell needed to get Ash home, to a soft bed and regular meals. If the only way to do that was to kill a dragon, then by fuck she would kill a dragon.

Ash had kept a camp in a river valley a mile and a half from the sea. Bluebell wanted to leave the ghost horse behind—just looking at the thing made her skin prickle—but Ash needed a mount and wasn't afraid of it. She would tolerate it for now, she decided, and together they set out.

On the journey, Bluebell observed Ash's posture, her actions, her continual glances at the sky. Her desire to escape from this situation was written all over her face. At any moment, Ash expected the creature to come for them. More than once, she cried and told Bluebell to go home, to leave her to her fate, but Bluebell didn't. She wouldn't even let Ash out of her sight on any of their rest stops. Bluebell had to end this quickly. One or two days more, then the weight of worry and guilt would grow too heavy and Ash would disappear again.

They returned to the cold ashes of Ash's fireplace while the sun was beginning its long summer descent. Bluebell dismounted and took Torr to drink, then began to unsaddle him. Ash's mount needed no such luxuries: She climbed down and it headed toward the shadows of the woods.

"Do you not fear it?" Bluebell asked her sister.

"He's a well-tempered horse," Ash replied. "I understand him."

Bluebell remembered what Ash had called herself last night. *A thing of the shadows.* Perhaps now was the time to ask about the story Grimbald had told. "Ash, I stopped at an inn where you and Unweder stayed . . . there had been an incident . . ."

She immediately regretted bringing it up. Ash hunched her shoulders as though to protect herself from a blow. "Not me," she said. "My elementals. I am learning to control them, but sometimes . . . What a horror that night was! I sometimes think, maybe she lived. Burnt, but recovered yet. Maybe."

"Maybe," Bluebell lied, then found the ghost horse with her eyes, standing still and silent at the hem of the wood. "Will you keep him? I don't know a stableboy in all of Thyrsland who will have him near."

"He doesn't need a stable."

"If you keep him, you should give him a name. How about Wraith?"

Ash shook her head. "If we survive, then I will name him."

Bluebell thought Wraith was a really good name. "We will survive," she said. "Let me see that spear."

Ash handed her the spear, and Bluebell inspected it closely. The workmanship was superb.

"The smith said she'd worked on the Widowsmith," Ash said.

"Is that right? Father gave her to me so I never knew who forged her. This spear and my sword are sisters, Ash. Like us. It bodes well."

The pinched look around Ash's mouth told Bluebell she was imagining the worst again.

Bluebell reached out and stroked her ragged hair. "Sister, I came to find you for a reason. Are you ready to hear that reason now, or shall we wait until the dragon is dead?"

"I—tell me. Tell me now."

"A randerman of Hakon's forged a sword to kill me. He said one of my sisters has it. But which one?"

Ash blinked twice. "Bluebell, you know which one."

"No, I need you to reach out with your mind and—"

"Who else would it be but Willow?"

This fact, stated so plainly by Ash, hit Bluebell hard. She realized that as long as the wielder of the sword had remained a mystery, she was able to believe her family all loved and served her. But now Ash said it, Bluebell knew that of course it was Willow. Rose was often angry at her, but had been her closest friend of childhood. Ash shared a special bond with Bluebell. Ivy was too silly and too weak to take up arms. Only Willow, with her head full of Maava's hate, and her height and reach, could be any threat to her.

"But she's a trimartyr . . . she wouldn't touch heathen magic."

"Perhaps she believes it is Maava's magic," Ash said. "All magic looks the same from the outside."

"I need to find her," Bluebell said.

"If she has the sword and intends to use it, I expect she will find you."

Bluebell let that thought settle and sink inside her. The trollblade existed to kill her. Willow intended to use it. And so here she was, faced with having to kill her sister first.

But that was a thought for tomorrow. For after the dragon was dead. "I still have some good sisters," she said. "Sisters worth dying for. Let's do this. Let's kill this dragon."

"Now?"

"Why not now?"

"Should we not . . . wait a night? Until you are recovered?"

"I'm recovered. What's our plan?"

Ash fell mute for a full minute, and Bluebell waited patiently.

"There is only one way to kill this beast. A soft spot between its eyes." Ash drew a triangle on her own face, on her brow and the bridge of her nose. "Unfortunately, the front of its head is where the fire comes out."

"I have my shield."

"It will burn."

Bluebell shrugged. "Not quickly."

Ash continued. "It lives in a cave on a rocky island just off the coast. But it will come to us—it will come for me. It hates me because I tried to drown it. So we can choose a place to stand that suits us, out in the open where you can get a clear shot."

"It will come?"

"I believe so. Eventually."

"Then let us go and wait for it."

Ash trembled, and Bluebell grasped her hand. "Let me put my armor on and we will go down to the shore."

Bluebell crouched among her possessions and pulled on her mail byrnie and helm, then lifted her shield. Her sword, as ever, hung by her side, but if the creature was in flight, the spear was the best way to kill it. She thought about Gytha and her famed spear arm, then reminded herself that Gytha owed her fame to Bluebell's training. Heavy with her armor, she strode down to the sea.

Ash flitted around her, begging her not to go in one breath and offering her advice in the next. The cloak she wore rattled softly as she moved. Bluebell told her, over and over, that she had no intention of dying and to please stop worrying. And so it continued all the way through the valley and out of the trees, and down over rocks, and finally to the shore.

The sisters stood side by side. The gray sea was swollen with the high tide. Only a thin strip of sand stood between rocks and water. The waves lapped close.

"That's the island," Ash said, pointing to a humpbacked rock standing out of the water, no more than a mile and a half away.

"And it sees you from there?"

Ash shook her head. "The entrance to its lair is on the other side, facing out to the horizon. It *senses* me."

"Come on, fucker," Bluebell shouted, bashing the handle of the spear on her shield. "We're here!"

Bluebell knew she wasn't the most patient person in the world, but it seemed a long time passed. The sun drew lower, the afternoon breeze came rattling in, the tide began to pull out.

"Nothing's happening," Bluebell said at length.

"It will come for me."

"What if you're wrong?"

"It has before. Ever since I tried to drown it."

Bluebell turned to Ash, whose eyes remained fixed on the island. The breeze plucked at her cloak, and it made that soft noise again.

"Ash, why does your cloak make that noise?" Bluebell asked.

"The hem is full of charms."

"What kind of charms?"

"Sea charms, protection charms, found for me by the same little sea spirit that reunited us." Ash's eyes widened as realization came to her. "Protection charms."

"Were you wearing it last time the dragon came looking for you?"

"No. Nor was I wearing it the day it nearly roasted me alive between rocks." Ash began to untie the clasp that held the cloak on.

Bluebell stopped her. "What are you doing?"

"Taking it off."

Bluebell held her by the shoulders. "No," she said. "I have a better idea."

Ash said she could move the water, but the dragon might sense the magic and Bluebell would have her protective cloak. Besides, Bluebell believed anybody with an ax, a knife, and a good brain could build a vessel. They worked on it together, chopping wood and tying ropes as dusk deepened around them. Bluebell relied on the withdrawing tide when Ash finally handed her the cloak. It settled around Bluebell's shoulders, its hem clattering softly. She shivered with the thrill of it. If she had her hearthband, even Thrymm . . . but no, it was she alone who would kill the dragon, and she would wear the glory. She took Ash's spear on her back, her sword against her hip, her knives around ankle and wrist.

"Stay under cover," she said to Ash.

"When it is done, pull me a scale from its belly. I . . . need it."

"Yes, you said." Bluebell wasn't sure why Ash had made this request, but she would comply nonetheless.

"Remember . . . between the eyes, but up a little."

Ash had already drawn her a diagram in the dirt by firelight, and she knew what to do. "I know," she said, pulling her helm on, presuming that if the dragon breathed fire on her head, her brain would cook inside. Still, she couldn't imagine going into battle without it. She lifted her shield over her shoulder, the raft between her arms. "Here I go."

Ash's bony, cold hand shot out and wrapped around her forearm. "Return to me alive, Bluebell. For I cannot live if you have died on my behalf."

"It's my duty to die for my family," Bluebell said, feeling the surge of pride and purpose in her blood. "And I am on fire to fulfill it." When she saw Ash's stricken face in the amber glow, she added, "But I'm not going to die."

Bluebell made her way toward the sloping cliff path, throwing the raft ahead of her onto the sand. It landed with a whump. The sun was an orange ball, just above the horizon. The clouds were dark blue against a pink sky. Bluebell climbed down, then dragged the raft out into the waves, laid her shield upon it, then stretched across it on her stomach and began to paddle.

The waves tried to bring her back to the shore, but she had strong arms and the tide was in her favor. A current caught her, hard, and swept her out over the bar. The next challenge was to steer the vessel. Water spurted up through the rough raft and washed over the side. She was soaked in minutes, but that didn't matter. Aching shoulders, wet clothes—none of it mattered. Her body was alive with the thrill of anticipation. It throbbed in her veins like a drumbeat, filling her with extra strength, extra courage.

The humpbacked rock was coming up fast on her left, and she could see other rocks protruding from the sea, black shapes in the gloom. She put both her arms in the water and tried to steer herself toward them. Waves brought her close, then far, then close again, crashing onto the rocks, grazing her left arm. The raft began to splinter and fall apart under her. Bluebell climbed to her feet, grabbing her shield, and leapt onto a rock, leaving the raft to batter itself to pieces in the swirling water. She stood for a moment, gaining her balance and bearings, and then began to pick her way up and around, from one rock ledge to the next, until she could see the opening of the cave. Faintly, the first stars of evening began to glow in the east, behind her, where she hoped Ash sat safely by the fire. Bluebell took only one glance back, then climbed hand over hand to the cave's mouth.

She heard the dragon before she saw it. It was sleeping, breathing roughly. Ash's wet cloak clung to her, ensuring the dragon didn't know she was here. Bluebell pulled herself up the last few feet, then stood inside the cave, allowing her eyes to adjust to the dark. The cave smelled of blood and fish and brine. The dragon was a curled shadow, iridescent skin shimmering as its ribs expanded and fell with its breath. Bluebell realized she couldn't see its head clearly in the dark, and she needed to be able to see it to know precisely where to plunge the spear.

She inched closer, slowly, so she didn't rattle too much. She rounded the front of its body, still trying to make out the exact location of the parts of its head. A shell crunched loudly as she stepped on it.

And the dragon opened its eyes.

Bluebell lifted the spear, lurched forward.

The dragon's head went up, recoiled. Bluebell's spear pinged uselessly off its hide as the thing kept recoiling, drawing in a huge gulp of breath.

Bluebell knew what was coming next.

She fell to her knees, crouching into a ball behind her shield as the flame came roaring down. The heat was immense. She struggled to breathe. Her hands were stinging from trying to hold the shield. It caught alight; another moment and she would have to drop it.

The fire stopped. The dragon took another breath.

Bluebell dropped her shield and it crumpled to embers at her feet. She leapt forward, grabbed the dragon around the head, and pulled herself onto its back, one arm wrapped around its neck. Its rear leg came up to push at her, the claw raking her mail but connecting hard with her calf. The pain flashed at her heart, but she held firm, withdrawing the Widowsmith and curling forward, finding the spot between the dragon's eyes. A great jet of flame came thundering out of its mouth, illuminating the scene in yellow-bright light and smoking shadows. The dragon threw its head back and Bluebell lost her grip, thudding to the ground with a dizzying jolt. The Widowsmith flew from her hand, landing on the other side of the dragon. Another giant breath. No time to run for the sword. She scrambled backward on her rear and dived behind a tall jutting rock just as another blast of flame rocked the cave. Bluebell could smell her hair singeing as the heat surrounded the rock. She flattened back on the ground. A huge clawed foot appeared over the top of the rock and began to slash at her. She drew her legs up to her chest, mind whirling. She needed her sword, but a dragon stood between her and it. The wound on her leg gushed blood and she pressed Ash's cloak hard against it to stem the flow.

The dragon withdrew. She could hear it turning around, the slither of its scales across the hard ground. Perhaps the cloak was still confusing its sense of where she was. Bluebell got to her knees, rose into a crouch, and peered around the rock.

It was looking in the other direction, head lifted, sniffing for her. The Widowsmith lay on the ground, point half raised where it had landed on a stone.

Bluebell closed her eyes, took a deep breath. Ran for it.

The sound of metal against stone as she picked up her sword; the sound of the dragon whirling. Its tail caught her behind the knees. They nearly went out from under her. She righted herself as it opened its mouth again.

Blindly, she lashed out with the sword and felt it strike the dragon's teeth, then plunge in farther to the creature's mouth. It snapped its head back, swallowing the flame, spitting blood. The claws came up again, and Bluebell felt the air beside her head split savagely as it missed her by less than an inch. She slashed out again, her blade bouncing uselessly off the scales of its leg but finding a soft spot between its toes.

The creature wrong-footed, the bottom of its jaw slamming the ground. Before it raised its head again, Bluebell once again climbed onto its back. This time, she wasn't letting go, locking her free hand on one of the horny protrusions on its brow. The dragon writhed and bucked, and blood and sweat began to loosen her hand. She tightened her grip, inched the sword into position, and pushed.

Nothing happened. Even though she knew she was in precisely the right spot. She pushed the tip of the blade harder, the muscles of her right arm bulging and cramping, her left hand slipping . . .

Then, with an audible twang, the tough hide finally gave. Bluebell plunged the Widowsmith deep, deep inside the dragon's brain. Blood spurted with such force that it stung Bluebell's arm, and the dragon let loose a screech that seemed to gather all the air around it, then release it in deafening waves of fire and sound. Bluebell held firm, hanging over the dragon's head, wrist-deep now in the dragon's skull and bathed in gore, until the fire blinked out and the dragon slumped against the cave floor. Bluebell waited, breathing hard and ragged in the dark. The dragon didn't move.

She withdrew her sword. She could taste blood in her mouth, though she didn't know if it was hers or the dragon's. She slid off its back, and sat, leaning against its body, for a while. Then she remembered Ash's request, for a scale from the palest part of the dragon's belly. She limped the length of its body, squinting in the dark. Here it was so pale it almost glowed. She closed her bloody fingertips around a scale and wrenched, slipped. Tried again. With a pop, it came away. Bluebell tucked it in the side of her boot. The pain in her calf was excruciating and she didn't want to look at it too closely. Outside, the restless sea roared. Bluebell closed her eyes.

Then opened them again. The sound of the sea had grown louder, water withdrawing hard over sand and gravel. She stood, hobbled to the mouth of the cave, and looked down. The water was rolling away from itself, revealing glistening sand in the half-light. Bluebell grabbed the spear and climbed down far enough so she could see back to the shore. A small black figure, holding up one hand that glowed white and bright. Ash. And she'd parted the ocean for her sister.

Ash had heard the screech of the dragon, and nothing could have compelled her to stay in hiding any longer. She'd run down, hope against hope, too big for her heart. A long quiet, in which she'd decided she needed to go out there herself, to see who had lived and who had died.

And then Bluebell was there in the distance, a lanky black shape climbing down from the rocks. Ash began to run, wet sand sucking at her shoes.

"Bluebell!" she cried.

Bluebell was favoring one leg. Ash put on a burst of speed, losing one shoe and stopping to slip off the other, then running heedless over rocks and broken shells. Closer now, she could see that Bluebell was drenched in blood. Alarm tapped at her heart. Her sister stopped and sat down on the wet sand.

Ash finally reached her and crouched, pulling her to her feet. "Here, lean on me."

"My leg," Bluebell managed.

Ash glanced at it. Even in the dim twilight, she could see a huge gash. "I can stitch it."

Bluebell leaned heavily on her. She stank of sweat and burnt skin and blood. But then she muttered the sweetest words Ash had ever heard. "It's dead, Ash. I killed it."

Only the need to continue supporting Bluebell kept Ash from falling to her knees. "Are you sure?" she said in a trembling voice.

Bluebell spread her arms. "This isn't my blood. At least, most of it isn't."

"It's dead," Ash said, and something about saying this aloud made sobs bubble out of her. Now Bluebell was supporting her, even on her wounded leg, lifting Ash into her arms as though she were a child, and striding unevenly toward the shore with dragon blood dripping in her wake.

Steady hands, now. Sharp eyes. Ash sat by the fire and stitched the wound that ran up the back of Bluebell's calf. Bluebell lay on her front, propped up on her elbows, wearing one of Ash's shirts that was far too short for her. Half her bare white arse was visible in the firelight. Ash couldn't understand why Bluebell was hardly wincing as the stitches pierced her skin and pulled the wound together, but then reminded herself that her sister was hard from battle, and courageous of heart. She was not known as Bluebell the Fierce for nothing.

"I have nothing to dress this wound to keep it from growing an infection," Ash said.

"You said yourself that Stanstowe is a day's walk. We'll go there tomorrow and see a physician. I'll need my hands dressed, too, though I've had plenty of salt water already."

"Stanstowe is very crowded, though," Ash said.

"So? The dragon's dead, Ash. And I can't risk an infection in my leg."

Ash inserted another stitch, the last one. Pulled the skin together then knotted the thread and cut it with her knife. She ran her finger along the bumps. "This will leave a big scar," she said.

"I'll add it to the collection," Bluebell replied, flipping over and sitting up, tucking the shirt between her legs and pulling her bony knees toward herself. "What's wrong?"

"Did you bring me back a scale?"

"Yes."

"From the palest part of its belly?"

Bluebell was already reaching for her boots. "I did." She plunged her hand inside one of them, then frowned and slid her hand into the other. She tipped them up and shook them. "Must have lost it," she said.

Ash winced.

"What's wrong?" Bluebell asked again.

Ash's cloak was in a sopping heap on the ground. She grabbed it and picked open the hem, extracted the white scales. "Open your hand," she said to Bluebell.

Bluebell did so and Ash tipped the scales in.

"What are these? What's this about?"

"These are the first scales I found, in a cave and a rock pool north of here. Do you think they came from the dragon you killed?"

"Of course they do. You think there are two dragons? Don't be ridiculous."

"Are you certain, though?" Ash asked, heart thudding hard with hope.

Bluebell handed her the scales. "I'd wager my kingdom on it, sister. White scales on its belly. Just like those."

Ash allowed herself a little exhalation. "When I saw the dragon, in the seeing fire, I thought they were pink. Not white."

"Seeing fires are no match for being there and killing it. Bluebell the Fierce, dragon-killer." She laughed, though Ash knew she was only half joking. Bluebell reveled in her reputation.

"Tomorrow we will go to Stanstowe and have your wounds seen to," Ash said, and the first spark of excitement glimmered in her heart.

"And tell everyone," Bluebell said. "But now I am tired and I will sleep. Good night."

"Good night, sister."

Bluebell turned on her side and within minutes was breathing deep and easy.

Ash sat up awhile longer, fighting the unwelcome thoughts tumbling through her head. She told herself that perhaps she had simply become inured to unwelcome thoughts, and eventually, through time and happy circumstances, they would lift away and disappear. One day. One day she would breathe freely again.

chapter 27

Seacaster was a town split in two by its deep, cold harbor. The dark-green water smelled of salt and old tin, and withdrew every afternoon to reveal gray mud and barnacled rocks. On either side, long wooden piers had been built with storehouses laid out behind them, and merchants' houses and fishing huts alike spread, crooked and narrow, up the sides of the sloping cliffs. Gunther's hall—Ivy's hall—and its satellite buildings sat at the highest point, the hall tower looking down on all from behind the bowerhouses. To get to the docks, Ivy had to exit through the duke's gate, the ruling family's private entrance, and walk down 112 stairs that Gunther's father had ordered carved into the rock fifty years ago. There was only one key to the duke's gate, and Ivy guarded it fiercely. Each steep stair had a curve worn in the center, and she never wanted the boys near these stairs. The barest imagining that one of them might slip and go cracking downward on rock made her skin twitch. She locked the gate carefully and made her way down to the port office, via the stairs and then the back alleys. It seemed whenever she appeared in public now, somebody took the opportunity to criticize her. Usually a trimartyr. Or a wharfman. Or a shop owner. She was due to meet with one of their wealthiest merchants, who had threatened to cease trading through Seacaster because of Ivy's burning of the chapels. Crispin had told her not to worry, that he was hardly going to move his entire business south to Brimheath. Ivy didn't know if that was true; all she knew was that she regretted burning the chapels. It had been a step too far, and the strongly worded messages from Wengest about reinstating them continued to arrive on a daily basis. Bluebell had told her to close the chapels, quickly and quietly, not set them alight.

Too late now.

Crispin was already deep in conversation with the merchant, a tall man with a long black beard and robes dyed red. Crispin's dark curls gleamed in the sun and her heart leapt, as it always did at the sight of him. Ivy struggled to remember the merchant's name—Bertric? Bertstan?—but she was glad she'd dressed for the occasion, in a deep-blue dress over a saffron shirt, gold and silver and amber hanging from her ears, arms, and throat.

As her foot left the stairs and struck the first board outside the port office, she saw a woman sitting among the rope cables on the end of the nearest pier, crying. She hesitated.

"Ah, here is Duchess Ivy now," Crispin said, turning and taking her by the elbow. "My lady, you remember Bertmond."

"Of course," she said, taking his hand and offering him her most appealing smile. "How good to see you."

"I wish I could say the same," he offered grudgingly, dropping her hand.

"I know, I know. You are upset about the chapels. I must assure you that my orders were taken completely out of context. I never ordered them burned, did I, Captain?" She turned here to Crispin, who nodded.

"She speaks the truth, Bertmond. The room was crowded, my men heard the command incorrectly."

"Even now, I am setting aside a small tax on every coin that flows through our port for a chapel-rebuilding scheme."

Bertmond was not convinced. "You are of Almissia. You are no trimartyr. If you were, you would have the decency to hand the ruling of this city to a man."

Ivy steamed but kept her smile applied. Her eyes kept returning to the crying woman, whose back was turned to her, her scarf drawn across her face.

"She's been out there for hours," Bertmond said, catching the direction of Ivy's gaze. "Probably crying because of the poor government here in Seacaster."

"I can assure you, I am not governing poorly," Ivy said, but her patience was wearing thin.

"No? I received two demands for wharf taxes that I had already paid. And today, when I brought my ship in, I was delayed before docking for hours. Your workers are incompetent and crooked. They are taking advantage of your weak rule."

The accusation stung, and she turned uncertain eyes to Crispin.

"No, no," she said. "Many of them are new. That is all."

"I am aware of that. I have heard tell of the families that were banished from the city for protesting the chapel burnings."

"I didn't banish families."

"The wharfmen's families," Crispin pointed out.

Of course they had families. How could she be so foolish? And neighbors and friends. Little wonder that so many dark whispers swirled in her wake whenever she appeared in public.

"If you take your business through Brimheath, you are reliant on the currents of the Wuldor River to move merchandise in and out of Blickstow," Crispin said smoothly, leading the discussion back to business. "We offer a direct route to Folkenham and, via the Giant Road, to both Fifelham and Blickstow."

"Yes," Ivy snapped. "If you trust to river currents more than you trust to the rule of a woman, then feel free to take your business wherever you please."

"I see you are making me choose between money and Maava," Bertmond said.

Then the crying woman turned, pushed her scarf off her face, and Ivy recognized her as Durwin's grandmother. Leaden guilt settled in all her crevices.

"I have to . . ." she began, then didn't finish. Couldn't finish. She walked toward the old woman. Bertmond was calling behind her, using words such as "outrage" and "disgrace," but she paid no heed, striding across the wooden boards and up the pier, dodging crates and barrels and stepping over ropes.

The woman sensed her and turned.

Ivy knelt beside her. "Are you well, my lady?"

The woman turned her eyes back to the sea, reached out a bony hand. "Just there, they found him. Just there."

Ivy took the woman's hand and folded it in her own soft, young fingers. "I knew him," she said.

The woman cried harder, and Ivy folded her against her bosom. "I am sorry," Ivy said, and she felt it the truest statement she had ever made. "I am so very sorry. He was a good man, and too young to die."

"There are worse fates than dying young," the old woman said. "There is growing to old age like me, and having nothing left to love."

"Ivy!" This was Crispin, his tone peremptory. She glanced over her shoulder. Bertmond was striding off; the set of his shoulders told her he remained unappeased. Crispin was beckoning her vigorously, and she felt the first prickle of irritation with him. Who was in charge here, after all?

"I will make sure you are taken care of," Ivy said to Durwin's grandmother. "Durwin was good to me, and I will be good to you." Then she was on her feet, hurrying back to Crispin.

"He left?" she said.

"Obviously."

"He won't take his ships to Brimheath."

"If he doesn't, it will be because of nothing you've done."

Ivy stared him down, and he grasped her—rather roughly, she thought—around the upper arm and propelled her toward the port office and through the door, where he let her go.

"Out!" he barked to the assembled guardsmen. The little dark room was full of misplaced merchandise, stacked untidily and crammed in corners. Bolts of cloth, broken pottery, bags of spices that filled the space with tingling aromas.

Once they were alone, Crispin closed the door and turned to her. "What happened?"

"The woman . . . it was Durwin's grandmother."

"Durwin?"

"The stable hand. The one you had killed the same night you had Elgith killed."

"I know who he is, and I know what I did; but why was his grandmother more important than making nice to Bertmond?"

She glared back at him defiantly, and his whole demeanor changed. He pulled her close, gently, and said, "I am trying to help you."

"You said yourself that Bertmond wouldn't move to Brimheath."

"But we needed to make him feel good about the decision."

"Yes, but—"

He nuzzled against her throat a moment, then said, so close to her ear that his breath tickled her, "Nobody else is going to help you but me, Ivy. They all hate you."

A cold barb to her heart. "Who hates me?"

He stood back, squaring her shoulders and looking her in the eye. "The merchants. The thanes. The trimartyrs. Half your army hates you. I am all that stands in the way of your boys losing everything. Can you not understand this? Can you not simply trust me and my advice?"

"It isn't true. Nobody hates me." The thought made her feel desolate; the desolation made her angry with herself.

"You're losing your nerve. Does a stable hand's death really trouble you? Can you not imagine what would happen were the world to know we are lovers? My authority would be in tatters; you would be the butt of every crude joke. Neither thane nor king would believe anything we had to say." He paused a moment, then said, "I thought you were smart, but here you are foolish. I thought you brave, but here you are weak."

Her pride prickled and rose up and she said, "I am not foolish."

"Crying over old ladies."

"I am *not* weak," she said, flicking him off her. "You killed a simple stable hand and an old woman. I killed the duke."

Crispin's eyebrows shot up and Ivy was at once satisfied and afraid.

"You killed Gunther?"

Ivy nodded, heart thudding but determined to seem cool. "I poisoned him. It took four years." Why was it hard to swallow suddenly?

"Does anyone else know this?"

"Of course not."

"Elgith suspected?"

"I think so."

"Then others would suspect." He glanced away, rubbing one fist against his opposite palm.

"No, not a one. Not Hilla, or any of his thanes, or his own sons. I was very careful."

"Who sold you the poison?"

"An old witch."

"Then she knows," he said, stilling his hands.

Ivy's stomach felt loose. "She's no threat to me. To us."

"Take me to her."

Ivy shook her head.

"I just want to ask how much she knows," he said with a soft smile. "Don't think me a monster, Ivy. I am your Crispin. Your lover. I am a gentle man."

Ivy knew this wasn't true. She knew it. Sunlight had shot through the shutter, making a striped pattern on his cheek. She could see fair light in his dark stubble. She wished it could go back to how it had been: when they spoke of nothing more consequential than kisses.

"I won't take you to her," she said at last. "She wouldn't suspect a thing. I told her it was to poison rats." She smiled, though her lips felt stretched and stiff. "Trust me. I am not weak and I am not foolish, and I don't care if everyone hates me."

He shrugged, grudgingly. Then said, "Did you poison Gunther so we could be together?"

Ivy didn't know how to answer. She didn't know how to say that she had never set out to kill her husband, just to keep him away from her. That it hadn't been a plan so much as an idea that evolved over time. That she had really just done it to see what would happen. If she told him that, he would believe her foolish.

Perhaps she was foolish.

"I'm tired of talking about this," she said.

"As you wish, my lady," Crispin said with a deep bow. "I am sorry I questioned you."

She tried a smile, but he turned and was gone, closing the door behind him. Ivy felt she had let him down, and wondered if he still loved her.

How deep she was in dark waters, now. She would have to warn Dritta, give her money, help her to leave the Tanglewood. She couldn't let the old woman die the way Durwin had.

The sea was wild and thunderous in the distance, and the clouds roiling over the moon when Ivy rose, dressed, and slipped outside with an oil lantern. She made her way down to the gate, where she ordered the guardsmen to open it for her.

One of them, a burly man whose face was grim in the shadows, looked at her suspiciously. But she was the Duchess of Seacaster and he was paid to do as she said, even if it was leaving the city alone at midnight.

Lantern in one hand and clutching her cape around her against the wind with the other, Ivy set off. The path to the Tanglewood was made unfamiliar by shadows and the strange noises of night creatures. Dark wings flapped overhead. She kept her head down, eyes on the path in front of her. Distance and time led to unwelcome thoughts, but she resolutely refused to think them.

When she arrived outside Dritta's cottage, she was surprised to see flickering light behind the shutters. The old witch was awake.

Ivy rapped hard.

A voice from within, alarmed, called, "Who is it?"

"It's Ivy," Ivy said in a harsh whisper.

Dritta took her customary two minutes but finally opened the door. "I don't know anyone named Ivy," she said.

Ivy could see past her into her crowded cottage. Potions bubbled over the fire. "You have to leave," Ivy said. "It's not safe for you here anymore."

"I can't leave," the old woman said, fear creasing her forehead. "What do you mean?"

But before Ivy could answer, footfalls sounded behind her. She whirled around to see Crispin detaching himself from the shadows of the trees.

"Crispin?"

"Stand aside, Ivy."

"No! I—"

Crispin pushed her aside so she overbalanced and had to steady herself against the threshold. He loomed over the old woman, who cowered, not screaming, but making a soft mewling noise. Crispin slammed the door and Ivy withdrew her fingers just in time. She heard the bar drop into place and began to pound on the door.

"Stop! I order you! Stop it, Crispin! Leave her alone!"

On and on she shouted and banged and kicked, then the door gave and she was falling into Crispin's arms. He smelled like blood and smoke.

"Leave it, Ivy," he said, as she tried to get past him.

"Why did you do this?" she cried. "Why?"

"To protect you." He closed the door behind him. The firelight inside still flickered.

"Did you follow me? Am I being watched?"

"The guardsmen at the gate told me you left."

"I am your duchess. I tell you what to do. Not the other way around."

"Shh, shh. You are young. You need me to be strong." He wrestled her into a hug and she felt the rough material of his shirt against her cheek and his heart thudding, and she pressed herself against him, hungry for comfort. Then he released her and the cold, damp wind chilled the tears on her cheeks.

"Don't kill anyone else," she said, and knew she sounded young and petulant.

"There's nobody else to kill. You are safe now."

Ivy didn't feel safe. Crispin had control of an army, but she had lost control of Crispin.

Hakon told Willow it was midnight. Marvik's cold harbor was dark silver and still under a clear, twilit sky. The air seemed white, shivering with pale light and frost. The days didn't end this far north, but the cold still bit as hard as winter. The winds on their journey had been bruisingly unfavorable. What should have been one long day's journey turned into two, with Hakon growing so tired and irritable that he snapped at Willow repeatedly. Willow endured the hardship, thinking of the story that would be told of the high waves and the cold and the rain, to bring the name of Maava to the heathen lands of the north. She tried to encourage Hakon to do the same, but received a tongue-lashing in his native language for her trouble. Willow brushed it off. She had already submitted to the will of her Lord. Raging against the weather was not her style.

In the low light, she caught her first glimpse of Marvik. Since childhood, she had heard tales of the mighty city of the raiders with its mountain hall, but the city in front of her seemed small and ill formed, somehow. Yes, the harbor was like a mirror, just as the stories said, and yes, the entrance to Gisli's hall, carved into the mountain and closed up with a giant, elaborately decorated wooden door, impressed her. But the other houses were a mismatch of little earth bungalows with turf roofs, or strange, round wooden buildings with double-peaked roofs painted in different colors. There weren't the many ships in the harbor or clatter and color of port that she had seen in Seacaster, and the natural world around the city seemed vacant and hostile: tough yellow grasses, rocky promontories, and snow on the mountains behind the city.

The north was a cruel place, and it had bred cruel people. It was Willow's task to make them see their privations as their blessings, giving them good standing in the eyes of the Lord. Somehow this would come to pass, although she wasn't sure how—and between this moment and that moment lay the assassination of King Gisli.

Willow wouldn't think of that. Not yet. Instead, she prayed.

She was still praying, although silently, when Hakon pulled their boat into a tiny jetty at the farthest end of the harbor. His hood was up as he tied their boat and helped her onto the creaking boards, and she did likewise, so that they were two hooded figures, one tall and one less so, skulking into the city at midnight.

"Stay close" was all Hakon said. He had told her of his many allies in Marvik, and she presumed they were heading to meet one of them now. She kept her head down and her steps even, her thoughts focused. Angels sighed and breathed all around her ears and eyes, and her blood sizzled and popped with anticipation.

They moved away from the mountain hall toward the outer ring of the city. Standing among the turf-roofed huts was a tall, bulky wooden building, more like the buildings of the Southlands, but with the strange double-peaked roof. Willow thought it was painted red and blue, although the colors were made inky by the low light. All the shutters were down and no noise came from within. Hakon approached the front door and knocked twice, hard. The sound echoed around them, but Hakon seemed unconcerned.

A few moments later, a voice from the other side. It must have asked who was there, because Hakon said, "The raven has returned," in her own language so she could understand.

The sound of a latch moving and then the door opened, and Willow found herself looking at a portly man of about her father's age, with a well-kept silver beard, thick gray curls, and a crooked grin. "Ah, so he has. And he has brought a little bird with him."

"A rare bird," Hakon said, pushing her in ahead of him then closing the door behind them. "Willow, meet Modolf, who was my father's most trusted adviser, demoted to minister of trade by my double-dealing brother, Gisli. Modolf, she doesn't speak our language."

"No matter, for we speak hers," Modolf said, going from one

lantern to another and lighting them so the room was bathed in amber light. "You must have studied hard, Hakon. I didn't think you had the brain for languages."

"I had a good teacher," he said. "But she's always cold so perhaps you could light a fire?"

"In the middle of summer? She will have to grow a little harder if she is to live here in the north. Is that your plan? Are you to marry? Lucky girl. What is she, some kind of Southlander peasant?"

Willow had been glancing around the room, looking at the vast array of exotic objects: bowls and combs and mirrors and cages with birds in them, tapestries and rich woven blankets shot through with gold thread. Every inch of space was crammed with things. When Modolf mentioned marriage, however, she snapped her head around and gave him her most ferocious stare.

"I am Princess Willow, daughter of Athelrick of Almissia," she said, and instantly regretted her pride. How Maava would be judging her now, aligning herself with heathens just to impress this stranger. Why, she should be happy to be a peasant if she was a good, humble peasant who loved her Lord well.

She was so busy with these thoughts that she didn't hear what was said next, but the two men were laughing together so she presumed it was some joke about marriage and who would rule their roost. She didn't care for such base nonsense so she ignored them imperiously, lips pressed tightly together, until they stopped laughing and Modolf got on with lighting a fire in the hearthpit and invited her to sit.

"I have bread baked fresh this morning," he said, offering her a blanket, which she took and spread across her lap. "Would you eat, my lady?"

She shook her head and Modolf sat across from Hakon, and Hakon pushed back his hood all the way and showed his mutilated cheek to Modolf.

"What do you think?" Hakon said, with a big grin.

"Of . . . ?" Modolf asked.

Willow's heart picked up its rhythm.

"Do you not remember what I looked like when I left? The ax wound in my face, when Bluebell the Fierce nearly took my head off and then sold me to Gisli?"

Modolf peered at Hakon's cheek across the fire, narrowing his eyes.

"All healed," Hakon said.

"It truly is," Modolf agreed. "What a miracle. You must forgive me; it is so long since I have seen you I only remembered you whole and handsome."

"A miracle indeed," Hakon said, and reached for Willow's hand. "Willow did it."

"Maava did it," she corrected him.

"Maava, eh?" Modolf said thoughtfully. "The trimartyr faith is a good way to run a kingdom, my friend."

"Yes. Divine rule. Gisli doesn't have that." He smiled grimly. "*Bluebell* doesn't have that."

"Under Maava, she never will," Modolf agreed.

"Maava is worth more to all of us than political expedience," Willow said hotly.

Modolf turned his face to her. "So you're the full trimartyr, Princess Willow?" he said. "Your father must be in agony." He laughed heartily, and so did Hakon, and nobody pointed out that when Hakon laughed spit flew from the side of his face and hissed into the fire.

"Willow hasn't seen her family for many years," Hakon said. "I've been training her. She has a trollblade, forged to kill Bluebell. I will show you tomorrow what she can do. It's impressive."

"Why are you back, Hakon?"

"It's time. I have Willow, and I have a plan. Are there still allies here for me?"

"I have been sowing the seeds, Hakon. I had to go slowly and silently for a long time after I released you from prison."

"Gisli didn't suspect you, then?"

"No. I had two of your jailers executed for the crime." He grinned, his top lip curling back unappealingly. "Gisli sees me as he always has: He thinks I am old and eccentric and a little incompetent but mostly harmless. Only guilt about my long service to his father keeps me employed at all, I suspect."

They spoke for a little longer in her language, and Willow gleaned from the conversation that Modolf had always been devoted to Hakon, and Hakon had promised him a return to his role as adviser should he become king. But then they lapsed into their own language and Willow lay on her side and began to drift to sleep. She heard Maava's name mentioned a few times, and hoped that it was being said with enthusiasm and love.

At some point, the two of them went outside. She heard the door open and felt the blast of cold air, then it closed again and she was alone. She shivered, imagining her body's vulnerability, so far from home in hostile territory, alone. But then she remembered that she was always held in Maava's grace, and she was safe wherever she was. She didn't need Modolf and Hakon; they needed her.

As she drifted off again, she puzzled over Modolf's acceptance of Hakon's self-deception. Was he too afraid of Hakon to state clearly that his face was the mess it ever was? Or did he see the advantages of allowing Hakon to live inside his own story?

For a little while, remembering Hakon's proud grin, she almost felt sorry for him.

When she woke in the morning, both Hakon and Modolf were asleep on the other side of the fire. She lay there a few moments, considering them in the dim room. The air smelled like ashes and sweat. If Hakon was determined to marry her, he would have to start bathing more regularly.

She pushed aside her blanket and went looking for a private place to relieve herself. Modolf probably had a piss pot in here somewhere, but she didn't want to wake him to get it for her and then use it in front of him. It had been bad enough going over the side of the boat while Hakon, back turned as she requested, shouted at her to hurry up. Something about being urged to pee quickly made everything freeze up.

She was wise enough not to use the door they'd come in last night, and found instead a shoulder-height back door that led to an overgrown garden with chickens scratching around in it. She crouched in a far corner by the henhouse, then took a few eggs and went back inside to stoke the fire and cook.

The sounds and smells of cooking woke her companions, and Modolf rose to cut bread and hold it on a long skewer over the fire so that it was crispy. He also offered Willow a jar of pickled fish, which she politely declined. They ate as though the mismatched company were unremarkable—the duplicitous counselor, the Crow King, the converted trimartyr princess—but Willow was well aware that this was just one more verse in the story that would be told of them by Iceheart trimartyrs for generations to come.

"Come on then, Princess," Modolf said as he wiped his plate clean with his toasted bread and brushed crumbs off his fingers. "Show us this sword of yours, then."

Willow stood, pushed back her cloak, and unsheathed *Grithbani*. The shutters were still closed so the room was dim but for firelight, and the orange glow caught the welding patterns and the strange runes on the blade.

Modolf nodded, smiling. "Very nice. Wait right there." He moved to the corner of the room. There was a clattering sound among his many objects, and then he turned suddenly and lunged at her with a sword of his own.

Shocked and angry, she blocked him and pushed forward. He overbalanced on his back foot and went down on one knee. Willow brought *Grithbani* down swift as lightning and he rolled out of the way, his flailing feet sending his plate and cup clattering to the ground. Willow stepped forward again. Hakon boomed, "Don't kill him," and she stopped, the point of the blade over Modolf's heart. He gazed up at her, one hand, palm out, trembling over his head. When he saw she had stopped, he grabbed the end of her blade and thrust it away from him.

"Away with you," he said. "You've proved your point."

Willow sheathed the sword, her heart returning to its normal rhythm.

"I believe you now, Hakon," he said.

Hakon shrugged and kept eating. "I'm not a liar."

"Sometimes we deceive ourselves," Modolf said, and fixed Willow with a meaningful gaze as he climbed to his feet.

She looked back at him with a flat expression, her mind turned as ever to Maava and His angels, listening for their song.

"You are . . . something," Modolf said quietly, and she wondered if she was meant to hear it at all.

Hakon finished his eggs and put his plate aside, wiping his face on his sleeve. "Willow, today you will meet my brother. Modolf will get you in by telling him you've arrived as a trimartyr pilgrim, estranged daughter of Athelrick, who wants to help him destabilize or even overthrow Almissia."

"He's been favorable toward your family," Modolf explained, "but only because he's afraid of them. He will take the chance to get inside and destroy the current rule in Blickstow, annex it to Iceheart, use it as a place to take the entire west coast of Thyrsland. Bradsey will fall in a day without Almissia to protect it."

"He *needs* you, Willow," Hakon said. "There's growing discontent up here about his reluctance to raid the south. He will see a resurgence in support when he declares war on Almissia."

"He can speak your language, but not well."

"He was never as smart as me."

Willow watched their shadows on the rough wood of the wall, her own shadow dwarfed by them. Doubt stirred inside her. But no. This was the business of earthly men and she served a greater Lord, so she kept her mind and will turned to Maava and let the conversation swirl around her.

"I need to teach you an important phrase," Modolf said, facing her. "Are you ready?"

She fixed her eyes on him and nodded.

He recoiled a little. "You have the strangest eyes," he said.

"What would you have me learn?"

Modolf spoke in his lilting mother tongue, the same phrase three times over.

Willow duly repeated it, then asked, "What does it mean?"

"It means, 'I must speak with you alone, away from the eyes and ears of your guardsmen.'"

Willow repeated the phrase again. Hakon winced at her bad pronunciation, but Modolf declared it would do.

"Once you are alone with him, you kill him," Modolf said.

"Won't he call out for help?"

"The walls in the mountain hall are very thick. I will be waiting on the other side of the door. You knock twice, quickly, and I will open the door and see you out."

"But the guardsmen will know I killed him."

Modolf was already shaking his head. "Let me take care of them. I promise you, when you emerge from the inner rooms of the mountain hall, there will be nobody to witness you." He smiled; perhaps it was meant to look reassuring. "We will raise the alarm, tell them some assassin of Almissia came after you and killed Gisli instead. Would you mind wounding yourself, too?"

"Modolf—" Hakon started.

But Willow nodded. "Of course," she said. "Maava will honor me if I do."

Modolf and Hakon exchanged glances, but Willow didn't care what they thought of her. As long as they intended to help her bring Maava to the Iceheart, they could think what they wanted.

"Will he be armed?" Willow asked.

"I think it unlikely," Modolf said.

Unlikely. Willow turned her eyes to Hakon.

"Strike him while his back is turned," he said. "For Maava." He rose and moved toward her. He gently took the edges of her cloak and pulled them forward so that her sword-belt was hidden, then untied her scarf and removed it so that her long plait swung free. He said something in his own language, then, "May Maava bless your steps and your actions, Willow." He dropped his hands. "I must stay in hiding, but I have every faith in you and in our Lord."

"Is this a glimpse of my future?" Modolf said with a theatrical lift of his hands. "Endless talk about Maava?"

"Just replace the name of the Horse God in every sentence," Hakon advised. "It's simple enough."

Willow held her tongue. There would be a time for debate about how to use Maava's name. She would make them all see. When she was queen, she would bring the angels down upon them all to beat their mighty wings and raise their terrible voices.

For now, she nodded as though entirely compliant. "Very well," she said. "Let us go."

chapter 28

By the third time she told the story of Bluebell's defeat of the dragon, Ash was as drunk as her sister. The crowd in the inn at Stanstowe had grown thicker and the room hotter since they'd arrived in the late afternoon. Ash embraced company and mead in equal measure. Both made her forget her fears. Bluebell bragged for a while, then decided Ash instead should be the teller of her tale. It was a tale that hardly needed embellishing, reported to her by Bluebell on their ride to Stanstowe: the raft that broke on rocks; the shield in ashes; the fire and blood. She played down her own role, still superstitious about her truth and power. But the listeners weren't interested in her in any case, not while Bluebell was among them in the firelit room. They gathered around to gape at Bluebell's singed knuckles, to inspect the deep claw mark in her calf. Some of the old folk said they'd always suspected there was a dragon down there. Tales were told of decades of missing pigs, children who didn't return from collecting chestnuts. Gartrude, the smith, was there, bathing in the reflected glory of her family's contribution to the tale. Bluebell returned the spear to her to keep, so that she might tell the tale again and again. Gartrude was delighted by the idea of being so associated with heroic deeds, and began the cry that they should send a party out to the dragon cave to cut off its head and hang it over the village gate. Bluebell approved vigorously and said that she would accompany them in the morning, but by this stage she was so drunk she could barely slur out the sentence, and the chance that she would remember anything in the morning grew very remote.

One by one, the revelers left to stumble back to their houses. As the inn began to empty, a hunched man so old he creaked approached them. Bluebell smiled at him, eyes not quite focused. "Look at the winters upon your brow," she said to him. "Yet I'd wager you've never heard such a tale as Bluebell the Fierce and the red dragon of Stanstowe."

"That tale?" he said, and Ash noticed the cruel glimmer in his eye that spoke of his resentment of Bluebell. There were many who hated her, but many more who loved her. "I have heard many more tales, of a dragon that circles the western capes of Almissia, and in every story that dragon was not red, but white."

Ash's heart went cold. Bluebell leapt to her feet and bellowed, "Do you dare doubt me?"

The old man shrank back, but he smirked nonetheless, happy to have landed a blow, however small.

"Perhaps I was mistaken," he said, and slipped off.

Bluebell watched him go with hard eyes.

"Bluebell," Ash said, her skin prickling. "The white scales."

"Its belly was white," Bluebell said slowly and forcefully, as though talking to a child. "If it had been seen from below, perhaps it might look white. But you and I, we were close to it. We are daughters of kings." She sat down again. "More mead!"

"It's very late."

"One more!"

Ash went to fetch her a drink. Her fears were all awake now, despite her drunkenness. The impulse to run was strong. But so, too, was the desire to believe Bluebell. Her older sister was always right. Usually right.

When she returned, her sister was nodding off into her chest.

Ash roused her. "Come, sister. Time to sleep."

"I *was* asleep," Bluebell protested blearily. Her hair was lank and hanging half over her face.

"In a bed."

"Where's the bed?"

"Gartrude has a spare room for us." Ash rose and put her hand under Bluebell's elbow, felt the sinew of her sister's mighty arm.

Bluebell stood unsteadily. "I like her."

Gartrude saw them and hurried over, beaming. "My lord, you will be so comfortable at my house."

"Why are you talking so loud?" Bluebell said.

"This way, sister," Ash said, and they followed Gartrude out into the cool night air. Her head spun.

"I will cook you a breakfast fit for a champion," Gartrude was saying. "Eggs and salted pork and porridge. Will that make you happy, my lord?"

"My sister is coming home with me," Bluebell said, grasping Ash around the waist and nearly knocking her over. "I couldn't be happier." She stumbled, fell.

"My, but she's long," Gartrude said, considering Bluebell flat out on the ground.

"Come on, up you get," Ash said, but the thought of home was so overwhelming that she almost fell to her knees.

Between Ash's coaxing and Gartrude's thick muscles, they managed to get Bluebell back on her feet and across the village to the little house behind the smithy. Here, out of the cold, Gartrude showed them to a neat room with a soft mattress for them to share.

"Thank you," Ash said, because Bluebell was already spread out on the mattress with her eyes closed.

"It's an honor," Gartrude said, and closed the door behind her.

"Come on, Bluebell," Ash said. "You can't sleep in your mail."

" 'Course I can."

"At least take your boots off." But Bluebell's eyes were closed. Ash went to the end of the bed and pulled off her sister's left boot, then the right. As she did so, a small ping sounded off the floor. Ash knew immediately it was the scale, freed from its sticking place in Bluebell's boot. She crouched on the floor. The candlelight picked up its iridescent glow.

The scale *was* pink, not white. Nor was it the same shape or size as the white scales in the hem of her cloak. Even though she had suspected it, this new certainty made her moan with weary dread.

"C'mon, Ash," Bluebell slurred. "Sleep time."

Ash lay down next to her sister. Bluebell rolled onto her side and put her heavy arm over Ash, then dropped into sleep, snoring loudly.

Ash listened to her awhile, listened to the wind over the eaves. She would wait an hour, maybe two, until she was sure Bluebell wouldn't wake and stop her. Then she would run, take herself back out into the empty world she never should have left. Mead and exhaustion swept her along. She slowly began to descend toward slumber, thoughts blurring against one another . . .

Fire. Fear. It's coming for you.

Ash startled awake, every nerve in her body alive. The dream again. The dream that had driven her into exile, driven her on the quest to find and destroy the dragon. The dream that seemed to tell her that she would bring death and destruction to those she loved. In that dream, the dragon had been red, not white. But a dragon was a dragon.

And it seemed that her nightmare had not yet ended.

Ash woke, leaden in heart and limb, while the sky was still dark. Cursed herself for sleeping at all. Bluebell slumbered on, a lank strand of fair hair falling diagonally across her face. Ash studied her for a moment, memorizing every scar and line, in case it was the last time she saw her beloved sister.

She pulled on her shoes, but her cloak lay half beneath Bluebell's hard shoulder. Ash tugged it gently. Bluebell stirred. Ash froze.

Then her sister rolled over—farther onto the cloak—and went back to sleep.

Instead, Ash picked up Bluebell's cloak. It didn't have protection charms in the hem, but perhaps she could gather more. She needed something against the winters when they came, however, and she wouldn't be returning to any towns or villages ever again.

Her knees nearly buckled at the thought. The empty roads, the empty years. She opened the door quietly and slipped out.

Forty yards up the road out of town, a soft whinny and relaxed hoofbeats told her Wraith was nearby. She kept walking, head down, and at the head of the road the ghost horse joined her.

Ash grasped his bridle. "You do know what you are getting yourself into with me?" she asked him, climbing onto his back. Again, that strange buoyant feeling. "Dragons and so on. Though I suppose you don't care if you're already dead." The thought made her smile. At last she had a companion who needn't fear what happened.

Wraith whinnied, straining to be away.

"Toward the sea," she said to him, patting his chill flank. "I will see that dragon's corpse with my own eyes." The last shred of hope. Perhaps the cave had been dark. Perhaps Bluebell had missed some white scales.

They moved off, away from the town. Away from anyone she could hurt.

Ash sat on a sun-drenched rock, vertical noon light on her shoulders. In her lap lay eight shining dragon scales. Each of them she had plucked herself from the dead dragon's belly, in the cave that smelled of fish and blood. She had cut her index finger retrieving one of them, and it throbbed softly. All of them were pink.

The sea wind pulled at the hood of Bluebell's cloak, which was too long for her by a mile and pooled around her feet. One by one she tossed the scales out over the rocks, toward the sea, then sat a little longer, contemplating the horizon, that blue arch of the world, and wondering how long it would take to find the other dragon. And if she had a hope at all of killing it.

And why her dreams had shown her a red dragon when the only one still alive was white.

She closed her eyes. The sunlight made her field of vision red. Unweder had plunged himself in a trance to see the location of the dragons, but perhaps Ash, with her strong attunement to elemental forces, could seek the last dragon with her mind.

A breath, and then a release. The unseen world teemed around her. She could feel their presences, like so many warm pockets of steam, layer on layer, retreating infinitely into time and sky, growth and earth, breath and sea.

"Dragon," she murmured, sending her mind's eye out among them.

A prickle ran from the base of her spine up to her skull, then collected on her scalp. A mad itch.

Too late, she clamped her mind closed. Her eyes snapped wide. *Unweder.* She had made herself too receptive and he had sensed her. She had to move, take herself into the woods where she was harder to find. She climbed to her feet and made her way back to Wraith.

The land to either side of the narrow, rutted path was rocky and choked with gorse and bracken. From a high point on the road, she could see a distant dark-green strip of woodland. Clouds moved in as she rode, casting a pattern of shapeless shadows on the ground. Her eye fixed on the woods, she urged Wraith forward. The horse didn't resist, or tire, or need to be fed and watered. They kept going. The woods were a mile away. Half a mile now. Quarter.

A scudding cloud, a breath of hot wind. A fast-moving shadow.

Her blood knew before her brain did.

"Wraith, run!" she cried as the shadow on the ground resolved itself into the shape of two giant wings. She clung to the reins, dared not look behind her. Wraith streaked away across the uneven ground as the shadow grew, covering her, overtaking her. She chanced a look directly up. White. Dazzling white with the sun on its wings, and easily twice the size of the red dragon Bluebell had killed. It began to circle overhead.

But it didn't try to kill her.

Ash pushed Wraith out over the bracken, cutting away from the path and straight toward the woods. The dragon realized what she was trying to do and glided toward the woods, circling and landing.

She yanked the reins. Wraith pulled up, whinnying. Ash's heart jumped in her chest, her mind scrambling for a solution.

Then, from the woods, a familiar figure on a muscular white destrier emerged.

"Bluebell, no!" Ash called, but her voice was snatched away on the wind.

Bluebell charged at the dragon, the Widowsmith held aloft. Her battle cry rang out over the moor.

The dragon spread its wings and took to the sky, spun and blew a huge gout of fire at Bluebell. Ash kicked Wraith and they galloped.

Torr, spooked by the fire, reared and ran toward the trees. The dragon circled and took off, back toward Ash. She was closing on the cover of the woods now, and urged Wraith to put on an extra burst of speed. She was horribly exposed out here; she expected the river of flame any moment.

But it didn't come. She made it to the hem of the wood, then farther in. Bluebell had Torr by the reins, trying to settle him. The wings passed overhead once, twice, slicing through the air with a whoosh. Ash braced herself for fire.

Nothing.

Bluebell grabbed Wraith's reins. "Get off," she commanded. "We'll get farther under cover without the horses. And don't run away from me this time. I've had enough of that."

"Bluebell, I'm sorry I—"

But Bluebell grabbed her arm and they began to run, farther into the wood, where the trees were dense.

Ash heard the wings move off, but Bluebell ignored it, found them cover behind a large rock, and sat.

A minute passed, then another, with only the sound of their ragged breathing and small animals moving in the undergrowth.

Finally, Ash said, "It's gone."

Bluebell nodded, mute.

"It didn't try to kill me, Bluebell. Do you know what that means?"

Bluebell rose lazily and started back to the horses. "That it wants revenge on me? I killed the other."

Ash scrambled to her feet, following her. "No. It's smarter than the other. It anticipated where I would go. It knew who you were. It wants me alive."

Bluebell flipped open the pack over Torr's rump and withdrew Ash's cloak. "Here, you forgot this. Can I have mine back now?"

Ash snatched the cloak. "Bluebell, listen. I think it's Unweder."

"Unweder? How?"

"Very powerful magic. Magic that I . . . may have given him." She thought about all the extra blood he had been taking from her. "I need to know, one way or another. If it's not him, if it's just the beast, then we will kill it and I will be free."

"And if it's Unweder?" Bluebell asked.

Ash shook her head. "If it's Unweder, he'll follow me forever."

When Ash pointed out the little chapel in the distance, on the crest of a rocky outcrop over the sea, Bluebell's blood heated up. Trimartyrs in her father's kingdom? Whichever pious idiot had built this chapel, she was almost glad he had been burned to death by dragon fire before he could spread his message of hate and oppression across Almissia.

Hate and oppression of women, mostly. That had been her observation.

"We should approach cautiously," Ash said, squinting into the afternoon sun. "In case Unweder is still in there."

Bluebell dismounted and drew her sword. "I hope he is," she said, and she didn't say that she was thinking it was long past time when she should have filled his guts with steel. Ash hurried behind her as she stalked toward the chapel. She kicked open the door. A cold, rank smell hit her face. The chapel was empty but for a bloody blanket.

Bluebell picked it up.

"My blood," Ash said. "It looks as though he hasn't returned since last time we . . . met."

Bluebell sheathed her sword, disappointed. "What did you hope to find?"

"Him," Ash said. "Evidence that he hadn't . . . become that thing."

"Where else might he be?"

"Down along the coastline, in the caves."

"Then that is where we will go."

"Can you not return to Blickstow, whole and alive, sister?"

Bluebell fixed Ash in her gaze. "I intend to. With you by my side."

"It would be easier if I just gave myself to him."

"It would be easier if I never went into battle. But I keep going." Bluebell yanked the door shut, and she took a gulp of brisk sea air to clear her nostrils. "Ash, this isn't just about saving you from him, it's about saving Thyrsland from him. If he can take dragon form, what do you think he intends to do with that power? Fly circles for fun?"

Ash blinked twice, as though it had never occurred to her. "He never gave any indication that he was interested in worldly power."

Bluebell made a dismissive noise. "Everybody is. We need to find him and stop him, before he makes an alliance with King Renward or that smug bastard Tolan and they decide to march on Almissia."

"I'm sure he doesn't want—"

"You cannot be sure of anything." Bluebell was already walking toward the cliff, her eyes scanning for a clear path down.

"This way," Ash said, leading her to the north. A path, rocky and steep at first but then sloping more gently, led them down to the sea. The tide was full, revealing only a thin strip of rocky sand.

Bluebell's boots sank into the damp sand. "Where now?" she asked.

"I found the white scale in a cave to the south, but Unweder was searching to the north."

Bluebell nodded. "Let's start with your cave." She turned and jumped with alarm. The sea goblin who had fetched Ash for her had appeared beside her. Bluebell put a hand over her heart.

Ash smiled and knelt on a flat rock before it. "Hello. I thought I might not see you again," she said, all gentle and warm with the ugly thing.

"Stand aside," Bluebell said.

"Be kind," Ash said. "This little fellow helped save your life."

"I don't like goblins," Bluebell muttered.

The goblin climbed up onto the rock next to Ash. "You seek your companion? The man in black?" it asked in its jagged, guttural voice.

"You have seen him?" Ash asked.

"The whole sea saw him," the creature said. "For he charmed a dragon away."

Bluebell could tell from the droop of Ash's shoulders that this was what she feared the most. "Where?" Ash asked. "Where is the living corpse of the dragon? If we hack off its head, Unweder will die."

"He took it far out beneath the sea. Farther than you could dive."

"Will it drown?" Bluebell asked.

"Dragons don't drown."

"Can you kill it for us? I could give you a knife."

Ash shot her a harsh glance.

"The sea is large and we are small," it said, spreading its little barnacled hands. "We are not much good with knives."

Ash climbed to her feet and stepped off into the swirling water, wading out a few yards with her gaze on the horizon.

"Ash?" Bluebell asked.

"Let me think," she called back, her small voice nearly engulfed by the sound of the waves.

Bluebell waited, aware of the goblin standing beside her. Eventually, it said to her in a quiet voice, "She is important, you know."

"I know. She's my sister."

"No. Important. To Thyrsland." The goblin paused a moment, then said, in a tone that was almost nasty, "More important than you."

Bluebell narrowed her eyes. "I don't take counsel from goblins."

"Maybe you should."

Ash turned and waded back toward them. "I can open up the sea," she said. "I can find the dragon where he's hidden it and open up the sea, and go down there and—"

"There's an easier way," Bluebell said. "You say Unweder wants you?"

"Yes."

"Then we draw him out, using you as the bait, and we kill him."

"Bluebell, that dragon is twice the size of the other, and he will be airborne."

"I'm not saying I will do it alone," Bluebell said. "We'll go to Withing and find my hearthband. Nobody has a spear arm like Gytha, and Sighere would spill his last drop of blood by my side. And you, Ash, have your own power. Among us, we will take the creature down."

Ash wavered.

"I will give you more charms," the goblin said. "If you wait only an hour I will bless more charms for you to sew into your cloak." It snapped its wet little fingers, growing excited, its voice rising in pitch. "They will be the strongest charms I have ever blessed: so strong it will mute your own magic while you wear the cloak, so he cannot find you."

Ash swallowed hard, her eyes going to the sea again. Her skin was so pale and thin she looked almost blue. "Yes," she said softly. "Very well. We will try it."

Several days on the road, and Ash and Bluebell had neared God-webb, a small town of wool growers and spinners a day's ride from Withing. Ash could tell that Bluebell felt a strong sense of relief, knowing they were now so close to her hearthband. Ash's apprehension, however, grew daily.

Ash reined in Wraith at the top of a rise, unwilling to go any closer. Bluebell cantered a little farther, then realized she was without her companion and turned Torr around.

"What is it?" she asked.

The village looked happy, welcoming. Wide rolling fields of green dotted with sheep, well-kept roads with high beech hedges, and a two-story alehouse of lime-washed wattle and daub, with large shutters to let the summer light in.

"We can't go down there," Ash said.

"But . . . mead."

"What if Unweder comes?" Ash said, and realized she had said it in a hushed voice, as if he might be nearby and listening.

"You have that." Bluebell indicated Ash's cloak, which she had spent hours every night by firelight sewing charms onto. It now crackled with objects from the sea: shells of all different shapes and sizes, coral and dried seaweed and driftwood, seahorses and starfish hard as rocks. The briny smell had accompanied them inland.

"I don't know how far I can trust it."

Bluebell shrugged. "He hasn't found us yet."

Ash could not expect Bluebell to understand. Every step of the way, she felt Unweder searching for her. She perceived his interest like a faint rubbing sensation in the air around her. She had no doubt he had turned to the strongest undermagic to do so. He needed her. If she took off the cloak, which made her own magic feel as though it were under mud, she could probably tell exactly where he was. But then he would be able to locate her, too.

If the feeling grew stronger before they found help in the form of Bluebell's hearthband, Ash knew she would have to run. Bluebell could not kill the white dragon alone, and Ash could not risk attracting Unweder to a small, happy village. "Please, Bluebell," Ash said.

Bluebell tilted her head slightly, looking at her. Ash could almost see her brain ticking over.

"It's fair weather," Bluebell said eventually. "Let us sleep under the stars."

If Bluebell was irritated about missing out on company and mead, she didn't show it. She got on with tending to Torr while Ash made a fire and cut the bread they had brought with them. The last of the afternoon light was leaving the sky when they sat down to eat by the fire.

"Look cheerful, Ash," Bluebell said through a mouthful of bread. "It will all be done with soon."

"You don't know that."

"I know everything."

Ash glanced up. Bluebell was smiling in amusement, but perhaps she still believed the claim.

"I cannot wait to have you home in Blickstow with some fat on your bones and your lovely hair grown long again, telling tales of your adventures to the cook's children," Bluebell said.

"Please. Do not speak of such things. They fill me with such yearning, and I am not at all certain that they will come to pass."

Bluebell shrugged. "Nobody knows what will come to pass."

Ash thought of her dream, the awful premonition. "It is not lost on me that, in trying to avoid my Becoming, I have brought it rushing toward me."

Bluebell dusted her fingers, swallowed, and said, "You are not your fate. You are your deeds. Your Becoming is only the warp on the loom, the threads that are already in place that you cannot change. Your deeds are the weft. You choose the thread, the shuttle. You make the pattern." She leaned toward the fire, the glow illuminating her scarred face from below. "What happens next is not to be known, but if we die, we die having chosen our deeds, and that is right and good."

Ash's heart stirred at her sister's words. How she longed for them to be true. "I am not as brave as you, Bluebell," she said. "I'm afraid. Not just for myself, but for anyone else who might be drawn into this."

"Stop worrying," Bluebell said, leaning back on her elbows. "Tomorrow we will have enough weapons and warriors to kill any dragon."

chapter 29

The air outside was crisp. The sky was blue but cold, and the sunshine barely penetrated Willow's clothes. Yesterday's rain lay in swampy puddles in the grass and Willow carefully sidestepped them as Modolf led her out and toward the mountain hall. The soil here did not drain well, and moisture froze into it in winter, making it difficult to farm. To be the king of such a starve-acre place was no great thing, Willow understood. That was why Hakon needed more land, south beyond the mountain range, in her homeland. Hakon had told her that in the mountains where Gisli's hall was burrowed there had once been veins of rich ore— silver and bronze—that his great-grandfather's people had mined and sold all over the known world. Willow knew herself how valuable Iceheart silver was, if only from Ivy's preening about jewelry in their shared childhood.

"But my grandfather was a spendthrift," Hakon had told her. "He burned through the wealth of the land as though it would never run out, then spent more on mining deeper and deeper, finding nothing but rock."

Their feet struck the road and Modolf's hand remained under her elbow. Willow kept her head down, paying no mind to carts that rattled past or the little boys who called out, trying to sell her squid and oysters. Only when Modolf said, "We are here," did she lift her gaze and take in the magnificent oak entrance to the mountain hall. Easily twice her height and ten feet across, the doors were adorned with carved eels and squid and seaweed, moons and stars and stylized mountain peaks.

"Oak from Almissia," Modolf told her. "Almost like being home, yes?"

"Almissia is not my home," she replied.

He smiled at her. "You amuse me."

"I don't aim to amuse anyone."

"Come along, let's go in."

He pushed one of the doors in, and it creaked back on its mighty hinges. They found themselves standing in a portico lit only by arrow slits. The air was chill and stifling, the smell of oily candles and smoke thick in her nostrils. Two guardsmen, men in rich cloaks with well-combed hair and beards, stepped forward. Modolf spoke to them in his own language, and Willow kept her gaze still and let them talk about her.

Maava, angels, give me a sign. Will all be well? Will I survive?

What did it matter if she survived? To die in Maava's name was to die in glory.

Then why did her heart hammer so hard?

You lack faith. You are not worthy of His love.

Willow pressed her lips together hard and blinked away tears of shame and disappointment.

The internal doors were opening and the guardsmen were ushering her through. Modolf followed behind and Willow put one foot in front of the other and said Maava's name over and over in her head until there was nothing else, nothing but His name. The long, dark corridors of the mountain hall, lit only by torches in sconces, unraveled before them. So cold and so dark. How could anybody live in here? It would be like living in a tomb. When she and Hakon took control, she would insist on living somewhere brighter, with more air and less stone, no matter that it was exquisitely adorned with writhing art and set with darkly gleaming jewels.

They passed many doors, winding farther and farther into the mountain, then finally they came to a wooden door, lit on either side by blazing torches that created sinister shadows among the carvings. One of the guardsmen thumped on the door twice, and the sound boomed around the corridors.

A word was spoken from the other side, the guardsman opened the door, and Willow saw King Gisli for the first time.

He looked nothing like Hakon, but Willow wasn't surprised. She looked nothing like her own twin, Ivy. Gisli was handsome and fair, the very essence of an ice-man, with white-blond hair and light eyes and a strong jaw. His body wasn't lean and hungry like Hakon's either: He was soft in the middle, although enormous in height. He wouldn't be fast. She saw immediately that he was armed. His sword-belt hung at his left hip, over a tunic of dark blue and gold and well-tailored pants.

Modolf was talking quickly. Gisli's eyes flicked from Modolf to her face and back again. She heard her own name, her father's, Bluebell's, but the rest was a mystery. She took the time to look around the smoky room. Deep shelves had been carved all the way around in the walls, and they were full of war booty: gold cups and shield bosses and decorated daggers. With a bolt of heat to her heart, she recognized some ornate triangles that had clearly been stolen from murdered trimartyr pilgrims.

A long wooden table was positioned at the back of the room, in a corner that looked too dark to work in. The hearthpit was lit, the smoke escaping slowly through a tiny hole in the ceiling where a single shaft of distant daylight entered. She wondered how many feet of rock were above them, and her mind felt oppressed by the thought. Oil lanterns burned on the walls.

Finally, Modolf stopped talking and Gisli gave the signal for him and his guardsmen to leave. Willow wouldn't have to use her only phrase of Iceheart tongue. The door closed behind them and Gisli turned to her.

"Will you sit with me?" he said in a thick accent.

"Yes, I would like that," she said, slowly, aware that his grasp of her language wasn't good. She had found with Hakon in the beginning that talking to him slowly was best.

Her fingers twitched, expecting him to turn his back to lead her to the table, but he didn't. Instead, he indicated that they would sit on the floor by the fire.

"You Southlanders do not like our cold," he said with a smile.

She nodded, lowering herself cross-legged to the floor. He did the same on the other side of the fire, and her pulse flicked hard at her throat as she wondered how she was going to kill him now.

"Why are you here, Princess Willow?" he asked.

"To help you overthrow my father and bring the name of Maava to all of Thyrsland."

"I do not believe in Maava."

"You should. For He will punish those who have heard His name and do not come to His faith."

Gisli raised one eyebrow.

Willow reminded herself of what she was here for. "It is of no consequence when you come to Maava, King Gisli, for you and I share a hatred for my father and my sister Bluebell and for Blickstow. I am estranged from them, but they will accept me back into the fold readily should I show up there, and then I will let you and your men into the family compound and you will do what you need to do to end their reign. Without Athelrick or Bluebell at their lead, the army will fall into disarray. I will arrange you and your men safe passage into the city." All of this was a lie, of course. Her family would never welcome her back, there was no way of getting a band of assassins into the family compound, and no easy passage for an army from Iceheart to Almissia without alerting the strongholds or being seen disembarking ships at one of the harbors. Did Gisli know this? He must know at least the last fact, but her story had captured his imagination nonetheless.

"And what would your reward be, Princess Willow?" he asked. "Would you be queen of Almissia?"

"No, for Maava does not want women to rule. You would be its king. I seek only to avenge myself on my family, then I will lead a quiet life in a chapel, which you will build for me in the center of Blickstow."

Gisli smiled. "I can do that." He leapt to his feet and began to pace, talking in his own language, fast and excited.

Willow counted his steps, wondering if she had time to stand and draw her sword while his back was turned, but in five steps he was around and facing her again, so she watched him awhile. She needed him to be still. "I have another request, Gisli," she said.

He pulled up. "Anything," he said.

"I want to tell you about Maava."

He hesitated, then sat back down. "I suppose I can listen awhile," he said grudgingly.

She leaned forward and began. The first book of Maava, which told how the world came into being, shaped by His mighty hands out of crushed stars and sparked into life with His mighty breath. Then the second book, which told how Liava and her little twins were persecuted for still believing in Maava under a wicked king, somewhere in those warm dry parts of the world that Thyrslanders never saw.

His eyes glazed over. He wasn't listening. He was humoring her. So she stood and began to preach more slowly, telling of Liava and her children burned alive for their beliefs, their bones forming the triangle that became the symbol of the newborn religion, their martyrdom a constant reminder that all must suffer if they were to make their way to the Sunlands after this pitiful, trivial life lived on earth. He barely raised his head to listen. No doubt his mind was already working out the details of his invasion of Blickstow. He didn't even seem to register as she began to pace, perhaps attributing it to her zeal, her growing fervor as she spoke of the fate of all who refused to take Maava's name as their Lord.

"They shall be cursed," she said, feeling the weight of *Grithbani* on her hip. "They shall be sent to the Blacklands where there is no light, no hope, no warmth." Pacing back and forth in front of him, telling him stories of sinners impaled on frozen rocks and tormented by Maava's most terrible angels. By now, he had truly stopped listening. She was speaking too fast for him to understand anyway, and he didn't notice when she slipped beside and around him in her pacing. Once around the room, twice . . .

On the third time she drew her sword, slashed it down on his right arm so he couldn't draw. He called out, began to climb to his feet, but it was too late. She plunged the blade through his back, into his heart. He fell sideways to the ground, his head thumping horribly on the stone floor, and the dark shadow of his blood pouring from his wound in dying pulses, pooling around him.

That was the end of the reign of King Gisli of Iceheart, and the beginning of the time of Maava in heathen lands, she narrated in her head as she tore the front of her own gown as though brutes had set upon her, slashed open her left palm as though she had defended herself with bare hands, and smeared her face with blood for dramatic effect.

She strode to the door and knocked twice as Modolf had told her to do.

He opened it, peered inside, and took in the sight of Gisli lying in a pool of blood, the single beam of sun caught in the dead king's hair. A sharp intake of breath and he pushed Willow back into the room, half closing the door. He seized her sword and slid it up into the highest shelf carved into the wall. Then he hurried to the other side of the room, to the long table, and threw over some chairs. Behind the table, his hands found a secret door she hadn't known was there, and he opened it and then turned to her.

"Go that way," he said, pointing her back the way they had come. "Scream. Call for the guardsmen. Tell them an assassin came for you through the secret door and Gisli died in trying to save you."

"They won't understand what I'm saying," she said.

"It doesn't matter. Just make sure you sound frightened. Faint if you can manage it." He gave her a little push and she stumbled toward the door. "Act like a normal woman, not like your sister."

She knew he meant Bluebell, but in that moment she realized she had to behave as Ivy might in such a situation, as though she were helpless until a man came along to make everything right for her.

Willow began to run along the winding corridors, screaming and howling. Sometime in the first few feet of her flight, the howling grew genuine, as the morning's strain finally settled around her heart, as the pain in her hand became real. Halfway back to the entrance, the two guardsmen met her and others emerged from side doors. She stumbled and collapsed to her knees in front of them, surrounded by them, unable to count them through the blur of her tears, telling them the story the way Modolf had instructed her. Somebody lifted her gently under her armpits and held her close while they hurried back through the hall to Gisli's stateroom. The first body was Modolf's, a broken pot smashed around his bloody head. The guardsman dropped her next to him and she sniveled and cried while they discovered Gisli's body and Gisli's dropped sword, and the whole world was in an uproar of Iceheart language and shouting and blood.

Modolf's hand reached out and squeezed her fingers.

Hakon and Modolf had prepared it all the night before, of course. A mile from the secret back entrance to Gisli's bower, which adjoined his stateroom via a hidden door, they had created a little camp and kicked over the coals, left food scraps and even footprints that led through the mud and back again, down to the beach where scrape marks in the sand told the story of an assassin who had come for Gisli. Nobody suspected Willow of killing him, but they blamed her for attracting death to the king's court with her arrival. Modolf thought this was a good outcome: hardening sentiment against her family. But Willow couldn't see how she would rule over a community that held her responsible for the death of the king.

"You will be the new king's bride," Modolf said as he bandaged her hand back in his little house. "They will come to love you."

But Hakon, who had been sitting thoughtfully on a stool by the hearthpit since they returned, lifted his head. Willow saw sadness in his eyes, and it made her heart afraid. For if Hakon could be sad about his brother's death—the brother he hated with all his heart—then perhaps she would feel sad about Bluebell's death or Ivy's fate or her whole family's future. She said a quick prayer and pushed the thoughts aside.

"She's right, Modolf. It's too soon. I cannot come in today, or tomorrow, or even this week and say, *Look, here I am, here is my wife who caused Gisli's death, we are now all trimartyrs.* It must be done at a softer pace. It is clear now that the hot moment is over."

"You have many supporters, Hakon," Modolf said. "And as for being trimartyrs . . ."

Hakon stroked the gruesome side of his face and Modolf squeezed his lips together, giving Willow a meaningful stare, but she let no doubt shade her face.

"Look at him. Maava has made him whole again," she said instead, as though she, too, were under the same enchantment. "To turn his back on Maava now . . . only ill would come of it."

Hakon got to his feet and began pacing. "I can be a trimartyr king with a trimartyr army, can I not? Then our war on the Southlands will be a holy war. At least on Almissia and Bradsey, if we take the west. Maybe Wengest will assist us; he is a trimartyr king as well, and we know that love has soured between him and Blickstow. Between us, the trimartyr kingdoms will control the Giant Road and have reason to destroy every kingdom or tribe that remains heathen." He emphasized this point with a smash of his fist into his palm.

"And you are so sure you will turn your back on the Horse God?"

"Maybe all gods are one, Modolf. We can choose among them when we need to, name them what we like. Desperate men have always done so."

"The Horse God is a heathen devil," Willow said emphatically, then fell silent again.

"What would you have me do, then?" Modolf said.

"Start the rumor that I am coming back. That I have heard of

Gisli's death and I will return soon. Keep pretenders away from the throne. Send Gisli's widow and children away for their own safety. It will take me a fortnight, no longer, to capture Seacaster and for Willow to travel to Blickstow to put Bluebell to the blade. Then see any of them dare to question me or my queen."

"You will be returning to a city in disarray," Modolf warned.

"All the better to bring it victory and harmony." Hakon, fatigued from long stretches of the Southland language, lapsed back into his own tongue and he and Modolf debated some more.

Willow was tired and her hand stung. For a few minutes she was sorry for herself, but then she remembered that every hardship brought her closer to her Lord, so she rocked her cut palm back and forth on the hard ground beside her to make it bleed a little more.

Expectant silence and two faces turned toward her—she had been asked something.

"Yes?" she asked, wiping her bloody palm on her skirt.

"Modolf can marry us," Hakon said. "As a member of the king's council he has that authority."

"Marry us?" She didn't know why she said it aloud.

"Yes," Modolf said. "While we are still in Iceheart. Then you will return a queen."

"A trimartyr queen?" Willow asked.

"Yes, if you like."

She looked at Hakon. "I won't lie with you," she said.

"There will need to be an heir."

"I have a son. He can be our heir."

Modolf and Hakon said a few phrases to each other in their own tongue. Willow waited, her heart thudding. *Give me a sign, angels. Give me a sign. Is Maava working through me? Is my glorious destiny tied to this moment?* Before the thought had even unspooled in her head, there was a clatter of claws at the window. A crow sat there looking curiously at them through the open shutter.

It cawed once, clicked its beak on the windowsill, then its wings rattled and it took to the sky again.

Willow kept staring at the place where it had been.

"She is off in one of her trances again," Modolf said.

She turned, gave him her coolest stare. "Yes," she said. "I will become the Crow Queen."

At midnight, she and Hakon sailed away from Marvik, one full day since they arrived. Her sword was returned to her and hung comfortingly on her hip. Her scarf was tied once more around her hair. On the back of her right hand she wore a fresh, bloody tattoo. Raider custom was to marry with matching tattoos: She had persuaded Hakon that they would take the sign of the triangle.

"Good luck in Seacaster," Modolf said as he helped them aboard the boat, in their clandestine location beyond the eyes of the mountain hall.

"Good luck in your work here, Modolf," Hakon said, stroking his beard. What pleasure it gave Willow to see Maava's symbol in black ink on his hand. "Prepare them for a new and glorious king and queen."

"I will."

Hakon untied the last rope and picked up the oars. Willow sat in the front of the boat, facing him, knees under her chin. One stroke after another, they made their way out of the harbor. Then Hakon raised the oars and let down the sail. The wind caught it eagerly, as though Maava had sent it for them.

Of course Maava had sent it for them.

They began their journey to Seacaster—to her sister, her destiny— with all the angels singing in Willow's head.

CHAPTER 30

S kalmir's feet struck against a rock and then the ground gave out from under him and he was falling. Darkness, a long drop. He tensed against the landing, but it came sooner than he'd thought. Thudding into the ground, knocking the air from his lungs and the light from his brain.

Both restored themselves a moment later, and he opened his eyes and it was morning, and he was lying on his back at the foot of a huge, hollow tree. Was this where he had fallen? He turned himself around, wincing against the pain in his hip and back, and called back up the tree trunk, "Rose? Rose? Can you hear me?" But there was no answer. He backed out of the tree and climbed to his feet, blinking in the unexpected morning light.

And he heard it. Deeper in the woods, to the east. Singing. Sighing. Like wind in the leaves turned to music, a voice that sounded a million eons old, whispering like bark, rising to crescendos like a storm howling over branches.

He had found the singing tree.

Skalmir followed the sound of the singing toward the east, where the sun was rising yellow and warm, shooting beams between the trees. His footfalls were quiet but not silent, small twigs and dried leaves popping softly under him. There were no other sounds but the rustle of wind in branches, the peep of robins, the distant call of a crow. He heard no voices that indicated Rathcruick and his tribe were nearby.

But if he found the singing tree, he would find Rowan, surely?

The singing rose and fell in volume on the wind. It was music from a dream, not quite real. Deep in his heart, a flicker of suspicion. All those tales about First Folk, about wandering too far from the road, about their spirits singing men to their dooms. But he told himself he was going to find Rowan, he wasn't answering the call of seduction. He would keep a clear head.

The forest started to thin and yet grow dark at the same time. He looked up and saw an enormous oak canopy shutting out the light, choking off the growth. In moments, he had slipped through the last stand of hazel trees and caught his first glimpse of the singing tree.

It was a mighty oak, but not an oak, because flowers and fruit grew on it in colorful profusion. Nothing could grow in its shade, so the ground for two hundred yards around was thick with drifts of leaf-fall. When the wind shook its branches, it rattled like a money purse, gold and silver pieces jangling against one another. And the singing was exquisite. An ancient, evocative song that seemed to say to him, *I know you and I will always know you.* He approached its huge base, where roots were buttressed into the ground so high that he had to climb over them to circle the tree. Looking up, looking up, higher and higher its branches stretched into the misty sky. Skalmir barely noticed that the sun's rise had become the sun's set and now moonlight glimmered on the farthest arch of the sky.

Then he saw the cage, hung high in the branches.

"Rowan!" he called.

"Snowy!" she responded.

The point of an arrow was held to the back of his neck, cold and unforgiving.

"Surrender," said Rathcruick.

❖   ❖   ❖

Skalmir had many things to consider—captured now, held in a cage under the singing tree—but all he could think of was Rowan's face and body, lit by the firelight of Rathcruick's tribe.

Because Rowan had changed. She had left him a seven-year-old. The girl in front of him was not yet a woman, but she was not a child, either. If he had never seen her before, he would have guessed her age to be twelve. Her face, her arms, her legs, all longer and leaner than the Rowan he knew; the first curve of maturity in her waist and hips.

"I would have warned you," she said to him as Rathcruick and another man pulled a thick rope that raised the cage, inch by inch, back into the branches of the tree. The cage swung and the rope creaked.

"You look different," he said.

She turned her head so he could see the tattoo on her cheek, identical to Dardru's. Spirals within circles. "I have been here a long time," she said.

"It can only be weeks."

"Time passes differently here. Sometimes it feels like weeks, sometimes like years," she said with a sigh. "There seems to be no division from night to day, from sun to moon. I feel . . ." She slapped her palm against her temple twice. "I am not alone in here."

"You have me."

"Not in the cage," she said, pointing at her forehead. "In here. In my head. Dardru is with me."

"Dardru . . . ?"

"Rathcruick's daughter. The one Bluebell killed."

"Bluebell didn't kill her. She killed herself."

"For pride, to escape being one of Bluebell's trophies," she said. "I know all her thoughts."

"I don't understand. How did she get in you?"

"Rathcruick did it. He has gone mad in his grief. The First Folk believe the spirits of the dead stay around their loved ones until given leave to cross over. Rathcruick never gave Dardru any such leave. And I was open, vulnerable. I was out—out of my head for less than a moment, trying to find Mama as my shimmering self, and he slipped her in. At the first opportunity . . ." She took a deep shuddering breath. "He says I will be queen of the First Folk, and queen of Thyrsland thereafter. All I need to do is submit."

"To Dardru?"

"Yes. But I won't. She isn't as strong as me. I am descended from kings."

He gazed at her in wonder. His tiny foster child, grown into a young woman who boasted about her strength, her lineage.

"And so he keeps me in this cage, thinking it will make me change my mind." She looked down at the fire and called out, "I won't change my mind!"

Rathcruick didn't answer.

"He won't speak to me," she said. "They roast food right beneath me and give me leaves to eat. Then they cover the fire at night so I won't be warm, and they go sleep in their houses. There's a whole camp, about half a mile away." She indicated with one hand, poking it through the bars. "I had already decided that if you didn't come for me, I would refuse to eat and die in here just to spite him, and his wretched daughter can live inside my corpse and see how she likes that."

He smiled weakly, and didn't reveal his doubts. "You won't die," he said. "Do they keep you in here the whole time?"

She indicated the rough blankets around her on the wooden base of the cage. "As you see. They lower the cage twice a day to feed me and let me go to pot. Under guard, mind you. Other than that, I'm here in wind and rain and sun, and will be until I do as he says." Then her defiance leached away again, and she sounded very young as she said, "If only Dardru hadn't died. He was kind to me until then. I thought I would be happy when I found the singing tree. I believed he wanted to make friends. He says he knew my grandfather, that they had been allies . . ." She trailed off, uncertain.

Skalmir couldn't tell her that, now he'd come for her, he didn't know how to save her. He'd left his weapons back at the camp with Rose, Rathcruick had taken his knife, and the bars of the cage were forged of iron. He ran through possibilities in his mind. They would be let down twice a day. The camp was half a mile from the cage. He put these two facts in play over and over, and yet couldn't come up with a way to escape.

"Have you ever tried to get out of here?" he asked her.

"Of course. I've been here forever. I tried reaching under and loosening the latch. I tried to reach for the rope to gnaw through it with my teeth. I've tried swinging the cage until the bough creaked and cracked. But every time I get close, the tree warns them."

"The tree?"

"Yes, it stops singing and starts screaming." Her eyes went up to the branches around them. "It has no love for me. It does Rathcruick's bidding." Then Rowan looked at him sadly. "I don't suppose it will be any easier for you to help me escape, will it?"

"I don't know, Rowan," he said, and he grasped her hand and squeezed it. "But there's somebody else who might save us yet."

"Who?"

"Your mother."

And now Rose was alone. She knew it. She didn't need to go into the wood to see what had happened to Skalmir; he was gone. He hadn't answered any of her increasingly frantic calls.

She curled herself in a ball by the fire and closed her eyes as the morning sun began to flood the glade. Alone. For a few brief moments, her mind turned over the agonizing choice between continuing to search for Rowan or returning to Linden, but then she realized she had no choice. She was lost and had no idea how to get back to her own world, or into Rowan's. As far as she knew, she was the only human in this place—wherever it was—and she felt her isolation keenly. Her skin was covered in gooseflesh, and she hugged her knees and told herself she mustn't cry, but she cried anyway, big heaving sobs of self-pity that made her ashamed of herself. Who was there to listen and judge her, anyway? She cried until her stomach hurt, then she stopped, sat up, palmed the tears from her face, and started thinking about what to do next.

The sun was up by now, so she knew she should at least follow Skalmir's route and see if there was any evidence of what had happened. She had heard no sounds of a struggle, no roars of bears or howls of wolves, so she didn't expect to find him dead, but she trod warily and anxiously nonetheless. She listened carefully, heard nothing beyond the usual sounds of the wood. Skalmir's feet had turned up leaf-fall and left faint prints in the cold dirt. Rose followed them.

The footprints stopped. No scuffle. No mark of him having stood somewhere. Step, step, step, nothing.

Rose lowered herself to her knees on the spot, her hands reaching out to move twigs and leaves around. She found a stone, which at first looked as though it was entirely naturally formed. But on closer scrutiny, she became aware it was too symmetrical to be anything but hand-carved, too upright to be anything but placed deliberately. She cleared off the ivy growing over it, and saw that it was shallowly etched with a symbol. A circle, like a wheel with spokes that extended out and finished in spirals. She ran her fingers over it lightly, then more forcefully. "Take me where Skalmir has gone," she demanded, under her breath, but nothing happened. She was still in the wood, the sun already sweeping fast overhead. She looked up and could almost see it moving. It would be night again soon. Her eyes felt gritty with tiredness, her body limp with exhaustion. She couldn't remember the last time she had slept.

Rose climbed to her feet and headed back to their camp. Her stomach rumbled loudly, but she was too tired to hunt for mushrooms. Skalmir's pack was still here, and she went through it and pulled out a hunk of old bread, which she chewed on and swallowed without pleasure. She washed it down with water and kept looking through his pack. A knife, arrowheads, spare clothes. She tucked the knife into her waistband and repacked the rest. His bow and quiver were still here, too. She had never shot an arrow in her life and now it seemed a terrible oversight. She pulled the bow-string. It was much heavier than she'd imagined. Standing, she tried to fit an arrow in it and release it. The arrow fell at her feet, the bow-string slapping her hand.

Rose sat back down and went through her own pack. She still had blinding powder, so she tucked that under her cloak. Eldra had also given her a potion to help if she got the shits, and another to purify stagnant water. Solutions to problems she didn't have. She remembered the strange waymark magician, the one who foretold she would be lost again. How could she conjure him up, get him to point her in the right direction?

There was no right direction, though. She knew that. She was lost in the woods, lost in between the days and weeks. She thought about the gray that had appeared in Skalmir's beard and wondered if the woods had already robbed her of a year or two of her life as well.

Late-afternoon shadows came so quick they looked as though they were being poured onto the ground. She was weary enough to sleep, knowing too it would give her back her energy, chase away the mental fog. Sleeping alone among the enchantments of this wood didn't feel safe, but sleep she must.

Rose gathered the packs and the weapons close, wrapped them in Snowy's blanket, and gathered them against her chest. She closed her eyes and willed sleep to come. Her senses were too alert, and for an hour or more she lay in that position, unmoving, unsleeping.

Then the dark seemed to set in properly. Night noises came. She cracked her eyelids open and saw stars. Was Rowan under the same stars? Was she nearby? "I am coming for you, my child," she murmured.

Closed her eyes. Slept.

The warm shape against her back was familiar. She had felt it hundreds of times before, at home in her bed at Eldra's house. But this time, it wasn't still or quiet. Fingers poked her back.

"Mama, I'm here. Don't wake up."

Rose was dreaming. Her dream self came to consciousness, opened dream eyes on a silver-blue landscape of shadowy trees. "Rowan?" she asked, looking around, everything moving slowly, shushing softly as if under water.

"You won't be able to see me," the voice said, "but you can feel me." With that, a small, cool hand slid into Rose's.

Rose squeezed it tight. "Oh, my child," she said, overcome. "My child."

"There will be time enough for that," Rowan said, her voice a whisper among the folds of Rose's thoughts. "But I have only seconds. I have been trying to connect with you for days, but our hours and seconds run differently here. Any moment we could slide apart again. Let me show you where you must go."

The hand tugged gently, and Rose began to drift, a kite being pulled on a string, over rocks and uneven ground. The shimmering light moved and swirled around her, making whispering, murmuring noises. Rose felt weightless, made of moonlight. The dark parted in front of her and closed behind her again, and her thoughts became scrambled, blurred.

"Stay in the dream," Rowan said urgently, bringing her back to the dream-lit forest. "Stay in the dream, Mama. I need to show you where to go."

They had stopped in the forest and Rose tried very hard to concentrate, to look around at the shapes of trees and rocks so she could find this location again tomorrow when awake.

"Here, look down," Rowan said.

Rose looked down and saw the stone she had found earlier, with the spiraling pattern on it, where Snowy had disappeared. He must have crossed through here. "I know where this is," Rose said. "I didn't see the way."

"The way is shut. I will open it when I slide back into myself, and I will keep it open as long as I can. As long as Rathcruick doesn't feel me working the crossing, you will be able to get through. Listen for the singing tree."

"Does he control the crossing?"

"He controls nothing. He thinks he does, but the woods are just as capricious as he is. Just come, quiet and cautious. Snowy and I are waiting for you."

Rose snapped awake. The silver-blue forest of shadows was gone, replaced with bright sunlight. How long had she slept? Not long, she suspected, as her limbs still felt heavy. But her mind was alert, her heart thudding.

"Rowan," she said, and the idea that she was so close now, so close to her child after so many years . . .

She had to find the stone in the wood. Rose scrambled to her feet, left her pack covered by the blanket—and kicked a thin cover of dead leaves over it for good measure—grabbed Snowy's weapons, then retraced her steps back into the wood.

The stone was where she remembered it, and she knelt by it and put her hands on it, expecting to be transported that way. Nothing happened.

An awful suspicion that her dream had been just that: a dream, nonsense, wishful thinking.

But then she saw the shadow, eating the ground next to her. The shadow deepened, became a hollow, then a pit. The ground crumbled away around her knees and she scrambled back, only to find herself sliding into the pit on her palms and knees, tumbling over and falling. Her stomach went hollow and she screamed, but the scream stopped abruptly when she hit ground.

Somewhere else entirely. Rose took a moment to get her bearings. It was now nighttime. She appeared to be in the bottom of a hollow tree, and the other place, with the carved stone, had simply vanished.

She stood, careful not to hit her head, and brushed off her palms.

Rowan had said to listen for the singing tree, and she heard it immediately. Music made from wind in branches, sweet and strange and seductive. As much as she wanted to hurry her steps, the dark and Rowan's warning made her quiet and cautious. Nearly an hour passed before she saw the enormous oak, the smoldering campfire beneath it. She could see two silhouettes in a cage hanging from a bough against the deep twilit blue of the sky.

Rose slowed, crouching to inch closer, expecting to be discovered at any moment. But it seemed the fire had been left to burn down, the camp gone elsewhere. By the time she stood beneath the cage, looking up at Rowan and Skalmir, she was convinced Rathcruick and his tribe had left them up there to die.

Snowy looked down, motioning for her to be quiet. Rose glanced around, saw the rope that was used to pull the cage up and down. She could untie it, but had she the strength to lower it safely? Would they come crashing to the ground too fast and break their bones?

She eyed the tree. They were a long way up. The rope it was.

Rose began to work the knot. As she did so, the tree's melodious whispering and rattling began to intensify. False notes sounded.

"Hurry!" Rowan called.

Rowan, her daughter. It was finally happening, the reunion she had dreamed about for years. She felt unprepared. The circumstances were not right. They needed time, a safe place to hold each other.

The tuneless notes became more frequent, louder. Rose had the rope in both her hands. She dug her heels into the ground and freed the last loop and the weight of the cage tore the rope through her palms, lifting the flesh. She turned, wrapping the rope around her own waist once, then pulled it around the curve of the tree trunk. She stopped on the other side, her back hard against the trunk, and braced as she lowered the cage, in fits and jerks, to the ground. Her hands bled, her shoulders burned, but the cage was coming, faster and faster.

It fell the last few feet, thudded to the ground.

Now the tree wasn't singing. It was howling.

"They will come!" called Rowan, but it couldn't be Rowan. She was too old. Was this a nightmare? Who was this girl she was rescuing?

Rose's hands stung and she wiped the blood on her skirt. "Why are you—?"

"We have no time," Skalmir said. "Can you get us free?"

"How?" Rose looked around wildly for a latch, a lock, anything. The bars were iron, and they were fitted tightly into the wooden base. What tools could she use, especially now her own hands were torn and bloody?

Then she remembered the blinding powder. "Stand back," she said, reaching for it. "Right in the farthest corner. Snowy, protect her."

One small handful had been enough to blast a scorched patch in the ground. Perhaps the whole pouch would blast a hole in the cage.

Skalmir pushed Rowan into the corner of the cage, turning his back to Rose and holding his arms over the child's head.

"Close your eyes," Rose said as an ill wind whirled around the tree and made the branches scream and howl.

She threw the pouch into the closest corner of the cage, and then raised her arm over her eyes. An enormous crack sounded through the forest, sending the tree into a frenzy. A smell of sulfur filled the air. When she lowered her arm, she saw that the bars in the corner were curled up. There wasn't room for them to get out.

Not Skalmir, in any case. Rowan was already on her stomach, sliding under the bent bars.

"What about Snowy?" Rose asked.

Heavy, fast footfalls approaching.

"They are coming!" Rowan screamed.

"Go without me!" Skalmir said.

"Your bow—"

"I am too outnumbered for it to be of use. Give it to Rowan. I would happily die for her, Rose, if you stay alive for her."

"This way, Mama," Rowan said, already streaking past Rose on her way back through the woods. "Hurry!"

There wasn't time to make sense of anything. Rose turned and ran, following her daughter—if it was her daughter, why was she so long of limb?—back to the crossing.

Over rocks and branches. Running feet were after them. Rose was sure they were heading in a different direction from where she had come.

"Quick, Mama, we are almost there."

Rose banished all questions from her mind. For now, escape, get Rowan somewhere safe. Up ahead, a looming gray shape in the dark—a dolmen. Rowan skidded to her knees next to it, pulled Rose down next to her. Rose could hear her daughter's panting breaths as she whispered something.

And they crossed. Now Rose was blinking against early-morning light in a different part of the Howling Wood. Rowan looked up at her, grinning, and in that smile Rose saw her: the child she had lost so many years ago.

Rose pulled Rowan into a fierce embrace, smelling her hair, running her fingers over her soft skin, drinking her. "At last, at last, I have you," she said.

"Mama, you're squashing me," Rowan said, laughing.

Rose let her go and they sat back on the leaves and cold earth and stared at each other.

"You are exactly the same as the picture in my memory," Rowan said.

"You are so changed." Rose's eyes took the changes in, and she realized that the same incoherent shift of time in the Howling Wood had aged Rowan four or five years. "You're a young woman."

Rowan reached out and touched Rose's cheek, ran her fingers over her temple. "My mother," she said.

Rose heard a sound in the forest and snapped around in alarm, but Rowan said, "Don't worry. It was just a deer."

"Will Rathcruick follow us?"

"He might try, but he won't find us. We will stay ahead of him. Dardru was the crossing keeper in the tribe, and she's inside me."

"Who's Dardru?"

"Rathcruick's daughter. It doesn't matter. I'm free of him now, but we must save Snowy."

"Not us. We're not going back in there." Reality crunched down on her. "I have to get you back to your father . . ."

"Which one?" Rowan said, and a little flint of ice touched her voice.

"Wengest, of course."

"Mama, *Snowy* is my father. He has raised me for as long as I can remember. Wengest was a man who came to see me from time to time." She sighed, leaning back on her palms. "And Rathcruick wants to be my father, and no doubt Heath wants to be my father. Yes, Rathcruick told me about him. But I don't love them, not any of them. I love Snowy."

The barb about Heath landed squarely in Rose's heart. Guilt and shame. "Heath is a good man. As is Wengest. They are both worthy of your love," she said. "You and I are just a woman and a child, and we can't rescue Snowy. Wengest can send armed men in, raid Rathcruick's camp."

Rowan's eyes misted over. Rose remembered that look from her littlest years, a twitch of the eyebrows, a pink flush around her pore-less temples. She looked uncertain. Young.

Rose reached out and touched the awful tattoo on her face. "Heath says Rathcruick has a black heart."

"He is full of anger. Everything has been taken from the First Folk. They are pushed to the margins of the land. In Rathcruick's case, right into the folds of magic that still inhabit the woodlands." Rowan spread her hands. "I am meant to be their queen."

A wind whipped up and raced through the woods, sending up a swirl of leaves and setting the branches swinging. Rose shivered, then said to her daughter, "No. You don't have to be anything but a child. I am taking charge now, and that means I am returning you to Wengest, who has done his duty as your father since your birth. You are a princess of Nettlechester, and if you tell him you need somebody to go to Rathcruick's camp and free Snowy, then he will do it. I know this to be true."

Rowan nodded. "Perhaps you are right, Mama. And we ought to get your hands seen to; they are a terrible mess."

Rose looked down at the rope burns across her palms. She couldn't visit Wengest. She had to pretend she'd had nothing to do with Rowan's rescue. There would be time to explain all this to Rowan. For now, Rose let the knowledge of their inevitable parting ache inside her like a bruise.

"Here," Rowan said, leaning forward. "Give me Snowy's bow and quiver." Rowan shouldered the weapons, climbed to her feet, and began to walk. "We need to confuse Rathcruick, so we must find another crossing. This way."

Rose stood and followed her.

"There are crossings all over Thyrsland," Rowan called over her shoulder. "Usually remote places, but there is one in the Howling Wood—the *real* Howling Wood—outside Nether Weald. We can get horses in the village and ride to Folkenham together. I have so much to tell you!" Rose caught up with her at a small carved stone. Rowan put one foot on it, grabbed Rose's hand and—

It was early morning, dewy. The air was fresh and . . . different somehow.

"We are home," Rowan said.

"Home?"

"Back in Thyrsland. You can feel it. Time is moving normally. The press on my heart is gone."

Yes, she was right. That was what felt different. All that time in the hidden part of the woods, Rose hadn't realized that being there made her feel different. As though all the particles that made up her body had been buzzing too fast. Now she felt normal again. She took a deep breath of morning air.

Rowan took her hand carefully. Turned it over and looked at the wounds. "I know who can tend to these," she said. "Sister Julian. She's not far away. Let's go."

By midmorning they were on their way on a borrowed palfrey. Rose's hands were smeared in salve and bandaged, and they had proper cooked meals in their bellies. The sky was clear, and Rose had settled back into Thyrsland time—plodding, welcome, non-magic time—slowly, her daughter on a padded seat buckled onto the saddle behind her, arms around Rose's middle. They talked and talked. Rose told Rowan about Eldra, about her half brother Linden, about Heath, about what had happened and why they could never be seen together, not just for their own safety but for the peace of Thyrsland. Rowan took it all in with soft murmurs of agreement and understanding, and then she talked about life with Snowy, about hunting in the woods, and darker themes such as the ghost of Rathcruick's daughter lurking inside her.

"I have my own magic," Rowan told her as they passed over a hill and looked out over green fields baking under a summer sun traversing the sky at a natural pace. "Her magic is rough. I don't want it."

"Perhaps I should have taken you to Eldra," Rose said. "She could have—"

"Nothing is more important now than rescuing Snowy. Dardru can wait. She has no power outside of the hidden wood."

They approached a junction in the road, a waymark standing sentinel at its fork. Rose looked up. On one arrow was the symbol for Folkenham: the great hall carved with Wengest's insignia. This was the road home for Rowan, the road to separation for Rose.

But Rowan must have been looking at the other arrow. A picture of a crooked oak.

"Withing," Rowan said, in a dreamy voice. "Bluebell is heading there. I can sense it in my gristle. It's closer, and *she* will help Snowy."

"But your father—"

"My father doesn't love Snowy as Bluebell does. My father cannot send a guardsman or even a troop of guardsmen who are Bluebell's equal. We must go to Withing. We must find Bluebell."

Rose turned in her saddle to look at Rowan. She had become agitated, two pink spots appearing on her cheeks.

"Please, Mama. Every moment we waste is a moment Snowy is in danger."

Rose picked up the reins, eyes forward. "Very well," she said. "We head for Withing."

chapter 31

I vy despised the first morning of the week, when one by one the disgruntled citizens of Seacaster—and there were many—lined up on the stairs outside the hall tower for her to placate them. While Gunther had had an easy time of it, settling disputes between neighbors, and enforcing fines for petty merchants and opportunistic peddlers, Ivy had a far harder time. The protests about the chapel burning, rather than dying down, appeared to be picking up speed again. Not a week went by when she wasn't berated for it, and had to have a guard force them out. Then they'd sit outside the gate, howling and shouting about Duchess Ivy, the heathen fool who couldn't even read. Somehow Torsten had let that detail about her go public.

Steady rain fell, tapping against the roof and dripping miserably off the eaves. She was already weary before the first hour was up, and when the door opened and she saw Crispin there, she nearly wept with joy at the distraction.

"Out," he said, to the plump woman who stood in front of Ivy on her high seat, complaining that looters had been to the vacant house beside her four times and the guard had not come. The woman didn't need to be told twice. Crispin, in his deep magenta cloak with his mail and weapons rattling, looked fearsome.

Ivy hid a smile, struck by his handsome appearance at a welcome moment. Over the last few days he had returned to his usual reassuring self, and her doubts had begun to fade.

Once they were alone, he stood before her and bowed deeply.

"Oh, don't bow, Crispin," she said with a soft laugh. "Not unless you intend to stay down there between my knees."

He straightened and stepped forward, took her hand, and knelt in front of her. There was an urgency in his eyes that unsettled her. "Ivy, I have . . . news."

"What is it?" she said, her breath pressed in her lungs. Had he killed somebody else?

"Hold tight to hope, my love. At least we have advance warning."

"Of what?"

"We have a report from Littledyke. A child who had run away from home, who was hiding along the clifftops, saw raider ships concealed in an inlet."

"Raiders?" Her blood flashed hot.

"He ran back and told his mother, thank the gods, and the local reeve rode out there to confirm. He says he wasn't seen. A cluster of ships are gathered half a day's sail northeast. We can guess that they have their eye on Seacaster."

"What? Why?"

"No doubt news of Gunther's death and the resulting . . . instability have reached their ears. They seek to take advantage of it."

"But we aren't unstable, are we? We have a strong city guard— I have you." Her thoughts whirled. She was trapped in the disbelieving moment. This wasn't happening. The city was hers and would remain hers and all the lovely taxes would be hers and nobody could take it away from her.

"From the outside, perhaps we appear to be," he said. "The port is poorly managed. Protests divide the city."

"But we're safe?"

"Raiders are not to be dismissed, Ivy. Reports say seven large ships. That is at least three hundred men. We are outnumbered."

"Then we'll send for help. Wengest will come with his army. He must protect us; we pay taxes to him."

"That is what I'd advise you, Ivy. Send an urgent request to Wengest for reinforcements. If they are waiting for good weather to strike, it could buy us a few days. The raiders won't be expecting us to have an army here before they arrive."

She grasped Crispin around his upper arms, searching his face. "There isn't going to be a war, is there? I can't have a war. I don't know what to do."

He met her eyes steadily, softly. "I know what to do."

She swallowed hard, nodding.

Ivy released Crispin, and he stood and left. Ivy sat in her high seat, staring at the ground, overwhelmed by fear.

The door opened again and the plump woman tried to slip back in.

"Get out!" Ivy screamed at her. "Tell them all to go away. No more today. Get out!"

The woman scurried out. The door closed with a thud, shutting out light and air.

That night the weather worsened, and a squall rose out at sea and came sheeting over the bowerhouses, rattling shutters and pulling at the thatching. Ivy lay in Gunther's old bed listening to it, unable to sleep. Every time she dropped off, the storm became raiders raging through the city, murdering her children, burning the docks. A thunderous knock in the middle of the night made her heart jump so hard against her ribs that she hurt. She sat up, taking a breath to scream, but then heard Crispin's voice.

"Ivy, let me in."

She leapt out of bed, getting tangled in her covers and nearly falling flat on her face. She extracted herself and went to the door.

Crispin came in, sodden.

"What is it?" she asked, lighting the lamp by the door with unsteady hands. "What's happened?"

He sat on a stool and pulled off his shoes. "I came as soon as I heard. Wengest returned our messenger. Made him ride all the way back in a day, on a fresh horse, despite the storm."

"Returned our messenger?" Usually, their messenger would stay in Folkenham a day or so. If a reply came, it would be one of Wengest's men.

"Returned our messenger, yes, and refused our request."

"What?"

Crispin stood and pulled off his shirt, roughly toweled his curls with it, and threw it on the floor. "He has said we don't know for sure if the raiders are coming to us, and anyway he can't spare his army."

"What does he mean by that? Should I be reassured? The raiders don't want to come here after all?"

But already Crispin was shaking his head. "Ivy, he's punishing you for burning the chapels. For taking the city."

Wengest wasn't coming with his army. She let that sink in.

"Fuck him," she spat.

"I think if you went down there yourself, very humble, and—"

"I'll do no such thing. Beg Wengest for forgiveness? Fuck him."

Crispin fell silent, his dark eyes fixed on her.

"Send an overnight messenger to Blickstow," she said. "Tell Bluebell to come and bring my father's army, and when the raiders arrive and the Almissian army repels them, then Wengest can choke before asking me for taxes." As her anger ebbed away, she grew uncertain again. "Do you think that could work?"

"I would rather your father's army than Wengest's. Will they come?"

"My family are very loyal to one another. If they know I'm in trouble, they will most certainly help." She hesitated. "Am I in trouble, Crispin?"

He folded her into his embrace. The smell of his skin, his damp hair, overwhelmed her with sensation. Desire, fear.

"There is trouble afoot, my lady," he said against her ear. "But I have you sheltered in my arms."

She allowed herself to fall against him, and stood like that a long while, before he finally pulled away.

"Ivy, send the boys somewhere safe with Hilla. Just in case."

She tried not to sob with fear. "They are safest with me."

"As you wish it." He picked up his wet shirt and wriggled back into it. "I will organize the overnight message to go out the moment the storm abates."

"Can we afford the time?" She thought of the raiders, half a day's sail away.

"No man would take a horse out in this. The weather is awful, but it is awful in our favor. If raiders do intend to strike against us, it won't be until this rain and wind ease."

She reached for him, kissed him fervently, felt his wet body pressed against her nightgown, and began to reach for his trousers. But he extracted himself, stood back, and said, "This is not a time for love."

Ivy's cheeks flushed warm, embarrassed. A prickle of desperation. What if he stopped loving her? What would she do then?

"Sleep if you can," he said. "I can only offer you hope for the days ahead."

Then he was gone, and Ivy was alone in the storm.

Bluebell's long afternoon shadow speared ahead of her as she walked from the stable to the inn at Withing, Ash's smaller shadow at her side. Bluebell could feel the tension emanating from her sister's slim frame. Ash was thinking about running; Bluebell had no doubt.

"Perhaps I could sleep outside the town," Ash began as they crossed wooden boards laid over mud to the town square.

"It will be fine, Ash," Bluebell said, forcing her voice to sound patient. "He hasn't found you yet, and now we have my hearthband." Bluebell indicated a wooden inn, two stories high, with a huge hunting bird carved on its gable ends. "Come along, and stop worrying. You have never been safer than this moment."

"It's not my safety I'm worried about," Ash muttered, but she stayed close nonetheless.

Bluebell pushed open the door. The air was thick and warm with smoke and the rich smell of roasting deer. An old woman with knotted hands was stirring a soot-streaked cauldron on a chain over the hearthpit. As the light from outside fell into the room, the woman raised her head and offered them both a gap-toothed smile.

"My lord Bluebell," she said, gesturing to the cauldron. "I would be honored if you tasted my turnip-and-thyme soup."

Bluebell strode over, Ash in her wake. "Olwyn, you know I cannot resist your cooking." She took the ladle from the old woman's hand and lifted it to her mouth. The soup was hot and savory, with a hint of sweetness. Bluebell would have happily stood there ladling it into her mouth until she burst. "Meet my sister Ash," she said through a second mouthful.

Olwyn's eyes widened. "My lady Ash. May the gods all bless you and keep you."

Ash was pale, her lips barely able to form a smile. "I thank you," she said softly, and glanced toward the door.

"Is Sighere about?" Bluebell asked.

"Upstairs. The usual room. The others have been sleeping down here at night, among the dogs and ashes. I think some of them have been helping repair the chapel roof during the day. A chestnut tree dropped a branch on it during the last storm."

"Maava should have seen that coming," Bluebell huffed. She didn't like her hearthband helping at a trimartyr chapel.

"He might have done it on purpose," Olwyn laughed. "The preacher is no smarter than my old pig, Hambone."

Bluebell handed back the ladle and grasped Ash's hand. "Have my usual room made ready for me and my sister," she said. "I don't know how long we will stay."

"Surely only a night," Ash blurted.

"I need to talk to Sighere," Bluebell said, to both of them and neither of them. "Come, sister."

The stairs were narrow and steep, opening out on a dim, shut-tered corridor with four doors along it, the inn rooms. Bluebell knocked swiftly at the first door, and Sighere's voice came from within.

"Enter."

Sighere sat on a narrow straw mattress on the floor, his knees spread apart before him, oiling the blade of his sword. "My lord," he said when he saw her. "Lady Ash."

Bluebell sat on a low stool in front of him, Ash sinking to the floor beside her. "Sighere, my sister is so pale because a dragon follows her. We need to kill it."

Sighere raised the corner of his lips in a smile, directed at Ash. "Is this true, my lady?"

"I . . . yes," Ash stammered.

"How fortunate your father has an army nearby."

"What?" Bluebell snapped.

"Duchess Ivy has called for aid. Raiders are sitting off the coast of Seacaster."

"How many raiders?"

"Several ships."

"Has Gisli gone mad?"

"I do not know, my lord. Weather keeps them away for now, but Athelrick is marching there with Almissian troops. If you had not arrived by tomorrow, we were going to join them."

"Without me?"

"I would have left you word."

Bluebell nodded, a rush of thoughts tumbling through her mind. "So this is simple. We go to Seacaster, defeat the ice-men, then while the army is mobilized we draw the dragon out onto the battlefield and kill it."

"It isn't *simple*," Ash said on a harsh breath. "The dragon has the sky."

"We have hundreds of warriors with spears and arrows," Blue-bell said. "Don't you agree with me, Sighere?"

"It will be better if we can get it on the ground," Sighere replied.

"Him," Ash said. "His name is Unweder and he's a powerful and crafty undermagician."

"Undermagicians still bleed," Bluebell said, blustering over her uneasiness at the mention of magic. "Against an army? He has no chance. It's perfect, Ash, don't you see?"

Ash fell silent as Sighere and Bluebell talked through the size and abilities of the dragon, and made plans for getting Unweder on the ground with slings and nets. The only sign that she was listening was the incessant jiggle of her right knee.

They were interrupted by voices in the hallway, Olwyn calling Bluebell's name. Bluebell leapt to her feet and opened the door. Olwyn stood in the dark corridor with two women. She recognized the first instantly as Rose and enveloped her in a hug. Her eyes lit on the other woman, and she jerked back involuntarily.

"It's me, Rowan," Rowan said.

Bluebell tried to make sense of this and couldn't. A trick of the light? She took a step backward, and Rowan stood very still in front of her.

"Snowy is in trouble," the new Rowan said.

Snowy? Bluebell ushered them into Sighere's room. "Come inside. Tell me everything."

Bluebell had food and drink fetched for all, and allowed Ash and Rose to greet each other tearfully, all the while with an urgent press against her heart, before demanding to know what had happened. As they ate, Rose and Rowan told her their story in fits and starts until she had pieced it all together. Rowan had fallen under some enchantment, Rose had rescued her, but Skalmir had been left behind in the Howling Wood. Rowan, a seven-year-old, now looked years older. Bluebell had to stop herself from recoiling from the girl, so unnaturally grown. She forced herself to reach across and touch Rowan's tattoo. She felt as warm and soft as she ever had.

"And this is the same tattoo that Dardru wore?"

"Yes. It marks me as Rathcruick's daughter."

"You are no such thing," Rose exclaimed.

Bluebell had enough tattoos—across her back and collarbones, encircling both arms—to know how much they could hurt. The idea of her niece having to endure that pain on her silky child-skin made her shudder.

"You will save Snowy, won't you, Bluebell?" Rowan asked.

The question hung in the air. Athelrick and the army needed her. War was here.

But it was Snowy.

"If so, we must do it tonight," Bluebell said. "My father's army is on its way to Seacaster and I will need to join them."

"Seacaster? Is all well with Ivy?" Rose asked.

"The ice-men poised to strike." Bluebell glanced at Ash. "There are . . . other reasons we need to be with the army, but each thing in its turn."

"Rowan can't go tonight," Rose said. "She has already traveled too far today."

"I will go," Rowan said. "I don't want to leave Snowy there a second longer."

"I should go alone," Bluebell said.

"You need me to open the crossings. I am going." She set her shoulders square. "I will need a bow and a quiver full of arrows."

Bluebell eyed her niece, half admiring, half amused. "Certainly. I will arm the seven-year-old before we leave," she said on a laugh. "Rose, you stay here with Ash. Olwyn should have my room ready by now. It's the next along. Go, sisters, both of you. Leave me with my niece and my thane."

Rose helped Ash to her feet. "You are skin and bone," Rose said. "A ghost of yourself."

"I have wandered like a ghost these four years," Ash said. "I ought not to have come back among the living."

Rose slid her arm around Ash and turned to Bluebell. "Take care of my daughter. As I know you have these past four years."

So there it was, the accusation Bluebell had been expecting. She shrugged it off. Once Rose and Ash had left the room, Bluebell said to Sighere, "If I'm not back by dawn the day after tomorrow, take them all to Seacaster with you. They will be safer in a strong keep near the Almissian army than they would be unprotected here."

"If that is what you wish."

"And put a guard on their door."

"Do not concern yourself, my lord. Nobody will get in to their room."

"No. I want to stop Ash getting out," she said.

Sighere did not blink. "Yes, my lord."

Ash sat by the window in Bluebell's room at the inn in Withing, with the shutter open so she could watch the clouds rolling in from the east against the evening sky. One by one, the stars disappeared, and soon enough the rain came, spitting soft drops through the window. Still she sat and stared.

"Ash?" Rose's voice, sleepy, from the bed.

"Go back to sleep," Ash said. "I'll close the window if you are cold."

Rose peeled back her blanket and climbed to her feet, approached Ash. "What is on your mind?" She put her hand in Ash's hair and softly stroked it. "Why did you cut all your hair off? Lice?"

"One bloodsucking louse," Ash said, but she leaned into Rose's touch.

"What have you seen, you poor thing?" Rose said. "You are my favorite sister. I hate to see you like this."

"Bluebell would not want me to tell you."

"Bluebell does as she pleases and cares little for what anyone thinks," Rose said dismissively. "Are you not tired of that?"

"I had four years to miss her," Ash replied.

Rose went to the basket that hung from the beam, where the candles and flints were kept. Ash watched her as she lit a candle and set it on the table by the bed in a little bronze holder. The candleglow bathed the room in amber. Rose grasped her hand and pulled her away from the window, down onto the bed beside her.

"Tell me," she said.

"You remember Unweder?"

"Yes."

"He has taken dragon form and is hunting me. I have dreamed many times about a dragon that comes for me and destroys thousands of people. I believe this is my Becoming."

Ash noticed Rose recoil a little.

"Then what—?"

"Bluebell wants to draw it out and have the army kill it."

"Will our father be involved?"

"I expect so. She wants to do it after we've seen the ice-men off." She dropped her head. "If we see them off."

"We've never lost a war against raiders," Rose said.

"Yes, and they know that. Which means they have something different this time. Some new horror to bring with them."

Rose turned her eyes to the window for a moment, thinking.

"What is it?" Ash asked. Something about the cool, damp air and the candlelight made her apprehensive.

"In the woods, when I was . . . lost, I saw a vision. An old washer-woman, washing blood out of Father's clothes."

Ash knew, in an instant, that her father would be a casualty of her feud with Unweder. She jumped to her feet. "That's it. I have to leave."

"Ash, no. Perhaps it was just—"

"I cannot expose so many to danger, and especially not my father, the king of Almissia." She went to the door and started hammering. "Open up! Open up!" she shouted.

The door opened, and Sighere stood there, blocking the way with his broad shoulders. "My lady Ash?"

"I need to leave. I never should have come."

"I cannot allow that."

Ash wanted to wrench off her cloak and blast the door off its hinges. But that might mean Unweder would find her. Instead she tried to appeal to Sighere's good sense. "Sighere, Bluebell is mistaken about the dragon. She killed one, yes. A small one. This one is twice as big and it will burn a dozen men before you get near it. You cannot kill it. Only I can appease it, and I want to do that. I want to do that right now. Let me go. Please, let me go. At least let me get out of Withing. I will take myself into the woods." She realized that she had descended into sobs. Rose was behind her, curling an arm around her.

Sighere looked from Ash to Rose and back again. "Stay in here," he said.

"But I—"

"I will arrange it," he said. "I will arrange for you to leave Withing, but I cannot allow you simply to walk out into the world unguarded."

"Do you not see? I'm dangerous to whoever accompanies me!"

"My life would not be worth living if Bluebell knew I'd let you go alone," Sighere said. "I will send one of my strongest spearmen with you. When the battle at Seacaster is over, Bluebell will come for you herself."

"I'll go with you," Rose said.

"I cannot allow you to, Rosie," Ash said. "It's too dangerous."

"She's right, Princess Rose," Sighere said. "Keep your sister calm and quiet tonight and tomorrow I will come for her."

Rose nodded and Sighere backed out, closing the door.

"Do you feel better?" Rose asked.

"I'd feel better if I was back on the empty coast," Ash said, but even as she said it she knew it wasn't true. The thought of exile made her soul grow chill. "But this idea of Sighere's will work for now." She forced a smile so Rose didn't know that she had already made up her mind. The moment she was alone with the spearman, she would run.

Chapter 32

Despite her protestations otherwise, it was clear from the dark shadows around her eyes that Rowan was tired. Bluebell pulled her onto Torr, between her arms, and told her to sleep on the way.

"Will you make sure I don't slide off Torr's back?"

"That I will, little chicken," Bluebell replied, aware that the pet name no longer suited this young colt.

Rowan fell silent for a long time. Perhaps she did sleep. Hours passed. The remaining light disappeared from the sky. The road moved under Bluebell, a dark ribbon. Bluebell was aware that she would be tired when she arrived in Seacaster for war; that this was folly.

Rowan's voice suddenly piped up in the dark. "Whose daughter am I?" she asked.

Bluebell wasn't sure how to answer.

"Oh, I know who provided the seed from which I grew," Rowan continued. "Heath is his name."

"I know. But you oughtn't—"

"Yes, I'm aware I oughtn't. The peace between kingdoms relies on me not telling anyone. But my question goes deeper than that. Who should I consider my father? The man who provided the seed?

The king who thinks I'm his, who has seen me kept from harm all these years? The hunter who raised me in the woods and whom I love with all my heart? Or Rathcruick, who wants to elevate me as the queen of the Howling Wood and from there all of Thyrsland?"

"Is that what Rathcruick wants?"

"Yes. So he says. I'm to accept him as my father before that can happen. But answer my question: Whose daughter am I?"

Bluebell was silent a long time. Rowan's sudden intensity reminded Bluebell that she wasn't a little girl anymore.

"Perhaps you are nobody's daughter," Bluebell said. "Perhaps you are your own thing." She thought of her father, how she loved him and worried for him and grew frustrated with him. "Perhaps you are just Rowan."

"Do you think we will be able to save Snowy?" Rowan asked.

"Of course."

"Will you kill Rathcruick?"

"If he gets in my way. Yes. Why?"

Rowan shifted in the saddle, bony elbows and shoulders poking Bluebell in the chest. They were entering a wooded valley. Shadows grew around them. "I feel sorry for Rathcruick."

Bluebell told herself to be patient. "He imprisoned you. He forced that tattoo on you. He robbed you of part of your childhood. Why exactly do you feel sorry for him?"

"Because he lost his daughter, and he loved her so much. And I feel sorry for all the First Folk," Rowan continued. "They have lost their lands and been forced to the margins of the world."

"They lost them fairly, in battle, as all people who lose their lands do. As would we, should the raiders come south and win." Bluebell made her voice softer. "Little one, you will one day be a great queen, and compassion is one of the marks of a great queen. But so are firmness and decisiveness. Toughness."

"There is First Folk blood in me," Rowan said.

"And Thyrslander blood in larger measure. The First Folk aren't your people. We are your people. Your mother's family. Wengest and his family."

Rowan lost a little of her stiffness of spine. "Wengest," she said simply. "Will I have to return to him?"

"Yes. Do you bear no love for him at all?"

Rowan sagged a little. Bluebell wished she could see the child's face. "In fact, I bear too much love for him, for somebody who is not in any way my blood. The other man, Heath, is a stranger."

"You've met him. When you were little."

"I don't remember."

"You liked him."

"What is he like?"

Bluebell considered how to answer this. Finally, she said, "Your mother loved him so much that she risked everything. She defied every demand I made not to see him."

"She defied you?" Rowan chuckled. "I cannot imagine it."

"Rose does what her heart tells her," Bluebell said. Was that why she was rescuing Skalmir? Because her heart told her? Bluebell dismissed the thought. The important thing was to send a clear message to Rathcruick that he could not challenge her sovereignty. "Rose's heart told her to love Heath and keep loving him, despite good sense," Bluebell continued. "If your mother loves him, he must be a good man, don't you think?"

Rowan didn't answer.

After a while, Bluebell asked, "Why don't you want to go back to Wengest?"

"It's not that. I just don't want to leave Snowy."

Bluebell didn't reply, but she understood the sentiment only too well.

The weary night seemed to go on forever. Bluebell almost dozed off once or twice, rocked to sleep by the rhythm of Torr's hoofbeats. When light began to glimmer in the horizon, Rowan suddenly snapped awake, jerking upright in the saddle.

"We are here," she said. "The gate is nearby. We should leave Torr here."

Bluebell reined Torr in and dismounted. She walked him about for a few minutes then hitched him to a tree and patted his withers, taking down her shield. "Back soon," she said, though she didn't know how soon. Then the thought came to her that maybe she would not defeat Rathcruick, or that maybe the strange passing of time would affect her, and she worried for Torr and untied him. She didn't want him here for days without any chance to find food or water. She thought about Seacaster. The army. Her father.

"We need to get in and out quickly," she said to Rowan.

Rowan took her hand and said, "This way."

They walked a hundred yards away from the road, uphill, and came to a dolmen that stood to about Bluebell's hip height.

"This?" Bluebell asked. She had been expecting a grand barrow, like the ones out on the moors of Almissia.

"Dardru's spirit is in me. I can cross any gate," Rowan explained. "They are all laid out in a pattern that the First Folk understand."

Bluebell struggled to reconcile Rowan's great power with the girl who stood before her. "I am in your hands," she said simply.

Rowan spread her fingers on the top of the dolmen, where a curlicue pattern had been carved. Bluebell braced herself for something to happen.

But Rowan said, "Before we go, I want something from you."

"What is it?"

"You expect me to go back to Folkenham, to Wengest, and to pretend I know nothing of my real father, that I haven't seen my mother and know nothing of her lies. He will see with his own eyes that I have spent time under enchantment and no doubt arrange for the fat preacher Nyll to pray over me daily."

Bluebell winced. "Yes, I do expect that. I expect it because I will have no heirs of my own, and you will be—"

"Yes, yes," Rowan said impatiently. "And I will do this, as long as you hold a promise to me."

Now Bluebell felt uncomfortable. The peace between Almissia

and Nettlechester would only hold if Rowan did as she said she would. "Well, tell me what it is and I will see how I feel about it."

"I want you to admit that you love Snowy."

This request was so unexpected that Bluebell laughed out loud. "What? No."

Rowan stood, spine erect, her hand on the dolmen. Deeper in the wood, a bird began to sing and it almost sounded like a laugh. "Admit it, Bluebell. I know it to be true; why do you not? You have left behind a battle to come to him. Admit it and tell him."

"Why do you want me to do that?"

"Because he loves you. Bring him to Blickstow, and love him, and he will be happy."

Bluebell didn't know if she was talking to a child with a silly idea stuck in her head, or a half-magic heir to First Folk blood who had cold flint in her heart. Then she realized: Rowan was both.

"What if I make him unhappy?" Bluebell said. "What if I change my mind about him? What if I am always away at war? What if I take—" She had been going to say, *What if I take other lovers?* but pulled up, remembering she was talking to a child.

"Snowy would expect no conventional behavior from you," Rowan said simply.

Bluebell considered her. The forest was very still. "And you will keep our family's secrets if I do this?"

"I promise to."

An image of Snowy came to her mind: his strong tanned hand spread across Thrymm's ribs, whispering softly to the distressed animal, close to her ear. He was gentle and capable in all things, strong of heart and straight of principle. Surely she was enough of a woman to know the difference between lust and love? She thought about her father, his loneliness making him morose. A king needed a companion. "I will do it," she said. It seemed a small price to pay, under the circumstances.

"Really?" Rowan giggled and sounded for a moment like her old self, and Bluebell regretted making the promise to the little girl. She was opening her mouth to caution Rowan to expect nothing too soon, but then the girl pressed her hand into the dolmen, and in a blink they were in a clearing among old woodland, hazel and oak. It was no longer predawn; it was late afternoon.

Bluebell fought to gain her bearings, but Rowan was already moving. "This way," she called.

Bluebell followed.

Skalmir didn't know how long had passed—minutes or weeks—in the hastily repaired cage in the singing tree. They had bound him hand and foot, now, so his time was spent wriggling in discomfort, unable to find a position that wasn't painful or constricting. Sometimes he fought against his bonds. Sometimes he lay in the bottom of the cage and wished to die, while the tree was singing in its uncanny beauty.

They never left him alone as they had left Rowan alone, and he understood now that leaving her alone had been a strategy to frighten her. This fact made him harden his heart all the more against Rathcruick. To frighten a child deliberately was cruelty beyond his imagining.

Then one late afternoon, a commotion arose below him. Two woodlanders came rushing along the path from the encampment, and spoke in urgent voices to the guardsmen who had been placed below him. He couldn't make out everything they said, but one phrase was very clear: "Dardru returns."

Dardru. They meant Rowan. She was coming back to rescue him. In his head, he said no a thousand times. He willed her away. He wanted her away and safe. Perhaps Rathcruick had always known she'd return. Perhaps that was the point of keeping Skalmir alive.

The cage began to move, and Skalmir realized they were bringing him down to the ground. They normally only did this when they were going to feed him, which they had already done two hours ago, so his spine prickled with suspicion. One of the guardsmen, a large, meaty fellow with an enormous flaming-red beard, pulled the key off his belt and unlocked the cage.

"Where am I going?"

"Rathcruick wants you at the camp."

The camp. Skalmir had never seen it. In fact, he hadn't seen Rathcruick this entire time. He was roughly pulled through the door of the cage and stood on his feet. They slashed the bonds around his lower legs, then marched him into the woodland.

It had been so long since he'd walked that at first his knees buckled under him. His feet were still bare, though the dog bite had healed. The woodlanders did not tolerate his weakness, taking him under each arm and half dragging him along the earthen path, layered with leaf-fall, to Rathcruick's camp. The woods opened up on a round encampment, surrounded by a wattle fence that stood to head height. The gate was unlatched and the woodlanders pushed him through. Inside the fence were a dozen small round houses, roughly built of mud and thatch. In the clearing amid them all, a pyre had been built of bracken and cut wood. And in the center of the pyre was the hewn trunk of an oak sapling.

"No," Skalmir said.

Two more of the woodlander men and one stocky woman descended on him, pulling his feet out from under him. He kicked vainly against them, but the bonds had been so tight that his muscles were feeble and they easily got him up the pyre and against the post, where they lashed him around and around with vines and ropes so that he was tied fast. Then Rathcruick himself emerged from one of the huts, the antlers on his head, dressed only in a deerskin, and poured fire oil on the kindling.

Skalmir had seen many people die, including those he loved the most, but he was unprepared for the sheeting panic that burned inside him now, and was ashamed and horrified to realize he'd wet his breeches in his fear. "Please spare me," he gasped. "I have never meant you harm."

"Dardru comes," Rathcruick said, as if it explained everything, and he stood aside, his back turned to Skalmir, eyes fixed on the gate.

They waited.

Bluebell sped through the forest after Rowan, who seemed to know it as well as if she had lived here her whole life. Bluebell understood this knowledge was from the other woman, Dardru, whose echo was lodged somewhere inside Rowan's lithe body. They passed a tree whose branches caught the wind in such a way that something like music radiated from it. Bluebell found the music too eerie to admire, but Rowan stopped a few moments to listen, and to point out the empty cage that lay on the ground.

"That's where they held me. And Snowy." Her face looked uncertain.

"Then where is he now?"

"They must have taken him to the camp. This way."

Deeper and deeper into the wood, swallowed by its shadows and its pockets of cold air. Then finally they came to the fence. The gate lay open.

"They are expecting us," Bluebell said, indicating the gate. "They want us to come in." She drew her sword.

Rowan touched her wrist. "Don't kill anyone if you don't have to." She cleaved close to Bluebell's side as they walked through the gate.

The moment they emerged from between two round houses, they found themselves in an open area with a pyre in the center. Snowy was tied to a post on top of the pyre, Rathcruick standing in front of him, branch antlers worn proudly on his head. An archer stood to either side of the pyre with flaming arrows nocked in their bows.

"No!" Rowan cried, pulling her hand out of Bluebell's and running toward Rathcruick.

Bluebell lurched forward and caught her, yanked her back in the crook of her arm and held her firm. Other woodlanders emerged from the little round houses, so that in all a dozen people now stood around the pyre. She heard a pig grunt. The whole place smelled of mud and shit. A dirty trough sat outside the largest round house: It seemed the king of the woodlanders had his own pig. Impressive.

Bluebell could rush at Rathcruick, but that would almost certainly result in the fire beneath Snowy being lit. If she tackled one of the archers, the other would still find his mark. So she stood and in her biggest voice boomed, "Let him go."

"Let *her* go," Rathcruick said, indicating Rowan with an imperious sweep of his arm.

"Let me go," Rowan said in a low voice to Bluebell.

"No, I—"

"Let me go," she whispered again, more urgently.

Bluebell looked at her, felt the tingle of uncanniness again, and released her.

Rowan walked directly toward Rathcruick.

"No, Rowan," Skalmir shouted. "Don't do this. I am not afraid to die."

Rowan took another pace, another, then swift as lightning had her bow in front of her, an arrow aimed directly at Rathcruick's head. "Tell the archers to stand down," she said.

Rathcruick blanched. "Dardru, I—"

"I am Rowan, not Dardru. I feel her inside me, I know you are the father of my spirit, but that man"—she indicated Skalmir with a nod of her head—"is the father of my heart."

The sky seemed to hold its breath, and Bluebell was alert as a cat.

But then, "Extinguish the arrows!" Rathcruick cried.

Bluebell exhaled softly. She sheathed her sword and took a step toward Snowy.

Then everything turned to noise and movement. One of the archers, either through pride or carelessness, loosed his arrow. The pyre at Snowy's feet blazed to life.

Rowan screamed, and she sounded like a little girl again. Bluebell rushed toward Snowy. The woodlanders all moved toward Rathcruick to close ranks around him, and the archer who had shot the flame crossed Bluebell's path and tried to trip her.

Red mist descended, and the Widowsmith was in her hand and his blood was on the ground a second later. Arrows whistled through the air and she held her shield aloft and heard one thunk into it, while another grazed past so close that her hair moved. She looked up to see Rowan trying to get close to the fire.

"Rowan!" she called, dropping the shield on the ground and reaching for the knife in her boot. "Catch!"

She threw the knife to the girl before thinking it through. It turned over in the air, then Rowan caught it by the handle. Of course she did. Bluebell didn't see what happened next because she was scooping up her shield and going after the archer that had shot at her. Rathcruick was surrounded by flame-haired men and women now, some with arrows trained on her, another who rushed at her with a spear. She had her sword up, ready to bring it down on his head when Rowan called out, "Stop! Please, all of you! Stop!"

Bluebell held her blow, shouldering her shield up and not taking her eyes off Rathcruick and his men. Rowan had thrown the knife to Skalmir, who was even now hacking at his own bonds. The fire crept higher. He'd never be free in time.

"You! The trough!" she ordered, and when the gingery fellow with the spear didn't move, she ran him through and turned to the next one. "The trough. Now."

This time, it worked. Not only did the woodlander move, but so did two of his companions, leaving Rathcruick exposed. Bluebell moved in and seized him, shouldering off anyone who tried to stop her and holding the sharp edge of the Widowsmith across his belly. She could feel his heart beating through his hot back. As calm as he wanted to appear, his racing pulse gave him away.

The fire was extinguished. Skalmir finished with his bonds and stumbled down, trousers smoking and black. Bluebell could see one side of his trousers had been burned off, and black bloody skin showed through. Her rage flared and she pressed the blade a little harder.

Rowan got under Snowy's arm and helped him across to where Bluebell stood.

385 SISTERS OF THE FIRE

385 SISTERS OF THE FIRE

"You stink," she told him.

Rowan put her hand on Bluebell's wrist once again. "Lower your sword, Bluebell," she said.

"And have these wild beasts kill me?"

"They won't, because if they do I will never come back."

Bluebell felt Rathcruick flinch.

Rowan lowered Skalmir to the ground and came around to face Rathcruick. "I will want to know you one day," she said to him, "but you cannot demand my esteem, you can only earn it. I will come to you when I am grown to learn about my First Folk blood, but only if you let us go now."

"Get your aunt to drop her sword."

"Bluebell, please."

"When everybody else drops their weapons," Bluebell said.

Rathcruick gave a nod, and bows and spears were dropped on the muddy ground. Bluebell, alert to the slightest movement, slowly withdrew her sword but did not sheath it.

"As you wish it," Rathcruick said to Rowan, with the slightest bow of his head. "But do not forget who you are."

"I know who I am better than you do," Rowan said. "Bluebell, Snowy, we can go."

Skalmir was on his injured feet now, moving away after Rowan. Rathcruick turned and gave Bluebell a withering look—disdain, loathing—and without thinking she lifted the Widowsmith and swiped it through his branch antlers, reducing them to an inch in height.

Woodlanders lurched forward, scrambling for their crude weapons, and Bluebell turned to fight them.

"Come on, then," Bluebell said.

"Stop it!" Rowan cried.

"Let her pass," Rathcruick said grudgingly. He was no longer the noble woodlander king, but a sad, slightly plump man with broken antlers. Bluebell liked him better that way.

She ushered Rowan and Snowy out of the encampment, backing out behind them with her sword ready. The woodlanders watched her go but didn't follow. She kicked the gate closed and Rowan was already running into the wood.

Bluebell got Skalmir back to Sister Julian's house in Nether Weald on Torr's back, while she and Rowan walked alongside. All the while the press on her heart: the dawn deadline in Withing retreating farther and farther from her. But Skalmir could barely move due to the damage to his leg and feet, and could barely speak for pain. Bluebell had seen many burns in her life, and she knew how easily they filled with infections. She couldn't allow him simply to return to his home and hope for the best.

Sister Julian took one look at the wounds and said they were too severe for her to treat, and that he would have to go to Folkenham and see a physician from the Great School. "Do not delay," Julian said. "I will fetch some milkberry-leaf sap to soothe the pain, but it will make it sticky and attract dirt. You will have to clean it every few hours on the journey."

Bluebell was not going to Folkenham. That was entirely in the wrong direction.

Julian left Bluebell and Rowan with Skalmir and went to fetch her milkberry leaf. Skalmir grimaced up at her. "I will make my own way to Folkenham. You have to meet your father."

"They have a full infirmary in Seacaster," Bluebell said. "I'm sending you there, in a padded cart, with two swift horses. Rowan, you go with him and tend his wounds."

"There is no need," he said.

"Seacaster, Bluebell?" Rowan said. "While there is a war and many injuries for the city infirmary to treat?"

"Raiding bands have been in these parts, and you can wager that any one of those raiders would like to be the one to cause me sorrow. I want you both behind the walls of the shorefort. It's the safest place for . . . those I love." Her pulse thudded at her throat and she glanced at Rowan, who was smiling.

"My lord," Skalmir said, a laugh in his voice, "did you just say you love me?"

Bluebell could barely hold his gaze. "Yes, I do, Skalmir Hunter. I love you. But I won't say it again, so never ask me. You can trust me to tell you if the situation changes. Now both of you wait here while I go to the village square and organize a cart. I need to get back to my hearthband. I have been away too long."

CHAPTER 33

By evening on the second day, Ash was almost crazy with frustration. She began to suspect Sighere had promised her a freedom he never intended to give her. He had not been to see her, and she and Rose were locked in. "For your safety," the strapping young man with the hawk's nose on the other side of the door told her. Ash didn't feel safe. She had not felt the press of Unweder's interest at all that day, but she knew it would return. He would never stop trying to find her.

When supper arrived and Sighere still had not, she tried to get through the door and past the armed warrior.

"I am under the strictest orders to keep you safely in this room," he said, an arm as dense as stone shooting out to block her exit. It would have taken barely a thought to have him blasted backward by air elements, or for a roof beam to crack above him, but her protective cloak muffled her magic.

"Where is Sighere?"

"He is organizing your transport," the young warrior said.

Ash's heart lifted. "Really?"

"You will be traveling under cover of the night."

The relief. Ash's knees wobbled. "And will Sighere accompany me?"

"No, you will be accompanied by Gytha, who is your sister's first spearman."

"Nobody else?"

"The driver."

"Driver?"

"A closed cart, my lady, so you cannot be seen from the road." This was Sighere, striding down the corridor with his shadow looming ahead of him. "You can sleep on the way."

"I will be happier if I can walk."

"You have walked far enough these last few years, Princess Ash. The driver will also be an armed warrior. He will leave you and Gytha somewhere safe, until Bluebell comes for you. After Seacaster."

Somewhere safe? There was nowhere safe. But she didn't say it. Let them believe she would happily wait in some obscure hovel with Gytha the spearman until Bluebell decided it was time to kill the dragon. Ash would be gone long before her sister got there.

Within an hour, Ash was saying goodbye to Rose in the cobbled town square. Ash held her close, knowing it might be the last time she saw her; but not so close that Rose suspected Ash intended to flee. Night was closing in; rain threatened.

"They say we go to Seacaster at dawn," Rose said, and she sounded fearful. "Bluebell and Rowan haven't returned. Can you . . . see anything?"

Ash shook her head. "I cannot, but good sense would tell you that Bluebell will keep Rowan safe. You will see her again, at Seacaster." Ash thought about the dragon. Would he seek Bluebell out, hoping she would lead him to Ash? But no: Some kind of connection between them would be needed. His focus would be on Ash for now. Soon, Ash would let herself be found and Unweder would leave her loved ones alone.

"Thank you," Rose said. "The thought gives me comfort. Now here is a comforting thought for you. Your premonition of the dragon, Ash: You do not know when it will come to pass. Perhaps it is not now. Perhaps it is in the distant future, when we are old and used up. Take heart. Nothing is over yet."

Ash smiled tightly, tears stinging her eyes. "Thank you, Rose."

The closed cart was built of wood, with a superstructure of beams hung with moleskin. Gytha, the muscular woman who would be joining her in the cart, held apart an opening in the moleskin for Ash to climb in. "My lady," she said. "There are blankets. Make yourself comfortable. We will be quite invisible from the road."

Ash gave Rose's hand one last squeeze and climbed up. The cart smelled of old onions and dirt. Gytha climbed in, too, and pulled the moleskin flap closed. Voices outside, somebody giving the order, and then they moved.

Gytha sat in the back corner, her spear erect beside her. "Sleep," she said. "I will keep watch."

Ash lay down, pulled the blankets around her. Rain deepened overhead, making a soft rhythm on the moleskin. She didn't close her eyes. She glanced at Gytha from time to time. The woman kept her eyes on the back of the cart, never wavering. Her spear looked sharp. Proof against dragons? The rhythm of the cart and the rain-drops soothed her. She drifted off to sleep.

When she woke, it was still dark. Voices, shouting. She didn't know how much time had passed, but she heard the unmistakable sound of wooden boards under the cart. Hollow, as though laid over a great flanking ditch.

Ash sat up with a start.

Then Gytha's hand was on her shoulder, pushing her back down. "My lady, you will not resist."

"What is happening? Where are we?"

"Seacaster."

Ash's blood flashed hot. "Seacaster? But that's— But Sighere said—"

"On my lord's behalf, I apologize for the deception. You are to be guarded here in the hall tower."

"Your lord? You mean Bluebell? She is in the Howling Wood. How could she make such an order?"

"Sighere made it for her. He knows her mind."

Of course he did. She was a fool to think that Sighere would be any less stubborn than the lord that he served.

"You must let me go," Ash hissed, grabbing Gytha hard around the wrist. "Death by fire follows me."

Gytha easily withdrew her hand. "I have orders," she said. "You will either follow me or be carried."

In the end, they had to carry her: four strong men in jingling mail with Gytha bearing a flickering torch shouting orders the whole time. Ash called out threats, she called out pleas to be brought before Duchess Ivy, but the end result was still the same. She found herself locked in the hall tower, high above Seacaster, with an open view of the theater where her nightmare would play out.

Ivy woke to shouting. Footfalls thundering past. Dark under her shutter. She sat up, the dream she'd been having falling away. A meadow, running with the boys, no weight upon her mind. Now her heart was thudding, her knees like water as she tried to stand in the dark, steadying herself. Robe on, door open.

She stepped out to a whirl of noise and motion, men running.

"What's happening?" she croaked, though she knew what was happening.

Crispin was there a moment later, catching her under the elbow. "My lady," he said.

Firelight. The glow of firelight from the docks. She began to hurry toward it, to see, although she didn't want to see.

But Crispin caught her. "Go back to your bed."

"They're here, aren't they?"

"I will take care of everything."

"Have we heard from my father? Is he sending his army?"

"We have heard nothing yet, my lady." He glanced around, ensuring nobody was watching, then leaned in close and hissed into her ear. "Ivy. You are safer inside. With your boys."

"I feel so—"

"How you *feel* is not of issue. Raiders are setting fire to merchant ships. It's only a small group, but they are likely to be ahead of something much worse. If your *feelings* are all you have to offer, then take them inside the bower where they belong, and let me get on with the business of war."

She turned her eyes to his, saw he was angry, and flinched.

He thrust her away. "Go," he said. "Hold your children. Let me be in charge. It's what you wanted, wasn't it?"

"Yes, yes, I—thank you, Crispin. Thank you."

Then he was gone.

Eadric was at the door, looking out at her with frightened eyes. "Mama? What is happening?"

She took a deep breath, controlling her tears and her tremors. "Inside, my darling," she said, scooping him up and holding him close. "There's a fire but Crispin will put it out."

"Is it a big fire?" he asked, his little face stricken.

"It's a—let's get you back to bed." She kissed his plump cheek, nearly crumpled to her knees. Steadied herself once more. "All will be well. You'll see. Dawn will be here soon."

Ivy got the child back to bed then opened the door to the stone staircase and went up to the lookout on the second floor. From here, she could see the fishermen and dockworkers and merchants and their wives and children pouring toward the walls, shouting and crying, being let into the city square. Down at the docks, twenty or so raiders, dressed in wolfskins, brandished torches and axes. Though made small by distance, the wolfskin raiders still caused terror in her blood. Everyone knew they were full of reckless fury, heedless of pain. She watched as two of Crispin's men leapt on one. Even with shields, even outnumbered, one of them died taking down the raider, who struggled to his feet only to be cut down again.

Ivy closed her eyes, but the patterns of firelight still shifted against her eyelids; she couldn't make the horror go away.

❖   ❖   ❖

Bluebell caught up with her father and his army twenty miles out-side Withing. A short break at an inn, to combat her weariness, had seen her too far behind to meet Sighere by dawn. She galloped down the trade road instead, taking the side road toward Seacaster, when she saw from up on a rise her father's red-and-gold banner flying from the crest of his tent in the bright morning light. All around it were other small white shelters staked into the ground, men and women busy cooking or grooming horses or sharpening weapons or simply talking to one another, taking a last relaxed moment be-fore the fighting began. Bluebell estimated this was only half the army, about seven hundred warriors.

She made her way down the rutted pathway into the valley, and Sighere saw her and met her at the bottom. She reined Torr in.

"What do you think, Sighere?" she huffed.

"What's wrong?" he asked.

"I would have brought more."

Sighere turned to survey the camp. "It will be enough. We out-number the raiders, and our army will be better equipped."

"I still would have brought more," Bluebell said, then turned her attention to Sighere. "My sisters?"

"Rose is here, but I had to send Ash ahead. She wanted to run. I've had her transported to Seacaster, and she should be secured in the hall tower there."

Bluebell winced. Ash would be angry. "You did the right thing. Come. Let's find my father."

She handed her horse over to a steward and walked among the soldiers. The fields were overgrown with weeds, and the churning of many feet and heavily laden horses had made mud of the ground. Some of the warriors saw her and began to cheer. By the time they approached Athelrick's tent, he had already heard she was coming and was standing ready to greet her. He was richly dressed in mail and a deep-blue cloak, his thick silver hair warmed to gold by the morning sun. "I was not expecting to see you," he said.

It sounded almost as though she was unwelcome. No, she was imagining it. "I've ridden hard and traveled light," Bluebell said. "I will need armor before we head to Seacaster."

"Everything you need is here," he said. "Rose said you found Ash."

"Yes, but she is little more than a walking shadow. We have . . . business to finish, after this battle."

"I will see her then," he said. "For now, my mind is focused on Hakon."

"Bluebell!" This was Rose, calling from the opening of a small tent. She came hurrying over, ducking around a pack of war dogs sleeping. "Rowan? Where is Rowan?" Her cheeks were flushed and her eyes were wild with fear.

"I have sent Rowan directly to Seacaster with Snowy," Bluebell said. "He's injured and needs the infirmary there. She is tending him. They will be along in time. She is free of Rathcruick. For now."

"Rathcruick?" Athelrick said, frowning. "There's a name I haven't heard in a long time."

"I will explain all, Father, on the other side of this battle. Rose, will you excuse us? We need to discuss our strategy."

Rose nodded and turned away. When she was gone, Athelrick said to Bluebell, "Walk with me."

"My lord." She fell into step beside him, noticing he walked with a barely perceptible limp. She didn't mention it, waiting to see if he would offer an explanation himself. The noise and activity of the camp buzzed on around them. Flies rose from the mud and hung about Bluebell's hair. She swatted them away irritably.

"There are seven ships," Athelrick said. "I sent a scout off at first light to see if they've made it to Seacaster yet."

Bluebell sidestepped a pair of sleeping dogs, thought about Thrymm and wished she was there; she loved the taste of raider blood. "Perhaps they don't have Seacaster in their eyes. Perhaps they are intending to sail farther south to Brimheath."

He was already shaking his head. "It is widely known Seacaster is unstable. Gunther is dead, and Ivy burned all the chapels and took charge."

"She burned the chapels?" Bluebell didn't know whether to be amused or horrified.

"And took charge," Athelrick repeated. "Our Ivy. In charge of perhaps the richest port, and certainly the largest shorefort in Thyrsland."

Bluebell didn't tell him she had suggested Ivy do just that, even though she had specifically instructed Ivy to do it quietly. "She will be fine if she has good counsel."

"She has counsel. The captain of the guard is a clever enough fellow, I have heard. I fought my first battle alongside his father." His eyes became distant, remembering back through the years. Then he was back with her in the muddy camp. "He's ambitious, they say."

Bluebell shrugged. "Ambition is not a bad thing."

"I suppose not, unless it is in the company of unkindness." They had arrived near the outer edge of the camp and now began to circle it slowly. "Bluebell, it's Hakon. Not Gisli. They saw his flag. The raven."

"Fucker," Bluebell spat. "Of course it is. What is his game? How has he managed to amass seven ships full of men? Why hasn't Gisli stopped him?"

"Maybe Gisli couldn't. There was always strong popular support for Hakon, and Gisli has been seen by some as weak and pandering to us."

Bluebell turned this over. Maybe Gisli was dead. The thought chilled her. What cold and vengeful fury could be stirring in the breasts of those who loved Hakon?

"If we engage them at Seacaster, we will beat them," Athelrick said. "But Iceheart will remain far from stable and Hakon will be back."

"He hates me," Bluebell grumbled. "I need to kill him."

"You stay away from him. Let someone else kill him. I haven't forgotten about the trollblade."

"Nor have I." Bluebell wondered if Willow was with Hakon, but that was ridiculous. A trimartyr prig like Willow wouldn't go near a stinking heathen like Hakon. They walked wordlessly a few more minutes and finally Bluebell asked, "What's wrong with your leg?"

He responded with a blank expression. "What do you mean?"

"You're limping. Did you think I wouldn't notice?"

"I'm fine."

"Are you going to let me lead the army?"

He shook his head. "No. It might be my last campaign." He smiled, but the smile crossed his face and was gone like a ghost, clearly forced over deep sadness.

"Did you injure it?" she persisted.

"No. Maybe in my youth. It's simply getting stiff with age." A flicker in his glance. He was embarrassed.

Bluebell couldn't comprehend this: embarrassment? Because he was getting old? Anger, she could understand. Or regret. Sadness. But embarrassment? It was so unexpected that she was undone by it, but knew that to reassure him there was no shame in age would only intensify the feeling in him. She was saved from having to say anything by a shout from the far side of the camp.

The scout had arrived back, and was hurtling toward them on her horse. A steward came and helped her down, took the horse away. The scout was a little woman, slender and nearly a foot shorter than Bluebell and her father, dressed in plain brown clothes.

"What did you see?" Athelrick asked her.

She was still panting. "There are two hundred, laying siege to the gate at Seacaster."

Two hundred wasn't so bad. "Raiders? Definitely?" Bluebell asked.

"Raiders under the sign of the raven," she said. "But that's not the only flag they're flying."

"What do you mean?" Athelrick asked.

"The triangle."

"The trimartyr symbol?" he said, aghast.

Bluebell knew then that she had been wrong. Willow was with

Hakon. Somehow she had spent long enough in his company to convert him, which meant she had spent long enough in his company to learn how to wield a weapon. All her nerves lit up with white heat.

She turned to her father. "Two hundred at the gate. We need to leave now."

Athelrick nodded, then said to the scout, "Find the other war leaders, give orders to prepare to march directly on Seacaster."

Bluebell touched the gold embroidery at the edge of his sleeve. "Father, we need to go north first."

"North? Why?"

"If they have any inkling that Ivy got word out in time, they'll be expecting reinforcements from Wengest, not us. He's the king of Nettlechester. They'll be looking to the south for his army, out across the open meadows. We can come down through the woodland on the northern flank of the city." She vigorously hoped that he wouldn't look embarrassed again because he hadn't thought of this obvious strategy.

Without flinching, he turned back to the scout and said, "Tell them we're marching north." Then returning his attention to Bluebell, he said, "Find my steward and have him dress you. I want you in the best mail we have, and I want you behind a stout shield, and I want you nowhere near Hakon or whoever else he might have gathered along the way."

They both knew he meant Willow, but he was unable to say it aloud, unable to believe his own flesh had turned on the family.

"Yes, Father," she said, but only to appease him. Her blood pulsed hard in her veins. The fire had been lit inside her. She and her sister were on the opposite ends of a path, heading inexorably toward each other.

Every battlefield Bluebell had ever seen was originally a peaceful field or meadow. The meadows that lay in front of the ditch and banks that protected the mighty front gate of Seacaster were teem-

ing with wildflowers: daisies and marigolds, knapweed and but-
tercups, cowslip and harebell. All of it doomed to be bathed in blood
by sunset. Her father had already run down and dispatched the
small guard standing at the northern wall before they could warn
the rest of Hakon's army what was coming; the noblemen's horses
had been left in the woods with the stewards, and now Bluebell
marched behind her father's left shoulder, as the Almissian army
poured into the meadow.

The raiders had so far not succeeded in breaching the wall. Evidence of their attempts included hastily lopped tree trunks that had
rolled into the ditch, raiders fallen by arrows around the foot of the
wall, grappling hooks and chains lodged into the gate with a team
of men wrenching from every angle. The sky was sunny and windy,
and the twin flags of raven and triangle that had been raised over
the raider encampment flapped and snapped in the stiff breeze.
Shouts in their strange language rose on the wind, as they realized
who was behind them and turned to assemble and run back into the
meadow. Bluebell scanned for Hakon's mutilated face, for any sign
of Willow, but could see none. She adjusted her helm and drew her
sword.

Large battles excited Bluebell to such a degree that her senses
seemed to intensify until they outgrew her body, and merged into a
blur of light and sound around her. Through this divine fog, she
perceived all as happening slowly and deliberately, while her actions at the center of it were quick and faultless. The raiders began
to run and so did she, outstripping her father and plowing into the
fray with the Widowsmith raised, slashing and hacking, enemy
blades thudding against her shield. The battle stirred up whirls of
dust, coating her tongue and stinging her eyes. Blood flowed, slippery under her feet, but she stayed upright, whole. She was aware
of her father nearby, and he moved as a man half his age, the limp
banished by the war rush as it took him in its thrilling grasp.

A mighty thud sounded from across the meadow and Bluebell
glanced up to see that the city gates had opened and the footbridge
lowered into place. The city guard came thundering out across the

ditch, arrowing for the rear of the raiders' army. Athelrick cried out orders, and the flanks of the Almissian army flowed outward and around, trapping the raiders between Athelrick's men and Seacaster's guard. Fully surrounded now, with no way to escape, they became increasingly desperate. Their desperation made them deadlier but more vulnerable, and Athelrick and his army were known for precision and care. From front to back, from north and south, the raiders fell to the swords and spears of the Southlanders.

chapter 34

It was after, when Bluebell's senses had returned to normal and her body began to ache, that she met Crispin, the captain of the city guard. Two bonfires were being built: one for dead raiders, the other for their own fallen men. Already crows were circling the battlefield, drawn by the tang of blood. Bluebell was picking through the bodies, flipping over any who were facedown to see if Hakon or Willow was among them. The shadows had grown long and the air had cooled, when she looked up to see her father talking to a tall, handsome man with curling dark hair.

She strode over to them, and the tall man bowed deeply then offered her his hand. "Crispin, my lord. The captain of the guard and defender of Seacaster . . . and defender of your sister." The last was said softly.

She eyed him. Knew instantly he was fucking Ivy. "The raiders aren't all here," she said simply.

He nodded. "I was explaining to your father. Seven ships were seen. If they were full, there could be another two hundred of them unaccounted for."

"Wolfskin raiders came last night and set fire to the docks," Athelrick told her. She noticed he stood very still and stiff. "They were repelled swiftly, but they were clearly just a distraction to set up the siege at the gate."

"They nearly breached the wall before dawn," Crispin said. "But we forced them back and they settled there and camped until daylight. But now you are here we suspect they might try to come up through the docks. Every citizen is safe within the walls, but there are many frightened people in Seacaster, certain their possessions will be looted and their homes will be razed. If you and your father and your army would be willing to come in and stay, they would be soothed."

"Of course we will," Athelrick said.

Bluebell wondered where Snowy and Rowan were. Had they been able to get to Seacaster before the raiders? "They will have to fight uphill if they come from the docks," Bluebell said.

"Yes. I suspect it's why they tried to come in the front entrance. But we aren't as well fortified from the east gate. There is no ditch, just gates."

"And many hiding places," Athelrick added. "The city is like a rabbit warren." He shifted his weight onto his right leg, hiding a wince.

"We will spend the evening examining the lay of the city," Bluebell said. "Father . . ." She needed to tell him she was taking charge of the army, that he ought to sit out the next wave of raiders. But she could not bring herself to say it to him, and certainly not in front of Crispin.

"My men are tired from the march, Crispin," Athelrick said. "Could you send some members of your guard back to the camp to fetch our retinue and my daughter Rose and bring them within the city walls?"

"As you wish, my lord. We will need a guide."

"This way," Athelrick said, leading Crispin away.

Bluebell watched them go. Her father was limping, much worse than before. The sea wind was picking up, pulling her hair into knots. The pyres were lit now, and slowly men dragged their enemies and their friends alike toward them. All just flesh in the end. Someone had the pole that was attached to the raven flag and the trimartyr flag and was feeding it to the flames. A shout went up as bright orange flared on the flags and embers rose into the coming dusk.

Rose arrived among the cooks and stewards and grooms, in a large retinue of horses and carts, that evening. The pyres were burning low and the smoke hung over the meadow. The bridge was lowered and the retinue assembled in the crowded town square. Rose slipped away, not waiting for Bluebell or her father to find her. She needed to know if Rowan had arrived safely.

"Excuse me?" she asked a guard hurrying past. "Which way is the infirmary?"

The guard jerked a thumb over his shoulder. "Last building at the end of the laneway," he said. "Keep going until you think you've come to the wall of the fort."

Rose headed off down a lane between two buildings. Lack of sun had made the grass grow thin and thready, and many feet had churned up mud, carrying the wounded from the battlefield.

The lane grew darker, and she did indeed feel that she had reached the wall of the fort: rough stone seemed to stretch off in both directions. But then she saw the door to the north, a torch burning low in a sconce outside it, and she hurried her steps.

Rose pushed the door to the infirmary open and was immediately greeted by the smell of blood. In her agitated state, worried about Rowan, the smell made her feel ill. The room was brightly lit, full of movement, but terribly quiet. Laid on bloody blankets on the floor were thirty or more wounded warriors. Healers moved among them, wrapping wounds and applying salves. She quickly scanned the room, but Rowan was nowhere to be seen. Just to her right, inside the door, a trimartyr preacher sat with an injured warrior, holding his hand while he groaned softly. It was clear from the crimson wound in his head that he would not last long.

"There is no need to fear," the preacher said softly to him. "If Maava is in your heart, He will take you to the—"

The warrior grunted, snatching his hand away.

A tall woman with a hooked nose approached. She was dressed all in black, a physician of the Great School. "Are you here to help?" she asked Rose in a peremptory tone.

"I . . . I'm looking for my daughter. She looks about twelve years old. She would have come in with a tall, fair man."

"I have seen nobody who answers that description."

Rose's heart dropped. "If you see them, can you . . ." Rose looked around again, at the wounds that still needed tending, at the dying soldier who needed to be reassured he was joining the Horse God's train, at the pile of filthy blankets. "I am here to help," she said. "What would you have me do?"

Rose barely had time to look up for the next hour. She boiled water and washed wounds and wrapped bandages, and spoke softly to two men who left life behind. She heard the door of the infirmary open and close many times, as the walking wounded came in and out, but it was only when she heard a familiar voice that she glanced up.

It was her father, and he stood by the fire talking to the hawk-nosed physician.

"Father!" she exclaimed, and picked her way past patients to join him.

As she spread her arms out to hug him, he took a faltering step back and held up his hand. "Slowly now," he said.

"King Athelrick's knee is troubling him," the physician said. "Don't knock him down with your adoration."

"This is one of my daughters," Athelrick said, and he gently squeezed Rose around the waist, leaning close to her ear and saying softly, "Don't tell Bluebell."

Rose stood back and looked at her father. Alarm crept up her spine. He was injured, yet he intended to go to war. "Father, you ought not—"

"I have very overbearing children," Athelrick joked to the physician.

Rose wanted to tell him about the vision she'd seen, but held her tongue. She didn't know the words to use to warn somebody they might be doomed, and she doubted such a warning would induce Athelrick to stay out of the battle.

No, she would tell Bluebell. Bluebell would know what to do.

Ash stood at the open shutter, gazing out into the dark. The fog had rolled in, engulfing the view little by little. First the horizon disappeared, then the sea, then the harbor, the docks, and finally the houses and shops and even the city wall. But still she stood and watched the world she had rapidly been reabsorbed by, and wished Bluebell had never found her.

She pulled her cloak tight around her. It was the only thing keeping her from descending into complete despair. Unweder couldn't find her. Nearly two days had passed without the feel of him around her and she even allowed herself to imagine that he had died without her blood. Not given up, just run out of magic and spiraled out of the sky. And perhaps destroying the red dragon had negated her Becoming.

Within the walls, the city was crowded and noisy, with people making camp wherever they could find a few square feet. The icy fog would not be welcome among them, she supposed, but it might protect them from raiders from the sea for a little longer: All the guide beacons had been extinguished so sailing into the harbor would be dangerous. Ash had been locked into a warm room in a tower adjoining the duke's hall, where hundreds of rolled maps and deeds and contracts were shelved behind a small wooden table and a carved chair. A plain-faced serving girl had brought her blankets and soup, but she had appetite for neither sleep nor food. She had only an appetite to run. Nobody from her family had come to see her or speak to her. She had seen and heard the revels in the city square after the battle this afternoon, but Bluebell had not come. Was probably isolating her on purpose, so she infected nobody with her frantic fear.

At length, the air became too chill for her, making her fingers feel raw. It surprised her. She had been inured to hardship, had lived through four long winters with Unweder huddling in damp or drafty shelters a long way from comfort. She closed the shutter and climbed underneath the table with her blankets.

Ash thought sleep might take a long time to come. But she did slip off, quickly and deeply. At first her sleep was dark, shapeless, but as her body's natural rhythm brought her up to dreaming speed, the old familiar vision began to flash across her mind's eye.

Wings. Fire. The sea. The crowds of people.

Ash sat up, startled. Her pulse thudded heavy in her head.

"He can't find me," she said, grasping the cloak tight about her. "He can't find me."

No, not with his undermagic. But he only had to be in human form at an inn or crossroads to know that Athelrick had marched to Seacaster. That Bluebell would be there, too. And last time he'd seen Ash, she'd been with her sister.

Ash leapt to her feet. She cracked open the door and saw that her guard was dozing into his chest on the top stair. There was no time to consider; she made her way down the steps, silent as the grave, to the hall. Some of the local families—highborn types or important merchants—were camped here, their sleeping bodies still in the dark. By the hearth, armed men talked in low voices. She willed nobody to see her. But then, a short, round guardsman approached her and blocked her exit.

"My lady?" he asked.

"Let me go," she said, her voice thin and desperate.

"I have orders to ensure nobody leaves."

"But I have to leave Seacaster immediately."

He looked Ash up and down. "I take my orders from your own sister, my lady."

"Neither of my sisters would want me treated as a prisoner." She stepped forward again, and he moved once more to stand in her way.

"My lady, we are in a state of war," he said, kindly but firmly. "I will not stray from my orders. To do so would endanger my reputation, if not my life."

She considered the possibilities. He wouldn't kill her, would he?
Of course not. If she shoved him aside—she thought about her thin
arms, her insubstantial body—he'd leap ahead, bar the door, hold it
closed. Even if she raised spirits to push him aside and slip out, he
or somebody like him would catch her. And the city gate was closed,
and nobody would open it for her. Nor did she want to blast it open
with wind or fire, and then leave the city vulnerable to raiders.

"Please," she said. "If you won't let me free then would you
please . . . just . . . fetch Bluebell for me? Or have a message sent to
her? She must come to speak with me. I must leave before dawn. If
I don't, terrible things might happen."

"Everyone is fearful," he said with a smile. "Rest your mind, my
lady. Return to your bed and sleep. Nobody will enter Seacaster
while this fog is so low."

The sleeping guard clattered down the stairs then, a look of alarm
on his face. "Princess Ash, I'm sorry I—"

"Will you? Please will you send the message?" Ash asked the
short guardsman.

"Of course I will."

Ash did not feel reassured, but she allowed herself to be led up
the cold stairs and returned to her room. If she could speak to Bluebell, she could make her see sense. At first light, Ash would get out
somehow. Far away, where she should have remained all along.

Bluebell stood on the city wall, peering into the fog in the vain hope
of being able to see the harbor, but it was as thick as parsnip soup.
Everyone else seemed convinced that the raiders wouldn't risk
bringing their ships into harbor in such conditions, but perhaps
even now Hakon and Willow were rowing some small vessel
through the fog, to slip into Seacaster unseen and hide.

A bell began to clang out of the gloom from the east. Bluebell
turned and listened for a few moments, then decided to go and in-
vestigate. She crouched and jumped to the wooden trestle that had

been set up that afternoon. From there, she climbed down to the ground and passed through the crowds of people camped in the village square on her way to the gatehouse. They sat or slept around small fires. Women with drawn faces stroking the hair of their little children. Men dozing into their chests while sitting up on watch. Worried dogs following her with their eyes. The bell clanged again, and she noticed members of the city guard hurrying toward the gate.

"What is it?" she asked one of them. "What does the bell signify?"

"The gatehouse guardsmen have seen something," he replied, head bowed respectfully. "Follow me, my lord."

Bluebell followed him to the gatehouse and pushed her way to the front, taking the stairs first. Surely the raiders wouldn't try the east entrance again. They had lost half their army there already. The fires still smoldered in the field.

"What have you seen?" she asked the guardsman who stood on duty.

He pointed. "Two raiders."

She peered down into the dark. Two figures had emerged from the mist and now stood on the other side of the ditch. One a man, tall and fair like a raider, leaned on a smaller hooded figure who waved her free arm wildly.

"It's Snowy and Rowan," Bluebell said with a gasp of recognition. "Let them in." She hurried down the stairs two at a time and leapt onto the grass. "Let them in!" she commanded, and the guardsmen gathered around the gate and hauled it open, lowered the footbridge. Bluebell ran across it and caught Snowy against her. He was burning with fever. "What is this?" she exclaimed. "What happened?"

She indicated to two of the guards they should carry Snowy, and they lifted him between them. He groaned softly.

"The infirmary!" she demanded, and dragged Rowan along beside her.

Rowan's face was pale and drawn in the torchlight. "The driver would not bring us any closer to Seacaster than Birchley," she said. "He was too afraid of raiders."

"Birchley? That's ten miles from here."

"I thought at first Snowy might be fine at the inn there, but then he began to get the sweats. We walked."

Bluebell turned into the lane toward the infirmary. "Snowy walked with those wounds? When there may be raiders on the road?"

"I thought he might die otherwise."

Bluebell stopped and grasped Rowan by the shoulders. She could barely speak; the idea of losing Snowy was too close and raw. "You are full of courage and strength. I thank you."

She grasped Rowan's hand and pulled her along toward the infirmary. One of the guards kicked the door open and then they were inside, in bright firelight. A woman who looked like a bird of prey, all in black, attended Snowy immediately. Bluebell knew she was of the Great School, who were trimartyrs, but their knowledge of healing was renowned.

Bluebell was dimly aware that Rowan had slipped off, but her focus was on Snowy. "Are you in pain?" she said.

"I'm aflame," he responded. "My head feels full of boiling soup."

She squeezed his hand. She was overcome by the idea that she should come to love somebody, to go so far as admitting it to him and to herself, and then face losing him. "Skalmir Hunter," she said impulsively, "if you survive this I will marry you."

His eyes widened in surprise, but before he could speak the physician interrupted.

"Is this man a soldier?" she asked, uncovering the wounds.

"A hunter," Bluebell answered. "It's a burn. From fire."

The woman in black lifted Snowy's tunic and placed a hand on his stomach. "He is feverish. An infection has set in."

If Bluebell ever met the driver of that cart, she would separate his head from his neck with delight. "Can you help him?" she asked.

"I will do all I can, but there are many here to be tended."

Bluebell opened her mouth to say, *But he is important to me,* then glanced around. All of these men and women, lying here bleeding and in pain, were important to somebody. Then she saw Rose, her arms around Rowan.

She strode over, mail jingling. "Rose, you are working in the infirmary?"

Rose looked up but didn't let go of Rowan. "I want to be useful."

"Then keep an eye on Skalmir for me," Bluebell said. "I cannot be here for him."

Rose gave her half a smile. "He means something to you?"

Bluebell glanced back to Snowy. Before she could answer, Rowan interjected with, "They are in love."

Bluebell turned back to Rose, offered no further explanation. "I must take a few hours' rest. We may be fighting tomorrow."

"Wait, Bluebell," Rose said, grasping the cuff of her sleeve. "Father was in here earlier asking the physician for help with his knee. He's in pain and favoring it."

Bluebell nodded. "I suspected as much."

"I know that Father is one of the most famous soldiers ever known to Thyrsland and that pain will not stop him performing brave deeds; but Bluebell . . ." Here Rose dropped her head, clearly choosing her words carefully. "I saw a vision in the Howling Wood, of an old washerwoman, washing blood from his clothes."

Bluebell's arms prickled with gooseflesh.

"Will you stop him from going into battle?" Rose asked. "Please?"

"I will find a way," Bluebell said. She squeezed Rose's shoulder and touched Rowan's hair, then headed out of the infirmary and into the fog.

She took a few moments to offer words of courage and kindness to some still awake in the village square, then found the refuge of the hall where the highborn families, their guards, and her hearthband were situated. She helped herself to a bowl of porridge from the hearthplace and sat on a stool by the fire eating it, turning Rose's warning over in her head. Father knew he was injured, and yet he was determined to lead the army. Did he hope to die tomorrow? By steel, rather than winter, as he had said? He was a fool if he thought she would let him.

One of the city guard, a small mole-like fellow, approached her. "My lord Bluebell, your sister Ash wants to see you."

"Is she well?"

"I do not know. She was trying to leave."

"Leave the hall?"

"Leave Seacaster. She was wound up tight, desperate. She says she must speak with you."

Bluebell knew that Ash could not rest for thinking about Unweder; but she had the cloak to protect herself. Raiders were nearby, a real threat in the present. "She isn't to leave."

"Yes, my lord. That's what I told her."

"She will be asleep now. I'll see her first thing in the morning." Bluebell had no intention of going to Ash and talking around in the same circles again.

"Very well, my lord."

Bluebell turned her eyes up, wishing she could see through the wooden ceiling into the room upstairs. Was Ash sleeping? Or was she desperate, pacing, consumed with thoughts of dragons?

It didn't matter. Ash would have to stay in Seacaster, whether she liked it or not.

chapter 35

The fog lifted in the early hours of the morning, while the sky was still velvety blue and stars were only beginning to fade. Willow opened her eyes when she heard men's voices. A deep, low chant. She was curled at the end of a ship, her puddle of blankets pulled around her and over her. Rough men surrounded her on all sides. She knew Maava would not blame her for being indecorous while she was doing His work. Such manners and niceties were for weaker women. But the men's stares and jokes, guttural and foreign, made her feel exposed. While she was nested in her bedding, they couldn't harm her. Now she sat up and looked around, only to see a group of men standing around a bleating lamb, chanting. Hakon was among them.

"What are you doing?" she asked, horrified.

He turned, held a finger to his lips to silence her. Ragnar knelt and cut the lamb's throat, and blood pooled on the boards.

They were making a sacrifice to their heathen god.

Willow was enraged, speechless. She closed her eyes and prayed for the angel voices to block out the sounds of their shouts and cheers. Just yesterday, she had felt such pride knowing the trimartyr banners were being raised over the battlefield, but the Almissian army had come—not Wengest, but Bluebell—and the raiders had lost. A bloodbath under the sign of Maava. And rather than seeing their fallen companions as martyrs who would now spend forever in the Sunlands, the scouts who had seen it all told tales of their souls returning to the Horse God's hall, for an eternity of drinking and wenching. It had made her shudder. Now this.

She opened her eyes again. They had hung the sacrificed lamb off one of the masts, where it dripped blood and fluid onto the boards below. The sails were dropped, and the ship began to move. All smelled of salt water and blood and seaweed and sweat and raw wet wood. Above her a tangle of ropes and square, colored sails clattered in the morning breeze.

She went through the motions, sick in her soul. Folding away her bedding, taking care of her morning routine with no privacy and only her anger to shield her from curious eyes. Eventually Hakon brought her some bread and cheese to eat and sat with her a little while on the wooden board that had become her seat.

She glared at him.

"What is it?" he said impatiently.

"I thought this was a trimartyr army."

"We lost one hundred and eighty men yesterday on Maava's watch," he said simply.

"It was nothing to do with Maava. It was Bluebell who killed them."

He slapped her knee. "And now you kill her—you see? And when you do, they will all say Maava's name again."

"Will you?"

"Yes."

"Because you believe in Maava deep in your heart and love Him with all your being?"

He shrugged, his gaze skimming out over the water.

Willow took a deep breath, told herself that some miracle would yet make him see.

"We may be able to take the city from the sea, and if that looks unlikely we will simply set fire to everything. Burn their houses, their ships, their docks to the ground. If we can't have it, then nobody else can, either."

Willow experienced a small twinge of regret, but then hardened her heart. Heathens. Burners of chapels. They had offered such high insult, and it could not go unrepaid. "My destiny is upon me," she said. Her hand went to the pommel of her sword, and her mouth grew dry. "Kinslayer," she said softly, her own voice foreign to her for a moment.

"Are you equal to this, wife?" Hakon asked, his eye glittering intensely.

"I am." A hot shiver moved through her and she knew it was Maava, filling her with strength. "I am glad she is here. It is time to end this."

Hakon leaned in and kissed her, lips tight against each other, then pulled back and began giving orders in his own tongue. Willow licked her lips. They tingled from the kiss. She looked to the sky and smiled, warm and safe in her Lord's grace. Today would be a day Thyrsland remembered forever.

Bluebell woke when the door to the hall was opened and a shaft of bright morning sun fell on her face. She was instantly alert, sitting up with her hand over her eyes to shield them. Her father stood in the doorway.

"I let you sleep," he said. His armor and weapons had been cleaned since yesterday, so he gleamed in the sunlight. "You were on watch until late."

"Who told you?"

"Everyone who saw you." He smiled, his eyes crinkling. "Eat and dress. They are in sight of the harbor."

"They are?" She got to her feet. "You should have woken me earlier."

"There is time." He indicated the soldiers who crowded around the porridge pot at the other end of the hall. "There are four ships. At most, they have two hundred."

"Two hundred raiders. They are like rats," she said, brushing out her hair with her fingers and weaving it into a rough plait. "They will be in among the crooked streets, setting fires and looting houses. We must drive them back at the docks." She wound her hair in a knot and searched about in her pack for pins.

"Of course we will. This is an easy battle to win."

"I don't like overconfidence," she said. "Are you recovered from yesterday?"

"Completely."

So he was going to lie to her.

"I will lead the army," he said.

Now she knew he had deliberately woken her late so she wouldn't ask too many questions about his stiff leg or interfere with plans already set in motion. Well, she could deceive him just the same. "As you wish, Father. Let me find my steward and eat, and I'll meet you at the east gate."

Athelrick nodded, then left her. Bluebell turned her back and went instead to find her steward. She was too angry to eat. It was time to put on her armor and go into battle.

Ivy was curled around Eadric and Edmund, but she hadn't slept even for a moment. Hilla had been reassigned by Crispin to cooking duties in the city square, and even though Ivy knew that every able body was needed to help, there was something about being left alone with the boys that made her feel boneless with vulnerability. She had hidden here in the bower, pretending to the children that all of the noise and commotion outside was a game, smiling and smiling over the fear. She daren't leave them alone even for a second, and so she hadn't even been to greet Bluebell. She remembered how fearsome Bluebell had appeared to Edmund in her mail and helm with her weapons rattling. Soldiers were steel and sharp edges; at such times as this, the boys needed skin and curves.

Ivy supposed she must be doing a good job of it: Despite her sleeplessness and her raw fatigue, they slept easily. She watched them in the gray light of the shuttered bower. Little Edmund's thumb was firmly wedged in his mouth. Eadric's eyes moved back and forth under his lids. How she loved her boys. How she feared for them.

Then the door burst open and made her jump. Crispin and several other men stepped in, all deep voices and beards and careless noise. The boys were awake in moments, looking around, sleepy and frightened.

"My lady, it is time for you to take the children somewhere safer."

"We are safe here," she said, but it sounded like a question.

Crispin sent the men forward with a confident hand gesture. "You will be taken to the hall tower where the rest of your family wait."

"The rest of my . . . ?"

"Your sisters Ash and Rose are here, and your niece Rowan."

Ivy took a moment to process this, then said, "Why the tower?"

"You can lock it from the inside if you need to, and it's stone so it won't . . ." He glanced at the children and dropped his voice. "It won't burn easily."

She stifled a gasp.

"We hope for all to be over within a few hours, and there is a standing guard at the hall. I can't spare men to watch the bower-houses as well."

Ivy rose. She hated it when he spoke to her as though no sweet words had ever passed between them. "As you wish, my captain," she said. "Come on, boys, we're going up to the tower for a little while."

"Mama, I'm hungry," Eadric said.

"We will eat something soon, darling, I promise you. You're going to meet some of your aunties." They were herded out into the morning light, then up to the hall. Crispin didn't even say goodbye.

Ash opened the shutter and peered out. The ships were plowing into the harbor and raiders were torching warehouses, causing a great conflagration of flame and choking orange smoke. The combined forces of Seacaster and Blickstow were pouring out the gate and down the cobbled hill to meet the invaders. Then lightning seemed to flash across her field of vision and her mind's eye transformed them all into walking corpses. Before she could even catch her breath, the vision was gone.

She turned her back to the shutter and closed her eyes.

"Ash?"

Her eyes flew open.

It was Rose. The door had opened and she was ushered in by a new guard, a stocky woman with straight black hair. "Are you all right?"

Ash shook her head, agitated. "I should go."

Now Rowan entered the room with Ivy and her children behind her, and the door was closed again.

"You look like death," Ivy said, by way of a greeting. "So skinny! Where have you been?"

"I *am* death," Ash said. These babies were so soft-skinned and sleepy-faced that she hardened her resolve. She didn't care if she was murdered by raiders. She was leaving. She brushed past Ivy to the door, slammed out, and thundered down the stairs with the stocky guard in pursuit.

At the bottom of the stairs the guard grabbed at Ash, seizing her cloak. Ash unfastened it and let it slide from her shoulders. Another two soldiers stepped in front of her to stop her leaving. "You can't—" one said, but his words were cut off by the blast of wind that wrenched the door off its hinges and sent it crashing to the ground outside. The wind whirled into the hall, sending all the tapestries dancing, the ashes in the hearth swirling up.

"Stand out of my way!" Ash shouted, and they crept back, fearful. She swept out into the open air.

Bluebell watched as they marched out the gate: There was no doubt Athelrick's limp had worsened. Only yesterday he had fought as hard as any of the young men against the raiders, but today he was paying for his vigor. She wanted him to have his last battle, but not like this. Not leading an army that could see him favoring his leg. Not on ground so steep and uneven that he could easily overbalance and fall prey to the rough steel of a much lesser man.

"Father, a word in your ear," she said, grabbing him around the upper arm.

As they stood on the road, the others separated and flowed around them like water. Athelrick gazed at her curiously.

"You cannot," she said simply.

"I can."

"On stairs and cobbles and steep roads?"

"I have been doing this much longer than you," he said, pulling himself up straight and puffing out his chest.

She gestured to the duke's gate—the small, bolted opening to the compound where the bowerhouses stood. "We need somebody to guard the duke's gate, the family, the tower where your daughters wait in fear."

"The tower is well guarded."

She held his gaze and his watery eyes blinked back at her defiantly. Anger and fear rose in her.

Bluebell kicked him. Hard. In his bad leg.

He cried out, bent to cradle his knee. "What have you done?" he shouted. "Foul, ungrateful child!"

"You cannot," she spat. "I will not see you killed at the hand of a filthy raider. Stay behind and guard the duke's gate."

He lifted his head and cursed her with his gaze.

"Come," she said, grasping him under his arm and helping him to hobble into place. She left him there at the top of the narrow spine of stairs that led straight down to the harbor.

"One day, you will see I did the right thing," she said to him.

"One day, you will be wise enough to understand what 'right' is," he shot back, but he didn't follow her.

Bluebell hurried down the stairs to lead her army, her guilty pulse thudding in her ears.

❖　❖　❖

Ash knew she would never get out the huge west gate of Seacaster. The footbridge was up, the ditch was fortified, and she would have to cross the entire city square and pass all the mobilized soldiers to get there. But from here, she could see a route down past the un-guarded bowerhouses to the duke's gate. It was high and narrow, bolted and locked, but on the other side was a staircase that led to the harbor. If raiders killed her, so be it. Once she was dead, she was of no use to Unweder, and he would have no reason to come for her.

By now her scalp was itching so violently that she could have happily ripped it off her skull. He was looking for her, finding her, but she had no idea how far away he was.

Ash didn't want to blast off the door and leave an entry point for raiders, but beside the bowerhouse she found a thick, fallen bough among the tangle of trees that screened the northern flank of the wall. She bent over and closed her hands over the rough wood and tugged it toward her. Bugs and ants began to run madly in all direc-tions, off the bough, over her hands. A sharp smell of decayed leaves and mud rose. The bough was cracked at one end, and rattled with dried leaves at the other. Ash pulled it all the way to the gate but couldn't lift it. She breathed, spread her palms, and the little hands were all around her, pushing the bough into place with its split end resting on top of the gate. Ash dropped her hands, waded through the dead leaves, and then carefully crawled up the bough to the top of the gate. The bough bent underneath her. Her skirts were tangled around her knees and ankles and she barely gained her balance on top of the gate before she dropped heavily to the other side, falling sideways onto her hip and grazing her palm.

It was only then that she saw her father, halfway down the stair-case, still and silent. He hadn't seen her yet. He was trying to keep people from heading into the city, not out of it.

Athelrick wouldn't let her leave.

Would he even recognize her?

She hesitated a moment, studying his profile. How sagging his jowls were now, how silver his beard. All her body and heart bent toward him; she wanted nothing more than to go to him and be embraced and told all would be well, just as she had when she was a child.

But that time had passed, as all times do.

Ash studied her surroundings. A high cliff face flanked her on one side, the crooked city on the other. She could vanish among the buildings, make her way to the docks through the narrow winding streets. Slowly, quietly, she stood, ready to disappear. Creeping down the stairs, seeing an opening into a side street . . .

But then her body began to tingle. Dread crept over her, into her. Mortal fear, cold as death. Her eyes went out to sea in time to see the harbor erupt with boiling steam and fire, to see the white dragon rise, salt water sheeting off its wings, and take to the sky. Fire reflected off its white scales, turning them crimson.

Ash was frozen. It was her Becoming.

And Unweder had found her.

chapter 36

"C lose the shutter!" Ivy cried. "I hate the sounds of war."

Rose glanced over her shoulder. Ivy had been sitting on the floor, clutching her boys and crying since the first horn of battle had been blown. "Ash has gone out there!"

"Ash is a grown woman and can do as she pleases. My children are just babies and they are coughing from the smoke. Close the shutter!"

"Close the shutter, Rowan," Rose said softly to her daughter, who was the one who had opened it in the first place. But Rowan did not respond.

"Please," Rose said to her, dropping her voice. "Your aunt is worried about her boys."

Rowan lifted her hand and extended it toward the sea. "Look. Both of you!"

Rose peered out and gasped. Ivy leapt to her feet and joined them. A monster, glittering in the summer sun, was rising from the sea.

"Mama?" Eadric said, his voice shaking.

"No!" Ivy cried. "No, not a dragon! They don't exist anymore." She descended into hysterical crying, pulled her boys with her under the table as though that could protect them.

Rose's stomach was hollow. Now the tower seemed the very worst place for them to be. It may have been made of stone, but it was the highest point of the city. If the creature was determined to attack Seacaster, it would come here first.

"Rowan, get under the table with Ivy and the boys," Rose said.

"No," Rowan said, striding to the corner where her belongings were and seizing her bow. "Help me out the window."

"What? No!"

"Help me out the window, Mama. I can kill it."

"You're a child!"

Rowan's mouth tightened, her nostrils flaring. Rose remembered that expression from her babyhood, the expression that came just before a tantrum. But Rowan simply brushed roughly past Rose, hanging the bow and quiver over her shoulder, and seized a chair.

"We need that!" Ivy said.

Rowan roughly shoved the chair in front of the window and climbed onto it. Rose, terror clawing at her heart, tried to pull Rowan back down. With strength and force unnatural in one so young, Rowan flung Rose's hands off her. She bent to look Rose right in the eyes, and Rose became aware that her daughter's eyes were different now. Harder. Older.

"I must protect my family," she said in a low, hissing voice. "I can kill the dragon. I *must* kill it." Then she pushed herself through the window with her back against the sill, took hold of the brickwork outside, and pulled herself up and out.

Rose threw herself under the table with Ivy, putting her arms around her sister. "Hush, all will be well," she said. The city was on fire, their children and sisters were in mortal danger. "All will be well," she said again, although it couldn't possibly be true.

Willow took her time. Swords were waiting for them on the docks, but the wolfskins went first with their flaming torches, then the raiders armed with spears and axes began to hack their way through the crowd. Willow was last to leave her ship, unused to the heavy mail whose weight lay across her shoulders, Hakon pushing her in the middle of the back. Smoke and bodies and shouting and confusion. *Grithbani* was in her hand and she refused to let the noise and blood distract her. Her instincts were homing in on Bluebell as easily as if she could see her. Maava was showing her the way. To the north. Bluebell was not among this mob; she was approaching from the east.

Hakon cleared a path for her, his mighty arms slashing and slicing. He was terrifying, a machine of death, hacking through heathens as they screamed for their mothers and for mercy. Many deliberately sidestepped him, some jumped in the water rather than face him. Willow could see they were outnumbered. She could foretell that Hakon's army would not be taking Seacaster—which made it all the more important that she take Bluebell.

Then, for a moment, the crowd cleared and she saw her sister, and her sister saw her. Charged recognition passed between them, and Willow plowed ahead. Bluebell shouted an order to somebody nearby and stood, waiting, the Widowsmith raised, an overturned rowboat on fire behind her so that she was outlined in orange flames, as Willow had seen her countless times in her mind's eye.

Willow's knees turned to water. Her hand felt moist on the hilt of *Grithbani*.

Hakon stepped aside. "Maava be with you," he said, and with this one simple phrase, Willow felt once again Maava's will rushing unfettered toward her. The surge of strength and faith in her body made her tall, powerful, and she ran at Bluebell with a guttural roar and the blessings of angels.

Bluebell deflected the first blow, but was unprepared for the speed of the second, twisting around awkwardly to block it. Willow was pleased to see her sister almost lose her footing, and even more pleased to see the expression of shock on what was visible of her face under her helm.

Willow drove at her again, received a shield bash in the face for her trouble, and stumbled onto her backside, heart thudding. But then a huge shadow passed over them, and a rumbling, sucking, drawing of mighty breath split the air. Bluebell's eyes went sky-ward, and Willow glanced up, too, and her heart leapt with joy when she saw it.

An angel had come. Glittering white wings spread across the heavens, spewing fire down on the heathens battling for Seacaster.

The dragon made one pass over the armies, indiscriminately breathing fire down upon the city.

"Ash!" came the cry, and Ash took her horrified eyes off the dragon's glittering wings long enough to see her father hobbling toward her.

"No, stay back!" she called, with a sweep of her arm. But a moment later the dragon arrowed straight for him, opened its jaws, and a long stream of flame shook down from the sky.

The last Ash saw, Athelrick lifted his shield and crouched. Then smoke and flame obscured her view. When it cleared, Athelrick lay on the ground shouting with pain. His shield was cinders on the stone, and his hands were two black smoking stumps.

Ash began to hurry toward him, but the dragon came to circle around her: once, twice, three times, as though saying, *See what I will do if you do not give me your blood.*

"I'm sorry, Father," she said under her breath, stopping in her tracks. She turned and put her face up to the sky. "All right, Unweder!" she called, her voice very small and thin against the roar of battle. "You win! Leave the city alone and I will meet you on the field outside to—"

Unsatisfied with this offer, the dragon shot off over the crooked streets of fishermen's houses, spewing down orange-bright fire. The heat made the air shimmer.

"What would you have me do?" she cried.

His voice was inside her head. *You will come back to the coasts of Almissia with me. You will give me a dish of your blood, every morning, and protect me with your elemental army. Vow you will do this, and I will leave the city be. Disagree, and I will burn the tower where your sisters and niece are.* As if to emphasize the threat, the dragon flew up toward the tower and circled it closely, the tip of its wing scraping across the stone. Ash could hear the terrified screams of the gathered citizens in the square. Then she noticed that Rowan sat in the window of the tower, her bow and arrow trained on Unweder.

"Rowan, you can't!" she called out.

Rowan loosed an arrow. It pinged harmlessly off the dragon's hide. Unweder lazily flapped away from the tower and then turned, Rowan clearly in his path, arrowing down.

Every morning. For the rest of her life. Living with Unweder again.

And she knew she could never agree to his terms; but neither could she disagree and let Unweder destroy everyone she loved.

There was only one way to end this, and that was to end the supply of blood magic that so effortlessly sustained his unnaturally extended life in all its forms.

Ash strode to where her father lay and pulled his sword from its sheath. "You want blood, Unweder?" she cried, and willed the air elementals to make her voice boom on the wind. "Come, then. Let us be done with this."

Athelrick tried to stand, but slipped and fell on his front with a shout of pain and distress. "Ash? Do not do this!"

Ash poised the tip of the blade over the hollow of her throat. Instantly, the dragon changed its path. Unweder's voice in her head shrieked, *Wait!*

The dragon landed, took two cumbersome steps toward her. She had thought facing death she would be frightened, but all she felt was bone-deep sadness for her loss of the world and all the beautiful people in it. Ash gripped the sword in two hands, ready to plunge it into her throat.

Bluebell abandoned Willow, on her arse on the ground looking stunned and shredded with exhaustion, and ran toward the staircase where the dragon was circling. Father was there. She had left him there, all but crippled, unable to defend himself. All the armies were in disarray, some running toward the sea away from the flaming city. She ran up the stairs, feeling the weight of her armor keenly. The dragon had plunged toward the ground, and as Bluebell ascended, it came into view. Father lay on his back over the stairs. She couldn't make sense of what had happened to his hands. He was pale and streaked with soot.

The dragon moved forward, but was too large and unwieldy in the cramped space. So with a strange shifting jolt of shadow and light, it transformed into a man in black.

Unweder.

With the dragon no longer crowding the view, she could see Ash before him, a sword awkwardly pointed toward her own neck.

"Ash, wait!" she cried, charging toward Unweder. If she killed him, then all Ash's problems would go away.

Then an arrow came whistling out of the sky, and Bluebell ducked and held up her shield. But it was Unweder who took the arrow, falling backward, bent at the knees like a ghastly puppet, blood bubbling from his chest. The arrow had struck him squarely in the heart.

Ash let out a cry: half a shout and half a sob. She dropped the sword and crumpled to the ground next to Unweder's body.

Bluebell ran to Athelrick. Panting, she fell to her knees. "Father, Father. My king," Bluebell cried, wanting to grasp his hands in hers. Never again. She would never hold those hands again. "You will be all right. I will fix you."

"You can't fix this, Bluebell," Athelrick said. Then he smiled through his pain and shock. "My granddaughter," he said. "Up on the tower."

Bluebell lifted her eyes to see Rowan standing on the peak of the tower roof, her bow held aloft in victory.

❖   ❖   ❖

Ash knelt over Unweder. There was yet a dull light in his eyes, but it faded fast. She had thought she might feel a sense of loss; he had been her companion so long. But she felt nothing but relief.

Bluebell strode over, placed her foot on his face. "Don't watch him die," she said. "He deserves our scorn, not our pity."

"There is no pity in my heart, Bluebell," she said. "Perhaps I have become hard."

"Perhaps you have simply become free."

Then the air around Ash began to buzz. As Unweder's life left him, a wave of energy was rising off him. At first only Ash could sense it, but then Bluebell was flung off him, and Ash could see a crimson-tinged fog of warm air around him.

As it expanded and touched her skin, she recognized this energy. It was her own blood magic, returning to her. Ash braced herself.

Then a hot wave crashed over her, knocking her on her back, tearing at her clothes and whistling into her ears, her nostrils, her gasping mouth, even the tiny pores on her skin. And as this energy entered her body, she felt every nerve and fiber swell with it, tingle and burn, then settle again but now pulsing with power. The wave was over as fast as it had come, and Bluebell was there, holding out her hand, helping Ash to her feet.

"Go to Father," Bluebell said. "I have to take care of Willow."

As Ash moved off toward the duke's gate with Athelrick, Bluebell turned to see Willow advancing on her, the trollblade in her hand.

"Come, sister," Willow cried and turned her wrist to flourish her sword. "I shall send you to the Blacklands!"

Bluebell wasn't in the mood for speeches about Maava, and no matter how good Willow was as a swordsman, she wasn't Bluebell's match, magic sword or not. Bluebell dashed down the steps, on the attack. Over, under, side. Willow blocked, but not fast enough. Bluebell caught her across the thigh and she staggered, cursed.

You could kill her.

Bluebell took a step back, held the death blow.

Just kill her.

A flash at the corner of her vision. Bluebell turned to see Hakon from between burning buildings, back where she had been standing moments before.

The hot slice of the sword on her exposed left shoulder. Bluebell rounded on Willow, angry, went hard after her. Over, under, side. Willow's other thigh opened up.

"Maava blesses me for my suffering," Willow said.

Bluebell knew she had to finish this quickly. "Drop the sword and don't make me kill you," she said.

Willow gathered herself, pressed forward, struck low from weariness, slashing across Bluebell's foot. Hot pain. Bluebell struggled to right herself. The stairs were uneven, steep. A flash of rage across her heart. Hakon's footsteps came fast, his ax held high.

Bluebell lifted her shield, caught Hakon's ax but exposed her middle. Willow lurched forward. With one swift movement, Bluebell brought her shield, with Hakon's ax still embedded in it, down on Willow's head.

Willow fell, striking her head on the ground. The trollblade clattered out of her hand. Hakon reached for it, but Bluebell reached for it, too, smacking him across the head with her shield. He sprawled flat on the ground, eyelids flickering.

Then the trollblade shot into the air. Bluebell leapt back and Willow cried out in triumph, "Maava be praised!"

But the sword spun in the air, then shot off toward the duke's gate. Bluebell turned to see Ash, her hands outstretched, a look of uncanny focus on her face.

"No!" Willow cried, struggling to her feet and stumbling past Bluebell on the stairs, falling on her backside.

Ash caught the sword, and Bluebell let go of a breath. If she trusted anyone with *Grithbani*, it was Ash.

Bluebell returned her attention to Willow and brought the Widowsmith down, stopped it half an inch above Willow's head. Her sister looked up, pupils shrunk to pinpoints.

"Don't make me kill you, sister," Bluebell said.

Willow remained silent.

Bluebell could see her pulse flicking at her throat. Hakon was rousing. She didn't have much time. She dropped her shield. Reached out her free hand to help Willow to her feet. "I don't want your blood on my conscience. The trollblade will be destroyed. Come back to Blickstow."

Willow's hand came up. Her white fingers closed around Bluebell's.

And she pulled with all her might, sending Bluebell pitching down the stairs.

Bluebell felt the first three thumps to her body, then everything went gray.

chapter 37

S eacaster burned. Willow was helping Hakon away. Father was horribly maimed. Unweder's body lay in a black and bloody heap. *Grithbani*, though safely slid inside her belt, was still intact.

But all Ash could focus on was Bluebell, long and blond and bloody and crumpled on the stone stairs at a horrible angle. She abandoned Athelrick and started down the stairs.

"Bluebell, Bluebell," she said, over the noise and heat and confusion. She picked up her sister's hand, felt its limpness. "Breathe. Talk. Be alive. Please, *please*, be alive."

She put her ear against Bluebell's back, listening for a heartbeat but unable to hear anything over the noise of war. She could see, though, that the raiders were pulling away, would escape on their ships.

Ash weighed the harbor with her mind and knew what Bluebell would want her to do. She stood and hurried down the stairs, calling out to all she passed, "Let them go! Let their ships sail!"

Crispin, the captain of the guard, caught her. "My lady?"

"Help me," she said, glancing back, molding the lie. "Bluebell wants . . . She wants them to leave unimpeded."

He gave her a curious look, but Bluebell's name worked the magic it always did. "Let them retreat!" he began to call, and slowly

Bluebell's army and Ivy's guard withdrew. One by one the ships limped away, some of them barely manned.

Ash planted her feet on the wooden boards of the dock, took a breath, and began to stir the water, pulling at the currents. It was easier than ever. Her returned power flexed in her muscles. With barely any effort of her mind's will, she grasped the tide and dragged it so that the raiders' ships were sucked out toward the mouth of the harbor. She could feel the ships resisting her and closed her eyes, shaking them off her. Then, once the open ocean's force was within her reach, she brought its mighty weight down upon them. Waves—giant rollers—began to crack and thunder around them, shattering them to pieces and carrying their debris far, far out to sea.

But now here came the tide, rushing back into the harbor. She opened her eyes and realized that the warriors were all still amassed on the docks. Ash had to stop the water crushing the wooden boards when it returned, so she desperately tried to grab its force and slow it. Her hands shot out reflexively in a stop gesture, but it was almost too late. The first waves were arriving.

She turned and crouched, a futile move to shield herself, throwing her arms up. The water followed the direction of her hands as though they were deliberately giving orders. Up and up a cloud of water went. When Ash saw, she only had to think of the flaming roofs of Seacaster for the sea to know where to go. The water, disembodied from the tide, fell like salt rain on the burning city.

She turned, soaked and gasping. All was in disarray. Bodies and men crying in agony, others on their knees with their faces turned to the sky. She wove her way between them, thighs aching and heart pumping as she ascended the stairs as fast as she could. Bluebell hadn't moved but Father had hobbled over and now sat with her, a look of terror on his face.

"Dead!" he cried. "She is dead! I see the Horse God standing over us."

Ash's heart seized in her chest. She dropped to the stair next to Bluebell and loosened her helm, pulled it off. Bluebell's face was slack, her skin pale. Ash's frantic fingers found the vein in her throat. Her pulse was weak and thin.

"Not dead," she said softly, sadly. "But dying."

Athelrick bent his head to Bluebell's chest, spreading his maimed and bloody arms over her ribs. "Take me!" he cried. "Take me into the Horse God's train, but leave my daughter. Give my life to her."

Ash could feel the air grow thick with the smell of horse and leather. It was true. The Horse God was nearby, and he had come for somebody. But did it have to be Bluebell? Along with her own power, some of Unweder's was in her, too.

"Father," Ash said. "You would give your life to save her?"

He looked at her. Tears ran through the soot on his face and beard. "What use am I?" He held up the blackened stumps of his forearms. "I am old and weak. There is enough life between us for one king; it should be her." Then his eyes grew sharp. "Ash? Can you . . . ?"

Ash closed her eyes, reached for the Horse God in her mind. She felt him as a huge, powerful force, hard as stone yet warm as sunlight. The question formed in her mind and was answered instantly. Yes, he would make the trade. She only had to be the conduit for Athelrick's life essence, and the echoes of Unweder's power would make that so. The air bristled. She opened her eyes.

"I love you, Ash," Athelrick said.

"I love you, Father." She withdrew *Grithbani* and held it angled up so the point was facing Athelrick. The runes on the hilt glowed blue.

Her father rose to a crouch, then fell onto the blade. A spurt of blood, and he collapsed over Bluebell's prone form.

Ash placed a hand on his back, the other hand around Bluebell's hip. Rushing through her, cold as frost and hot as fire, came Athelrick's life force. She was dimly aware that the Horse God had retreated. The thick air thinned, became smoky and briny again, but she was crushed under the weight of sensations and memories. Not memories of events that Athelrick had experienced on his senses; they all went with him and the Horse God. No, these were the memories of his living essence. Every heartbeat and breath drawn, every pulse of thought and twitch of limb. They rocketed through her and toward her sister, faster and faster, harder and harder, until Ash could not hold back the tide anymore, and her mind turned gray.

When Ash opened her eyes, her hand was still on Bluebell's hip. Neither Bluebell nor Athelrick was moving. A small group of Seacaster's guardsmen had assembled, looks of horror on their faces.

"Bluebell!" Ash cried, clambering to her feet. With a huge effort she tried to roll her father off Bluebell. "How can you stand there?" she said to the guardsmen. "Help me!" Two of them pressed forward and rolled Athelrick. He thudded onto his back on the stairs, the trollblade protruding from his chest.

Ash leaned down next to Bluebell and shook her. "Wake, sister. Wake."

Bluebell murmured. Her eyes flickered open. She looked at Ash, then her head fell to the side. Her eyes fixed on her dead father, then closed again. "No," she managed.

"She lives!" Ash cried. "She lives! Get her to the infirmary!"

Ash stood and reached for *Grithbani*. She couldn't leave the deadly blade out here for anyone to take. She yanked hard and it came free from her father's chest, then began to crumble in her hand. Startled, she dropped it. When Ash held the sword for Athelrick to fall on, *Grithbani* had fulfilled the kin-slaying purpose for which it was forged. As it hit the ground, it turned to dust.

Ivy grabbed the boys and raced downstairs to the hall to welcome back the city guard. Men everywhere, stinking of sweat and blood and victory. She couldn't see Crispin anywhere in the hall so she went out into the sunshine, with baby Edmund on her hip and dragging Eadric by the hand. The wounded were being laid out on the grass. Her heart ran hot with fear. She didn't dare to look at their faces to see if one of them was her beloved.

Then he was there, and all her fear evaporated. She let go of Eadric's hand and impulsively threw her arm around his neck. "Crispin!"

He gently pulled her hand away and stepped back. "My lady."

She smiled at him. "If I cannot publicly kiss the captain of the guard on such a day, then when can I?"

He leaned toward her and said in a low, barely audible voice, "Be sensible."

She noticed then the smears of blood on his mail, and felt very young and foolish.

Rose joined them a moment later, with Eadric's hand in hers. "You have a little runaway here," she said.

"Rose, this is Crispin, the captain of my guard. Crispin, my sister Rose."

He nodded once at Rose. "I am sorry about your father."

"Thank you."

He began to pull away. "If you'll excuse me, my ladies, I have to assist with bringing in the injured."

Ivy wasn't ready for him to leave. She had been longing for the comfort of his arms, of some tender words that restored her to her usual place in the world. "Must you go just yet?" she blurted.

He fixed her in his gaze and the expression he wore . . . Was it pity? Scorn? She recoiled from it.

"I will see you in good time, my lady," he said tersely. "When the dead and wounded are accounted for."

He turned away from her and moved into the crowd. She followed him with her eyes until he was lost among jostling, shouting bodies. A little flint of fury lit in her heart. How dare he? She turned to Rose and took Eadric's hand, her protective instincts flaring into life.

"Thank you," she said. "We don't want him lost in this crowd."

"You are in love with Crispin, aren't you?"

Ivy averted her eyes.

Rose pressed on. "Do you want my advice?"

"No, I don't," she said, and when Rose opened her mouth to give it anyway, Ivy raised a finger to her lips. "I don't," she said again. "Especially not from you." She knew what Rose would say, about love and about good sense and about the fates of kingdoms that rested on their soft shoulders. But her sister underestimated her if she thought Ivy could not manage Crispin. Was she not born of kings?

Bluebell ebbed in and out of gray, aware of noise and voices, but experiencing it all as though it were a dream. A bad dream, where Father had died and his hands were missing. A howling pain sat around the crown of her head. She remembered something about Ash, and a dragon, but surely that had been another dream.

But then a glimmer of thin light, and she opened her eyes and Ash was sitting there, wet and bloody, right next to her. "Ash?" she said. "Where am I?"

Ash smiled weakly. "The infirmary. Seacaster. How much do you remember?"

And with that simple question, the pain came roaring back. It had been real. Father was dead. She groaned.

Ash stroked her hair. "Go slow, sister. You have been badly hurt."

Bluebell licked her lips. "Where is Willow? Hakon?"

"They headed to their ships. I crushed them in the harbor. Listen, can you not hear the horns of victory?"

"Victory?" Bluebell said, and she struggled to sit up. Every bone in her body ached. "My father is dead . . ." Her breath caught and she bent over her knees, moaning.

"Are you in pain?" Ash asked.

Bluebell lifted her head. "I have never hurt more than I hurt now."

The physician bustled over, past the rows of other wounded, when she saw Bluebell was awake. "Lie down," she commanded. "I have not yet assessed all your injuries. Though how you are still alive, I do not know."

Ash smiled tightly. "It's a miracle," she said. "The gods were on her side."

The physician did not smile in return. "Well. My lord Bluebell, there is somebody here who may yet cheer you on this dark day."

"Who is that?" Bluebell asked.

The physician stepped aside and indicated Skalmir, who was limping toward her. She climbed to her feet, despite Ash's protestations.

"Snowy," she said, the crushing weariness and grief of the day roaring over her.

Slowly, he approached, stopped in front of her with an expression of empathy and concern. "My love," he said.

"My father died," she managed to say, then stopped speaking in case she cried.

Snowy stepped forward, opened his arms, and she let herself fall into his embrace.

Willow drank the sea. Over and over she tried to claw toward air, only to gulp then slide under again. Her eyes stung; water bubbled around her ears. And she put her fate in the hands of Maava.

If you want me to live and give you heathen lands, you will save me.

Something hit her head. Every nerve alert, she reached for it. A piece of a ship, about as big as a table. She grabbed on with all her might, groped her way forward until her upper body was out of the water. Above the surface, it was a calm clear day. Her piece of wood was being thrust toward the shore, north of the harbor. She shook her head to clear her eyes of water, and blinked around her.

Bodies floated on the heaving currents. She counted them with her eyes. Dozens. Some, like her, grasping the surface of the water then disappearing again. Too far away for her to help. She would be the only survivor. *Many hundreds of martyrs were made at the battle of Seacaster, but Maava's favorite, Willow, was spared.*

Then she saw Hakon. She would have thought him any of the

raiders, floating facedown in the water, but she recognized the black triangle on the back of his hand. Their wedding tattoo.

The angel voices brewed, began to rub against each other. *Will you honestly leave your husband to die?*

"He's a heathen," she said to them, her voice creaking over the salt that lined her throat. "He's already dead."

Are you sure?

A sign. Where was the sign she needed? Her piece of driftwood would soon crash directly into his body.

She looked to the sky for a sign.

Perhaps Maava was sick of her, always asking for signs. She lay on her belly and reached out. As the wave pushed her forward, she grasped the back of his shirt. The weight of his body pulled her off the driftwood. Splinters sliced through her palm as she tried to hang on. One hand on Hakon, one hand on the driftwood, feeling her weight slowly sinking.

"Hakon!" she screamed at him, making her throat raw. "Hakon!"

With all her might, she pulled his upper body onto the driftwood, then climbed over him. Pulled again, heaving him up. Her shoulders burned. She turned him on his side and sat across his ribs.

Water spewed from his mouth. He coughed. He was alive. The driftwood was crashing toward the shore. There were rocks. There would be pain.

Willow braced herself.

A short period of black followed, then she was blinking her eyes open and feeling pain in every part of her body. She was on gritty sand, Hakon kneeling over her. Warm blood ran down the side of her face.

"What happened?" she said.

"You are safe. You are cut, but nothing seems broken."

Willow closed her eyes, relished the feel of air moving in and out of her lungs. Maava had saved her.

"Willow?"

She opened her eyes again and saw that Hakon looked down on her mournfully. "What is it?" she asked.

He hooked his finger inside the wound on his cheek and said, "Maava's miracle has passed."

If Willow was not so full of pain and exhaustion, she might have thought to run. Now he would know she had deceived him. Now he would not bring Maava to the heathens.

But then he put his head in his hands and said, "We failed to take the city in His name. We slaughtered a lamb to the Horse God. Maava has punished me."

Willow realized that failure had convinced Hakon of Maava's great power more than all the small successes had. She knew then that it had been right to save him, and she promised she would stop asking the angels for reassurance, stop asking her Lord for signs. She had a rightness inside her, and she would trust it from now on.

Willow struggled to sit. She could see now that her legs were bruised and grazed and cut; the mail had protected her upper body. Her head swam and she put her hand on the back of her scalp and felt another gash. Her fingers came away bloody.

She put her bloody hand on Hakon's shoulder and said, "He may yet forgive you."

Hakon lifted his head.

"When Iceheart is converted. When the war on the Southlands begins. Who knows when His favor will once again turn to us? All I know is we must keep trying."

Hakon nodded, took her hand roughly. "I promise Maava. I promise you. We will wipe all of the heathens out of Thyrsland together."

Bloody and bruised, they rose to their feet and began to walk north.

chapter 38

Rose spent two days in Nether Weald with her daughter after the siege of Seacaster, in the times of confusion and chaos as the world righted itself. But then it was time to say goodbye, as she always knew she would. Rowan, for her part, seemed easily able to separate, and Rose felt keenly her own foolishness at having taught her to expect the departure of loved ones.

Rowan had taken Rose to a barrow in the river valley, given her a perfunctory kiss, and sent her across the gate to the moors near Eldra's house. From there, Rose walked.

With aching feet, she approached the place she had lived these last four years, across grass wet from recent rain, under gray clouds lowering on the distant flat horizon. When the small white house became visible, she hurried her steps. Sun sliced through the clouds, and it was then she saw them. Heath and Linden, sitting on a wooden bench in front of the stable. Heath was showing Linden how to carve. Their heads were bent together: Linden's dark curls, Heath's long golden locks.

She stood still a moment, watching them. Heath was clearly much recovered, and had regained some of his masculine denseness of muscle. He looked like the Heath she remembered. But more than that: She could see in him now, as he smiled at Linden, that he was kind, reasonable, reliable, loyal . . . qualities she might once have found dull, but now seemed to her to be the qualities that a real enduring love might be made from.

Then Linden looked up and saw her, eyes wide.

He jumped to his feet and ran, leaping into her arms. Rose let the tears fall, feeling his dear little body against hers again. A few moments later, Heath joined them, reached across Linden's head to touch her cheek.

"You're back," he said.

"And all is well," she replied. "I will tell you everything over supper."

"If all is well, then it's time for me to return to my tribe."

Linden turned to him, his mouth upside down. He reached out his chubby little hand and grabbed a hank of Heath's hair. Rose had to laugh. She wanted to do the same.

"I see you and Linden have grown fond of each other," she said.

"That we have."

Her heart sped a little. Her words spilled out, tumbling over each other. "Then we will come with you, and live as a family," she said, then paused. "If you will have us."

Heath smiled and even though his face was still gaunt, she knew that smile and loved it with breathtaking force.

"Of course," he said. "Of course I will have you."

The day they burned Athelrick's body was gray and gloomy, with drizzle setting in at sunset. The sky cried where Bluebell could not, would not. She stood beside the pyre in her mail and waited until it had burned to the ground, her face like a stone, then scooped up a handful of ash to keep in a bottle in her bower.

The day of Bluebell's wedding, the weather conspired to persuade her that love and marriage were things of wonder: endless blue skies and soft sunshine, ripe blackberries heaving on the vines, and white ribbons tied to every building in Blickstow as they all came out to feast in honor of Lord Bluebell's new husband. Little children dressed up in hunting gear in his honor and shot rough toy arrows at one another. Ash bound their hands together with ribbons and they made vows and Bluebell grimaced through it all, feeling exposed and slightly silly. Her heart was still sick from the loss of her father two weeks before, but she knew she had made the right decision in taking Snowy as her husband. Skalmir Hunter was well loved by the people of Blickstow and everyone said they made a handsome couple, though nobody really meant it about Bluebell.

The night before Bluebell took the throne of Almissia, exactly a month after her father's death as was custom in Blickstow, fog had settled among the bowerhouses and the hall and the ruins. She couldn't sleep, her guts churning and thudding, her long legs twitching. Snowy slept on peacefully beside her. Curse Rowan for making her declare her love for a man who could sleep peacefully in the dark before the world tilted on its axis.

"Snowy," she said at last, when midnight was surely long behind her. "Snowy, wake up."

He rolled over, his voice croaking with sleep. "What is it?"

"I will be king tomorrow."

He reached out a warm hand and rested it on her hip. "Are you afraid?"

"What? No," she said. "Of course not."

A long silence. The air was very still.

"Snowy, wake up."

"I am awake," he said.

"If I was afraid, what would you say?"

"I would say that only a fool would be unafraid at such a time. That your fear only proves that you will always be a vigilant steward of Almissia. I would say that to be afraid of becoming king honors the memory of your father."

Bluebell smiled in the dark. "Well, then," she said. "Perhaps I will sleep now."

The next day, her eyes gritty and her heart bruised, Bluebell took her place on the great carved oak seat that had been in her family for over a hundred years. It was the middle of the day, and the sun should have been streaming through the windows of the hall, but the fog was thick and cold and the shutters had all been closed against it. She was the only light in the room, all in coronation white with her long, fair hair brushed loose. The hall was crammed full of people, mostly soldiers in full armor, standing shoulder-to-shoulder. Old Dunstan was there, stooped and white-haired. Somehow he had outlived Father. Other gray old men looked at her with eyes both sorrowful and hungry. How they longed to be young again.

Bluebell's arse was aching. Whoever had designed this chair hadn't put much thought into comfort. Thrymm sat at her heels, demoted from war dog to hearth dog but not seeming to mind too much.

The chatter of voices died away as Sighere walked solemnly to the front of the hall, holding Athelrick's crown. No—Bluebell's crown. She swallowed hard. Her whole life had been tending toward this moment; why was she so unequal to it? Nervous like a virgin on her wedding night?

Bluebell turned her mind to higher things, away from the hall and the watching eyes, and the self-doubts that she would have sworn she would never feel. Instead she thought of Father, and his ancestors, all in the train of the Horse God now. One day she, too, would join that train. Father was right to remind her: She would grow old and die. But to die having brought fierce glory to herself and her ancestors was rich indeed. That was the new horizon toward which her life would tend.

Sighere, as her first-ranked thane, laid the crown on her head, then knelt in front of her, his hands on her knees. "Long may you live, my lord," he said.

And the cry went up around the hall: "Long may she live!"

She stood and spread her arms and they cheered wildly. The Horse God moved inside her, and to the gathered assembly, Bluebell seemed ten feet tall.

❖   ❖   ❖

The day after her coronation, Sighere entered the stateroom late in the afternoon while Bluebell was sorting the maps her father had left of all the civic districts in Almissia. He closed the door behind him and waited for her to look up.

"Sit down, Sighere. I really should get somebody else to do this, but many of these are his own drawings and I feel close to him when I touch them."

Sighere did not sit down, and Bluebell raised her head warily. "What is it?"

"We have news from Marvik."

"Go on."

"Gisli is dead. Hakon is king."

Bluebell held her breath.

"Willow is queen."

"And they have converted?"

"It would seem so."

Bluebell nodded. "What is your opinion of the stronghold at Merkhinton?"

"It can keep raiders out. But the stronghold on the northern border of Bradsey, at Harrow's Fell, is vulnerable."

She looked around at the maps, thinking about her civic duty and how dull it all was. With Sighere's words, a feeling of purpose surged in her body. "Then we must secure Harrow's Fell as a matter of priority." She bit her lip, remembering the old curse that forbade her to travel in Bradsey. "Ash will have to come with us," she said.

"As you wish, my lord."

Bluebell smiled up at him, her blood leaping at the thought of moving. "Make all preparations. We head north tomorrow."

Willow traveled under a heavy cloak with her hood raised, and every ferryman and horse trader thought her a grim specter of some kind. She had gold, though, and they happily took it when she offered it. Long enough had passed now since the unsuccessful siege of Seacaster, the failure of Hakon's plans to kill Bluebell, and the first wave of forced and bloody conversion through Marvik. Now it was finally safe to bring Avaarni to Iceheart.

As Willow walked the familiar route up the rise to Bramble Hill, her heart thudded with excitement. Would Avaarni now be in his male body, ready to begin his training as heir to the kingship of a united, trimartyr Thyrsland?

The gate was not locked, and it opened with a rusty creak. Willow was still so full of thoughts of the glorious conversion that she didn't notice the gardens were overgrown, that long grass surrounded the carts near the stables, that the flowering pots outside the front door of Gudrun's house contained only dead plants.

When she removed the key from her belt and opened the door, she realized.

The smell hit her first. Empty, yeasty, faintly malodorous, as though windows hadn't been opened in an age. But then the silence. No Penda or Olaf. No dogs. Not even Parsley, the cat.

"Gudrun?" she called, advancing into the stone-tiled front room. "Avaarni?"

She pushed on, her eyes finally confirming what her heart already knew.

The house was empty.

Her child was gone.

EPILOGUE

Rowan kept many secrets. She had learned that anyone who had power and influence in this world had to keep secrets, because they were the hidden glue that held all things together. She liked having secrets. They reminded her that her life was bigger than the daily mundanity of her existence in Folkenham.

She couldn't complain about the trimartyr praying. Nyll, horrified by the heathen tattoo that would forever mark her cheek, subjected her to daily prayers that the magic depart. Yet those prayers had taken nothing from her. She could still feel the gates opening and closing all over Thyrsland, still feel her First Folk blood latent inside her, waiting for a moment of destiny to rouse it to action, the return to Rathcruick, the father of her spirit.

She couldn't complain about Wengest, who had heard of her great feat of archery at Seacaster and now gave her time, equipment, and a trainer to help her hone her skill even further. At the end of a boring day of sewing and reading, to stride into the garden and send arrow after arrow thunking into the targets cleared her head and allowed her to feel less trapped by life at court. Her father often came to watch her, and cuddled her fiercely afterward as though she were still a little girl, as though they were blood, as though he were more than just the father of her memories. She loved him in her own way.

She didn't complain about Marjory, Wengest's new wife, who was as horrified at the notion of mothering Rowan as Rowan herself was. They seemed to have come to an unspoken agreement to pretend to like each other, while actually avoiding each other at every opportunity. She much preferred Sister Henrietta, who had been given the thankless task of helping Rowan improve her cross-stitch, but who at least had some good stories to tell of the times of the giants and dragons.

She didn't complain about how far she was from Blickstow and Snowy, the father of her heart, because Wengest had agreed to let her go there every Yule, and that was only a few months away.

And even though she was circumscribed when she longed to be free, she knew the years would pass and her time would come and she would choose her path. In the meantime, the nights were hers and nobody had to know what she did in her sleep, when she sent her shimmering self out over fields and forests, moors and marshes, and found her mother's body: the body to which she always wanted to return. The bed was more crowded now, with her half brother on one side and Heath, the father of her blood, on the other. But her shimmering self took up no room, and she found her way among them, and settled happy and fulfilled there every night.

The four of them all curled together, a family that nobody could see.

acknowledgments

My thanks are due to my support team: Anna Madill, Paula Ellery, and Heather Gammage, without whom I don't know how I'd ever get a book finished. Love and appreciation always to my cheer squad: Ollie, Mary-Rose, the Sisters, and Mum. I wrote a great deal of this story on my travels in the United Kingdom in 2015, during which time I shared the delightful company of Louise D'Arcens, Lisa Hannett, Kate Forsyth, and Elizabeth McKewin. A special mention to Gerald Pimm, who told me I needed a man just like Snowy in my book, and he was right. I have the loveliest people in publishing working with me, particularly Sue Brockhoff, Jo Mackay, Airlie Lawson, Anne Groell, and Kylie Mason. Much love to my children, Luka and Astrid, who are patient and kind. Finally, I offer my most heartfelt thanks to Selwa Anthony, who has now been my literary agent for more than twenty years. Since 1996, her love and faith, her business acumen and passion for books, have sustained me and inspired me. There is nobody in publishing like her, and it is a blessing and a privilege to have her on my side.

about the author

KIM WILKINS is the author of *Daughters of the Storm*. She was born in London, and grew up at the seaside north of Brisbane, Australia. She is an associate professor of writing and book culture at the University of Queensland. She writes a lot, usually by ignoring unimportant things like cooking and washing her children's clothes. She has enduring obsessions with Viking-age England, misty landscapes, pagan mythology, Led Zeppelin, and really, really small dogs.

kimwilkins.com
Facebook.com/KimWilkins2014
Instagram: @hexebart

about the type

This book was set in Palatino, a typeface designed by the German typographer Hermann Zapf (b. 1918). It was named after the Renaissance calligrapher Giovanni Battista Palatino. Zapf designed it between 1948 and 1952, and it was his first typeface to be introduced in America. It is a face of unusual elegance.